...s in Montana...
...e springer spaniels.
...boats and plays tennis.
....com, on Facebook or on Twitter

...nor

...lay **Maggie Wells** is buried in spreadsheets. At night ...pens tales of intrigue and people tangling up the ...ts. She has a weakness for hot heroes and happy ...ings. She is the product of a charming rogue and a ...meless flirt, and you only have to scratch the surface ...this mild-mannered married lady to find a naughty ...eak a mile wide.

CF

Also by B.J. Daniels

Also by Maggie Wells

Discover more at millsandboon.co.uk

STICKING TO HER GUNS

B.J. DANIELS

FOOTHILLS FIELD SEARCH

MAGGIE WELLS

MILLS & BOON

First Published in Great Britain 2022
by Mills & Boon, an imprint of HarperCollins*Publishers* Ltd
1 London Bridge Street, London, SE1 9GF

www.harpercollins.co.uk

HarperCollins*Publishers*
1st Floor, Watermarque Building,
Ringsend Road, Dublin 4, Ireland

Sticking to Her Guns © 2022 Barbara Heinlein
Foothills Field Search © 2022 Harlequin Enterprises ULC

Special thanks and acknowledgement are given to Maggie Wells for her
contribution to the *K-9s on Patrol* series.

ISBN: 978-0-263-30341-4

0522

MIX
Paper from
responsible sources
FSC™ C007454

This book is produced from independently certified FSC™
paper to ensure responsible forest management.

For more information visit: www.harpercollins.co.uk/green

Printed and Bound in Spain using 100% Renewable electricity at
CPI Black Print, Barcelona

STICKING TO HER GUNS

B.J. DANIELS

This book is number 115! I dedicate it to all my loyal readers. Thank you so much for making it possible. I always wanted to write stories when I grew up. It took me a while to grow up, LOL, but this is what I love doing. What a joy it is that I can share these stories with you. I hope you enjoy this next Colt Brothers Investigation book. Welcome to Lonesome, Montana.

Chapter One

Bella Worthington took a breath and, opening her eyes, finally faced her reflection in the full-length mirror. The wedding dress fit perfectly—just as he'd said it would. While accentuating her curves, the neckline was modest, the drape flattering. As much as she hated to admit it, Fitz had good taste.

The sapphire-and-diamond necklace he'd given her last night gleamed at her throat, bringing out the blue-green of her eyes—also like he'd said it would. He'd thought of everything—right down to the huge pear-shaped diamond engagement ring on her finger. All of it would be sold off before the ink dried on the marriage license—if she let it go that far.

As she studied her reflection though she realized this was exactly as he'd planned it. She looked the beautiful bride on her wedding day. No one would be the wiser.

She could hear music and the murmur of voices downstairs. He'd invited the whole town of Lonesome, Montana. She'd watched from the upstairs window as the guests had arrived earlier. He'd wanted an audience for this and now he would have one.

The knock at the door startled her, even though she'd been expecting it. "It's time," said a male voice on the other side. One of Fitz's hired bodyguards, Ronan, was waiting. He would be carrying a weapon under his suit. Security, she'd been told, to keep her safe. A lie.

She listened as Ronan unlocked her door and waited outside, his boss not taking any chances. He had made sure there was no possibility of escape short of shackling her to her bed. Fitz was determined that she find no way out of this. It didn't appear that she had.

In a few moments, she would be escorted downstairs to where her maid of honor and bridesmaids were waiting—all hand-chosen by her groom. If they'd questioned why they were down there and she was up here, they hadn't asked. He wasn't the kind of man women questioned. At least not more than once.

For another moment, Bella stared at the stranger in the mirror. She didn't have to wonder how she'd gotten to this point in her life. Unfortunately, she knew too well. She'd just never thought Fitz would go this far. Her mistake. He, however, had no idea how far she was willing to go to make sure the wedding never happened.

Taking a breath, she picked up her bouquet from her favorite local flower shop. The bouquet had been a special order delivered earlier. Her hand barely trembled as she lifted the blossoms to her nose for a moment, taking in the sweet scent of the tiny white roses—also his choice. Carefully, she separated the tiny buds afraid it wouldn't be there.

It took her a few moments to find the long slim silver blade hidden among the roses and stems. The blade was sharp, and lethal if used correctly. She knew exactly how to use it. She slid it back into the bouquet out of sight. He wouldn't think to check it. She hoped. He'd anticipated her every move and attacked with one of his own. Did she really think he wouldn't be ready for anything?

Making sure the door was still closed, she checked her garter. What she'd tucked under it was still there, safe, at least for the moment.

Another knock at the door. Fitz would be getting impatient and no one wanted that. "Everyone's waiting," Ronan said, tension in his tone. If this didn't go as meticulously planned there would be hell to pay from his boss. Something else they all knew.

She stepped to the door and opened it, lifting her chin and straightening her spine. Ronan's eyes swept over her with a lusty gaze, but he stepped back as if not all that sure of her. Clearly he'd been warned to be wary of her. Probably just as she'd been warned what would happen if she refused to come down—or worse, made a scene in front of the guests.

At the bottom of the stairs, the room opened and she saw Fitz waiting for her with the person he'd hired to officiate.

He was so confident that he'd backed her into a corner with no way out. He'd always underestimated her. Today would be no different. But he didn't know her as well as he thought. He'd held her prisoner, threatened her, forced her into this dress and this ruse.

But that didn't mean she was going to marry him.

She would kill him first.

Chapter Two

Three weeks earlier

Bella smiled to herself. She'd just enjoyed the best long weekend of her life. Now sitting in a coffee shop with her closest friend, Whitney Burgess, she blurted out the words she hadn't even let herself voice before this moment.

"I'm in love."

Whitney blinked. They'd just been talking about Bella's new online furnishings business she'd started. "You're in love?" her friend repeated. "With the new line?"

Bella shook her head. "With a man. The man I want to spend the rest of my life with." This was a first so Bella was sure it came as a surprise.

"Love? Marriage?" Whitney laughed. "Seriously? Anyone I know?"

"Maybe. I just spent a long weekend with him in that luxurious hotel downtown. It was amazing."

Her friend shook her head. "And you aren't going to tell me his name?"

"Not yet."

"Well, at least tell me about your weekend," Whitney said, dropping her voice and leaning closer. "Don't leave out a thing."

"We watched old Westerns, made popcorn, ate ice cream, ordered the most wonderful breakfasts in the mornings and had hamburgers and fries at night."

"Wait, you skipped the best part," her friend joked.

"We didn't even kiss." Bella laughed. "It was the most fun I've had on a date in forever."

Whitney sat back. "Sorry, you didn't even *kiss*? So you didn't…for a whole long weekend together?" she asked incredulously.

Bella shook her head. "It was *perfect*."

"Not my idea of the perfect date, but clearly it has you glowing. Come on, who is this amazing man?"

Bella hesitated. "Tommy Colt."

"That wild boy your father ran off the ranch with a shotgun when you two were teenagers?" her friend asked in surprise.

Laughing, Bella nodded. "I think I've been in love with Tommy for years, but I never admitted it, even to myself, until now. We were inseparable from about the time we were five, always sneaking away to see each other. Our ranches are adjacent so it was just a matter of cutting through the woods." She smiled at the memories. "We built a tree house together at ten. That's about the same time we became blood brothers, so to speak." She held out her finger and touched the tiny scar.

Whitney was shaking her head. "You're really serious?"

"I am. It feels right," she said. "I wanted to wait before I said anything."

"Wait. He doesn't know how you feel about him?"

"Not yet," Bella admitted. "But I think he might suspect. Maybe."

Her friend laughed again. "Why didn't you tell him?"

"I'm waiting for the right time, but I will soon. My dad called. I have to go back to Lonesome. I told Tommy that if he was around…"

Whitney was shaking her head again. "You amaze me. When it comes to business, you don't hesitate. But when it comes to love…"

"I'm cautious."

"No," her friend said. "You're scared. And truthfully, I didn't think anything scared you. Are you worried he doesn't feel the same?"

"Maybe."

"Tell him! He's a rodeo cowboy, right?"

"He's on the circuit right now. I think he has a ride in Texas coming up."

"You could meet him there, surprise him," Whitney suggested, clearly getting into this.

"I could." Bella smiled, the idea appealing to her. "I definitely could." Her smile faded. "But first I have to go to the ranch and see what my father wants." She didn't add that there had been something in his tone that worried her. She just hoped this wasn't another ploy to try to get her to join his business partnership. She didn't trust his other two partners, Edwin Fitzgerald Mattson senior and his son, Fitz.

"I am going to tell Tommy how I feel about him," she said, the decision made. "I'm glad we got together today. I think I'll surprise him in Austin." She just hoped he felt the same way about her.

TOMMY COULDN'T BELIEVE he was home in Lonesome— and for good.

"Okay, Davey and Willie are gone," his brother James

said after the others had cleared out. The four brothers had gotten together for the weekend, but now Davey and Willie were headed back to the rodeo circuit, leaving Tommy and James alone.

"Why are you really here, Tommy?"

They were in the upstairs office of Colt Investigations, what would soon be Colt Brothers Investigations, if Tommy had his way.

Before answering, he walked to the second-story window and looked out on the small Western town of Lonesome, Montana. It was surrounded by pines and mountains and a river to the east. He'd grown up here but had been gone for years on the rodeo circuit.

"I told you. I'm done with the rodeo and living my life on the road. I want to join you in our father's private eye business and stick around here."

"What's her name?"

Tommy laughed and turned to smile at his older brother. "So like you to think it has something to do with a woman. Speaking of women, how is Lorelei?" Lori, as they all called her, was his brother's fiancée. They were in the process of having a home built for them on the Colt Ranch.

"Lori's fine. Don't try to change the subject." James leaned back in the old high-backed leather chair behind the marred oak desk. Four years ago it would have been their father sitting there. James looked enough like Del that it still gave Tommy a start. They all had the thick dark hair, the same classic good looks and a dark sense of humor. They all had loved rodeo for as long as they could remember.

Thinking of their father, Tommy felt the loss heart deep. They'd lost their father way too soon. Worse, none of them believed Del's death had been an accident. Tommy had known that coming back here would be painful.

"I want to be part of the business," he said. "I can do this. I know I can."

"You don't know anything about being a private investigator."

"Neither did you," Tommy said. Everything about this room reminded him of their father and the Colt legacy. "But look at you now. A major cold case solved and business picking up."

James shook his head. "I never thought you'd ever quit the rodeo. Not you."

He could feel his brother's gaze on him as he moved around the room. "I used to dream of following in our ancestors' footsteps," Tommy admitted as he studied an old Hollywood poster featuring his great-grandfather Ransom Del Colt. Ransom had been a famous movie star back in the forties and early fifties when Westerns had been so popular.

Their grandfather, RD Colt Jr., had followed in Ransom's footprints for a while before starting his own Wild West show. RD had traveled the world ropin' and ridin'. Tommy and his brothers had grown up on the stories.

He could see himself in their faces as well as his father's and his brothers'. They shared more than looks. They were all most comfortable on the back of a horse—even when it was bucking.

"So what happened?" James asked.

Tommy shook his head. "Recently rodeoing just didn't have that hold on me anymore."

"Uh-huh," his brother said. "You going to tell me about her or not?"

He smiled and continued around the room, looking at all the photographs and posters. The Colts had a rich cowboy history, one to be proud of, his father always told them. And yet their father, Del Colt, had broken the mold. After being a rodeo cowboy, he'd had to quit when he got injured badly.

Del, who'd loved Westerns and mystery movies, had gotten his PI license and opened Colt Investigations, while he'd encouraged them to follow their hearts. He'd taught his sons to ride a horse before they could walk. Their hearts had led them straight to the rodeo—just as it had Del and the Colt men before them.

Tommy had thought that he would never stop living and breathing rodeo. That love had been in his soul as well as his genes. But he didn't need to get hurt like his father and brother to quit as it turned out. He was home—following his heart.

He was the third-oldest behind Willy and James, and like his brothers he had enjoyed life on the road and made enough money to put quite a bit away. But for a while now he'd been feeling the need to grow roots. It had made him restless. When James had taken over their father's business back here in Lonesome, Tommy had felt the pull.

But that wasn't what had made the decision for him, James was right about that. He turned to face his brother. "Did you hear that Bella is back?"

James swore. "I thought you'd lost your nerve bronc riding in the rodeo," he joked. "Instead, you've lost your mind. Not Bella Worthington?"

"Afraid so," Tommy said. "She and I ran into each other in Denver a couple of weeks ago."

James opened the bottom drawer of the desk and pulled out what was left of the bottle of blackberry brandy and two paper cups. "If this conversation about Bella is going the way I suspect it is, then we better finish this bottle." He poured. Tommy took his full paper cup, stared at it a moment before he downed it.

His brother laughed. "So maybe you do realize that what you're thinking is beyond crazy. Do I have to remind you who her father is? Not a fan of yours or the rest of us, for that matter. I'm sure he has aspirations of her marrying some biz-whiz with big bucks."

"It's not up to him," Tommy said as he smiled and traced the scar on his right temple. The scar was from when they were kids and he'd made the mistake of suggesting that Bella, being a girl, shouldn't try to cross the creek on a slippery log. She'd picked up a rock and nailed him, then she'd crossed the creek on the log. He smiled remembering that he'd been the one to slip off the dang log. Bella had come into the water to save him, though. It was what best friends did, she'd told him.

"The woman can be a firecracker," Tommy agreed. "Maybe that's why I've never gotten over her."

James shook his head. "What are you going to do? I suspect you won't get within a mile of the Worthington ranch before the shotgun comes out if her father is around." He shook his head and downed his brandy.

As he refilled the cups, his brother asked, "How'd this happen? You wake up one day and say, 'Hey, I haven't been kicked in the head by a bucking horse enough lately. I think I'll go home and see if Bella wants to marry me'?"

Tommy shrugged. "Something like that. I can't explain it. I guess I did wake up one day with this feeling." He met his brother's gaze. "I think it's meant to be. Running into her again in Denver, I suddenly knew what I wanted—what I've always wanted."

James studied him for a moment. "I just have one question. When she sends you hightailing it, are you planning to tuck your tail between your legs and leave Lonesome and Colt Investigations?"

"Nope," he said. "I'm serious about going into the business with you." He glanced around. "The way I see it, you need me maybe even worse than she does."

His brother laughed. "You're serious about the job—and Bella?"

"Dead serious," he said.

James shook his head. "Dangerous business going after Lady Worthington. That is one strong, determined woman."

Tommy grinned. "That's what I love about her. I can't seem to quit thinking about her. I think it's a sign."

"It's a sign all right," James mumbled under this breath, but he smiled and raised his cup. "Fine. You start work in the morning."

Tommy looked down at the paper cup full of blackberry brandy in his hand. But this time he took his time drinking it. Tomorrow, he would learn as much as James could teach him, start an online class and apply for his private investigator's license. He hadn't seen Bella yet, but he wanted to accomplish something before he did.

When he went out to the Worthington ranch to see her, come hell or high water, he planned to ask her to marry him. He had the ring in his pocket. As terrified as he was, he was doing this.

BELLA COULDN'T HELP being worried as she drove out to the ranch. She'd heard something in her father's tone when he'd called her in Denver and asked her to come see him at the ranch. There'd been an urgency that surprised—and concerned—her.

Maybe this wasn't about trying to get her to go into business with him. He often made her feel guilty for striking out on her own, but he knew why she'd declined. She didn't like his other partners, Edwin Fitzgerald Mattson and his son, Fitz. As generous as her father's offer had been, she'd also wanted to start her own business.

Her father had started his from the ground up. She thought he should understand why she wanted to succeed on her own. But the more she thought about it, she wondered if this visit would be about something different entirely.

"I need you to come home," her father had said.

She hadn't been back to Lonesome River Ranch in months because of her business. When he'd called, she'd given legitimate excuses as to why she couldn't come home right now.

"Bella." His voice had broken. "I have to see you. If you'd prefer that I come to you—"

"Are you sick?" she'd asked, suddenly frightened. Was it possible he was worse than sick? It seemed inconceivable. Her larger-than-life father never even got a cold.

"No. It's not that. I have to see you. I wouldn't ask, but…" His voice had broken. "I'm sorry."

"I'll come right away," she said and then hesitated before asking, "Are you there alone?"

"Except for the staff," he said, sounding both annoyed and resigned. He knew that if Edwin and Fitz were there she would refuse. The last Christmas she'd spent at the ranch had been so miserable because of the two Mattsons, she'd told her father that there would be no encore.

Parking, she got out of her vehicle in front of the ranch

house and took a deep breath. The Montana summer air was ripe with the smell of pines and river. She'd missed this, another reason she was ready to make some changes.

As she started up the steps to the wide front porch that overlooked the river, her father stepped out and she felt a jolt of shock. He'd aged. While still a large, imposing man, Nolan Worthington appeared beat down, something she'd never seen before. She was instantly taken aback. He had to be sick. Her heart fell.

He quickly ushered her into the house, going straight to his den. This had always been his favorite room in the ranch house with its leather furniture, huge oak desk and small rock fireplace.

"What's wrong?" she asked, her pulse thundering with fear.

Tears filled his eyes. "I've been a fool," he said and broke down. "I'm in terrible trouble and the worst part is…" He looked up at her. "I'm afraid that I've dragged you into it."

Chapter Three

Tommy Colt woke to sunshine—and as usual, a good strong jolt of reality. For days now, he'd been learning the investigations business from the ground up. And each morning, he'd awakened with a shock.

He'd come back to Lonesome, Montana, for a woman. A woman who had no idea how he felt and might not feel the same way. Not only had he blindly returned home for love, but he'd also quit the first and, for a long time, *only* love of his life. The rodeo.

Because of that, he'd thrown himself into a new job with his brother as a private detective for Colt Investigations. The two of them were following in their father's footsteps, both knowing the job had gotten Del killed.

In the light of day each morning, the whole thing seemed pretty risky on his part. But his brother James, as Jimmy D was going by now, had already solved his first case, gotten his PI license and was making money at it. Tommy had jumped in feetfirst with no training.

But then James had learned on the job when he'd decided to take over their late father's agency, he reminded himself. Clients were now pouring in.

Maybe more like trickling in, but enough so that his brother could use the help. Tommy told himself that he wanted to prove he could do this before he went out to the Lonesome River Ranch and told Bella how he felt about her. He was planning to go out to her family ranch as soon as he got settled in. He wanted to make sure he had a job and a place to live first before he asked her out on a real date, told her how he felt about her and asked her to marry him.

He had to have some experience under his belt before he told her what he'd done, quitting the job he'd had and taking on one he currently didn't know for beans. All he knew was that she'd returned to Lonesome to her family ranch—after that amazing long weekend in Denver with him. It had been platonic. That was another crazy part of this.

Tommy was planning to ask a woman he'd never even dated to marry him. What was the worst that could happen? She could say no.

James had agreed that him learning more of the business before going to see Bella was a good plan.

"I'd like to get some work out of you before you go out there and her old man shoots you," James had said. "I doubt his feelings about you have changed."

Tommy doubted it, too. Nolan Worthington had his own aspirations for his daughter. None of those aspirations included one of the wild Colt brothers.

Since moving home, he'd found a place to live in a cabin down by the river that he could rent cheap for a while. He'd saved most of the money he'd made rodeoing. But to say his life was up in the air right now was putting it mildly.

Forcing himself out of bed, he showered and changed

for work. It was an alien feeling. Could he really do a nine-to-five job?

"More manuals?" Tommy asked as he came through the door of the office later that morning. This was the most studying he'd done since college when he'd also been on the rodeo team. He figured James would start him out doing something like filing once he finished with his studies.

"I have a skip for you," James said now, shoving a sheet of paper across the desk at him without looking up.

Tommy couldn't help being surprised. "A real job?"

"What were you expecting, a soft, cushy desk job?" James laughed. "It's an easy one, Ezekiel Murray."

"Wait, *Zeke*?"

"I would imagine you'll find him downtown at the Lariat."

The Lariat bar was one of three bars in Lonesome. Like a lot of Montana towns there were more bars than churches, more pickups than cars, more Stetsons than baseball caps.

Tom checked the time as he picked up the paper, folded it and stuffed it into pocket. 8:45 a.m. If Zeke were already at the bar, it would mean one of two things—he'd been there all night, or he was starting earlier than usual. Either was trouble.

"Is this like my initiation? Bringing in Zeke?" Tom asked half-jokingly.

"I hear that he's mellowed," his brother said, still without looking up from his desk.

Tom laughed doubtfully. Even Zeke mellowed would be wilder than probably any bronc he'd tried to ride.

James looked up. "If you can't handle it…"

In the Colt family, those words were tossed out as a challenge at best. At worse, foreplay for a fistfight.

"I'm on it," Tom said as he headed for the door. This was definitely a test—just not one he'd expected. But there was no turning it down.

Colt Investigations was housed in an old two-story building along the main drag. Their father, Del, had bought the building, rented out the ground floor and used the upstairs apartment as an office.

But James was currently working on moving the office to the ground floor now that Tom was joining the business. The upstairs would remain an apartment where James was living while his house was being built on the old Colt Ranch outside of town. He and Lori, who owned the sandwich shop next door to Colt Investigations, would be getting married on the Fourth of July weekend.

"What did Zeke do this time?" Tommy asked, stopping just inside the office door before leaving.

"Drunk and disorderly, destruction of property, resisting arrest. The usual. His mother put up the bail. He missed his court hearing yesterday."

"Great," Tom said. "So all I have to do is walk him over to the jail."

James chuckled as he looked up from what he'd been working on. "Easy peasy for a guy like you."

Tommy grinned, nodding. "I knew you were jealous of how much bigger, stronger and tougher I am than you. Better looking, too."

"Yep, that's it," his brother joked. "The longer you stand here giving me a hard time, the drunker Zeke will be. Just a thought."

"Uh-huh." He put on his Stetson and strode on out the door.

It was only a little over a block to the Lariat. The town was still quiet this time of the morning. Not that there was much going on even later. Lonesome was like so many other Montana towns. Its population had dropped over time, but was now growing again as more people left the big cities for a simpler lifestyle. That was Lonesome. Simple.

He pushed open the door and was hit with the familiar smell of stale beer and floor cleaner. In the dim light, Tommy thought that this could have been any bar, anywhere in Montana. There were mounts of deer, elk, antelope and rainbow trout on the knotty-pine walls. The back bar was a warbled mirror with glowing bottles of hard liquor under canned lights.

At the end of a long scarred wooden bar sat Ezekiel Murray. His massive body teetered on a stool, body slumped forward, his huge paws wrapped around a pint of draft beer that he had just dropped a shot glass of whiskey into—shot glass and all. The whiskey was just starting to turn the beer a warm brown. Tommy would bet it wasn't his first boilermaker and would win.

In Lonesome, Zeke was known as a gentle giant—until he got a few shots in him. Tommy tried to gauge how far gone Zeke was as he approached the man.

Chapter Four

Other than Zeke, the bar was empty except for the bartender, who was busy restocking. A newsman droned on the small television over the bar, with neither man paying any attention.

"Hey Zeke," Tommy said as he joined him.

A pair of unfocused brown eyes took him in for a moment before the man frowned. "Which one are you?"

The thing about the four Colt brothers…they all resembled each other to the point that often people didn't bother with their first names. They all had the same thick head of dark hair that usually needed cutting and blue eyes that ranged from faded denim to sky blue depending on their moods.

They were all pretty much built alike as well and all liked to think that they were the most handsome of the bunch. Close in age, they'd spent years confusing their teachers. They were simply known around the county as those wild Colt boys.

Having been gone on the rodeo circuit now for so long, Tommy wasn't surprised that Zeke might not remember him.

"I'm Tommy Colt."

Zeke nodded, already bored by the conversation, and lifted his glass to his lips.

"I need you to take a walk with me," Tommy said standing next to Zeke's stool.

The big man looked over at him before the drink reached his lips.

"Your mother... She posted your bail."

"I don't want any trouble in here," the bartender called from a safe distance.

"Won't be any trouble," Tommy assured him. "Zeke doesn't want his mother upset. Do you, Zeke."

He wagged his big head and started to put down his drink, but then thought better of it and downed the whole thing. The shot glass that had been floating in the beer clinked against the man's teeth and rattled around the beer glass as he slurped up every drop of the booze before setting it down with a loud burp.

Okay, this probably wasn't going to go easy peasy at all, Tommy thought as Zeke got to his feet. Even at six foot four, Tommy had to look up at Zeke. And while in good shape from years of trying to ride the wildest bucking horses available, he knew he was no match for the big man.

Zeke pulled a few bills from his pocket, slapped them down on the bar and turned to Tommy. "Ready when you are."

They left the bar as the sun crested the mountains to the east. It was a beautiful summer day filled with the scent of pine from the nearby forest and that rare smell of water, sunshine and warm earth that he loved. There was nothing like a Montana summer.

Tommy couldn't believe his luck. Was it really going to be this easy? The courthouse was kitty-corner from the bar. Tommy was tempted to jaywalk, but Zeke was insistent that they walk up to the light and cross legally.

Lonesome had begun to wake up, a few cars driving past. Several honked, a couple of people waved. Tommy could just imagine what he and Zeke looked like, the gentle giant looming over the cowboy walking next to him.

The light changed. They were about to cross the street when Zeke seemed to realize where they were headed. "I thought we were going to see my ma?"

"But first we need to stop by the courthouse." The jail was right next door. Once inside, Zeke would be the deputy's problem.

"This about what I did the other night?"

"I suspect so," Tommy told him. "But once you go before the judge—"

Zeke turned so quickly Tom never saw the huge fist until it struck him in the face. He stumbled back, crashed into the front of the electronics store and sat down hard on the pavement. He could feel his right eye beginning to swell. Blinking, he looked up at Zeke.

"You realize I'm going to come after you again if you don't go peacefully with me now. Next time I'll bring a stun gun. If that isn't enough, the next time I'll bring a .45. I'm working with my brother James at Colt Investigations now and my first job was to bring you in. So, sorry, Zeke, but I gotta do it."

"I didn't say I wasn't going," Zeke said. "But I have to at least put up a fight. How would it look if I just let you take me in?" With that the man turned and walked on the crosswalk toward the courthouse.

Tommy got to his feet, only then starting to feel the pain. This was worse than getting thrown off a bucking bronco. He hurried after the man.

Once Zeke was in custody, Tommy headed back toward the office. He'd taken a ribbing from the deputies, but growing up with three brothers, he was used to abuse. He'd known this job wouldn't be easy, but so far it wasn't making him glad he quit the rodeo.

Worse, he could well imagine what James was going to say when he saw him. *Gentle giant my ass*, Tommy was thinking as he looked up and saw her. Bella Worthington.

She'd just come out of the bank and was starting to put on her sunglasses. She was crying.

"Bella?"

She hurriedly wiped the tears on her cheeks and lifted her chin, defiance in her gaze, before covering those amazing more-green-than-blue-today eyes with the sunglasses. He'd known her since they were kids playing in the woods together since their family properties were adjacent to each other.

Bella had been defiant even at a young age. Her father had forbidden her from playing with any of the Colt boys, but she'd always snuck out to meet him at the tree house they'd built together. They'd been best friends. The kind of friends that would let the other take a splinter from a finger with a pocketknife. The kind that would fight the town's worst bully even knowing the linebacker was going to kick your behind bad. The kind of friend the other would lie to protect.

"You all right?" he asked, thinking of the last time he'd seen her—just weeks ago. She'd been laughing, her head tilted back, the look in those eyes warm with emotion. They'd spent a few days and nights together, curled up on the couch in her suite at the hotel and watching old movies until they both fell asleep. They'd ordered room service breakfast and drank champagne promising that they would do it again soon.

He thought about the sweet scent of her, the way her long dark hair shone like a raven's wing, floating around her shoulders as she moved. He thought of the way she threw back her head when she laughed, exposing the tender pale flesh of her throat. And that laugh... He smiled to himself. But it was her voice he heard at night when he closed his eyes. A conspiratorial whisper next to his ear.

He and Bella had always been best as a team. Best friends for life, he thought, touching the tiny scar on his finger that they'd cut with their pocketknives to take their blood oath. It was as if they'd both always known how it would end, the two of them falling in love and getting married. Together forever.

Or at least that was what he'd thought, especially after their weekend in Denver. While they'd spent the time only as friends, he'd seen the promise in her eyes when she'd given him her cell phone number. "Call me. I've missed you, Tommy." She'd hesitated. "If you're going to be in Lonesome..."

He'd been surprised that she was going to the ranch and said as much. "Dad" was all she'd said with a shrug, as if it explained everything since he knew Nolan Worthington only too well. It would have something to do with business. He was always trying to get her to join him in the partnership he had with the Mattsons.

"Maybe I'll see you there," he had said, not realizing that within the next few weeks he would completely change his life for a woman he hadn't even kissed yet.

"I'm fine," Bella said now, looking embarrassed and not all that glad to see him. Even as she said it, she shook her head, denying the words out of her mouth. As her hand went to her cheek to snatch away the last fallen tear, he saw the ring and felt his eyes widen, the right one widening in pain.

"You're *engaged*?" He couldn't help his shock. He felt gutted. She hadn't been engaged the nights they'd spent together and that was only a couple of weeks ago, or had she? *"Since when?"*

"It just happened," she said, clearly avoiding his eyes.

He shook his head, trying to make sense of this. If there'd been someone special in her life, she would have told him the weekend they were together, wouldn't she? He thought they told each other everything. Or at least used to. *"Who?"*

She cleared her throat before she spoke. He caught the slight tremor in her lips before she said, "Fitz."

He laughed and said, "That's not even funny." Of course she was joking. They'd grown up with Edwin Fitzgerald Mattson the Third. Or the *turd*, as they'd called him. Fitz had been two years older and the most obnoxious kid either of them had ever met. His father was the same way. Edwin Fitzgerald senior was Bella's father's business partner along with his son.

Because of the business arrangement, both Fitz and his father often came to the Worthington ranch. Whenever they did, Bella's father always insisted that she spend time with Fitz. But he cheated at games, threw a tantrum when he lost and told lies to get Bella into trouble if she didn't let him get his way.

Often when she knew Fitz and his father were coming to the ranch, she and Tommy would take off into the woods. They could easily outsmart Fitz as well as outrun him. Spoiled rotten, Fitz loved nothing better than making the two of them miserable. Bella had always despised Fitz, who Tommy had heard hadn't changed in adulthood.

He stared at her. "You wouldn't marry Fitz."

Anger flashed in her gaze. "Why not?"

"Because he's a jerk. Because you can't stand him. Because you can do a hell of a lot better."

"What? With someone like you?" She raised an eyebrow. "Run into a doorknob, Tommy?" she asked, indicating his right eye, which was almost swollen shut now.

"Zeke punched me, so it could be worse. Don't try to change the subject. Were you engaged when we met up in Denver?" She shook her head. "So you got engaged in the past week or so?"

She pushed her sunglasses up onto her long, dark hair and stared at him. "I don't want to talk about this with you, all right?" Instead of anger, he saw the shine of tears.

"Why would you agree to marry him?"

"Maybe he was the only one who asked," she snapped.

Tommy shook his head. "Come on, you aren't that desperate to get married or you would have asked me."

She bit her lower lip and looked away. He saw her swallow. "And what would you have said?"

"Hell yes. But that's only if you had gotten down on one knee," he added in an attempt to get things between them back like they had been not all that long ago.

Bella shook her head. "What are you doing in Lonesome? Don't you have a ride down in Texas?"

He glanced down at his boots and sighed. This certainly wasn't going the way he'd seen it in his dreams. "After we saw each other again in Denver, I came home." He met her gaze. "You said you were going to be here. I left the rodeo circuit."

"Why would you do that?" she asked, her voice break-

ing. She knew he'd loved being part of the family legacy.
He'd been on the back of a horse from the time his father
set him in a saddle while he was still in diapers and told
him to hang on.

He'd grown up looking at the old Hollywood poster of
his great grandfather Ransom Del Colt, the Hollywood
cowboy star; his grandfather, RD Colt Jr with his Wild
West show; his own father, Del Colt. Rodeo was in his
blood and if anyone knew how hard it was for him to give
up, it would be Bella.

He met her gaze. "Maybe after I saw you in Denver,
I wanted more."

She looked away and he could see that she was fighting tears again. "You're a fool. So now you're jobless?"

Her words felt like the flick of a whip and smarted
just as much. "I'm working with James at the detective
agency. The eye? I brought Zeke in after he skipped out
on his bond. I've applied for my PI license. I'm staying
in Lonesome."

She let out a mirthless laugh. "Great job. Bucking
horses trying to kill you wasn't enough? Now you're
going into the detective business? Look where it got
your father."

He let out a low curse of disbelief. She knew how
much he'd idolized his dad, who'd started Colt Investigations after his injury. Del had never made a lot of money
but he'd helped a whole lot of people.

"I can't believe you would really go there, Bella, especially after all these years of being contemptuous of
your father using money to control you."

"I'm supposed to be happy about you going into a business that got your father killed?" she snapped, sounding
close to crying. "But it's your life."

"Right, and you're marrying Fitz, so what do you care?" Her chin rose in defiance. "What exactly is he offering you?"

"You wouldn't understand," she said and shifted on her feet as she slid the sunglasses back over her eyes and looked down the street away from him.

"Looking for your fiancé?" he asked. "I suspect Fitz wouldn't want you anywhere near me."

"You're right, Tommy. The best thing is for you to stay away from me." Her voice broke and he saw her throat work as if she'd wished she'd swallowed her words rather than let them fly out like she had.

"Wow, the difference a couple of weeks can make," he said as he took a step back. "I sure misread that weekend with you. Maybe a whole lifetime spent together. Guess I didn't know you as well as I thought. I take it back. Fitz is perfect for you." He started to turn away.

"Tommy?"

He heard the tearful plea, felt her fingers brush his sleeve and he stopped to look back at her. What he saw in her expression nearly dropped him to his knees. Just then he saw Fitz appear behind her, all decked out in a three-piece suit that probably cost more than Tommy's horse. The man didn't look happy to see him talking to Bella, but Fitz's displeasure was nothing compared to Tommy's.

"Good luck," he said to Bella and turned away before he put his fist in Fitz's face. He felt shock and disappointment and an unbearable sense of loss as he walked away. He and Bella had had something special. He was sure of that. Why would she agree to marry Fitz? It was inconceivable, especially after the two of them had been together just like the old days merely weeks ago. It wasn't possible that in that period of time she'd gotten engaged.

And yet he'd seen the large diamond on her finger. He'd heard the words come out of her mouth.

So why was he still unable to believe it?

He slowed his steps. He kept thinking about the last look that Bella had given him in Denver. Could the woman change her mind that quickly? Especially a woman he'd known all his life. He thought of the hours they'd spent in their tree house. They'd shared their secrets, they'd shared their desires, they'd even shared their blood with their prized pocketknives. He thought of the two of them together in Denver. That lifetime connection was still there—only stronger.

He stopped and looked back. Fitz put his arm around Bella, but she pulled away only to have him grab her hand and jerk her roughly back toward him. Lovers' quarrel? Or something else?

He caught a glimpse of Bella's face. Something was wrong. He knew this woman. She wasn't acting like a woman in love.

Chapter Five

Bella was still shaken when she reached her car after seeing Tommy—only to be accosted by her so-called fiancé. Fitz. She hated everything about him. The way he brushed back his blond hair with that arrogant shake of his head. She really hated that smug expression that marred an otherwise handsome face. He was strong and fit. No doubt he had a trainer who kept him that way. But he wasn't agile. Even as a kid, he couldn't climb a tree or jump a ditch or run fast enough to catch her.

He'd always been a bully and that hadn't changed. She shoved away that image of the pudgy Edwin Fitzgerald Mattson. The man she was dealing with now was much more formidable.

Looks were everything to Fitz. Like his car, his fancy condo in the city, his gold jewelry he seemed so fond of. She'd caught the glint of a few inches of gold chain at his neck. It must have been new because he kept reaching up to touch it as if to make sure it was still there.

But it was that self-satisfied look on his face that had made her want to attack him on the street, her hatred of him growing by the hour. The problem was she didn't know how she was ever going to beat him at his own game. He had her neck in a half nelson and wasn't about to let go until he got what he wanted.

She warned herself that she had to keep her cool and pretend she was going through with this ridiculous wedding that Fitz was planning. He had invited everyone in the county. He was so sure that there was nothing she could do to get out of it.

The only way she could keep from losing her mind was by telling herself she was merely stalling for time. She would get this sorted out. She would see that her father's name was cleared so Fitz could no longer blackmail her—or die trying.

Just the thought of Fitz made her stomach roil. Worse was the thought of Tommy Colt because that made her want to sit down and bawl her eyes out. He was right. She was in love with him. She'd been from as far back as she could remember. He'd been her bestie. He'd been her everything growing up.

Her father had been immersed in his business. When Nolan was around, so was his partner and Fitz. It was no wonder that she preferred the company of wild boy Tommy Colt and his equally feral brothers. They'd been her true family.

Now, as she drove toward the ranch, she knew that feeling sorry for herself wasn't doing her any good. She had to figure out what to do next—and quickly. She'd never felt more alone. Or more scared. The clock was ticking, the wedding coming up fast.

Looking down at the pretentious huge diamond ring on her finger, she wanted to rip if off and throw it out the window. But what would that accomplish? She had to help her father. Losing her temper would only make matters worse.

TOMMY WATCHED BELLA and Fitz part at her vehicle. Clearly angry, Fitz drove off in an obnoxious mustard-yellow sports car, the tires smoking. Bella sat in her SUV for a few minutes before leaving as well. He recalled that she'd been crying as she came out of the bank. He knew what it took to make Bella cry.

What had happened inside the bank? Was it about Fitz? Or something else? He had to find out what was going on and felt better as he turned back to the bank, even though his right eye was now almost swollen shut. He'd finished his first job for the detective agency. Now it was time for him to start believing that he could do this work.

Having grown up here, Tommy knew most everyone. One foot in the door of the bank and he spotted a young woman in one of the glass-wall offices. Carla Richmond had long black hair and large brown eyes. One of his brothers had dated her for a while, though he couldn't remember which one.

He stuck his head into her office doorway. "Have a minute?"

After her initial surprise, he could see her trying to figure out which one he was. "It's Tommy," he said as he stepped in and closed the door behind him. "I could use your help."

It was clear that Carla thought he'd come in for a bank loan. She started to reach for an application form, but he stopped her as he took a chair in front of her desk.

"This is awkward," he said, leaning forward. "I wouldn't ask but it's important. It's about Bella. Bella Worthington?"

She nodded and carefully replaced the form she'd been about to hand him. "You realize that I can't talk about—"

"She left here crying."

"I'm sorry to hear that," Carla said carefully.

"I don't want specifics, okay? I just need to know what might have caused the tears." He saw her jaw set. "Her father's rich. I would think she would come out of a bank all smiles." He caught that slight change in her expression. Something in those dark eyes. He felt a start.

"Tommy, you know I can't talk to you about bank business." She started to stand.

"Please, just tell me if you know why Bella was crying." He put his hand over his heart. "She means everything to me."

She sat back down and shook her head, but he could feel her weakening. "How is your brother Davy?" she finally asked as if changing the subject.

So it was Davy she was interested in. "He's still rodeoing, but I suspect it won't be long and he'll be coming home. You want me to let him know that you asked after him?"

She started to shake her head but stopped. "I suppose. If it comes up. We dated for a while in high school."

He smiled at her. "That's right. Look, how about you say nothing and I just run some thoughts past you." Before she could argue, he went on. "I doubt Bella is having any financial problems. Her business is going great guns from what she'd told me."

Carla's expression confirmed it.

"So who does that leave?" Again, that quick flicker in her eyes. He frowned. "Her father? Is he ill?" Tommy would have heard. Bella would have mentioned it. It dawned on him what Carla was *not* saying.

He let out a curse. It was a bank, not a hospital. "It's financial to do with her father." She looked past him again, clearly nervous. He could tell by her pained expression that he'd guessed it. "He's in financial trouble?"

She avoided his gaze as she rose and stood with her palms pressed to the top of her desk. "As I said—"

"I get it. You can't tell me." Tommy stood up. "I'll take one of those loan forms if you don't mind."

Carla looked relieved as she pulled out one and handed it to him. "I didn't tell you anything. Not a word."

He nodded. "Thanks." He held up the form. "I'll tell Davy I saw you."

Was it possible that Nolan Worthington was in financial trouble? If so, it would certainly explain what Bella was doing back in Lonesome at the ranch. With a curse, he realized it could also explain why she had agreed to marry Fitz. He thanked Carla and left her office.

He had to see Bella again.

But first he needed his brother's help.

James looked up from his desk and grinned as Tommy came into the office. "Nice eye. Zeke?"

"Good guess." He pulled the signed, delivered form from his pocket and tossed it on his brother's desk.

James picked it up, saw what it was and blinked. "I thought that might be your resignation letter."

"I told you, I'm in this all the way. We have a new case."

His brother lifted a brow. "A paying case?"

Tommy shrugged and pulled up a chair in front of his brother's desk. "If you don't agree it's a case we should take, well then I'll pay for it as your new partner."

"I'm not sure you understand how the business works," James said as he leaned back in his chair, but Tommy could tell that he was intrigued. He quickly told him about running into Bella as she was coming out of the bank crying.

"She's engaged to Fitz!" James shook his head. "I thought you said you and she—"

"Exactly." He told him about their conversation and then about Fitz showing up and the two arguing on the street. "I could tell something was wrong so I went into the bank. Did you know Carla Richmond works there?"

"Davy's old girlfriend. They were pretty serious back in high school."

"Right, anyway, she couldn't divulge anything about bank business…"

"But you got it out of her." James was sitting forward now, clearly interested.

"It's Nolan Worthington. He's in financial trouble."

James blinked. "Bad investments?"

"I don't know. It still doesn't make any sense. Why would a self-made man who went from nothing to filthy rich be so stupid as to make bad investments?"

"Is the partnership in trouble or just him?" James asked.

"No idea." He hadn't even thought of that. Maybe his brother was a better investigator than any of them had thought—and the one big cold case he solved wasn't a fluke.

James opened his computer and started to type, then abruptly stopped. "Wait. You were just with her in Denver. She didn't mention any of this, including the engagement?"

"She wasn't engaged but she said she'd gotten a call from her father and was headed for the ranch. She didn't sound happy about it. Something is wrong for her to even consider marrying Fitz." James looked away. "What?" Tommy demanded, knowing the look all too well.

"I didn't want to be the one to say it, but…" James looked up. "Maybe she's marrying Fitz because her dad's in trouble financially."

"I already thought of that, but we're talking about Bella. She isn't like that."

When James raised a brow, Tommy swore, wanting to cuff his brother upside the head for not believing him. "Then how do you explain it?" James finally said. "Did you ask her?"

Tommy sighed, got up and walked over to the Hollywood poster of his grandfather. Her being engaged to Fitz made no sense. Was it possible this woman he'd loved for so long was that shallow? Had he been a fool to quit the rodeo and come back here?

He turned back to his brother. "She said Fitz was the only one who'd asked."

"You think she's just trying to get you to step up?" James asked.

Tommy shook his head. "She knows how I feel about her. Even if I haven't spelled it out, this engagement is too sudden. Knowing what I do know about her father, I have to help her."

"That's just it," James said. "You don't know anything for certain. You need facts."

"You're right," he said as he came back over to the desk. "I need to find out the truth—with your help, bro. I need a quick course in PI."

"Then pull up a chair and let's see what we can find out about Nolan Worthington and his business and partners, Edwin Fitzgerald Mattson and his obnoxious son, Fitz."

THAT FIRST DAY BACK AT the ranch, Bella had been forced to drag the sorry tale out of her father. He'd said he hadn't been paying enough attention to what was going on with the business. Edwin had him sign papers all the time. He hadn't thought anything about it.

"What did he get you into?" she demanded. She'd never trusted Edwin Mattson let alone his son Fitz, who was now invested in the business.

Her father shook his head. "I'm in trouble. The Feds are involved. I have no proof that I didn't do any of it. But these businesses it says I bought? They're money laundering operations." He broke down, dropping his face into his hands. "I sold them as soon as I realized what I'd apparently done, but I lost so much money and the Feds are even more interested in me now."

She had to pull every sorry word out of him, but she quickly got a picture of what Fitz had done to him. He'd tricked her father, who hadn't realized that at least Fitz—and maybe his father as well—had set him up to take away the business Nolan had started. Of course, if he were arrested on a felony, he would be forced out of the business he'd started.

"It's worse than even that," her father said. "Fitz says he has proof that I've been embezzling from the company for the past six months for my drug habit. I'm sure that if any money is missing, it's been going into his pocket. But while none of that is true, added to the mistakes I've made..."

"You look guilty." He was also acting guilty, she noted. "So basically they're about to fleece you," she said and frowned. "You've hired a good lawyer, right?"

He looked at the floor. "I made a bad investment. I'm afraid I'm broke. It's all gone. Everything but this ranch and now I'm headed for prison."

Her hatred for Edwin and his son had her pacing the den in fury. "Surely you have some recourse."

He lowered his head, shaking it slowly. "The judge usually goes easy on a first-time offender—if I agree to pay back the money, but that's impossible. On top of that, now with the Feds... Edwin and Fitz have been setting me up for months." He met her gaze. "They have our investors believing I have a drug problem. A few months ago at a restaurant I was drugged and appeared..." He broke down again. "There'd been rumors going around about me, I guess, started by them. I found drugs in the glove box of my car and got rid of them, but I never know where drugs are going to turn up. They have me tied up. There is nothing I can do."

Her blood boiled, but she knew she had to keep her head. One of them had to be strong right now. "There must be a way to prove that this is all a setup." She stared at her father. It couldn't be possible. There was no way the man she'd known all her life was taking this lying down. Nolan Worthington had gotten where he'd been by being smart and doggedly determined. He'd built the business that Edwin and Fitz were now stealing from him. "There has to be something we can do."

His gaze lifted to hers. She caught hope in his green eyes so much like her own. "Fitz said he can make it all go away."

She waited, knowing that whatever her father said next would be bad. She just didn't know how bad. "What do you have to do?" she asked in a whisper.

"Fitz has been taking over his father's part of the company for some time now. He's the one who's in control, according to Edwin. If so, Fitz has me right where he wants me. You know he's always been jealous of what I built, this ranch—"

"What is it Fitz wants?" she demanded, fear edging her voice. She knew Fitz, knew the kind of boy he'd been, the kind of man he'd grown into. "What?"

Nolan Worthington held her gaze tremulously. "You. He wants you."

She shook her head and took a step back, too shocked to speak for a moment. "Well, he can't have me."

Her father nodded in resignation. "I can't say I blame you."

They both went silent for a long moment. "What happens if he doesn't get his way?" she finally asked, remembering the deplorable child she'd known.

Nolan Worthington looked away. "It doesn't matter. I can't ask you—"

"Tell me." She waited.

He finally looked at her again. His eyes filled with tears. "This isn't your problem. I got myself into this and—"

"Tell me what happens if he doesn't get me."

"He'll send me to prison," her father said. "He'll plant more drugs. He'll see that I get the maximum time. Twenty years."

Twenty years. A life sentence at his age. She swallowed and said, "Fitz is going to have to say that to my face."

"You won't have to wait long. He said he plans to meet you here at the ranch." Her father pulled himself together. "I need to tell the staff. He's replacing them all and basically kicking everyone out but you—even if you agree to marry him. I'd rather let them go than have him do it."

"Wait, he can't just take over the ranch. You said it's in my name."

Her father stared at the floor. "He said he plans to stay here until the wedding and if you didn't like it, you could discuss it with me in my jail cell."

Bella was unable to speak. If Fitz thought he could bully her... But even as she realized it, she knew that it wasn't an idle threat.

Her father stumbled to his feet and reached for her. "I knew I had to tell you what was going on. I'm so sorry, but I can't ask you to—" He hugged her and she felt him trembling.

"And if I do this?" she asked, her anger making her blood thunder through her veins.

He let go of her to step back so he could see her face. She saw a glimmer of the father she'd known flash in his eyes as anger. "Then he will produce evidence that proves I'm innocent. He said he'd even buy my share of the business. I'm sure he will do it for pennies on the dollar, but at least I won't be in prison."

She wasn't able to believe this. "How can he make this all go away just like that?" she demanded with a snap of her fingers.

"Apparently he has another scapegoat."

Bella stared at him. "His father?"

"I don't know. Maybe this was Edwin's idea."

She shook her head wondering if her father really believed that. "So what do you get if I go along with this?"

"I'd be out of the company," he said. "But Fitz will pay me enough that I could live comfortably, but only if I left the country since my reputation is ruined, thanks to the two of them. Even with proof, no one will believe I wasn't guilty."

Chapter Six

As threatened, Fitz had arrived a few days after Bella's return to Lonesome. He'd driven up in his expensive yellow sports car—one that verged on ridiculous in this part of Montana. He'd be lucky if he didn't break an axle on the ranch road. Come winter, he'd high center the car in the deep snow and freeze to death. She could only hope.

Bella had warned herself not to lose her temper. It wouldn't help her father even though she knew it would make her feel better.

Fitz shook back his mop of blond hair to expose small blue eyes the color of twilight. He had that same haughty look on the classically handsome face that he had as a boy. It said, *I'm spoiled rotten and hateful and there is nothing you can do about it.*

She feared this time he was right as she opened the door before he reached it. She'd called him days earlier, wanting him to confirm what he'd told her father—and record the conversation. He'd ignored the calls.

He stopped, a smirk coming to his lips as he pushed his sunglasses up onto his head and met her gaze. Bella thought she could have started a fire with the heat radiating out of her eyes. For a moment, he didn't look quite so sure of himself.

"I'm assuming you talked to your father," he said as he looked around, clearly avoiding her laser gaze.

"My phone messages weren't clear enough for you?"

His gaze came back to her along with the smirk. He raised an eyebrow. "You called me?"

She said nothing, waiting. Let the bastard admit what he'd done. She had her hand around her cell in the pocket of her pants, her finger hovering over Record.

He finally looked at her again. "I suppose he told you. Damned shame. Your dad should have known better."

That she could agree on. She'd never liked him going into business with Edwin Fitzgerald Mattson even before Fitz got involved. There was something about the man that she hadn't trusted—even as a child.

"So now what?" Fitz asked, getting visibly annoyed to be left standing outside the lodge. Had he really expected to be invited in?

"You tell me."

"At least invite me in. After all, pretty soon this ranch will be mine." He laughed and started up the steps toward her. "Excuse me, *ours*. It will all be ours."

"Over your dead body," she said, making him stop in midstep.

He raised an eyebrow, his mouth quirking into a smirk. "I thought your father would have told you how much trouble he's in. I hope you have the money for a good lawyer for him. He's going to need it. My father and I were shocked when we found out what he's been doing behind our backs."

She couldn't believe Fitz would lie like this to her face. Then again, she knew she shouldn't be surprised. She said as much, daring him to tell the truth for once.

His expression suddenly changed as if he realized what she was up to.

He came at her, grabbing her arm and pulling her hand from her pocket with the cell still clutched in it. With a laugh, he pried the phone from her fingers. "You said you wanted to talk, when you left me all those messages."

"So you did get my messages," she said. "Too bad you didn't take any of them to heart."

"Threatening my life?" He shook his head. "You are only adding fuel to the fire. Like father, like daughter."

What made her even angrier was that he was right. She needed to keep a clear head and find a way out of this. Threats were a waste of time. But it would be next to impossible not to want to claw his eyes out.

"If anything, you should be nice to me," he said smiling broadly. "It's to your advantage."

"I wouldn't count on that," she snapped, unable to hold her tongue.

His blue eyes, a deep navy, darkened even further as he gave her a push back into the open doorway.

It was all she could do not to physically push back. She feared what would happen though if she could get her hands around his neck. But he was right. He had the upper hand. At least for the moment. She took a step back and then another, afraid of what she would do if he shoved her again. She needed time to try to find a way out of this. She wasn't letting her father go to prison. But she also wasn't marrying this fool.

Once in her father's study, Fitz closed the door. "I could use a drink. How about you?" he asked as he walked to the bar.

"A little early in the day for me." He went to her father's bar as if he owned the place. Apparently he would soon enough unless she could stop him.

"Where's the help?" Fitz asked as he turned from the bar, a full drink in his hand. "There's no ice in the bucket."

Since her father normally lived in an apartment near his office in Missoula, there had been only part-time staff at the ranch except during the months he came here to stay. "My father let the staff all go as per your instructions apparently," she said. It was hard to be civil to this man. But she'd try a white flag of surrender first. If she didn't get the information she needed, she'd resort to all-out war.

Fitz chuckled. "I think that is the first time Nolan has ever done anything I asked him to do." He smiled. "How times change."

She watched him take a slug of his drink, lick his lips and settle his gaze on her again before she asked, "Your idea of a marriage proposal is to frame my father?"

He had the good grace to drop his gaze to the floor for a moment. "Over the years, I've tried other approaches."

"I recall. Slamming me against a file cabinet to grope my breast. Cornering me in the kitchen and spilling your drink down the front of my blouse as you forcibly tried to kiss me."

"'Forcibly' is a tad dramatic," he snapped. "I've tried nicely to get your attention. I decided on a different approach after you rebuffed my every advance."

"You could have just gotten the message and backed off."

His gaze hardened to ice chips. "I don't want to back off. In case you didn't get the message, I want you and I will use any measures to have what I want."

She nodded. "Just like when you were a boy and didn't get your way. This is just another form of tantrum." She turned and walked to the window so he couldn't see how hard she was shaking. None of this was going to help her father. If anything, Fitz would tighten the screws.

Bella turned to look at him again. It was all she could do not to gag at the sight of him slurping down her father's expensive bourbon. She could never let him win, for her father, for the ranch she loved, but mostly for her own sake. She swore right then, she would kill him before she ever became this man's wife.

"What now?" she asked trying to keep the tremor out of her voice.

He smiled as if he thought she'd finally accepted the inevitable. "We get married. Didn't your father tell you that I want the whole package? A big wedding. I've already sent out invitations to most of the county. It's going to be in the barn here at the ranch. It's going to be till death us do part."

She nodded, thinking she could live with the death part. "I really can't see you married to anyone, let alone me."

He put down his empty glass and stepped toward her. She stood her ground even as the floor seemed to quake under her. Reaching into his pocket he pulled out a velvet box and shoved it toward her.

She didn't take it, didn't move. Instead, she looked down at the floor. Fitz was simple and spoiled, but he wasn't entirely stupid.

He let out a sigh. "Fine. We can do it your way if that's what will make you happy." She watched him drop to one knee and thought since he was already on the floor how easily it would have been to end this right now. One good kick with her cowboy boot and he would be helplessly writhing on the floor. But it wouldn't help her father if she went to prison as well right now.

"Bella Alexandria Worthington, I'm asking for your hand in marriage," he said with a sigh and opened the box.

The diamond engagement was gaudy and ridiculously ostentatious. She looked from it to him. "It looks exactly like something you would choose." If he caught the sarcasm, he didn't show it.

"Only the biggest and best for you," he said and took the ring from the box and reached for her hand.

She thought of her father and tamped down her fury. Was she really going to let this man blackmail her into becoming his fiancée? If she hoped to stall for time to figure a way out of this, she had to at least let him think she was.

She stuck her hand into his face and he put the ring on her finger. It surprised her that it almost fit. He must have found out her ring size. She met his gaze, wondering what else he'd found out about her. That she'd been with Tommy recently for an entire weekend? It wouldn't matter that they hadn't made love. Fitz had always been jealous of the closeness she and Tommy had shared over the years.

As Fitz awkwardly got to his feet, she realized how dangerous this man was. What he'd done to her father was diabolical. All because she'd spurned his advances?

Bella looked down at the ring on her finger. Maybe this was just a show of power. He wanted her to know that he was in control. He didn't really want to tie himself to a woman who couldn't stand the sight of him, did he?

"Why would you want to marry me?" she asked quietly.

The question seemed to take him by surprise. "Have you looked in the mirror lately?" he asked with a laugh. "I want other men to look at me with naked jealousy."

"I saw your sports car. You can have any woman you want, women who are better looking than me. So why me?"

"Because I can and because you and I are the same." She instantly wanted to argue against that, but he didn't give her a chance. "Bella, you go after what you want. Look at the way you turned your father down when you had a chance to go into business with him."

"With you and your father you mean."

He smiled. "Yes, with me. That was a mistake. You should have joined the partnership and not forced me to take other measures." He was blaming her for this? "You and I could own the world."

"I don't want to own the world," she said and swallowed back the bile that rose in her throat. The conceit of this man, the hollowness of his desires, his all-out criminal behavior, and for what? Just to feed his ego?

"Well, you'll be with me soon and I want to own the world any way I can get it," he said.

"I can see that." He seemed to take her words as a compliment until he looked into her eyes.

"You may not like my methods. Fight me all you want, but I'd hate you to have to visit your father in prison. That is, if he doesn't overdose before then. Or jump out a window from our office building. Desperate men do desperate things."

Her hands knotted into fists at her side. She heard the threat and knew it wasn't idle. It was all she could do not to lunge for his throat.

"As your fiancé I'll be moving into the ranch right

away since the wedding is going to be here and it's coming up soon. Your large new barn is the perfect place for the wedding, don't you think?"

She shook her head. "You're not moving in here."

Fitz moved swiftly for a man of his size. "When are you going to realize that you no longer have a say in anything?" He grabbed her by the waist and pulled her into a kiss. She bit his lip, making him howl. He took a step back and slapped her so hard her ears rang, but he didn't try to touch her again.

As he'd gone back to the bar, Bella had promised herself that Fitz would never be her husband. One way or another, she would stop this marriage.

Chapter Seven

Tommy pulled up a chair as his brother began to type at his computer. "Let's see what we can find out." He watched James go to a variety of sites, taking notes, determined to learn as much as he could quickly.

"This is interesting," James said. "Six months ago, Nolan bought some small businesses. During those six months, he'd gone through a lot of money on top of what appears to be several bad investments."

"So he is broke?"

"This does not look good. Car washes are cash-heavy businesses like casinos and strip clubs. Simply owning businesses like that is a red flag for the Feds. This could get him investigated for money laundering even though it appears that he turned around and sold them quickly at a loss, which frankly I would think makes him look even more guilty."

"You think he's involved in money laundering?" Tommy asked in surprise.

James lifted an eyebrow and shrugged. "The thing is, in most business partnerships, if one of the partners is arrested for a felony, the remaining partners can buy him out for pennies on the dollar."

"So you're saying that Nolan Worthington could lose everything."

"It certainly looks that way," his brother said. "I always thought he was a smart businessman. Didn't he start the investment business from the ground up? No wonder Bella's upset." James began to type again on the keyboard. "But at least it looks as if the ranch is in her name. That's good."

"Until she marries Fitz," Tommy said. "Then he'd own fifty percent should there be a divorce." Tommy thought about the ranch that Bella loved. She wouldn't jeopardize it to save her father, would she? "How did this happen?" He knew he was asking why Bella would have ever agreed to marry Fitz under any circumstances.

"Greed? The business with Edwin Mattson seems to be doing fine," James said. "Maybe Nolan wanted to make more money. Maybe he got involved with the wrong people." He seemed to hesitate. "I did hear a rumor that he might have gotten involved with drugs."

Tommy shook his head. "Nolan? That's not possible."

James shrugged. "Fitz started his own business no doubt financed by his father. He's doing fine. Didn't Bella start her own business?"

He nodded. "But she's barely gotten it off the ground. She wouldn't have the funds to bail out her father."

James closed his computer. "Could explain why she's agreed to marry Fitz, though."

Tommy wanted to argue that James didn't know Bella the way he did. She'd never marry Fitz under any circumstances, let alone marry any man for money. But there was that huge rock he'd seen on her ring finger. Not to mention the words out of her mouth. He stood and shoved back the extra chair. "I've got to talk to Bella."

BELLA KNEW THAT she had to move quickly after Fitz's visit. The wedding day he had chosen was coming up fast. She realized that her father hadn't really explained how Fitz had left him so bankrupt. Conning him out of the partnership was one thing. What about her father's other investments? He shouldn't be this broke.

She called Fitz's father, wondering what kind of reception she would get. Edwin senior had always been kind to her even though she'd never trusted him. But when it came to Fitz, Edwin had almost been apologetic. Had that changed? Surely he was aware what Fitz was up to.

"Edwin, it's Bella," she said when he answered his phone at the office. For a moment all she heard was silence on the other end. "I'm sure you know why I'm calling. There's a few things I need to know. Starting with my father's finances."

There was a deep sigh. "This is something you should be asking your father."

"I'm asking you," she said, hating that underlying regret she heard in the man's voice as well as the pleading in her own. "Please. There is so much going on right now with Fitz... Tell me why my father's broke." She could understand Fitz and Edwin using the clause in the partnership to get him out of the business. But there had to be more going on here.

Edwin cleared his throat. "Apparently you are unaware of your father's indiscretions."

"Indiscretions?"

The man sounded embarrassed. "You really should take this up with your father."

"I would but I don't know what *this* is," she said losing her patience.

"Ask him about Caroline."

The name meant nothing to her.

"That's all I can tell you. I'm so sorry." Edwin disconnected.

Bella knew he could tell her much more, but he wasn't going to. Apparently she would have to hear it straight from the horse's mouth. How much more had her father kept from her?

He had gone back to his apartment in Missoula, which was only blocks from his office. She'd been so busy starting her online Western wear business that she hadn't been to his apartment since he'd first rented it. Instead, what little she'd seen of him had been at the ranch—usually at his request. Now she wondered if that was because he kept this Caroline at the apartment.

On the drive to Missoula, she had too much time to think about all of this. As she reached the new high-rise apartment house and parked, that stupid engagement ring on her finger caught the light, winking at her as if in on the ruse. She took it off and tossed it into her purse.

Her father's SUV was in the lot, but when she reached the reception area on the lower floor, the man behind the desk wasn't going to let her go up.

"He's had movers in and out all day," the man dressed in a security uniform told her. "Other residents are complaining about him tying up the elevator."

"You can take it up with him," she said. "I'm his daughter and I'm going up to see him."

The man looked as if he wanted to argue. "Fine, but please tell your father that the movers he hired need to use the service elevator."

Her father was moving? So much for her theory that he was keeping this Caroline woman in the apartment. But where was he moving? Surely not back to the ranch.

Or was he preparing for prison? she thought with a sense of panic as she took the elevator up to his floor and rang his doorbell.

Her father opened the door, clearly surprised to see her after their discussion at the ranch a few days ago. She was equally surprised to find him in such disarray. He hadn't shaved for a couple of days and appeared to be wearing the same clothes he'd had on the last time she'd seen him.

Past him, the apartment was filled with boxes. She caught the scent of old takeout and saw the food containers discarded on the breakfast bar along with several nearly empty alcohol bottles before she closed the door behind her and stepping past him. Her father never drank much, just a nightcap of his precious bourbon— not the rot-gut stuff that had been in the discarded liquor bottles she was seeing.

"I haven't had time to pick up," he said, stepping to the breakfast bar and beginning to toss items into the trash.

She moved deeper into the apartment. "What is going on?"

He stopped cleaning up, seeming surprised. "I already told you."

"You apparently left out a few things," she said. "Who is Caroline?"

All the blood drained from his face. He planted a hand on the breakfast bar as if to steady himself. "Who...who told—"

"It doesn't matter who told me."

"Fitz? Or his father?"

She'd never seen Nolan Worthington look more defeated. She wanted to reach for him and assure him that they would get through this. Except she didn't know the extent of what this was. But from the look on his face, this was even worse than what he'd told her before. "What have you done?"

He bristled and straightened taking on the stature of the father she'd always known. "I'd appreciate you not using that tone with me." She waited. "Could we at least sit down?"

She looked around for a place to sit, moved a couple of half-packed boxes and sat. He went to the breakfast bar. Picked up one of the almost empty bottles of bourbon and poured what there was into a dirty glass.

"I'd offer you one but…" He drained the glass, then came into the living area, moved a box and sat down some distance from her. The alcohol put a little color back into his face. "I made a mistake. It happens."

Bella sighed. How many mistakes had he made? Even more than he'd admitted to so far. "Just tell me so we can deal with it."

His Adam's apple bobbed for a moment before he spoke. "I met a woman. Caroline Lansing. I… I fell in love with her."

"She took all your money." It was a wild guess, but she saw at once that she'd hit a bull's-eye on the first try even as she told herself that her father was too smart to be swindled by a gold-digging woman. But he'd been alone for years since her mother's death. Lonely men could be easy prey for a female with criminal designs.

And Bella hadn't been around. "How bad is it?" She knew it had to be very bad.

"She… I…thought we were getting married. She let me believe that she had money, but that it was tied up in real estate, so I…" He shook his head. He didn't need to continue.

"She's long gone?" He nodded. "With your money?"

Another nod. "None of that matters right now," he snapped. "Fitz is trying to put me in prison."

When she said nothing, he added, "Go ahead and say it. I was stupid. I was played for a fool." His voice broke. "I was in love for the second time in my life."

Bella didn't know what to say. There really wasn't anything she could say. "Is there nothing left?"

"Just the ranch."

She had a feeling that her father would have probably raided the ranch for this woman if he hadn't legally put it in his daughter's name. She would bet money Caroline, whoever she was, had wanted every last cent he had and would have gotten the ranch if she could have.

"So this is why you're broke, this woman? Do you have any way to get your money back from her, legally or otherwise?" she asked.

He shook his head. "It's gone. She's gone."

"How long did you know her?"

"I met her six months ago," he said. "I was...distracted and Fitz took advantage."

Six months. Was that when Fitz began plotting to destroy both her father and her? Bella glanced around at all the boxes. "Where are moving to?"

"Everything is going into storage." He met her gaze. "My life is so up in the air, and I can't come back to the ranch. I know Fitz is moving in."

"That's what he says." She had much bigger problems. If she didn't marry Fitz, her father would be going to jail and then prison. Even if she did marry Fitz, her father's future was still uncertain. He was broke. Fitz was threatening to enforce the breach of contract clause in the partnership so that her father would lose everything, including his reputation.

"How did you meet this woman?" Bella asked.

"She came to the office, wanted advice on an investment," he said sheepishly. "One thing led to another."

She didn't doubt that Fitz had taken advantage of her father being distracted by this woman. But she couldn't help being suspicious that he'd been set up, and not just by Caroline. It seemed odd that the woman just happened to be sent back to her father's office.

"Do you have a photo of her?" Bella asked.

Her father looked surprised. Who kept a photo of the woman who had fleeced him? A man who'd truly believed he'd been in love. He started to reach for his cell phone.

"Send it to me and everything you know about her." She got to her feet. Her father looked better than when he'd opened the door. He had raised a strong, resourceful, smart daughter. However, she doubted even she could save him from himself. But she would try because he was her father.

She kissed him on the cheek as she left. The tears she'd seen in his eyes made her hate Fitz even more than she thought possible because all her instincts told her that he'd had something to do with everything that Nolan Worthington was now going through—and her as well.

FITZ STOOD ON the steps of the ranch house, considering what he would do with the place once it was his. Once Bella was his. He touched his tongue to his lip where she'd bitten him. Anger made him see red. Once they were married, she was in for a rude awakening.

He'd moved up the wedding from the original date he'd planned, anxious to teach her how things were going to be. That was if he could wait that long. She would soon be his in every way whether she liked it or not.

Smiling to himself, he realized that he wouldn't mind if she fought back. It might make taking her all the more enjoyable. He knew it would be an even bigger thrill to get her on her knees than the excitement and joy he felt when he took over businesses and crushed the life out of them.

A truck pulled up out front. He saw it was from the locksmith shop in town. An elderly man climbed out. "You the one who needs the locks changed?" the man asked, glancing around. "Where's Nolan?"

"He's away on business. He asked me to take care of it. Unfortunately, I'm locked out."

The locksmith looked wary.

"I'm Edwin Fitzgerald Mattson the Third. My father and I are Nolan's business partners." At least for the moment. "Bella's my fiancée."

The man didn't move. "Where's Bella? Going to need either her or her father before I change the locks."

Fitz was about to let out a string of curses when he heard a vehicle approaching. With relief he saw it was Bella. He wondered where she'd been. He was going to have to clip her wings. She couldn't just come and go without a word to him about where she was going, but one step at a time. Clearly, she needed more convincing about who was in control here.

"Here's Bella now," he said, seething inside at how she'd locked him out of the ranch house. He really needed to bring this woman to heel and soon, he thought, narrowing his eyes at her as she climbed from her SUV. And he knew exactly how to do it.

"I understand you want the locks changed," the elderly locksmith said to her as she approached.

Bella glanced from the man to him. Her look was so defiant that for a moment Fitz worried that she would embarrass him in front of this old man.

"Oscar," she said, turning to smile at the locksmith. "I appreciate you coming all the way out here." She turned to Fitz. The challenge in her eyes sent a spike of pure fury straight to his gut where it began to roil. So help her, if she defied him on this—

"Let me open the door, Oscar, so you can get the work done and be on your way. I know that you like to have lunch with your wife. How is Naomi doing these days?"

"She's fine, thank you for asking, Bella." Oscar grabbed his toolbox from his pickup and started up the steps after her.

As the man passed Fitz, he didn't even give him a glance. "I have some wedding arrangements to take care of," Fitz said from between clenched teeth. "I'll see you later." Not that either Bella or Oscar was listening. Bella was busy offering the locksmith a glass of iced tea for when he finished the job.

Fitz was almost to town when he realized his mistake. What were the chances Bella would give him one of the new keys? He swore, slamming his palm against the steering wheel. He should have stuck around until he had the key. She thought she was so much smarter than him and always had.

He considered what he would do if she locked him out again. It was time to teach that woman how things were going to be from now on.

He pulled out his cell phone and made the call.

Chapter Eight

Oscar had just finished changing the locks and given her the new keys when her phone rang. She didn't recognize the number, but something told her to take the call anyway. "Hello?"

"Bella." She could barely hear her father's voice, but she immediately picked up on its urgency. "I've been arrested. I need you to get me a criminal lawyer. I'm so sorry." There was noise in the background. "I'm about to be booked on a drug charge. I got pulled over. They found drugs hidden in the door panel on the passenger side of my car. He put them there." His voice broke. "I have to go." The phone went dead.

She clutched her phone, closing her eyes and trying hard not to cry. Fitz. She'd childishly locked him out of the ranch house and this was how he was getting back at her. When they were kids, he'd been sneaky and vengeful. She knew better than to taunt him.

The new keys in her hand, she threw them across the floor, angry with herself. If she was going to do something to him, then she had to be more careful. She had to be smarter. Taunting him would only make her father.

She had no idea how bad the drug charge would be—

depended on how much was found in his car. While her father probably wouldn't get any time as long as it didn't appear he was selling the drugs, this would only add to the story Fitz was concocting against him.

Opening her eyes, she looked around the ranch. She and her father loved this place. She'd missed it desperately being away as she started her business. Now they were about to lose it. Her father was going to have legal fees, she thought as she made the call. Because of Fitz.

There had to be a way to stop the man before this ridiculous wedding. If she were stupid enough to marry him, he would find a way to take the ranch, she knew that, and her with it.

She spoke for a moment with a prominent criminal attorney a friend had used. As she hung up, she heard the sound of a vehicle pulling up. She took a deep breath. If it was Fitz, she feared what she might do that would only make things worse yet again. But it didn't sound like his sports car.

Bella stepped to the entryway, picked up the new keys from the floor and opened the door. Tommy Colt was climbing out of his pickup. Her heart leaped to her throat. He stopped to look up at her and she felt tears of relief fill her eyes. She'd never been so glad to see anyone in her life. He'd always been there for her—even after what she'd said to him on the street in town.

Propelled by nothing but raw emotions, she rushed down the steps and into his arms—just as she had in Denver.

THIS WAS NOT the reception Tommy had expected. Far from it. He breathed in the scent of her, the feel of her in his arms and held her tightly. She smelled wonderful, felt wonderful. He didn't want to let her go.

When she finally pulled back to look at him, he saw that she'd been crying. Again. "I'm in so much trouble, Tommy."

"I know. At least I suspect. That's why I'm here." He let her go as she stepped back and wiped her eyes.

"If Fitz catches you here—" Her voice broke. "There is so much I need to tell you. But not here." She seemed to be trying to come up with a place that was safe. Her green eyes widened. "Meet me at the tree house in ten minutes and I'll tell you everything."

He didn't want to leave her, seeing how upset she was, but quickly agreed.

"Take the back road out of here. Fitz can't see you," she said.

He could see how frightened she was and, while he didn't like leaving her alone, he had to do as she asked. Clearly, she was afraid of the man. Tommy had never known her to be afraid of anything. What had Fitz done to put this much fear in her? He drove out the long way before circling back to the ranch's adjacent property— Colt Ranch property.

The road in wasn't as bad as the last time he'd seen it. They'd had a mobile home on the property to stay in when they were home from the rodeo circuit but one of James's girlfriends had rented it to some meth makers and had gotten it blown up. James had had the debris hauled off when he and Lorelei began building their house on another section of the property. Each brother had his own section to build on, if they ever decided to settle down.

Tommy parked and hurried through the pines toward the back side of Bella's ranch. He was scared for her, worried Fitz would come back and keep her from meeting him at the tree house.

But as he came through an open area, he saw her standing at the bottom of the ladder waiting for him.

The tree house looked as if it had weathered the years fairly well considering. "You'd better let me go up first," he said to her, seeing how nervous she was. He doubted her worry though was about the wooden structure the two of them had built together all those years ago.

One of the steps felt loose as he climbed up and pushed open the door. It looked as if some critters had made themselves at home in one corner, but other than that, the space looked better than he'd expected. He wondered if some area kids had discovered it and been keeping it up. There were several wooden crates someone had brought in. He dusted off one of them.

Turning he started to hold out a hand to help her up, but Bella was already coming through the door. He moved back to let her enter and handed her a crate to sit on.

For a moment they simply looked at each other, then she put down her crate and sat. He grabbed the other one, shook off the worst of the dust and sat down as well. The wooden crate creaked under his weight but held. He couldn't help but think of the hours he and Bella had spent here together, and the weekend they'd spent together recently. They had a bond that couldn't be broken, he told himself.

"A little different from that suite we shared in Denver," he said to break the silence. They'd watched movies, played cards, ordered room service and gone for long walks. They'd reconnected in a way that had made him realize that he no longer wanted to live without this woman by his side.

"So you're engaged?" he said even as he knew it couldn't have been her idea. He couldn't have been that wrong about her. Or how they both felt about each other.

Bella gave him a wan smile, tears sparkling in all that green before she dragged her gaze away. "I don't even know where to begin." He said nothing, waiting. "I told you that my father had called me and that I was headed home?"

From there she spilled out a story that shocked and infuriated him. "I'll kill the son of a—"

"No, that's just it. If either of us do anything, he'll just send my father to prison. He isn't bluffing. He planted drugs in my father's car and just had him arrested because I locked him out of the ranch house."

"You aren't seriously going to marry him," Tommy said, trying to tamp down his fury. He'd felt such relief when she'd told him that she'd been coerced into the engagement. But he hadn't realized how serious it was until now.

"I'm not marrying him," she said with a shake of her head. "But unless I can find evidence that proves my father is being framed…" She met his gaze. "I want to hire Colt Investigations."

He blinked. He had little PI experience. The skin around his eye was still bruised from taking Zeke in. "Bella, I appreciate your confidence in me but—"

"I'm so sorry for what I said on the street—"

"No, what I'm saying is that you need to hire an experienced investigator."

She shook her head. "You and your brother are the only people I can trust right now. I'll help. I know enough about my father's business and I have a key to his office—if Fitz hasn't had the locks changed. Will you help me?"

"You know I will," he said. He'd do anything for her. He realized sitting there, a shaft of sunlight coming through a slit between the old boards and lighting her face, that he would die trying to save her because he was crazy in love with her.

"But we can't be seen together," she said. "Fitz can't know that we've even talked after seeing us together in town. You probably shouldn't call me on my cell, either."

"I'll get us burner phones. I'll find us a safer place to meet." He grinned. "We grew up here. We know all kinds of places where we can be completely alone."

She smiled and let out a sigh. "I feel better than I have since my father called me. We can do this. We have to."

He nodded. "If you need to reach me before I can get the phones, call Lorelei and she'll get a message to me." He considered the trouble she was in and wished he could do more. Nothing like diving into a new job headfirst and blindfolded. But he was a fast learner and James would help from the sidelines.

She reached across the space between them and held out her pinkie finger. Tommy laughed at their old ritual they'd enact before leaving the tree house. He hooked his pinkie with hers.

"Best friends forever," she said and met his gaze.

Till death do us part, he thought.

Chapter Nine

Bella hoped she hadn't made a mistake by dragging Tommy into this, but she needed help and he was the only one she trusted right now. She'd left the ranch house front door unlocked and was glad she had when she returned.

Fitz's sports car was parked in the drive. She circled around so it would appear she'd come from the trail along the river—rather from the woods that led to the Colt property.

"Where have you been?" Fitz demanded when she walked in the front door.

"For a walk along the river." She met his gaze. "My father's been arrested."

He nodded and smiled. "Drugs, huh. Such a shame. I see you left me a key to the house." His look said he hoped that she'd learned her lesson. He looked way too pleased.

But she had learned her lesson, she thought, heart pounding. It still took all her control not to attack him with her words let alone her bare hands. She warned herself to be smarter as she started past him toward the kitchen.

He grabbed her arm. She froze, telling herself to play along—but only so far. Glancing over at him, she gently pulled her arm free. "Unless you've hired new staff, I was just headed for the kitchen to see about dinner. I don't know about you, but I'm hungry."

He seemed surprised that she could cook. Let alone that she might cook for him. "What are we having?"

"I'll surprise you." Before she started away, she saw the wary look come into his expression and smiled to herself. Let him worry about her poisoning him.

In the kitchen, she turned her thoughts to Tommy Colt. She'd made the right decision telling him. He was her bestie. She'd realized how much he meant to her in Denver. The feelings had always been there, but she'd never acted on them. Neither had Tommy.

It was as if the two of them were giving each other space, knowing that one day... She shook her head at the thought. No wonder he'd been so upset to see the engagement ring on her finger. She couldn't bear that she'd hurt him. But everything had been happening so quickly.

Tommy. Just the thought of him made her heart ache. Once this was over... Right now she needed her best friend more than ever. Tommy was the only one she trusted with this news. With her life. He might be new to PI work, but he was smart and resourceful. Together, she had to believe that they could outsmart Fitz. They had to, because the clock was ticking. Fitz had already sent out the invitations to the wedding that was just over a week away.

BACK AT THE OFFICE, Tommy told his brother everything that Bella had told him. His gut reaction had been for the two of them to find Fitz and beat him senseless.

"Not an option," James agreed.

"But definitely what I want to do. Not that it would do

any good. He's really set up Bella's father bad. We have to stop this before the wedding."

When he told him the wedding date, his brother groaned. "Nothing like a challenge. Are you sure about this? Bella is strong-willed as you already know. You sure she won't refuse to marry Fitz?"

Tommy shook his head. "She won't let her father go to prison. And neither of us think it's an idle threat. Fitz just had Nolan arrested in a drug bust. He planted the drugs. He did it because she locked him out of the ranch house. He's serious."

James shook his head. "He wants Bella that badly?"

Tommy looked away. "Maybe we should have been nicer to him when we were kids."

"Come on, I remember the kind of kid Fitz was. He's just grown up into a meaner adult. He sees Bella as something he can't have so he's determined he will have her," his brother said. "She's probably the only person who's ever said no to him."

"So what do we do?" Tommy asked as he banked his anger.

"We need to get the proof. The truth will be in the real bookkeeping," James said. "Which means it's on a computer somewhere. Didn't the partnership have an accountant? I'd start with him." His brother thought a moment. "You've got to hand it to Fitz. He came up with the drug addiction as a way to show where the embezzled money went. Otherwise, there would need to be evidence of large expenditures like boats, cars, big vacations."

Tommy had a thought. "If you were her, wouldn't you demand to see the evidence he's holding over her head before she agreed to marry him?"

His brother beamed at him. "Very smart. That way

we know where it is and how hard it will be to get. You think Bella will do it?"

He laughed. "We're talking about Bella, remember? She has more guts than anyone I know. But that doesn't mean that Fitz will go along with it."

As BELLA CAME in from the kitchen, she saw Fitz nervously rearranging the salt and pepper shakers, straightening the cloth napkins on the table and shifting his chair to put himself directly in front of the place setting in front of him.

She frowned as she put two plates of food on the table, one in her spot and the other in front of Fitz. She realized this wasn't the first time she'd seen him do something like this. When he was a boy, he had to have everything just so from his clothing to his room.

As she started to sit down, he suddenly grabbed her plate and switched it with his. She looked over at him and smiled as she picked up her napkin and laid it carefully in her lap. "Have you ever seen the movie *The Princess Bride*?"

"Of course. It's…" Fitz frowned and then quickly switched the plates back, making her laugh. He looked miserable. Did he really want a lifetime of this?

Picking up her fork, she took a bite of her dinner. She'd had a lot of time to think while she was cooking. She would have to tread carefully. He'd proven today how vindictive he could be. Anything she did could have major repercussions for her father.

Bella looked up. Fitz hadn't touched his meal. "Is something wrong?"

He scowled at her. "I'm hiring a cook. You won't be allowed in the kitchen," he said angrily.

She shook her head. "Whatever you want, but I made that meal especially for you." She reached across the table, purposely knocking over the saltshaker as she did, and jabbed her fork into a piece of the sweet-and-sour chicken dish she'd made.

Gaze locked with his, she brought the bite to her lips, opened her mouth and popped it in. As she began to chew it she watched Fitz pick up the saltshaker and put it back exactly as he'd had it before. She reached over, this time just moving the saltshaker a fraction of an inch out of line, and skewered a piece of pineapple.

She'd barely gotten the bite to her mouth when he grabbed the saltshaker, his hand trembling as he squeezed it in his big fist. She recalled how Fitz had always had to control things when he was a kid. Apparently, he hadn't changed—only gotten worse because now he thought he could control her.

"There is nothing wrong with the food on your plate," she said. "Cross my heart." She made an X over her heart and smiled.

Angrily, he shoved back his chair, knocking it over as he rose. "You like messing with me? Tormenting me? You should know better. Have you learned nothing today?"

"I haven't done anything but leave you an extra set of keys to *my* house and make you dinner." She reached over and stabbed one of the sliced carrots on his plate and popped it into her mouth. "You can't blame me if you're paranoid."

He was breathing hard, his face flushed. "I can't wait until we're married. I will make you pay dearly. Nolan always held you up as an example. 'Look at Bella. Isn't she amazing? So smart, so talented, so independent.'"

She looked into his eyes, feeling his hatred like a slap. "Just because my father loves me and is proud of me—"

Fitz let out a bitter laugh. "He put you on a pedestal and stood next to you, just asking for someone to knock you both off."

"I'm sure he didn't mean to make you feel—"

"Like I could never measure up?" Fitz grabbed the chair up from the floor. For a moment, she thought he was going to hurl it at her. But he seemed to catch himself. He slowly lowered it to the floor and gently pushed it in. She could see him trying so hard not to reposition it perfectly.

"He was just proud of his daughter," she said again, quietly. But Fitz had seen it as her father comparing her to his partner's son. "With my mother gone—"

"Well, soon I will have his daughter and then we'll see how proud he is of you when he has to watch what I do to you."

Bella felt a shudder move through her. She had no doubt he would make good on all his threats. Now at least she had some idea why he was doing this.

"I'll be back with my things and a new staff, including a cook, first thing in the morning," he said. "I wouldn't suggest you do anything to stop me. Once we're married..." He sneered at her. "You will be mine to do with as I see fit in every way and there won't be anything you or your daddy can do about it." With that, he turned and left.

She felt a sob rise in her throat and tears sting her eyes. He planned to tear her down, dominate her, destroy, her and all to prove that he had always been smarter, more talented, more everything. He was fool enough to think it would make him feel better about himself.

Taking an angry swipe at her tears, she made a solemn oath that he wouldn't beat her down no matter how hard he tried. Nor would he destroy her because she was never marrying him.

She finished her meal, although she'd lost her appetite, but she wasn't going hungry because of Fitz. His hatred for her and her father scared her. She regretted involving Tommy and Colt Investigations. It terrified her, what Fitz would do if he found out.

Yet a part of her needed Tommy for support, needed his help. After their time in Denver, she'd missed him. Something had happened between them during that long weekend. Not that either of them had acted on it. But their feelings for each other had grown into something special that she hadn't anticipated. Or maybe she had, she thought with a laugh. Maybe that was why she'd looked up his rodeo schedule and made sure they'd crossed paths.

Given the way she felt about him, she told herself that once she got the burner phones he was picking up, she should fire him. This was her mess. She shouldn't have dragged him into it. Knowing how cruel and heartless Fitz could be, what would he do to Tommy if he got the chance?

She shuddered at the thought. But even as she thought it, she knew that Tommy would keep trying to help her even if she did fire him. The thought warmed her. The truth was she needed Tommy on so many levels. She couldn't do this without him. She'd just have to make sure that Fitz never knew.

When she finished dinner, she took their dishes to the kitchen. She was loading the dishwasher when she remembered something. About a year ago, she'd been home to the ranch and overheard her father on the phone arguing with Edwin. He'd been upset about some deal Edwin had made with a company called Mammoth Securities Inc. Her father had warned Edwin not to do it. She was pretty sure the man had gone ahead.

There might be something there she could use. With a sigh, she knew she'd have to ask Tommy to look into it. But with luck, they might be able to fight fire with fire.

She turned on the dishwasher and left the clean kitchen. She had no idea where Fitz had gone or when he would be back. She didn't trust anything he told her. She called Lorelei, James's fiancée. "Can you get a message to Tommy? Also, could you pass on a photo and some information I have for him?"

Chapter Ten

Tommy had spent the day finding out everything he could about Edwin Fitzgerald Mattson the Third. Fitz looked good on paper, but the more he dug, the more questionable behavior he found.

He'd been reprimanded at boarding school for bullying. He'd also gotten into a cheating scandal at university. His father bought him out of both by making donations to the schools.

But Tommy had tracked down one of the former administrative assistants who'd been involved and gotten fired over it. The man had been most happy to give him the dirt on Fitz.

Unfortunately none of that would help the current situation, though. They already knew what kind of man Fitz was. What he discovered more recently was that Fitz had fired the partnership's long-time accountant six months ago. He felt that might be important since it was about the same time that Nolan Worthington had met the mysterious Caroline Lansing.

"How do we find this woman when we can't even be sure she gave Nolan Worthington her real name?" Tommy asked his brother.

James considered that for a moment. "Remember that kid in school, Lance Black's little brother?"

"Ian?" Tommy nodded.

"He's FBI. I think you should give him a call. Didn't you save his life that time in the river?"

Tommy laughed. "It wasn't quite that heroic. I did haul him out of the water, that much is true. But if you think he might help, I'll give him a call."

Ian sounded glad to hear from him. When he told him what he needed, Ian promised to see what he could find out. Tommy sent him the photo of Caroline and what information Nolan had given Bella and she'd sent to him through Lorelei.

"It's good to hear from you," the FBI agent said. "So you and your brother have taken over your father's PI business. Congrats. Probably safer than riding bucking horses."

Tommy wasn't so sure about that. "It's been interesting so far." He thanked him and then left to meet Bella.

He was already waiting for her at the abandoned old fire tower high on a mountain outside of town when she drove up. He could tell something more had happened even as she tried to hide it.

"You can talk to me," he said after they climbed up the four floors and took a seat on the landing. From here the view was incredible of the river valley and the mountains around them. They used to come here and drink beer with a friend who manned the tower during fire season. Now it was an empty locked shell that hadn't been used in years.

As the sun sank in the west leaving the sky blood orange, Bella nodded without looking at him and told him what Fitz had said to her. "I'm sorry I involved you. Fitz is dangerous. I can't let anything happen to you."

Tommy fought his anger, knowing, as James had said, if they did what they wanted to the bastard, it would only make things worse for all of them. He reached over and took her hand. "Nor can I let anything happen to you. I'm helping you no matter what you say. That's what we do, you and me."

She looked at him, those green eyes filling. "Tommy."

He put his arm around her and pulled her close. She felt warm and soft in his arms. He pulled back a little to look at her. All around them, darkness began to fill in under the towering trees. The air felt cool and crisp, scented with pine. The beautiful summer night filled him with memories of the two of them—and such love for this woman.

Tommy leaned closer, slowly dropping his mouth to hers. He brushed his lips over hers. He'd dreamed about kissing her from as far back as he could remember. He'd always feared that it could spoil their friendship. He was way past that now.

Her lips parted on a sigh as she leaned into him. He pulled her closer, deepening the kiss. She wrapped arms around his neck and drew him down for an even deeper kiss. Their first kiss to the music of the summer night was everything he'd known it would be.

He drew back slowly and looked into her eyes. "The marriage isn't going to happen. We're not going to let it."

She nodded and snuggled against him as they looked out over the darkening land. After a while, he took one of the burner phones out of his jacket pocket and handed it to her. "Keep it close. My number is the only one in there."

She nodded and took the phone before telling him

about the conversation she'd overheard between her father and Edwin Mattson.

"We're going to need to get into his office and Fitz's."

"I have the key to the main office door."

Tommy smiled over at her. "If Fitz is moving into the ranch tomorrow, I think we'd better break in tonight."

"I know the security guard should he stop by. He won't think anything about me being there. I just can't make things worse for my father. I got him a lawyer. He should get out on bail. At least for the moment. We discussed what he should do until his hearing and he's signing himself into rehab even though he doesn't have a drug problem."

"Smart. But I'm worried about you alone in that house with Fitz," Tommy said.

"There will be staff. I can hold him off until the wedding." She didn't have to mention that the wedding was coming up fast. He knew that Fitz had moved it up from the original date. The man certainly was in a hurry.

"There isn't going to be a wedding," he said again. "Let's go see what we're up against at the office. More than likely he wouldn't leave any evidence lying around. It's probably in a safe. Know a good safecracker?"

"No. I know a good locksmith, though," she said. "I also know Fitz." Then she leaned in and kissed him. "For luck," she said smiling.

THE OFFICE OF Lonesome River Investments was in the older part of Missoula on the river. The partnership had bought the narrow two-story brick building. It had a vintage clothing store on one side and a coffee shop on the other side, both leased to the businesses.

Bella used her key to open the outer door. They

stepped into a stairwell and she locked the door behind him before they started up the stairs to the second-floor offices.

This floor had been completely remodeled with lots of glass and shiny metal. Her father, who'd originally started the business, had been content with the original exposed brick and worn hardwood floors. But Edwin had insisted appearance meant everything when dealing with other people's money.

She used her key to open the door off the landing and quickly put in the security code. She felt Tommy's worried gaze. Wouldn't the first thing Fitz would have done be to change the code?

No alarm sounded. Bella let out the breath she'd been holding, but grew more wary as she neared the separate offices. Edwin's was the first along the hall across from her father's. Fitz's office was behind his father's with storage and a conference room at the end of the short hallway.

She passed Edwin's dark office and headed straight for Fitz's. She told herself that while Edwin had to be in on this scheme, Fitz would keep the evidence close—not trusting anyone—including his father.

As she reached the door to his office, she was only a little surprised to find it locked. She and Tommy had expected this.

"I've got this," Tommy said and pulled out his lock pick set. "Thanks to my misspent youth." It took him only a few moments to get the door open.

"Nice job," she said. Both of them had gotten quite good at picking locks as teenagers. It was a skill though that they'd never imagined using at this age, she thought.

Once in his office, she turned on the overhead light knowing it would be less suspicious from the street to alert security. Her father paid for a security patrol in the area.

Bella went right to Fitz's desk. It was too clean. No desktop computer. No laptop, either. Which meant that Fitz always had it with him in that large briefcase he carried.

She wondered what he actually did for his pay here. She opened each drawer. All too neat. The bottom drawer was locked. She motioned to Tommy that she needed his lock pick when he was finished.

Tommy had gone to the filing cabinets against the wall, picked the lock and was now going through the files.

She was rusty at this, but the desk drawer lock was simple enough it didn't take her long. She opened the drawer. Empty except for a single folder. She pulled it out and placed it on the table. As she did, photos fell out and spread across the table.

Tommy was at her side in an instant, having heard the shocked sound she'd made. Every photo was of Bella. They appeared to have been taken over the years, most with a telephoto lens from some distance. Tommy was in many of the photos.

"What the hell?" he said as he went through them. "Sick bastard."

"He's apparently been spying on us for years," she said, surprised her voice sounded almost normal given the trembling inside her. She'd become the man's obsession long before she had any idea of what was going on in Fitz's mind.

"Has he been planning this for years?" Tommy said more to himself than her. He started to throw the photos in the empty trash can under the desk, but stopped himself. "This could be evidence if things go south." He pulled out his phone and spread the photos across the desk next to the calendar with "E. Fitzgerald III" on it and snapped a half dozen shots.

She put the photos back into the file and locked them in the drawer again. She felt uneasy and realized why. Had Fitz known she would break into his office? Had he put them in the locked drawer for her to find?

"Did you find anything?" she asked Tommy.

He shook his head as he started around the room, peering under the artwork until he found what he'd been looking for. Removing the painting that had been covering the safe, he took a photo of the safe. "You really do know a locksmith who might be able to open it?" he asked as she joined him.

"Maybe." Bella thought of the single file in the locked drawer. Fitz had known she would break into his office, break into his desk. She couldn't shake the feeling that he'd wanted her to find it.

She touched the dial on the safe and slowly began to turn it.

"Bella?" Tommy said next to her.

Not answering, she finished putting in her birthday. Something clunked inside the safe and the door popped open.

Tommy let out an oath. "What the—"

The safe was empty except for an envelope addressed to her. She hesitated before she pulled it out. It wasn't sealed. Taking out the folded sheet inside she read:

Did you really think I would leave anything here at the office, Bella? You think you know me so well, but the truth is I know you better. I've been watching you for years. That's why I can predict your every move. Speaking of moving, you should get out of there. The moment you opened the safe a silent alarm went off. Security will be all over this building within four minutes.

She crumpled the note in her fist even as she and Tommy quickly exited the building. They had planned to look around Edwin's office. Another time, she thought. Except next time, Fitz would have had the locks or the security code changed.

They were a block away when they heard the sirens and saw the lights as security descended on the Lonesome River Associates offices.

They would have already called Fitz.

FITZ SMILED TO himself as he hung up the phone. Bella thought she could outsmart him. He couldn't wait to see her face. But not tonight, he thought as he turned back toward the woman lying in bed. She was waiting for him, the covers pulled back, exposing her lovely breasts.

Bella was right. He could have most any woman he wanted, like this classic beauty waiting for him. He could do anything he wanted to her. That was what money and power got him.

Yet even as he had the thought, he felt his desire fade. There was only one woman he wanted. Bella. He told himself he would have her soon.

"You should go," he said, turning away to reach for his robe. "It's late."

"Are you sure?" She sounded disappointed even though he'd already had his fill of her.

For a moment, he reconsidered. A bird in the hand…

Or in this case, a breast. He dropped his robe knowing this woman would do anything he asked her and come back for more.

"There's something I would like," he said and opened the drawer next to his bed. Her eyes widened and she drew back a little. "Is there a problem?" he asked as he pulled out the device.

She shook her head as he tossed her a gag and watched her put it on with trembling fingers. All he could think about was seeing that kind of fear and then pain in Bella's green eyes. She would learn soon enough who was in charge now.

"I HATE THE thought of you out at the ranch with that man," Tommy said when they reached the fire tower where they'd left his pickup earlier.

She'd turned off her engine, letting the summer darkness and quiet in. For a few moments, they sat in silence. "He thinks he knows me."

Tommy saw her shift her gaze to him in the darkness of the car. Overhead the sky was splattered with stars, but down here in the pines there were deep pockets of darkness.

"I'm afraid he proved tonight that he knows me better than I know him," she said, her voice breaking. "He's been one step ahead of me."

He reached for her, drawing her to him. She rested her head against his chest as he smoothed her hair. "He won't win. We won't let him. We can beat him, the two of us."

She nodded against his chest and pulled back, biting her lower lip for a moment. "What now?"

"James said you might want to demand to see what he's got against your father. That would let us know where he's keeping it. You could also demand an audit of the books. If Fitz wasn't expecting that move—"

"But if he is expecting it, that would alert the IRS of the embezzlement."

Tommy nodded. "It would mean calling Fitz's bluff. If the auditor suspected at all that there was a second set of books…"

She shook her head. "I don't know. So far Fitz seems to have thought of everything—the drugs in my father's car, the embezzlement, the setup at his office. Clearly, he's been planning this for a long time."

Tommy nodded. "It's a risk, but it could buy us time."

"Let me think about it," Bella said. "Maybe I'll talk to my father. I don't know that Fitz showed him the doctored books. You could be right and they don't even exist."

Tommy nodded and said, "Exactly," but he thought she was probably right the first time. Fitz had planned this. There would be doctored books. What if an audit only put her father in even more jeopardy with the law?

"What did you find out about Mammoth Securities Inc.?" she asked.

"Edwin dumped it at a loss," Tommy said. "That's all I've been able to find out."

Bella started the car. "I'll call you tomorrow the first chance I get."

He wanted to warn her to be careful. But she knew better than anyone what was at stake—and how dangerous Fitz was. "I did want to ask you to marry me." The words just came out as he reached for his door handle and looked back at her.

She smiled. "Is that right?"

Tommy nodded. "I still plan to." With that he got out and headed for his pickup. Had he looked back he would have seen her smiling.

Chapter Eleven

Bella had seen the vehicles pull up in the ranch yard last night from her bedroom window. As she watched a half dozen men exit the vehicles, Fitz drove up and got out of his car before leading the men into the house. Even from where she stood watching, she could see that the men were armed. Several of them looked like thugs. She noticed that those two were the ones Fitz had pulled aside to talk to.

Fitz was preparing for war, she thought, imagining the ranch becoming a fortress to keep only one person in— her. After that, she'd had a fitful night, sleeping little. This morning she'd showered and dressed, determined not to let Fitz get to her.

Her cell phone rang and she saw it was Whitney. She hadn't spoken to her since they'd gotten together after her weekend with Tommy. "Hey," she said as she picked up.

"What is going on? I just heard that you're engaged to Fitz and getting married in a matter of days?"

"It's a long story. I can't get into it right now," she said, wondering if one of the guards was listening outside her bedroom door. "Needless to say, things have been a bit complicated since I returned to the ranch."

"What happened with Tommy?" her friend asked, sounding sad.

"I still feel the same and I'm pretty sure so does he. It's going to work out." Her voice broke. "It has to." She hoped she sounded more positive than she felt right now. "Think good thoughts for me."

"You know I will. I'm a hopeless romantic."

She disconnected and started down the hallway to the stairs. As she did, she heard Fitz's raised voice coming from the guest quarters. Glancing around, she checked first to make sure none of his security was around before she moved down the hallway. Stopping at his door, she listened. He was angry with someone. She didn't catch a lot of his words. He seemed to be walking around with the phone.

"I don't care what you think," Fitz snapped. "I want this and damned if I won't have her."

Bella felt a chill as she realized that he was arguing with someone about her.

"You will back me on this or I'll take you down with him," Fitz yelled. "That's right, you don't think I didn't see this coming?" The laugh made her shudder. "That's right, you did teach me everything I know. Thanks, Dad. But if you bail on me now you'll wish you hadn't."

At the sound of footfalls coming up the stairs, she hurried down the hall before she turned and pretended to only just now be leaving her room. Her heart pounded so hard she thought for sure the security guard who appeared would be able to hear it.

She gave him a smile, but he barely gave her a glance, confirming what she'd suspected. They'd been told not to interact with her in any way. Of course Fitz would want them only loyal to him. The rough-looking guard continued on down the hallway toward Fitz's room. She heard him knock and Fitz open the door and call him by name. Roman. Fitz asked about Milo.

Roman said Milo was on his way. Then the door closed and she could no longer hear their voices. She swallowed, straightened her spine and went downstairs, but had barely reached the first floor when she heard someone coming. The men he'd called Ronan and Milo exited the house without a word.

Right behind them was Fitz. He saw her and he gave her that annoying smirk. It had changed little from the time he was a boy. But now she saw satisfaction in his eyes. They were dark, brooding, so different from Tommy's sky blue eyes that spoke of summer days and sunshine.

"Have a nice night?" Fitz asked as if he'd secretly put spiders in her bed. She could imagine what he'd been like at camp—if he'd ever gone.

"Actually," she said, thinking of Tommy's last words to her, "I did." She smiled, turning his smirk into a frown. "I see you *bought* some friends."

He started to correct her when he realized she'd purposely not said *brought*. She watched him grind his teeth for a moment. "I want you to be safe so I've hired some men to make sure you are."

They had lined up in the living room as if waiting for assignments. Bella knew it was Fitz's idea, a show of force. None of them scared her as much as Fitz himself.

"One of them is a cook?" she inquired. "I hope so because I haven't had my breakfast yet." She knew that needling Fitz wasn't smart, but she couldn't stand how self-righteous he'd looked when he'd entered her house last night with his soldiers as if it were his own. It would be soon enough if he got his way, she reminded herself.

"Roberto," Fitz snapped. "You're in charge of the kitchen. I don't want Bella to lift a finger in there. In fact, I don't want her in there at all. Can you make sure she has no reason to enter?"

"Yes, sir," Roberto said and looked toward her. "Just tell me what you would like for breakfast, Miss Worthington."

The man showing her respect clearly grated on Fitz. She could see him struggling to keep from saying something.

"It's Bella and thank you, Roberto. Surprise me."

As if he could take no more, Fitz barked orders to the five other men to act as security for the ranch house and her. She realized he must be putting them up in the bunkhouse, which meant they would be on the property 24/7 until the wedding.

Bella took a seat at the table in the dining room to wait for her breakfast even though the thought of food made her sick to her stomach. But she would eat every bite even as her stomach roiled. It was clear what Fitz was doing. How long before he ordered the men not to let her leave the house?

Roberto made her huevos rancheros. When she told him that she loved Mexican dishes, he promised to order chorizo, pinto beans, all kinds of peppers and tortillas to make some dishes she might like.

She thanked him and ate her breakfast, which was delicious and seemed to calm her. Her thoughts ricocheted back and forth from dark ones of Fitz to happier ones of Tommy. When she finished, she knew better than to take her plate to the kitchen. She unhooked her shoulder bag from the back of her chair and headed for the front door.

Her burner cell phone was hidden in her car. She'd felt it would be safer there than in her purse or even in her room. Fitz had already shown how low he would stoop. She knew it wouldn't be long before he started going through her things.

She had just reached the front door when she heard Fitz behind her.

"Wait!" he called, his footsteps heavy on the stone floor. Her skin crawled as he came up behind her. "Where do you think you're going?"

She took a deep breath and let it out slowly before she turned to face him. "I'm going into town to get my hair trimmed and my nails done. Do you have a problem with that?"

"I don't think it's safe, you running around with that big rock on your finger," Fitz said. "I'd prefer you take one of our security guards with you."

"I'd prefer not." She pulled the ring from her finger and dropped it unceremoniously on the entry table. It rattled as it skittered across the glossy top, coming to a stop on the edge before almost plummeting to the stone floor. "Problem solved," she said and reached for the door handle.

He grabbed her arm and jerked her back around to face him, squeezing her wrist until she let out a cry. "Haven't you caused enough trouble for your poor father? You don't want to underestimate how far I will go. You will do as I say."

"So you think," she spat over the pain as he continued to grip her wrist nearly to the point of breaking it. "But you will keep your hands to yourself and I will do as I please. You take it out on my father again and I will slit your throat while you sleep. Try me, if you don't believe me."

Fitz let go of her, flinging her arm away. "Once we're married—"

She didn't wait to hear the rest of his declaration as she held back tears of pain, turned and walked out the door. She figured he would station a security guard at his door tonight—and probably one at hers as well.

TOMMY HAD BEEN expecting Bella's call. "Hey," he answered, relieved. Every moment she was in that house with Fitz she was in danger. "You all right?"

"Fine."

He heard too much in that one word. "What's happened?"

"Just Fitz being Fitz," she said, brushing it off. "I'm on my way to Edwin Mattson's office. I heard Fitz arguing with him on the phone this morning. He might help us."

"I'll meet you outside of town at Four Corners. We can leave your car there," Tommy said and disconnected. Four Corners was an old café and gas station where two county roads crossed.

On the drive into Missoula, he broached the subject. "Maybe you should move off the ranch."

"Even if I would give him the satisfaction, he wouldn't allow it. He's made it clear that he'll do even worse to my father. Last night he moved a half dozen security guards onto the ranch. Earlier…" She seemed to hesitate and he saw her touch her wrist. "He tried to keep me from leaving."

"If he hurt you—"

"I told him that until the wedding, he wasn't to touch me and that I would do as I pleased."

"And he agreed to that?"

"*Agreed* probably isn't the right word, but he didn't try to stop me." She turned to look at him as he drove. "Don't worry about me. I can hold my own."

He didn't doubt that under normal circumstances. But this was Fitz. And now he had security guards at the ranch?

"We just need to get our hands on whatever he tricked my father into signing. Maybe Edwin will help us."

Tommy had his doubts, but he didn't voice them. Edwin and Fitz had always seemed a lot alike, two peas in a pod. But if Bella was right and Edwin was against this, then maybe he would help. Unless he was just as scared of what his son was capable of doing as the rest of them.

"Did you know that six months ago, your father and Edwin's company changed tax accountants?" She shook her head. "I suspect it was Fitz's doing. He didn't want their old accountant to catch any red flags."

"So six months," she said. "That at least narrows it down."

He nodded. "Which means past tax returns won't help until we have the current records. I'm wondering if it would do any good to talk to the former, fired accountant."

Bella smiled over at him. "I knew coming to you was the right thing to do."

Tommy took her hand and squeezed it, hoping she didn't regret it. "But first we see Edwin. Fitz already knows that you broke into the office. I don't think it hurts for him to know that you're not alone in this, that I'm doing everything I can to help you."

She nodded but he could tell she was worried. "Just be careful."

"I will. I don't think he'll do anything more to your father at this point," Tommy said, hoping that was true and glad when she agreed.

There was no one at the front desk when they entered the main office. He saw Bella glance at the empty assistant's desk and frown. The nameplate on the desk read Dorothy Brennan, he noticed as they passed.

They walked down the same short hallway they had the other night. Edwin's door was slightly ajar. Bella pushed it open.

The white-haired man behind the desk looked up. Tommy hadn't seen Edwin Mattson in quite a few years and was shocked by how much he'd aged. He seemed surprised to see them. Not just surprised, but nervous.

"What are you…" He looked at the landline phone on his desk as if wanting to call someone for help. Dorothy? Or Fitz?

Tommy closed the door behind them and locked it.

Edwin's eyes widened. He stumbled to his feet. "Bella, what… If this is about Fitz… None of this is my doing. You have to understand—"

"I do understand," Bella said as she stepped into the room and took a chair. Tommy continued to stand, his back to the door. "I heard you on the phone this morning with Fitz. He's got something on you as well as my father."

Edwin slowly lowered himself back into his chair. "I don't know what to say."

"I thought you and my father were friends," she said. "You really won't help him?"

The older man wagged his head. "I can't, even if…"

"What is Fitz holding over your head?" she asked. "Mammoth Securities?"

His eyes widened. "How did you know about—"

"I overheard my father telling you not to get involved with them."

Edwin looked sick. "I should have listened to him."

"Which is also why you can't let my father go to prison for something he didn't do. Fitz has no conscience but I'm hoping you do."

The older man reddened as he looked up at her. "It isn't like your father is completely innocent. He's embezzled money from the partnership before."

"That's not true," she snapped.

"I'm afraid it is. That time, I caught it and we remedied the problem before it was discovered. I would imagine though that it is where Fitz got the idea to use it against Nolan."

Tommy could see that Bella was shaken. "When was this?" she asked and listened as Edwin gave her the details. "But this time?" she asked, her voice breaking.

Edwin shook his head. "I don't know. Fitz swears Nolan's at it again. Are you aware that he has a drug problem?"

"Fitz or my father? My father definitely doesn't. It's all part of this web of lies that Fitz is spinning to control me. That's why I need to prove that Fitz is trying to frame him," Bella said.

"It isn't that easy," the older man said with a sigh.

"Why is that?" Tommy asked.

Edwin seemed to recognize him then. "You're one of those Colt boys."

"Tommy Colt. I'm working with my brother at Colt Investigations."

The man nodded, looking sicker, as if things had gotten even worse. "You realize that if Fitz finds out you came to me…" Edwin shook his head. "You'd be wise not to cross him. Either of you. You have no idea how far he'll go."

"Oh, I have a pretty good idea," Bella said. "Surely you can see that he'll take you and my father down as well. He can't be trusted to keep his word—even if I did marry him."

"If you don't marry him…" Edwin looked terrified at the thought of what his son would do. "I wish I could help, but my hands are tied. You coming here with…" He glanced toward Tommy again. "You're only making matters worse for yourself. Once Fitz has made his point—"

"You don't believe that. He's determined to destroy me and my father. It sounds like he plans to do the same to you."

Edwin started to come around his desk. "I'll see you out."

Tommy shook his head as he unlocked the door. "Don't bother. You made this monster. You need to take care of it."

"Tommy's right," Bella said. "You're just as guilty as he is if you don't do something to stop your son."

"Don't you think I would have stopped him a long time ago, if I could?" Edwin demanded and followed them to the door to slam it behind the two of them.

As they were leaving, Bella slowed at Dorothy's desk

and picked up what appeared to be a dead potted plant before heading for the door.

"Are you all right?" he asked once they were outside. She was hugging the pot with the dead plant, looking close to tears. "Edwin could have been lying." He didn't believe that and he knew she didn't, either, but she looked as if she needed a little hope. He glanced at the pot. "I hate to even ask."

"Dorothy. Her plant is dead." Bella met his gaze. "Which means she not only got fired, but also left in a hurry without her plant."

"Sounds like Fitz is cleaning house," Tommy said. "First the accountant, now the administrative assistant. You thinking what I am?"

Bella glanced at her cell phone. "I want to talk to her, but I can't be gone any longer today. I'm hoping to get into Fitz's room when he leaves again."

"Please be careful," Tommy said.

"Believe me, I am," she said. "How are you doing on tracking down the company's former accountant?"

"Working on it." He hated to tell her that the man seemed to have disappeared.

Chapter Twelve

Fitz was waiting for her when she entered the ranch house. "Roberto has made us a special dinner."

"I'm not hungry," she said.

"Please join me. I have something we need to discuss," he said. "Unless you no longer care what happens to your father." He started to take hold of her arm, but then seemed to think better of it even though clearly she wasn't really being given a choice about dinner.

"Why don't you lead the way," he said and stepped to the side to let her pass. "We're having steak, my favorite. As I recall, you don't like steak. Probably because you had so much of it growing up. There was always beef in your freezer, wasn't there."

"I was raised in Montana on a cattle ranch," she said as she stepped past him. Even though they hadn't touched, she still felt her skin crawl. But what Edwin had told her about her father's earlier embezzlement had her shaken. If true, could it also be the case this time as well?

"Yes, growing up on this ranch," Fitz said. "That's probably why you didn't appreciate it and why you looked down your nose at me when I always asked for steak when we visited here."

"Stop pretending you were some poor kid who went

without food. If I looked down my nose at you, Fitz, it was because you were as rude, obnoxious and demanding as a boy as you are now as a man," she said as they entered the dining room, where Roberto was ready to pour the wine. "I see you've gotten into our wine cellar as well as into our freezer," she said under her breath.

Fitz seemed to clamp his jaw down as he took his chair and Roberto helped her with hers. The wine poured, Roberto went into the kitchen, leaving them alone. Bella watched Fitz straighten everything before settling back in his chair. She could imagine what life would be like married to this awful, self-absorbed man. She felt sorry for any woman innocent enough to marry him. It certainly wasn't going to be her.

"Did you have a nice day?" she asked as she took a sip of her wine. He wanted to play at being husband and wife? She'd play along—to an extent.

"Very much so," he said. "And you?"

"It could have been better," she said and put down her wineglass after taking a sip. It was one of her father's expensive wines, which came as no surprise. Of course Fitz would help himself to the best. But she had to keep her wits about her.

Out of the corner of her eye, she noticed that the door to her father's den was open. But it was what she saw inside that made her momentarily freeze. Her father's gun safe stood open. There were no guns inside.

She looked at Fitz, who was smiling. She smiled back. Was he so afraid that she might shoot him? Was he going to hide all the knives in the kitchen as well? She would have found it amusing under other circumstances, she thought, as Roberto brought out their meals.

"Your father made bail, I heard," Fitz said. "I suppose

you've talked to him. I hope he's doing all right. Maybe we should have him committed to rehab—at least until the wedding. What do you think?"

She met his gaze and laughed. "Actually, he committed himself. He needs a good rest and it will look good when he has to go before the judge."

Fitz's surprise that he'd been outmaneuvered was wonderful to see. She took pleasure in it, wanting to gloat. She and her father had anticipated what Fitz would do next and had beaten him to the punch.

He picked up his knife and fork and began to hack at his steak with angry jabs at the meat. "You didn't get your hair trimmed or your nails done."

She said nothing. He wanted her to know that he'd checked up on her. That he would be checking every time she left the house—if not having her followed. She'd never been fond of steak but sliced a bite off and put it in her mouth.

Moments before, she'd been gloating—a mistake. If she thought she could beat this man at his game, she'd better think again. She chewed and met his gaze head-on. "No, I didn't go. I changed my mind. I was too upset after I left the house."

"So what did you do?" he asked as he took too much time cutting his steak. He knew she'd posted her father's bail. She should have seen it in his smugness the moment she saw him before he'd insisted she join him for dinner. But he'd gone straight to rehab.

"I'm curious," she said, not answering his question. "Is your plan to marry a woman who you're determined to make hate you to the point that she would kill you in your sleep?"

He looked up from his steak. "Do you really think I

care how you feel about me?" He laughed. "This won't be a real marriage, Bella. Once I completely destroy you and your father, once you're flat broke and broken, I'll dump you in the street. I'll sell your precious ranch and I'll move to some exotic place where I can have any woman I want—just as you said."

His words shocked her more than they should have. Wasn't this exactly what she'd thought he would do? He'd never wanted her. This was about humiliation. He'd felt small around her and her father. Apparently he couldn't live with that unless he brought her down and her father with her. Which meant even if she agreed to marry him, he would still send her father to prison.

"You do realize how pathetic that makes you sound, don't you?" she asked and took a bite of the twice-baked potato on her plate.

Fitz bristled, slamming down his knife and fork. Both clattered to his plate. A piece of steak flew off and onto the tablecloth. "I know you went to see Edwin. You and Tommy Colt. Did you really think my father wouldn't tell me?"

Bella considered that for a moment. She'd seen how scared Edwin had been of his only son. She should have known he'd tell Fitz, fearing that Fitz would find out and punish him even further.

She could see that Fitz was having trouble leaving the bite of steak on the tablecloth. Grease had started to leave a stain. She leaned forward, warning herself that she was taking this too far, but unable to stop herself. She snatched up the piece of steak from the table and tossed it back on his plate.

"You know what I think?" she said at his horrified look. His gaze kept going from the stain on the tablecloth to the piece of steak balancing on the edge of his plate. "I think this has something to do with your mother leaving you when you were five." All the color drained from Fitz's face. "I heard your father tell mine that you cried for days. I can't imagine how traumatic that must have been for you. I think it explains a lot about why you're acting out now and why—"

Fitz shot to his feet, overturning his water glass and knocking his chair backward. It crashed to the floor. "If you ever mention my mother again—" The words spewed from his mouth along with spittle.

"I'm just trying to understand where all this hate comes from," she said. From the look in his eyes, she'd taken it too far and yet it didn't feel like far enough at all. Look what the bastard was doing to her family.

For a moment, she thought he might have a heart attack. He stood swaying slightly as if trying to speak, but no more words came out. He heaved, each breath labored, his eyes poison-tipped darts aimed straight for her. When he did start to move, she realized he might launch himself across the table and go for her throat.

She picked up her knife. *Let him come.*

"Mr. Mattson? Can I get you anything else? Dessert is almost…" Roberto realized he had interrupted something. "Ready."

It took a moment for both of them to acknowledge that they were no longer alone. Fitz seemed to take a breath, his gaze shifting from her to the table and finally to Roberto standing in the kitchen doorway.

"Clean up this mess," Fitz snapped and shoved away from the table to storm out of the room.

Bella slowly put down her knife. "I think we're finished, but thank you, Roberto." She hated to think what might have happened if the man hadn't interrupted them.

"I will see that some dessert is sent up to your room, Miss—Bella," Roberto said.

She smiled at him as she put down her napkin and rose. "Thank you." She almost warned him that being kind to her would get him fired. But her heart was still in her throat. How would she survive this? Unless she could find a way out, she wouldn't.

Chapter Thirteen

To Bella's surprise there wasn't a guard outside her door the next morning. She'd had a fitful night filled with nightmares. As she made her way down to breakfast, she wasn't looking forward to seeing Fitz after last night. She told herself she would try to be pleasant. Even as she thought it, she found herself grinding her teeth.

But as she approached the dining room, she heard the sound of his sports car engine rev. When she looked out, she saw him speeding away.

Was he going into Missoula to see his father? She wondered if she should call Edwin to warn him. Then again, Edwin had told Fitz about their visit and had refused to help, so she figured he was on his own. After all, Fitz was his son.

"Good morning," Roberto said as he came into the dining room. "I have a special breakfast for you. Please have a seat."

She felt as if she were in a fancy restaurant rather than at the ranch. Her father had a cook who made meals when they were here at the ranch and had company. The rest of the time, they did for themselves.

"I have for you this morning quesadilla frita," Roberto said with obvious pride. "Two crispy tortillas topped with black beans, layered with fried egg, ham and cheese, and topped with my special spicy sauce. Served with a side of fried plantain."

"This looks wonderful," she said, admiring the dish. She asked about this family and if he'd always enjoyed cooking.

"I would spend time with my grandmother in Mexico," he said. "We would cook together. Everyone loved her cooking. I hope you enjoy your breakfast," he said and retreated to the kitchen.

Bella dug in, surprised by how hungry she was before she realized that she hadn't eaten but a couple of bites of dinner last night. After she finished, she stuck her head into the kitchen doorway and thanked him.

Then she'd hurriedly gotten ready to leave before Fitz returned. Her first stop was the rehab center her father had checked himself into. It was small and expensive and more like a spa than rehab, but money well spent if it helped should this ever go before a judge.

She found her father sitting out in the garden. He heard her approach, his expression brightening at the sight of her. She joined him on the bench and let herself breathe. Her father looked good, although she could still see fear in his eyes.

"I can't stand the thought of you having to deal with Fitz alone," he said, glancing around to make sure no one was listening. They were alone in the garden except for a man trimming a hedge in the distance. The buzz of his saw sounded like a swarm of bees.

Bella turned her face up to the warm sun. She took a deep breath and caught the scent of freshly mown lawn and pine from the nearby trees.

"I'm not alone," she said. "I've hired Colt Investigations."

"You aren't serious?"

She turned to meet his gaze. "I trust them. They are about the only ones I trust right now. You didn't tell me that this isn't the first time money has gone missing. Only last time, you paid it back."

"Who told you that?" her father demanded.

"Edwin."

Nolan Worthington slumped a little on the bench and turned his face away. "I'd made a couple of bad investments. You were in college. I couldn't borrow any money from the bank without worrying clients… So I borrowed some from the business."

Bella shook her head. "Is there more I don't know about?"

"No," he said, turning back to her. "I swear. But that's probably what gave Fitz the idea. It was stupid, but fortunately Edwin caught it and I sold some assets over time and paid every cent back."

"How do I know that this time is any different?" she asked.

His face reddened. "I didn't take the money." Her father shifted on the bench. "But no one is going to believe me if my own daughter doesn't."

She said nothing for a few moments as she tried to breathe. The sky overhead was cornflower blue, dotted with cumulous clouds that morphed in the breeze. She loved Montana summers. They always reminded her of Tommy. Back when they were kids the summer seemed to stretch out before them with so many possibilities.

Now she could feel the days slipping past, headed for the train wreck of a wedding that she wasn't even sure would save her father if she was stupid enough to let Fitz force her into it.

Her father spoke, drawing her out of her thoughts. "About six months ago, I was considering retiring. I'd had enough of Fitz. Edwin was cowed by him. I wanted out of the partnership, but Fitz wasn't having it. He made me an offer for the ranch." Her father hurried on as he saw her horrified expression. "I told him he'd never have the ranch, that I had my lawyers put it in your name. He got really upset."

She stared at him. "You think that's when he decided to force me to marry him for the ranch?"

Nolan shrugged. "I doubt it's that simple. Fitz probably doesn't even know what he wants. It's just something he doesn't have. Maybe he thinks if he had you and the ranch, he would be happy."

She laughed. "Is he really that juvenile? I would make his life a living hell and enjoy every minute of it." Bella couldn't believe this. The ranch was safe as long as she didn't marry Fitz—if she did, under Montana law he would own half of it. But she thought her father was right. It wasn't the ranch Fitz wanted so badly. He wanted revenge for feeling less around her and her father and the ranch.

Nolan reached over and took her hand. "I got myself into this mess. You need to let me get myself out even if it means going to prison."

She sighed. "You know I won't let that happen."

"I'm not sure either of us has a choice," he said, letting go of her hand. "But if you marry him—"

"Don't worry," she said, getting to her feet. "I'm not going to marry him. I'll find a way out of this for both of us."

Her father still looked as scared and worried as she felt. She touched his shoulder. "I'll think of something."

As she left, Tommy called.

"I got an address for Dorothy Brennan, but we need to hurry," he said. "Her landlord said she gave notice and is in the process of moving out." He rattled off the address. "I'll meet you there."

DOROTHY BRENNAN HAD been with her father's company from as far back at Bella could remember. A tall, thin, serious woman, she'd kept small treats in her desk for when Bella visited her father at work. The one thing she knew about Dorothy was that she loved plants. The one on her desk had been started from a cutting her grandmother had given her.

While she'd never married or had children, Dorothy had kept this plant alive for decades. That was why when Bella had seen it sitting on the woman's desk dead, she'd known something was terribly wrong. Dorothy wouldn't have left that plant behind.

Tommy was parked down the block when Bella arrived. She parked and got out as he joined her. They walked up the driveway to where Dorothy was loading boxes into the back of her SUV.

When she saw Bella, she started and glanced around as if expecting…who? Edwin? Fitz? Or the cops? The woman looked haggard and scared. Her gaze lit on the pot Bella was carrying and hope shone in her eyes.

"Miss Brennan," Bella said, calling her by the name she always had, as she approached. Tommy quickly took the box from the older woman and put it into the SUV for her. "This is Tommy Colt, a friend of mine. Could we talk to you for a moment?" She held out the pot. "I'm sorry about your plant, but I couldn't leave it in that office."

Dorothy took the pot, looked down at the skeleton of

her dead plant and hugged the pot to her. For a moment she studied each of them, then nodded and led the way inside the apartment. There wasn't much left except a couch and chair and a bed in the one bedroom that had been stripped. Bella assumed someone would be picking up the larger, heavier items and taking them wherever the woman was headed.

"Please sit down," Dorothy said as she set the pot on a windowsill in the sun. "I'd offer you something to drink but…" She glanced around, her throat working.

"We don't need anything but a few minutes of your time," Bella said quickly. "What happened at the office?"

The woman's gaze was shiny with tears as she turned to her. "I was fired. In a text from the young Mr. Mattson. I tried to go back for my things, but I was met at the door by two security guards and told I couldn't enter. I asked for my plant and was told it had been thrown out."

"I'm sorry," Bella said, touching the woman's shoulder. "This was Fitz's doing?"

Dorothy shrugged. "He's the one who gave me notice, but I assumed the others knew."

"My father wasn't involved," she said. "He's been pushed out as well."

She saw concern in the woman's face. "Nolan was always kind to me. I'm sorry."

"You aren't surprised that my father was forced out."

Dorothy shook her head. "I knew something was going on."

"Do you know what?" Bella asked.

"I heard things about Nolan, but I didn't believe them."

"Fitz is blackmailing my father, saying that Nolan embezzled a lot of money. He says he has proof."

"We suspect he has doctored books that show the losses coming from Nolan," Tommy said.

"There was money missing," Dorothy confirmed. "I heard Fitz arguing with his father about it. Edwin said that if it got out to clients it would destroy the business."

"If my father didn't take the money…"

The older woman met her gaze. "It was Fitz. You've seen his sports car?" Bella nodded. "It's just the tip of the iceberg." For a moment, Dorothy didn't look as if she was going to continue. "There's the country club and his lunches with so-called clients. But his big expense is his gambling and the woman he's putting up in a penthouse in Spokane."

"Do you have the woman's name and address?" Tommy asked.

Again Dorothy hesitated but only for a moment. "I wrote it all down. I was angry. Not that I thought I could do anything about it." She went to the few items she had stacked by the door, picked up her purse and opened it.

From inside, she took out what appeared to be copies of expense sheets. "These are the real ones," she said, handing them to Bella. "These are the ones he turned in to the business. I've been keeping two sets and keeping my mouth shut. He told me that if I talked, he'd say I stole from the company and have me arrested. He made me sign a nondisclosure agreement in order to get my last paycheck."

"Don't worry, I'll make sure it never comes back on you," Bella said, knowing that this wasn't enough to stop Fitz anyway. But it was a start. "Do you have any idea where he's hiding the evidence that would show my father took the money?"

Dorothy shook her head. "I'm sorry. Clearly he didn't

trust me." Her voice broke. "But…" She hesitated, then Bella saw the woman make up her mind. "One time I walked into his office and startled him. He quickly pulled a thumb drive from his laptop and palmed it until I left. I think that is probably what you're looking for."

Bella looked around the almost empty apartment. "Where will you go?"

"To Florida. My sister's until I can find another job."

"Send me your address. I'll let you know how it all ends." If it ended the way she hoped, she would get Dorothy a decent severance package from the partnership or die trying.

"I hope Fitz gets what's coming to him," Dorothy said.

"So do we," Bella agreed. Her cell phone rang. She checked. "Speak of the devil," she said. "I have to answer this." She stepped outside. Behind her, she heard Tommy asking if he could help Dorothy load anything else.

"Hello."

"Where are you?" Fitz asked. When she didn't answer, he said, "I'm making wedding plans. I need to know what your favorite flowers are."

Tommy joined her. Having overheard, he nodded and mouthed, "Tell him baby white roses."

She frowned since things were never going to go this far. Nor were those her favorite flowers and Tommy knew that. "Baby white roses."

"Excellent. That was going to be my choice," Fitz said, sounding relieved that she wasn't fighting him.

"Lonesome Florist," Tommy mouthed. His friend owned it, but she couldn't see why that would make a difference.

"I like the ones they have at Lonesome Florist," she said. "Since you're asking."

Fitz chuckled. "Got it. Oh, and you have a dress fitting scheduled tomorrow at two."

Bella looked at Tommy and had to bite down on her lip for a moment. "How thoughtful. You didn't trust me to select my own wedding dress?"

"I think you'll find that I have excellent taste," Fitz said with his usual arrogance. "I might surprise you." She shook her head but said nothing. "I'll leave the information about your fitting on the entry table in the hallway since you're spending so little time here."

"Is that all?" she asked.

"I heard you went to see your father," Fitz said. "I hope he's doing well."

"I'm sure you do," she said sarcastically. "Goodbye." She disconnected.

"He thinks your father is why you're not being so difficult," Tommy said. "So let him think that."

"Let him think I'm giving in to him?" she demanded as she pocketed her phone and shook her head. "He'd be more suspicious if I played nice, trust me. What was that about the flowers and the shop?"

"Just covering our bets. The owner is a friend. If it gets down to the wire, I could get you a message hidden in baby white roses."

Her pulse rate soared at the thought of it going that far. "Now what?"

"It seems like it wouldn't be that hard to prove that Fitz lives beyond his means and that he's the one who's been embezzling the money," Tommy said. "Have you thought any more about asking him for evidence?"

Bella shook her head. "Don't forget he's already framed my father for drug possession. But I might ask him before the fitting tomorrow to show me the proof of my father's embezzlement."

"At least Nolan's safe where he is now. I think we should check out Fitz's woman in Spokane. It will take all day to go there and come back. Sounds like you're busy tomorrow."

She hated it, but nodded. "I think I'd better go to the fitting. I can only push him so far without it hurting my father."

Chapter Fourteen

Bella was relieved to see Fitz's car gone when she returned to the ranch. Several of the guards though could be seen on the property. She ignored them and hurried inside.

Roberto had made her a special dinner, but she didn't do it justice. She kept thinking about Tommy and their first kiss and smiling stupidly. She'd known it was inevitable and that once they stepped across that line there would be no going back. The kiss had been just as wonderful and magical as she knew it would be.

Sitting on the deck of the fire tower had been the perfect spot to finally kiss. The summer night, the closeness she and Tommy had always shared, the chemistry that had always been there all added to that moment. But now she felt herself aching to be back in his arms. She wanted more. But also she knew how careful they had to be. If Fitz found out…

She heard his car engine. A few minutes later he walked in carrying his briefcase and frowning. She wondered what he did all day. It hadn't crossed her mind until that moment that maybe things weren't going so well for him—and that it might not have anything to do with her. She thought about what Dorothy had told her. Was it possible her father wasn't the only one who was broke?

If Fitz was hurting for money, then he needed what he could get for the ranch. Which meant he had to get her to the altar post haste.

The thought gave her little comfort as he came into the dining room. Roberto must have heard him. "Can I get you some dinner?" he asked Fitz, who shook his head and waved him away.

The cook quickly slipped back into the kitchen, letting the swinging door close behind him. She wondered if Roberto stood on the other side listening. Not if he was smart.

"Did you already eat?" she asked pointedly.

He met her gaze, still standing over the table holding his briefcase. "No, I'm just not hungry, but I see you've had your fill."

Food shaming? It made her smile. "And I enjoyed every bite."

That wasn't what he'd wanted to hear. "Some of us have to work. How is your business doing without you?"

"Who says it's without me?" she said, even though she hadn't given it much thought since her father's call. Fortunately, she'd hired good help and they were keeping things going without her.

"I wonder what you do all day," he said, narrowing his eyes at her.

"I wonder what you do all day," she said, narrowing her eyes at him.

He shook his head. "I'm not up to sparring with you tonight." He turned his back on her and started to walk away.

"I want to see proof that my father was embezzling money from the partnership," she said before he could escape.

He stopped but didn't turn around. "Why now?"

"I was remiss in not asking sooner."

"You wouldn't be able to understand it all. But an auditor would, especially one from the IRS." His threat hung in the air.

"I'm a lot smarter than you think. I run my own business," she reminded him. "I'm going to need to see it or the engagement is off."

He turned then. The look in his eye made her shudder inside. She realized she could have chosen the wrong time to make any demands.

She watched him fighting to keep his temper in check, refusing to drag her gaze away first or move a muscle.

"Tomorrow. After your wedding dress fitting," he said, his voice hoarse with emotion. "I'm too tired tonight." With that, he turned and stalked off, his spine rigid with anger.

She watched him storm up the stairs and disappear before she let out the breath she'd been holding.

TOMMY KNOCKED ON the penthouse door. He'd brought a box of chocolates and a bouquet of flowers. He'd thought he'd have trouble getting past the security guard at the desk.

"Mr. Mattson was very specific. I am to take these to her door and make sure she gets them," he told the desk guard who started to argue. "He wants me to make sure she is alone," Tommy whispered. "If I don't call back soon…"

"Fine, but be quick. I'll call up to let her know you're coming."

Tommy stopped him with a look.

"Fine. Just go up. She's in number two. The passcode is 409." He waved him away as if to say that both the woman upstairs and Fitz were a pain in his behind. Tommy didn't doubt it.

The elevator let him out on the top floor. He walked down the hall to number two and knocked, wondering what kind of reception he would get. He couldn't wait to see what kind of woman Fitz would actually pay money to keep.

He made a mental bet with himself. The door opened. He lost the bet. Worse, for a moment, he was speechless. "Margo Collins?"

"Yes?" The resemblance to Bella was shocking. Long dark hair. Green eyes. On closer inspection, he could see that she looked nothing like her beyond the obvious. Bella's features were softer and she was a little shorter and curvier.

"I have a delivery," he managed to say around his shock.

"From Fitz?" Margo asked and frowned. "He never gives me flowers but especially not chocolates. He says they'll make me fat."

"I guess he changed his mind," Tommy said, seeing that he'd messed up already.

"Well, it's okay with me," she said with a giggle as she outstretched her arms for her gifts.

"Mr. Mattson also wanted me to pick up something for him while I'm here."

She studied him for a moment as if noticing him for the first time, then shrugged and said, "Come in."

He followed her inside the apartment. Everything was white from the walls to the ceiling to the carpet on the floor and the furnishings. There were large windows that looked out on the hillside and the city.

Margo headed for the kitchen with her presents. In the living room, the television was on a reality show. The place was so clean and neat, Tommy couldn't believe anyone actually lived here.

He noticed her rummaging around in the bouquet and realized that she was looking for a card from Fitz. "Mr. Mattson said he didn't need a card because you already know how he feels about you." Her face lit up. "I need a folder he thinks he left here."

"In here?" she asked and turned toward what appeared to be an office.

Margo busied herself, humming as she put her flowers into a vase and opened the box of chocolates. "Oh, Fitzy, you really are going to make me fat. You never give me candy. Are you being a bad boy?" She chuckled as she popped a chocolate into her mouth.

In the small office, Tommy quickly checked the desk. None of the drawers were locked. Nothing in them hardly. Nothing of interest, either.

He looked up. Margo was standing in the doorway holding her box of chocolates. "You must be a new one," she said. "Didn't find what you were looking for?"

He shook his head. "He said there were some papers…"

"I bet he put them in his briefcase and forgot he took them," she said with a chuckle. "That thing is practically attached to his arm lately, but I guess I don't have to tell you that. Kind of like that thumb drive around his neck. I asked him what was so important. He said it holds the key to his heart." She smiled and licked her lips. The scent of milk chocolate wafted toward him. "You won't tell him I said that. He says I need to say less and think more." She shrugged. "He's right." She looked sad for a moment, then considered her next piece of chocolate from the box and brightened.

"Don't worry, I won't mention it if you don't mention that I didn't find what he sent me for. Like you said, the papers are probably in his briefcase and he forgot. I don't want to tell him that he messed up."

She nodded knowingly. "Smart. Our secret."

"Maybe the flowers and chocolates should be, too. I have to confess. They were my idea. I thought it would be rude to just show up without something." He gave her his best sheepish look.

She looked guiltily down at the box in her hand. She'd already made a good dent in the contents. He watched her debating what to do.

"Probably best not to mention the chocolates especially," she said.

He nodded and smiled. She seemed nice enough, though naive. "Our secret. Want me to bring anything else if he sends me back?"

She nodded with a laugh. "Surprise me. And stop by anytime." As he started to leave, she added, "If he does remember why he sent you here, could you remind him about the rent? The landlord called again." She made a face. "When Fitz gets busy, he forgets stuff. But it's been a few months now."

Tommy nodded, feeling sorry for the woman. It appeared Fitz was phasing her out as he got closer to getting what he really wanted. Tommy wondered how to tell Bella what he'd found out. It gave him a chill as he recalled how much Margo had looked like her—at least at first glance and when she smiled.

The memory sent a sharp blade of fear through him. Apparently Fitz wanted more than revenge for what he saw as her ignoring him all these years. He wanted Bella.

Chapter Fifteen

The next morning, Fitz was already gone by the time Bella came downstairs. She'd lain awake wondering how Tommy's trip to Spokane had gone. She didn't dare get her phone from where it was hidden in her car to call him. She'd pushed Fitz about as far as she thought she should for one day so hadn't left the ranch the rest of the evening.

Roberto had made her another delicious breakfast. She ate it quickly and, grabbing the note Fitz had left her with instructions to her dress fitting, she left. Once out of sight of the ranch and the guards, she called Tommy.

They met at a spot on the river north of town. As she parked in the pines and followed the sound of the water to the river, she thought about all the times she and Tommy had come here. They used to love where the stream pooled in the rocks to make a deep swimming hole.

Tommy sat on one of the rocks near the pool. She hopped from rock to rock to drop down beside him. The rock under her felt warm in the sun. She closed her eyes and leaned her head back to enjoy the rays for a few moments, before opening her eyes and looking over at him.

The news wasn't good. It showed in his handsome face. Those Colt brothers, she thought as she smiled to herself. They were a handsome bunch. "What don't you want to tell me?" she finally asked as she found a small piece of rock and threw it into the pool. She watched it sink until it was out of sight before she looked over at him again.

He hadn't shaved, his designer stubble making her want to kiss him. She couldn't help herself. She reached out, cupped that strong jaw and drew him to her. The kiss was sweet—at first, almost tentative. She touched the tip of her tongue to his and felt him shiver before drawing back.

"You keep doing that and you know where this is headed," he said, his voice rough with emotion.

"Would that be so bad?" she whispered.

He brushed his fingertips lightly over her cheek. She closed her eyes as his callused thumb caressed her lower lip. She wanted him with every fiber of her being. Her body tingled at his touch. She wanted to lie in the nearby grass naked in his arms.

Opening her eyes, she met his gaze. His desire mirrored her own, but there was also regret there.

"Bella." She heard the pain in that one word. "All this isn't dangerous enough for you?"

She felt the impact of his words. Not for her, for her father. If Fitz knew, he would hurt her father. She leaned back, needing to put a little distance between them. Her pulse thrummed. Only moments ago, she was ready to suggest they go into the woods. This had been building between them for years and she wanted it more than her next breath.

Closing her eyes against the desire that burned inside her, she let the sun again warm her face. "You haven't told me about Spokane." She realized that whatever he'd found out yesterday, it hadn't just made him more cautious. It had made him scared. For her father? Or for her?

"So what's she like?" she asked without opening her eyes. The sun felt so good, the smell of the river and the pines so crisp and familiar, she could almost pretend that none of this was happening. Just another summer day in Montana, her and Tommy on the river.

Tommy was quiet for a moment. "Margo Collins is like you."

She looked over at him.

"She looks so much like you that when you first see her it's startling," he said. "But then you see the differences, until she smiles. She has your hair, your eyes, your smile. Or damned close. As close as Fitz could find."

Bella let out a ragged breath. A sliver of disgust at the perversity of it followed on the next breath by fear that worked its way under her skin to her veins before roaring through her. The woman more than resembled her? She wasn't sure what she'd been expecting. Just some woman Fitz was keeping, but she should have known it was more than that. He'd kept this woman secret. He didn't want anyone to know. Maybe especially Bella. "Did she tell you anything we could use?"

He shook his head. "She isn't involved in any way in his business from what I can tell. She's just…an ornament. Until he gets the real thing."

TOMMY WALKED BELLA to her car. "Call me later." He could tell that she was as shaken as he was by what he'd discovered. Now at least she understood. They both did. A man who just wanted to destroy didn't go to all this trouble. Fitz wanted Bella. The woman Tommy loved.

But for how long? Fitz had no idea what he was wishing for. A woman like Bella would never be dominated by a man or anyone. But it seemed Fitz wanted to try—and would do anything for the chance.

"I told Fitz I wanted proof of my father's crime. He was in a really weird mood last night and said he'd show me after my dress fitting today."

"How weird?" he asked.

"Like he'd had a bad day at the office. I don't think it was because of anything we did unless..." She met his gaze. "You don't think the girlfriend called him and told him about you stopping by?"

Tommy shook his head. "I don't think so. Maybe all this isn't going together as well as he'd hoped. I'll see what I can find out. I think I might have located the former accountant. I'm meeting with him later. If he shows up. He sounds scared."

She nodded, but he could see that she was distracted. He wanted to hold her, to kiss her and get back that moment by the river. But it was gone and any intimacy seemed like a very bad idea until they got her and her father out of this mess. Fitz was too dangerous. And not just to Nolan. Tommy worried what the man might do to Bella—the two of them basically alone in that house with Fitz believing he could do anything he wanted.

"I'll call you later," she promised. "Tommy?" He had started to walk away but turned back. "Be careful."

He smiled. "You, too."

"Yes, I wouldn't want to get stuck with a pin at my dress fitting." With that she started the SUV and drove away. He watched her go before heading to his own rig. He was anxious to talk to the partnership's former accountant. As he reached his pickup, he heard a vehicle engine start up in the distance and realized they might not have been alone.

THE BRIDAL SHOP was in Missoula so Bella had way too much time to think about everything that Tommy had told her on the drive. She felt as if Fitz had a life-sized doll of her hidden in Spokane. It gave her the creeps. Worse, it seemed Tommy was right. Fitz wanted the real thing—her.

He'd said this marriage was in name only, but she suspected he would never let her go once he got her legally bound to him. He wanted her, the ranch, everything he felt he'd been cheated out of in life. So basically, he had no idea what he wanted to fill the cavernous yearning hole in him.

She found the bridal shop, parked and climbed out of her SUV. As she did, she saw a black pickup pull in a couple of vehicles behind her. She recognized the man behind the wheel and felt her heart drop. It was one of the guards Fitz had hired.

Heart in her throat, she realized he could have followed her from the ranch this morning to the river. He would know that she met Tommy there. She felt herself flush, remembering the kiss and the embrace. Only a fool wouldn't have realized how intimate it had been.

She was thankful that they hadn't taken it further on the sunny shore under the pines. Fitz was dangerously close to following through with his threats. For her sake and her father's, she needed to be sure that he didn't snap.

Taking a few breaths, she tried to assure herself that if she had been followed, it had only been from Lonesome to Missoula. She watched him get out of his pickup. He didn't look in her direction as he walked into a boot shop, letting the door close behind him.

Was it possible she hadn't been followed at all? It could be the man's day off. He could have just happened to be in the area. She wished she could believe that as she entered the bridal shop. The bell over the door tinkled and a young woman appeared.

"Bella Worthington?"

All she could do was nod, her mouth was so dry.

"Why don't you come back? I have your dress ready. I'm Crystal."

Her legs felt like jelly as she walked toward the back. Before she stepped through a curtained doorway, she glanced back. She didn't see the guard from the pickup. She pushed through the curtain and tried to still her raging heart.

Tommy was right. They had to be more careful. Which meant they couldn't chance being together. The thought hurt her physically. She ached to lie in his arms, to feel his body against her own, to feel safe and loved and fulfilled.

"Step in here," Crystal said. "You can hang your clothes there while I get your dress. Did you bring shoes?" Bella hadn't. "It's all right. Your fiancé said you probably wouldn't. He thought of everything." The young woman turned and walked away. Fitz had thought of everything. Wasn't that her greatest fear?

She had a sudden urge to call Tommy on the burner phone and warn him to be careful. If she was right and the guard had followed them to the river, then he might have already given that information to Fitz.

But the burner phone was in the car. She reached for

her purse, thinking it wouldn't make a difference now if she called Tommy on her cell. Not if Fitz already knew that she and Tommy had been meeting secretly. Had the guard seen them kissing? Had he taken photos from a distance?

Fear for Tommy's safety had her fumbling in her purse when Crystal returned holding the wedding dress. Bella froze. Not because of the dress. But because of the man standing behind Crystal.

"Fitz?" Her voice sounded too high to her ears. "What are you doing here?" Her mind was working. Whirling. She grasped the only thing she could think of. "It's bad luck to see the bride in her dress before the wedding."

"Don't worry," he said, his expression souring at her response to seeing him. Crystal had noticed and was trying not to show it. "I was just dropping off your heels that go with the dress."

Bella swallowed. "Thank you. That's very thoughtful. You know how stressful this is for me."

His frown softened. "I know. But now you can relax. Crystal, I think my fiancée is going to need that glass of champagne we talked about before she tries on her dress."

Crystal snapped right to it, hanging the dress on a hook in the large plush dressing room and scurrying out.

Fitz stepped in. "I was thinking about this time when we were kids. I sprained my ankle and you got a bag of frozen peas for me to put on it. Which proves you can be nice to me."

She lowered her voice so Crystal didn't hear. "My father is the one who made me be nice to you when we were kids. Yes, the same one you're trying to put in prison."

"Not if you marry me."

She gave him a side eye. "That would require trusting you."

He seemed surprised. "What would it take? Actually…" He held up his hand to stop her from answering. "People have been wondering why we don't go out together. So I was thinking…dinner tonight at the steakhouse? Don't say no."

She started to tell him that it would take more than a dinner at the steakhouse, but he didn't give her a chance. No doubt he already knew what she was going to say.

"Please don't tell me you're too busy to have dinner with your fiancé." His smile never reached his eyes. "You have been awfully busy lately. Maybe if you had your friends to the ranch instead of meeting them elsewhere…at least until the wedding…" She heard what he was telling her loud and clear. He knew about her and Tommy. Did he know it had gone beyond just friendship? Did he also suspect that she'd hired Colt Investigations to help her? She figured he would find that more amazing than worrisome. He didn't think much of her intellect or Tommy's, she was sure.

"I appreciate your concern," she said, hoping he didn't hear the break in her voice."

"Of course I'm concerned," he said, looking as if he thought he had everything under control. "Soon we will be husband and wife. Then I'm going to take care of you." It sounded like the threat it was.

Crystal reappeared with her glass of champagne. Bella took it with trembling fingers as Fitz excused himself to take a call. She couldn't hear what was being said. Her heart was pounding too loudly in her ears. Tommy was in trouble. She could feel it.

"Great," Fitz said after finishing a quick call. "A romantic dinner tonight at the steakhouse. It's just what we both need." He stepped close again, leaning toward her. She jerked her head to the side and his kiss brushed her cheek. "I'll see you later," he said as his cell phone began to ring again.

"You are so lucky to have such an attentive fiancé," Crystal said as Fitz disappeared from view.

Bella saw the questioning look on the young woman's face. Downing the champagne, she handed back the empty glass, making Crystal's eyes widen. "You have no idea."

She could hear Fitz's voice on the phone. It sounded as if he were pleading with someone. The sound faded as the bell over the front door tinkled and he left. "I need to make a quick call," she told Crystal and dug out her phone.

"I'll get your veil," the young woman said and left with the empty champagne glass.

Bella called Tommy's cell, but it went straight to voice mail. The back of the shop was quiet. She was pretty sure that Fitz had left, but she never knew for sure, did she.

"He knows," she said into Tommy's voice mail. "Be careful, please." She disconnected as Crystal returned.

"Ready?" the young woman asked.

Bella nodded. She wondered how many nervous brides came through here and how many of them were having second thoughts. She doubted there were many like her, trying on a wedding dress she'd never seen before in heels she hadn't purchased with only one thought in mind: killing her fiancé rather than going through with the wedding.

FITZ LEFT THE dress shop congratulating himself on not losing his temper with Bella. When he'd gotten the call from Ronan earlier today, it had confirmed what he'd feared. Bella had been meeting Tommy Colt—just as she had when they were kids. Only Ronan had seen the two locked in an embrace that he'd described as "hot."

His first instinct was to throw her father to the wolves and then go after her. But he'd reminded himself that he had the upper hand only with the threat of sending her father to prison. If he hoped to get her to the altar, then he had to leave Nolan alone.

As for Bella herself... He'd wanted to grab her by the throat, and shove her against the wall in the bridal shop and... He shook his head. Fortunately, he'd kept his temper. She would be his soon enough. In the meantime, he had to deal with everything else going on.

He needed money. A few investments that didn't pay off like he'd hoped, the expense of this wedding and all that entailed and some bad luck. The past few times he'd gotten into a high-stakes game, he'd lost. Worse, he had some loans coming due—not to mention all the payments for his expensive lifestyle.

As he was driving out of Missoula, he saw a Realtor sign and swung into the parking lot. It was a little premature, looking into selling Bella's ranch. But once they were married, he had plans that didn't include keeping the place. He had a general idea of what all that land along the river might be worth. Add the house, stables and barn, it should more than take care of his problems.

Fitz told himself that everything was going to work out and when it did, he would have Bella. But first he had to make sure that Tommy Colt didn't go near her again. He pulled out his phone and made the call to Ronan, who was still tailing the Colt PI.

By the time he came out of the Realtor's office, he was humming "Wedding March." Things were looking up.

THE BAR WHERE Tommy was meeting the accountant was small and dark and on the wrong side of the tracks in Butte. Because of the hour, there were only a few patrons inside at a table and a couple at the bar. The only person by himself was a man sitting at the far end of the bar away from the couple.

Tommy took a stool next to him. "Bill McMillan?"

The fiftysomething man was dressed in a suit, his tie loosened at his neck. He smelled of men's cologne and sweat, his dark hair flecked with gray and slicked down with something shiny.

"I'm sorry I said I'd talk to you," the man said.

The bartender wandered down. Tommy ordered a beer and looked to Bill. He sighed and nodded as if resigned to getting drunk. He already had two empty drink glasses in front of him.

Tommy waited until their drinks came. He took a sip of his beer before he spoke. Next to him Bill took a gulp of his drink. He started to pull out a pack of cigarettes before apparently remembering that he couldn't smoke in a bar in Montana anymore. Swearing, he gripped his glass with both hands and stared into the dark amber contents.

"Why do you think Fitz fired you?" Tommy asked after a moment.

Bill glanced over at him. "For obvious reasons." He lowered his voice although no one was paying them any attention. "He was robbing the company blind, and I was tired of covering for him."

Tommy took a wild guess. "He wouldn't cut you in."

The accountant looked offended and for a moment, he

feared Bill would get up and walk out. "I was going out on a limb for this jackass. It was the least he could do to make it more worth my while."

"How'd you hide it from his partners?" Tommy asked and took another drink of his beer without looking at the man.

"I set up a shell company for him. I'd write checks for fictitious expenses. I'd cash the checks and he'd take the money."

"Is there any way to prove he was involved?"

Bill leaned an elbow on the bar to look at him. "That's the really stupid thing on my part. I made it where he could walk away clean. It would look like I was taking the money because his delicate little hands never touched a pen."

"Wouldn't all of this show up on bank records or corporate business filings with the state?" Tommy asked.

"They could. Why do you think I left without a fight? He has me right where he wants me. He wouldn't give me a recommendation. I'm having hell finding another job. He could send me to prison. I'm the one who was writing checks and cashing them," Bill said.

"What about his bank records?"

The man shook his head. "Fitz wasn't putting the money in the bank. There was no paper trail back to him—only me."

"So you cooked the books, hiding the money that Fitz was stealing from the partnership until he fired you and got a new accountant," Tommy said, trying to understand how this all worked. "Is the new accountant involved?"

"Hell, no. Right before he fired me, he shut down the operation by killing off the shell company, making it look as if he sold the businesses at a loss. The problem is, now there is no extra money coming in. The only money he has is from the partnership with his old man and Nolan Worthington. I'd say with his gambling problem and his flashy lifestyle, he's in need of a cash infusion."

Tommy thought about the marriage to Bella. He had no idea what she might be worth. Her business was too new to be making much. But the ranch was in her name. Was that what Fitz was after besides Bella?

Bill drained his drink and slammed down his glass. The bartender headed in their direction. "One more for the road."

The bartender hesitated.

"I can give him a ride," Tommy said. As soon as the bartender left to make that drink, he asked, "Isn't there a record somewhere that proves there was a shell company but no real businesses?"

"Sure, if you knew what you were looking for." Bill shook his head. "That's how these guys get away with it. They kept their hands clean and let someone else take the blame. Fitz didn't set up the shell company. He had one of the partners do it."

Nolan? Or his father? Tommy couldn't help his surprise. "Wait, you're saying one of the partners was in on it with him?" Bill shrugged. The bartender returned with his drink and looked at him pointedly. "I'm giving him a ride." He turned to Bill the moment the bartender was out of earshot. "Which partner?"

Bill took a gulp of the drink. His eyes were half-closed now. He seemed to be having trouble staying on the stool. He loosened his tie some more and shook his head. "Nolan, but he didn't know what he was signing. He'd made a couple of bad investments and was running scared. He signed whatever I put in front of him."

Downing his drink, Bill half fell off his stool.

"Come on," Tommy said. "I'll drive you home."

"I didn't drive," Bill slurred. "I walked. I live just down the alley. I can find my way home blind drunk, trust me."

"Well, I'll see you home anyway," Tommy said as the man staggered toward the back door. Throwing some money on the bar, he hurried after him.

Pushing open the door, he stepped out to see that Bill was already partway down the alley. Tommy had just started after him when he heard an engine rev and tires squeal. He looked down the alley to his right and saw a dark-colored vehicle headed directly for him.

Chapter Sixteen

Bella still hadn't heard from Tommy by the time her fitting was over. She headed back to the ranch, half hoping Fitz wouldn't be there. But of course he was there waiting for her, sitting outside in the shade of the porch.

"How did it go?" he asked as she climbed the steps.

"Fine." She headed for the door.

"You didn't say anything about the dress."

She stopped, her hand on the doorknob. "It's a nice dress."

He laughed. "That's the best you can do?"

Bella turned to look at him. "What do you expect, Fitz? You know I don't want to marry you and that none of this would be happening if you weren't blackmailing my father."

"I wish it hadn't come to this, either," he said. "But you've never given me a chance."

She sighed. "I don't feel that way about you. It's simple chemistry. I can't control it." She saw his expression harden and reminded herself that they weren't capable of having an honest conversation without him getting angry.

"But there's chemistry between you and that saddle tramp Tommy Colt?" he snapped. He seemed to instantly regret his words as he hurriedly got to his feet and moved toward her. "Bella, I'm sorry. Let's just go to dinner and not discuss anything but the weather. Montana in the summer. We can agree on how wonderful it is, can't we?"

She realized that she feared this conciliatory Fitz more than the angry one. It made her worry all the more about Tommy. She couldn't wait to get to her room and try his cell again. It was dangerous using her regular cell phone to call him. But maybe it made no difference—if as she suspected Fitz already knew about the two of them.

"I'll go change for dinner," she said and entered the house, leaving him on the porch. She hurried up the stairs to her room, locking the door behind her. In the bathroom she turned on the shower in case someone was listening outside her door. She made the call, but like before, Tommy's cell went straight to voice mail.

TOMMY YELLED FOR Bill to watch out and threw himself against the bar's back door he'd only closed moments before.

The vehicle blew past him, hitting several garbage cans lined up along the edge of the building. Tommy ducked as one of the cans careened into him, knocking the air out of him. Out of the corner of his eye, he saw the front of the vehicle strike Bill, tossing him into the air. As the vehicle sped away, Bill's body landed in a stack of cardboard boxes piled behind a business. The accountant crumpled to the ground and didn't move.

Hand shaking, Tommy pulled out his phone as he ran toward Bill and punched in 911. Crouching next to the man, he checked for a pulse, shocked that Bill was still alive as the 911 operator answered.

He'd stayed with Bill until the ambulance arrived along with the first cop. Tommy had turned off his phone to talk to the police about the hit-and-run. He was still shaken. "It happened too fast. No, I didn't get a license number or see the driver. All I can tell you was that it was a black SUV."

Another cop arrived at the scene and pulled him aside. This one was older with buzzed gray hair and pale intense eyes. "You say the driver swerved toward you first, then ran down Mr. McMillan?"

"It appeared that way, yes. Look, like I said, it happened so fast. I was getting ready to go after Bill to make sure he got home. The SUV must have been parked down the alley waiting. I hadn't noticed it until I heard the roar of the engine and the sound of the tires squealing."

"Is there anyone who might want to kill you?" He could feel the cop's gaze intent on him.

"Not that I know of," Tommy told him. Fitz hated him and had proved how low he would stoop to get what he wanted. But murder?

"I recognize your name. Rodeo cowboy, right?"

"Was," Tommy said. "I recently joined my brother at Colt Investigations."

The cop's expression changed. "So this could be about some case you're working on."

Tommy hesitated, not sure what to say. "I really doubt it."

"Let me be the judge of that," the cop said. "Who's your client?"

"That's confidential."

The officer stared at him. "Seriously? Someone tries to kill you and you prefer not to tell me who you're working for?"

"Like I said, I doubt it's connected."

With a disgusted sound, the cop put his notebook and pen away. "Have it your way."

"How is Bill?" Tommy asked.

"Last I heard he has a broken hip but was in stable condition. You said he was extremely intoxicated?" Tommy nodded. "Being inebriated probably saved his life."

The cop got a call on his radio. All Tommy heard was "stolen black SUV." When the cop finished he looked at him and shook his head. "Could have been some teen joyriders. Guess we'll know more when we find the vehicle."

With that the cop walked back to his patrol car and Tommy turned on his phone and saw that Bella had called numerous times. He quickly dialed her number as he headed for the hospital.

BELLA AND FITZ were about to be seated at the steakhouse when her cell phone buzzed in her purse. She started to reach for it when Fitz's hand clamped over hers.

"Not tonight," he said, his hand tightening on hers.

"Just let me turn it off." He glared at her for a few moments before his grip loosened.

She quickly dug out the phone. Just as she'd hoped, the call had been from Tommy. She turned off her phone seeing that he'd left a message she would check later as they were escorted to their table.

The moment she saw where they would be seated, Bella knew this was Fitz's doing. It was in a back corner, secluded. A candle flickered on the table and a bottle of champagne chilled in a bucket of ice next to two glasses.

Fitz pulled out her chair for her before going around to his. She could tell that he was determined to be pleasant—as hard as it seemed for him sometimes.

"Are we celebrating something?" she asked, relieved

that she'd heard from Tommy—otherwise she would have worried given how in high spirits Fitz seemed tonight.

"Our first real date," he said and gave her a look that dared her to argue otherwise. He poured her a glass and handed it to her before pouring one for himself and offering a toast. "To the future. May it be happy for us both."

She wasn't sure how that would be possible, but she clinked her glass against his and took a sip. The bubbles tickled her tongue. She tried to relax, telling herself that Tommy was fine. He had gone to talk to the accountant. Maybe it had taken longer than he'd thought it would, but if he'd found out something they could use...

"You look so beautiful," Fitz said.

"Thank you." She picked up her menu. She wasn't hungry, but she was determined to get through this so-called date.

"I know you're not much of a steak eater," she heard him say. "But they have seafood. I know you like lobster. Please, this is my treat."

She lowered her menu. "Is everything all right?"

"Why would you ask that?" he inquired, frowning.

"It's just that you're being so..."

"Nice?" He let out a chuckle. "Did you really not realize how I felt about you all these years?"

She shook her head and dropped her voice even though there was enough noise in the busy restaurant that she doubted anyone could hear. "I thought this wasn't going to be a real marriage. That you were just doing this to destroy me *and* my father."

Fitz reddened and dropped his gaze. "I was angry when I said those things. I wanted to hurt you because you've hurt me." He raised his eyes to hers again. She saw him swallow before he spoke. "That wasn't what I really wanted. I've been in love with you for years."

After what Tommy had found out in Spokane it didn't come as a complete surprise. "You just have an odd way of going about asking me out."

He took a sip of his champagne before settling his gaze on her again. "You would have laughed in my face, but let's not get into that now. I want us to have a pleasant dinner. Is that possible?" Bella nodded, not up to one of their usual battles, either. "Have the lobster. I'm having a shrimp cocktail before a steak entrée. Join me. I know how much you like shrimp."

The waiter appeared and she nodded as Fitz ordered for them. Anyone watching might have thought that they were really engaged and having a nice quiet dinner before their upcoming wedding.

Bella tried to relax, but not even the champagne helped. This whole thing was a farce and worse, she sensed there was something Fitz wasn't telling her. He was in too good a mood. She felt as if she was waiting for the other shoe to drop and when it did, she knew it was going to be bad.

The rest of the evening was uneventful enough as they both steered away from anything resembling the truth.

It wasn't until they were leaving the restaurant that two men came out of the shadowy darkness of the parking lot and accosted Fitz.

"Here," he said to her, shoving his keys at her. "Go on to the car and let me handle this." She took the keys but didn't move. The men were large and burly and clearly angry. "Go!" Fitz snapped and gave her a push.

She stumbled toward the car. When she looked back, Fitz was arguing with the men. One of them shoved him back into the side of the building. Clearly they were threatening him. She couldn't hear exactly what was being said, but she'd picked up enough of it to know it had to do with money and gambling.

At the car, she opened the door and climbed in. Fitz appeared a few minutes later. He looked shaken. "What was that about?"

"Nothing," he snapped. "Drop it, okay? Just a misunderstanding. Everything is fine."

Bella really had her doubts about that. However, she could tell by the change in Fitz's mood that unless she wanted trouble from him tonight, she needed to let it go. But she couldn't help but wonder if Fitz was in financial trouble. If he owed those two men from the parking lot, then he had more than money problems.

Maybe this wedding wasn't just all about her after all. She had a bad feeling that her ranch had even more to do with it.

Chapter Seventeen

Bella woke with a start. For a moment, she didn't know what had yanked her out of her deep, mentally exhausted sleep. Her cell phone rang. She blinked, still fighting the coma-like state she'd been in only moments ago, as she reached for it and realized it was early morning. She'd tried to call Tommy last night but with no success. His message on her phone had been short: *I'm fine. Will call later when I can.*

She checked the screen and saw that the call was coming from Lonesome River Investments, her father's office. "Hello?" She sat up, thinking it couldn't be her father. He was still in rehab. Or was he? "Hello?" She could hear someone breathing on the line. "Dad?"

"It's Edwin," said the male voice. Fitz's father. The man sounded drunk.

"Are you all right?" she asked and heard him chuckle as she leaned against the headboard. This felt like the extension of the dream she'd been having. She wasn't sure any of it was real. "Edwin?" She heard him clear his voice.

His words were slurred when he finally spoke. "I... I thought about what you said." She held her breath. "You're right. Fitz won't stop. Even when he was little we noticed something was… That he was a challenge." He sounded as if he was struggling for his next breath. "But he's my son." He broke down for a moment.

"I'm so sorry. I know how hard this must be for you."

The man seemed to pull himself together. "You can't marry him."

"I don't plan to. Give me something to stop him."

For a moment she thought he'd disconnected. "He has a thumb drive on a chain around his neck. He did that after he caught me checking his deposit box at the bank."

She realized that she'd seen Fitz toying with the gold chain around his neck and thought it must be a new piece of jewelry he wasn't used to yet. Since he often wore a suit or at least a sport jacket, she hadn't thought he was wearing anything but a chain. Fitz had always gone for flashy gold accessories from his expensive watch to his diamond pinkie ring.

"What kind of thumb drive?" she asked.

"Silver, thin, one of those new ones," Edwin said.

"Thank you for telling me about this," she said.

Silence, then, "I had to tell him that you came by and tried to get me to help you."

"I know."

"I—I…" She heard a noise in the background like a door opening. "I have to—" The last thing she heard was Edwin say, "What are you doing here?" before the phone went dead.

Bella quickly disconnected. Someone had walked in on Edwin. Had they overheard what he'd been saying? Her cell phone rang. Edwin? She didn't think so. She listened to it ring, hugging herself against the shudder that moved through her body. All her instincts told her not to answer the call because it wasn't Edwin calling from his number. It was whoever had walked in on him wanting to know who he'd called.

Now wide-awake, she leaned back against the headboard and looked across the room, her eyes unseeing. Was it true about the thumb drive? Even if it was, how was she going to get it from around Fitz's neck? Very carefully. Unless that had been Fitz who'd caught his father calling her. If he'd overheard what Edwin had told her, then he'd be waiting for her to try to steal the thumb drive hanging around his neck.

WHEN BILL MCMILLAN opened his eyes the next morning, Tommy was sitting in a chair beside the man's bed. "Hey," Tommy said.

He couldn't help feeling responsible for what had happened to the man. Apparently getting drunk at the bar and walking back to his apartment was a nightly thing. But Tommy kept thinking about how paranoid Bill had been about meeting him, afraid that Fitz would find him. Had he been followed? Had Fitz not just found his former accountant—but Tommy as well?

Last night when he reached the hospital, he'd finally checked his phone and saw the message from Bella. *Fitz knows. Be careful.*

Bill tried to smile. "Was I hit by a bus?"

"Pretty close. An SUV."

The man's gaze was unfocused for a moment, as if he was trying to remember. "An accident?" Tommy shook his head and Bill swore. "I have insurance."

Tommy thought he was talking about the hospital bill for a moment. Bill grimaced in pain as he said, "We had a deal. He broke it. Screw him. Get my insurance. It's hidden in my apartment under the floorboard in the bedroom. Get the bastard." Bill closed his eyes. "My apartment keys were in my jacket pocket. The hospital probably has them."

A nurse came in. "Mr. McMillan?" she said as she neared the bed. Bill's eyes opened. "A police officer is here who wants to ask you a few questions. Feel up to it?" Bill nodded.

Tommy rose. "I'll be going now, but I'll check back later."

Bill met his gaze and gave a small nod. "Thanks for taking care of things for me. My cat," he said, turning to the nurse. "He needs the key to my apartment so he can feed my cat."

The nurse nodded. "Your belongings are at the nurse's station." She turned to Tommy. "Just follow me. You'll have to sign the keys out," she told him as he followed the nurse down the hall.

"No problem." He called Bella and told her what had happened and where he was headed.

"Give me the address," she said. "I'll meet you there.

BELLA WAS STILL UPSET. The message Tommy had left on her phone last night just said he was fine and would talk to her today. This morning he'd filled her in on the accident. She knew he wasn't telling her everything. She'd been worried about him yesterday—and apparently with good reason.

He was waiting for her when she drove up. As she got out and glanced around, she couldn't help being surprised that the accountant lived just off this alley. She vaguely remembered seeing Bill McMillan at her father's office. As far as she knew, he'd made a good living but since being fired by Fitz, he seemed to have fallen on hard times.

Seeing her surprise, Tommy said, "He's been hiding out. I fear I led Fitz right to him and that's why he was almost killed. The police think it was an accident. Stolen SUV. Kids on a joyride."

"But you know better. This is a really narrow alley," she said, looking down it before turning to him again. She thought of Ronan and Milo. Fitz couldn't have been behind the wheel because he was at dinner with her. Was she his alibi? She felt sick to her stomach remembering him professing his undying love last night at the restaurant. She had wondered at his good mood. Now she thought she understood.

"It wasn't only the accountant Fitz was trying to kill," she said, but knew Tommy wasn't going to tell her what had really happened.

"This way," he said, no doubt thinking he was protecting her. As they walked he filled her in what Bill had told him. "He said he got fired. From what I gathered, he'd wanted more money on the deal. He did tell me that your father was so distracted that he signed anything Bill put in front of him."

Bella shook her head. "My father was always so trusting when it came to Edwin and Fitz. His first mistake. Add in his girlfriend Caroline... He really had no idea what was going on right under his nose." She was hesitant to tell him about Edwin's call and her dinner with Fitz. With luck they would find what they needed in Bill's apartment and put an end to this.

Tommy opened a heavy metal door with graffiti splashed across it and they stepped into a small landing at the bottom of a steep set of dark stairs. "It's number four," he said and started up, her close behind.

Their footsteps echoed as they climbed. She could smell a variety of unpleasant scents as they passed several apartment doors. Behind them were the sounds of cooking, televisions turned up too loud and raised voices.

At number four, Tommy pulled out a key, but before he could use it, the door swung inward. Someone had already been here, she thought as she saw the ransacked apartment. Her heart fell. Whatever insurance Bill McMillan had hidden here had to be gone.

Tommy let out a low curse. "Wait here." He entered the residence, wading through the destruction toward what appeared to be the bedroom. The bed now leaned against the wall exposing the wooden floor. Several of the planks had been removed.

She watched him look into the gaping hole in the floor and then turn back to her in defeat, shaking his head. Fitz won again. That was all she could think about as they made their way back down the stairs to their vehicles.

They found a coffee shop and sat in a back corner. Bella cupped her mug in her hands, wishing she could chase away the cold that had settled inside her as she told Tommy first about dinner with Fitz and then the two thugs who'd been waiting for him in the parking lot.

"It sounded like he owed them money," she said.

Tommy shook his head. "I'm not surprised. Bill said that Fitz has been living beyond his means for some time. Once Bill did away with the shell company and that free money, he'd wondered what Fitz had been doing for income to support his lifestyle and gambling habit."

"We may know soon," she said and told him about the call from Edwin this morning.

"A thumb drive?" he said when she'd finished. "Bella, if it's around his neck—"

"I know. But I have to try," she said quickly.

He shook his head. "You can't be serious. If he catches you—"

"How can it be any worse than what is happening right now?" she demanded. "He would just gloat that he'd won again." She feared that he would do a whole lot more, but she wasn't about to share that with Tommy.

"I don't like it," he said.

She took a drink of her coffee and felt the heat rush through her. "I don't like it either, but time is running out. I have to try to get the thumb drive. If Edwin is telling the truth—"

"Exactly. You sure Fitz didn't put him up to this?"

Bella wasn't sure of anything except the impending wedding looming on the close horizon—and what Fitz might do to her father before this was over. What hung between her and Tommy was the realization that Fitz had gone beyond just threatening people. He or one of the men he'd hired had tried to kill the accountant and she was pretty sure the driver had also tried to kill Tommy. Ronan? Miles? Either were capable, she thought.

"You know what scares me?" she asked, feeling the tightness in her chest as she realized that she'd underestimated Fitz. "Fitz is much more desperate than I thought. I should have realized it. He's buying drugs to frame my father, throwing this elaborate wedding, he's been stealing money from the partnership, he's blackmailing me and his father, and now attempted murder?" She looked up into Tommy's handsome face. "Now I suspect he not only knows about us, but that he had someone try to kill you last night. I can't see you anymore. I'm firing you."

AS SHE STARTED to rise to leave, Tommy reached for her arm. "No," he said, easing her back into her chair. "Not happening. You aren't doing this alone." He knew Bella. She wouldn't give up. She would do this alone if she had to. But he wasn't going to let that happen—even as much as he wished he could talk her out of doing anything dangerous.

"You're right. He's become more desperate." He met her gaze. "I know he wants you, but there has to be more. You're just part of the plan. I need to ask you something. How much money do you have?"

She blinked. "On me right now?"

"No," he said with a shake of his head. "What are you worth?"

"You think Fitz wants my money." She laughed. "I think you're right. I know he wants the ranch."

He twined his fingers in her hand. "I'm in this with you whether you fire me or not." He thought about Margo and the unpaid rent. Maybe Fitz could no longer afford her. Or no longer needed her. Either way, Fitz was getting more desperate, which meant he was getting more dangerous.

"So what's your plan to get the thumb drive?" he asked, knowing that she would try no matter what he said. He saw at once from her expression that she hadn't had a plan. "You're going to need some strong sedatives. I'll get them for you. What does this thumb drive look like?"

"Silver, thin," she said, her voice breaking as her eyes welled with tears. "Thank you. I'll need one like it to replace the one I take."

He nodded. "I'll get it," he said, his voice also filled with emotion. He couldn't bear the thought that he might get this woman killed. "We do this together. Just like when we were kids."

She nodded and wiped at her tears. "Please be—"

"Careful? Have you forgotten that as soon as my license comes back I'm going to be a private investigator? *Trouble* is my middle name now."

"That isn't funny."

"But it's true," he said, squeezing her hand. She was shaking and he knew that she was scared. For him.

He had to bite his tongue not to tell her how much he loved her. But damned if he would do it in some coffee shop. When this was over…

"I'll bring the sedatives and the thumb drive," he said, trying to hide how terrified he was of what Fitz would do if he caught her. "Can you meet me later at that old pine where we used to ride our horses?" She nodded. "You're sure you can get away?"

"He's still letting me ride my horse," she said through gritted teeth. It more than grated on her that he had moved in and thought he could tell her what to do. Unfortunately, he could. For now. "Later this afternoon before sundown?"

"I'll be there. I'll come by horseback."

THE COLT PROPERTY was large but because it wasn't on the river, it wasn't worth as much as the Worthington ranch. Still, Tommy loved the land his great-grandfather had bought but never built on. All of them had spent so little time in Lonesome that building a house had remained a pipe dream.

Until James came home and fell in love with Lorelei. The house was coming along nicely. One of the first things James had done was fence off some pasture and build a stable and corral for their horses. Tommy had been keeping his horse and tack out here since he'd returned home.

After saddling his horse, he rode up over the mountain to drop down toward the river. The large pine he and Bella used to climb when they were kids was in the far corner of the Worthington ranch far from any roads—right next door to Colt land. It was very private since there were no roads into it—another reason it had been one his and Bella's favorite places to hang out as kids. While their parents knew about the tree house, they didn't know about the other spots they went to. No one found them here because no one came this far to look for them.

He spotted Bella's horse tied up some distance from the tree and reined in. As he swung out of the saddle, he saw her waiting for him under the mighty limbs of the old pine. She'd spread out a horse blanket and now sat with her back against the tree trunk. The waning sun shone on her face as he tied up his horse and walked toward her.

She looked so beautiful it choked him up. He realized he couldn't wait any longer to tell her how he felt. He'd held it in for too long. Her gaze tracked him, the expression on her face intrigued—and expectant. He chuckled to himself. Bella was too sharp not to know how he felt—or why he'd wanted to meet here. Had she, like him, been waiting for this day?

Chapter Eighteen

Bella studied the good-looking, dark-haired cowboy headed her way and felt her heart bump in her chest. His expression stole her breath. His long legs, clad in denim, quickly covered the distance between them.

She pushed to her feet, feeling the air tingle around her like dry lightning. Tommy didn't speak, just took her shoulders in his large hands and pulled her into a kiss. She felt the electricity popping around her, felt the spark as his lips touched her. It sent a jolt through her, straight to her middle, as he backed her up against the smooth tree trunk and she wrapped her arms around his waist and brought him closer.

He made a sound deep in his throat as one hand dropped to her breast. She groaned against his mouth as he slipped his hand inside her shirt and under the cup of her bra to fondle her now granite-hard nipple. He caught the tip between his thumb and finger and gently rolled it back and forth.

She arched against him, a groan coming from her lips. Only then did he pull back from the kiss to look into her eyes. She saw the desire burning there as hot as his callused fingers still teasing her aching nipple.

"Tell me to stop," he said, his voice hoarse with obvious emotion.

She shook her head. "I've wanted this for way too long."

The words appeared to be his undoing. He swept her into his arms and gently laid her on the blanket she'd spread out for them. For a moment, he merely stared down into her face. She smiled up at him, and then taking his face in her hands pulled him down for a kiss.

After that, Bella vaguely remembered the flurry of clothing flying into piles on the blanket before they rolled around, both naked as jaybirds. She'd known that their lovemaking would be both wild and playful—just as they had always been. She wasn't disappointed.

She'd never wanted anything more than she wanted Tommy as she began to feel an urgency. She desperately wanted him inside her. He bent to lathe each hard nipple with his tongue before trailing kisses across her flat stomach to her center. She moaned against his incredible mouth as he lifted her higher and higher until she thought she would burst. Until she felt a release that left her weak and shaking.

She drew him up to her, still desperately needing to feel his body on hers, in hers. The weight of him, the look in his eyes, the warm summer evening's breeze caressing their naked bodies. Hadn't she always known that if she and Tommy ever got past just being friends, this is where it would happen?

He started to speak, but she pressed a finger to his lips and shook her head. If he told her that he loved her right now, she feared she wouldn't be able to hold back the tears. She hadn't let herself admit how afraid she was that they couldn't stop Fitz.

She guided him into her and began to move slowly, her gaze locked with his. Their movements grew stronger, faster, harder. She arched against him, filled with a desire that only he could quench. When the release came it was powerful. Pleasure washed through her as she rose to meet him again and again, before they both collapsed together, breathing hard.

"I knew it would be like that," she said as she looked into his pale blue eyes.

"Bella—" She slipped from his arms. "Come on." Reaching back, she took his hand and pulled him up to run toward the river where it pooled among the rocks. The sun was all but hidden behind the mountain and yet the evening was summertime warm as they ran into the water, laughing. Droplets rose in the summer air and seemed to hang there.

Bella filed it all away in a special place in her heart, memorizing the scents, the light, the feel of the water and Tommy for fear this was all they may get when the dust settled.

LATER TOMMY WOULD remember the water droplets caught in her lashes. Her laughter carrying across the water. She hadn't let him tell her how much he loved her. But she knew. He'd seen that moment of fear in her eyes and felt it heart deep. They had no future unless Fitz could be stopped.

It was the only thing on his mind as he rode his horse back to his brother's place. He and Bella had air-dried off in the evening warmth before dressing and riding off in different directions.

He'd given her the sedatives and thumb drive. "Call me when you can," was all he'd said. There was no reason to warn her to be careful. Or to try to change her mind about what she planned to do. The wedding was approaching too quickly.

"Don't come to the ranch," she warned him as she swung up into the saddle. "The place is crawling with the men he hired."

"How will you get me the thumb drive?"

"We'll meet tomorrow morning. Ten o'clock. At the fire tower."

"And if you don't make it?" he asked.

"I'll find a way to call you." She'd known that wasn't what he was asking, but he let it go. "Just don't try to come to the ranch. I'll get the thumb drive and find a way to get it to you."

He thought of their lovemaking and ached to feel her body nestled against his. He recalled the pale light on her skin and trailing a finger through the river water that pooled on her flat stomach before they made love a second time.

What terrified him was the way they'd parted as if they might never see each other again.

"Your bouquet," he'd said before she could ride away. "If things go wrong, there will be something in the roses from me."

Her eyes had widened but then she'd nodded. Neither one of them wanted this to go that far. But in case it did...

"Thank you. I'll see you tomorrow."

Chapter Nineteen

Bella fingered the small packet of crushed sedatives in her pocket for a moment before she took her seat at the dining room table across from Fitz.

She felt flushed from being with Tommy Colt and feared it showed on her face. If Fitz had known where she'd been and what she'd done… But if he'd noticed a change in her, he didn't show it.

"To marriage," Fitz said, lifting his full wineglass. She hesitated to raise her own glass that he'd already filled. She didn't want to drink tonight. Later, she would need to be completely sober, completely in touch with her every movement if she hoped to succeed, because there was no way she wasn't going through with this.

"To truth and justice," she said and raised her glass, holding his gaze.

He laughed. "Whatever." He took a long drink. He seemed to be in a good mood…for some reason. Which concerned her.

She pretended to take a sip and put down her glass. Roberto brought out their meals. She ate distractedly. Fitz ate with gusto, as if he hadn't eaten all day. He probably hadn't. She watched him out of the corner of her eye.

All she could think was that she needed a distraction

so she could get the powder into his wineglass, but he seemed settled in, his gaze on her when he wasn't shoveling food into his mouth. Did he know what she planned to do? Had Edwin confessed that he'd told her about the thumb drive?

Fitz's cell phone rang, making her start and him swear. She had to relax. If he noticed how tense she was—

"I have to take this," he said and, dropping his napkin onto his empty plate, excused himself to head for the den. "What?" he demanded into the phone before he closed the door behind him.

She had no idea how long she had. Maybe only a few seconds. Quickly, she pulled the packet with the pulverized sedatives from her pocket. It took way too long to get the packet open, her fingers refusing to cooperate. She could hear Fitz still on the phone, but he was trying to keep the call short. He could open that door any moment and catch her. She feared she wouldn't get another chance tonight.

The bag finally opened. She poured the contents into his wineglass. Some of the white powder stuck to the side. She hurriedly poured some of her wine into his glass and swirled it around, spilling a little on the tablecloth.

She heard the door open and Fitz's raised voice. "We're in the middle of dinner," he said into the phone, the door opened a crack. "We can talk about this tomorrow."

All she could do was cover the spot with his plate, moving it though from where he had it set perfectly in front of him. Would he notice? He might. She moved the plate back to where it had been. Or at least close.

As he came out of the den, she reached for the wine bottle to refill her glass. Then she began to pour more wine into his glass, spilling just a little on the already stained tablecloth.

Fitz grabbed the wine bottle from her hand. "Clumsy. That's not like you." His heated gaze burned her as he walked around the table. Picking up his cloth napkin, he covered the spilled spot on the tablecloth and called for Roberto to bring him another napkin and take their empty plates.

She could feel his eyes on her, suspicious. The two spots on the tablecloth. He would see it. He would know. She looked up at him. He looked disgruntled with her. Would he demand the tablecloth be changed just to show that he was still in charge?

He took a deep breath, let it out and finally sat down. As he did, he straightened the salt and pepper shakers. She hadn't realized that she'd knocked over the salt in her hurry to cover up her crime.

She picked up her wine and pretended to take a drink. Had she gotten away with it? Not until he drank his wine.

Roberto whisked away their plates, promising to return with a surprise dessert. She saw Fitz open his mouth as if to say he didn't want dessert.

"I do, please," she said quickly, cutting him off. Then she looked at Fitz and said, "I've been thinking." She lowered her eyelashes.

"Oh?" From under her lashes, she saw him pick up his wineglass and take a drink as he watched her.

"Maybe we could make a deal."

He chuckled. "You really aren't in a dealing position."

She met his gaze, ran her finger along the rim of her wineglass and wet her lips. She had his attention. More than that, she saw something in his eyes that surprised her. Yes, he wanted to punish her, destroy her, but he also wanted her as well as her ranch. His look was lustful. Maybe she had more to bargain with than he wanted to admit.

She took a sip of her wine and this time swallowed it. *Easy, girl. If this works, you need to be dead sober.* She continued to hold her wineglass. She'd heard somewhere that diners often mirrored their dinner companions. Reach for bread, they were apt to as well. Same with drinking?

Bella realized there must be some truth to it because Fitz took a healthy drink of his wine. She needed him to finish it, though. He was a big man. But there'd been enough sedatives in the packet to put down a farm animal. If he finished his wineglass, he should start feeling the effects fairly soon.

But not too soon, she hoped.

"So?" he asked. "What is this...deal you want to make?"

She could see that he was interested, and it had gotten his mind off the spilled wine on the tablecloth. "I feel like we should call a truce."

He grinned. "A truce? What do you have in mind?"

She took another sip of her wine. She could feel the heat of it rush to her chest. But she had to get him to drink all of his. He had put his wine down but now picked it up again and nearly drained the glass.

She noticed with a jolt that there was white powder in the bottom of his glass. "It's going to take more wine," she said with a little laugh and reached for the bottle, knocking it over. There wasn't much left to spill but enough to cause him to leap to his feet as the bottle banged into his glass, spilling the last of the contents onto the already soiled tablecloth and running like a river straight for him.

He swore and jumped back just as she'd hoped. He didn't want to get red wine on his linen trousers.

She leaped up as well and grabbed his glass and spilled hers as well. "Roberto," she called. "We need help." She giggled as she felt Fitz's hard suspicious gaze on her again. "We're going to need another bottle of wine," she said, laughing as Roberto came into the room.

"I believe you've had enough," Fitz said. "Clean this up." He stepped back from the huge red stain on the white tablecloth as if it were blood.

Squeamish a little? She swayed and pretended to have trouble focusing. "I think we should discontinue this conversation for the moment. I might have to lie down or throw up," Bella said and grabbed the edge of the table for support. Had he noticed that her wineglass was less empty than his?

She told herself to be careful. Fitz watched everything. If he thought that she wasn't as tipsy as she was... Or worse, that she'd put something in his wine...

Roberto appeared and quickly took the dishes and the stained tablecloth. He saw that they were both standing and neither of them had sat back down. "No dessert?" he asked, sounding disappointed. "I made something special—"

She cut him off before he could say what. "Save me some please, but I really have to..." She didn't finish, just exited quickly, hurrying up the stairs to her room where she locked the door behind her.

Her back against the door, she stood listening until she heard Fitz's footfalls. Then she made gagging sounds until the footfalls quickly faded back down the hallway in the direction of the guest hallway.

Going to the intercom, she called down to the kitchen. "Roberto, I could really use some hot black coffee."

"And maybe dessert?" He lowered his voice and smiled. "I made tres leches."

She couldn't help but smile. "Why not?"

A few moments later there was a tap at her door. She couldn't be sure that Fitz hadn't waylaid Roberto and she would find him standing outside her door holding the tray, waiting to be let into her room.

She grabbed a towel, wrapped it around her head and splashed water on her face. As she was leaving the bathroom, she remembered to flush the toilet.

Unlocking the door, she opened it a crack. To her relief, Roberto was holding the tray. She stepped back to let him enter.

"Thank you," she said. "I don't feel so well."

"There are some over-the-counter pain relievers on the tray as well," he said and smiled as he quickly left.

She locked the door and reached for the coffee. If the sedative worked, then Fitz should be feeling the effects right now. She glanced at the time. She'd give it another fifteen minutes.

Chapter Twenty

Tommy had taken his suspicions about Fitz's gambling debt to his brother James. It hadn't taken long before they had a completely different picture of Edwin Fitzgerald Mattson the Third. "He's in trouble. His lifestyle seems to have caught up with him."

"The car is leased," James said. "He's behind in his apartment rent and his credit cards are maxed out. Have you seen the wedding invitations?" He shook his head. "Cash-only gifts as the couple will be moving overseas."

Tommy swore and snatched the invitation out of his brother's hand. Did Bella know about this? He didn't think so. But since she wasn't planning to go through with the wedding, maybe she wasn't worried about it.

"So he does plan to sell everything, including the ranch," Tommy said. "Even taking all of this into consideration, it still seems like Fitz is too desperate."

James nodded. "I saw the police report on the hit-and-run. I have a friend in the police department. You didn't mention that the bastard tried to kill you first."

"If it was Fitz's doing. Did your cop friend also tell you that the SUV was stolen and that they suspect it was an accident?"

"Yeah, like either of us believe that. Still, you're right. Fitz wouldn't know how to steal a vehicle unless the keys were in the ignition."

"There's more going on here," Tommy said. "From what Bella told me, he's gotten involved with the wrong people." James nodded. "I think this might have started with him wanting Bella, but that he now needs her money. The ranch is in her name. With the way things are selling in Montana right now…"

"That place is worth a small fortune, being on the river with the main house, bunkhouse, stable, new barn and all that land," James said.

"She has a couple of trust funds and some other money as well," Tommy told him.

"If Fitz is as desperate as it seems, he'll be even more dangerous," James said.

"That's what has me terrified, because of what Bella has planned." He couldn't sit still. How could he let her go through with this? How could he stop her?

"It's Bella," his brother said at seeing how anxious he was. "I'd put my money on her any day of the week to come out a winner."

Tommy smiled at his older brother. "I can't help but be scared. I don't know what Fitz will do next. He's already proven how dangerous he is."

BELLA POCKETED THE empty thumb drive Tommy had given her to replace Fitz's. If she didn't switch them, then he would know too quickly that his was gone. She needed time to find out what was on the drive before she realized what she'd done.

That was of course if she could pull this off. She

checked the time. Now or never. Taking a deep breath, she unlocked her bedroom door, peered out.

The hallway was empty. This time of night most of the security guards were either at the bunkhouse or outside on the grounds. Not that one of them couldn't appear at any time in the hallway since she knew that they also made sure the house was secure.

She let her bedroom door close softly behind her before starting down the hallway in her stocking feet. The house seemed unusually quiet tonight. The moon would be up soon. But right now, it was dark outside, even with a zillion stars glittering over the tops of the trees. Shadows hunkered in the depths of the pines. Not a breeze stirred the boughs.

At the guest room wing she stopped to listen. She heard nothing but the pounding of her own pulse, as if the house were holding its breath.

Making her way down the short hallway, she stopped a few feet from his door and listened before she pulled out her passkey. As quietly as possible, she stepped to the door and slipped the passkey into the lock.

Breath held, she listened as she turned the key. It made a faint tick of a sound. She waited and then turned the knob and slowly eased open the door, terrified to think that Fitz could be lying in wait and about to ambush her.

The room was filled with pitch-black darkness. The drapes were partially closed. Faint starlight cut through the gap to cast a dagger-like sheen on the carpet. The room held a chest of drawers and a king-size bed with a club chair and two end tables. The door to the bathroom stood open, its interior also dark.

Over the thunder of her heart, she heard it. The sound of heavy rhythmic snoring came from the direction of the bed. She tried to breathe for a moment. She was shaking. If she hoped to get the thumb drive, she had to calm down.

Stepping in on her tiptoes, she let the door close quietly behind her and moved toward the bed and the snoring man sprawled there. With each step, she expected him to bolt upright. Surprise! Maybe the sedatives hadn't been powerful enough. Or maybe he hadn't drank enough. She tried to remember how much white sediment had been in the bottom of the wineglass.

She neared the bed, ready at any point to turn and run. It wasn't until she was next to the bed that she saw Fitz had lain down with all his clothes on. The way he was sprawled, it appeared he'd barely made it before passing out. She wondered how fast the sedative had hit him and whether he'd realized what was happening before he hit the bed.

Bella told herself that she couldn't worry about that right now. Once she had the thumb drive, once she got it to Tommy, then it wouldn't matter what Fitz suspected let alone what he knew.

But because she didn't know how long it would take or even how she was going to get the drive to him, she had to replace the drive with the empty one.

Edging closer she listened to his snores. He lay on his back, one arm thrown over his head, the other lying across his rising and falling chest.

The moon rose up over the mountains, over the tops of the pines, the bright light fingering through boughs to shine through the space behind the partially opened drapes. That dagger of faint light was now a river of gold that splashed across the room.

The light glinted off the chain around Fitz's neck.

Tommy paced the floor, unable to sleep. He should have talked Bella out of this. That thought made him laugh. Once Bella made up her mind… Still, he had to know what was happening out at the ranch.

His cell phone rang, making him jump. Bella? He snatched up the phone. "Hello?"

"Tommy, it's James."

His heart jumped into this throat. He couldn't speak, couldn't breathe. He gripped the phone, terrified of what his brother would say next. "Edwin senior is dead."

It took a moment before the unexpected news registered. "What?"

"I just got the call here at the office from my friend with the Missoula police," James said. "Apparently it was suicide. They think he's been dead since sometime yesterday."

Tommy didn't know what to say. He recalled Bella telling him about Edwin's call to her. She'd said someone had come in. She'd feared it was Fitz and that he might have heard what his father had told her. "Does Bella know?" he asked. "What about Fitz?"

"I have no idea if he's gotten the call yet. Can't imagine why anyone would call Bella."

But they would try to reach Fitz. Tonight. And given what Bella might be doing at this very moment…

"Bella's in trouble," he told his brother and explained about her plan.

James swore. "That's a bonehead idea if I ever heard one, but if anyone can pull it off it is Bella."

"If you're just trying to make me feel better—"

"I'm not. You know her. I'm sure you tried to stop her without any luck, right?"

"Right."

"What's the worst that can happen?" James said. "He wakes up and catches her. He isn't going to kill her. He can't."

"I hope you're right." But Tommy knew that if Fitz caught her trying to steal the thumb drive, he would make her life even more miserable and God only knew what he'd do to her father.

BELLA EDGED CLOSER to the bed. Her chest hurt from holding her breath. She let it out in a soft sigh as she kept her gaze on the bed and the man lying on it. Fitz hadn't moved. He continued to snore loudly. She assured herself that he couldn't hear her.

But once she touched him…

Her plan was simple. She would gently lift the chain at his neck. Except as she reached down, he let out a sharp snore and stirred. She froze. There was nothing else she could do. What would she do if he caught her? A half dozen lies flitted through her brain, all of them so lame they were laughable.

After a few moments Fitz fell back into more rhythmic snores again. She shook out her hand, her fingers tingling as if asleep. Then she reached down and with slow, careful movements, pinched the thick gold chain between her fingers. Slowly, she began to lift it.

As she did, she could see the shape of the thin thumb drive moving beneath his shirt as it headed for the V opening at this throat. Her mind started to play tricks on her, telling her that he was faking it, that he'd been expecting her, that once the thumb drive was visible his eyes would flash open and he'd grab her by the throat.

Her hand trembled and she had to stop for a moment. *Almost there, don't give up now.* She felt an urgency and yet she still pulled the chain slowly until she'd eased the thumb drive out from the shirt opening. It lay against his bare throat for a moment. She drew it over onto his shirt and let out the breath she'd been holding.

Now it was just a matter of unhooking the golden chain from around his neck. Hanging onto the thumb drive, she pulled on the chain until the clasp was reachable.

But in order to unhook the clasp, she had to lean forward over him closer than she'd ever wanted to be. She could smell his cologne and their long-ago-consumed dinner on his breath and tried not to gag. Her fingers shook with nerves. She tried not to look at his face as she worked at the clasp and yet she was still expecting his eyes to flash open, his hand to grab hold of her wrist. She was still expecting to be caught.

The chain came unhooked so quickly that she dropped one end of it. She hurriedly slipped off the thumb drive and pulled the new empty one from her pocket—and switched them. Now all she had to do was reconnect the clasp.

The whole process felt like it had taken too long and yet she knew it had only been a few minutes. Would Fitz be suspicious when he woke up to find his chain pulled out? She thought about trying to stick the thumb drive back under his shirt and was still considering it when his cell phone, right beside the bed, rang.

The sound was so loud in the room that she jumped and dropped the chain as she lurched back. Her gaze shot to his face. He'd stopped snoring. His eyelids fluttered.

Move! But her feet felt nailed to the floor.

The cell phone rang again. She took a step backward, then another and another, all the time watching his face as he attempted to drag himself up from the drugged sleep. She was to the door when she heard the phone stop ringing. She could only see the end of the bed from here.

Had he answered it? Her heart was pounding so hard she couldn't be sure. She eased open the door and stepped into the hall, pulling it gently closed behind her.

In those few seconds, she'd expected him to yank open the door and grab her. Inside his room, his phone began to ring again. Her heart banging like cymbals against her ribs, she turned and took off down the hall. At the end, she finally had the courage to look back—fearful that if she turned she'd find Fitz right behind her.

The hallway was empty, but she could hear someone coming up the stairs. She hurried down to her room, unlocked the door with trembling fingers and stepped inside. It wasn't until she had the door locked behind her and stood, trying to catch her breath, that she heard banging.

Someone was pounding on Fitz's door. In the distance, she could hear another cell phone ringing. She hurried to hers where she'd thankfully left it next to her bed. But as she picked it up to call Tommy, she heard a noise outside her bedroom door and then a knock.

"Bella?"

She recognized the voice. Ronan. The other guards called her Miss Worthington. He knocked again. She waited realizing she was supposed to be asleep. "Yes, what is it?" she called, hoping she sounded as if she'd just woken up.

"There's been an accident," Ronan called through the door. "Open up."

She reached for her robe, pulling it around her and hiding her clothes under it. "What kind of accident?"

She could hear him waiting. She looked around the room clutching her cell phone. The thumb drive was in her jeans pocket under the robe.

At the door, she eased it open a crack. "What is it?" She sounded as impatient as she felt. She could hear Fitz's phone still ringing. Something had happened, that much was obvious.

"It's Edwin Mattson. He's dead. Suicide," Ronan said. His dark eyes bored into her.

She pulled the collar of her robe tighter. "Does Fitz know?" she asked.

"I thought you would want to know. Your fiancé is going to need you." There was censure in his words, in the look in his eyes.

Bella felt sick to her stomach. What did Ronan know? But when she met his gaze, she realized he was probably the one who'd followed her and Tommy to the river. He knew. So Fitz knew as well—just as she'd feared. "I need to get dressed." She slammed the door and quickly locked it an instant before he raised his hand to stop her.

She leaned against the door. Just minutes before she'd been home free. She had the thumb drive. She'd done it. Now this? Edwin? Suicide. A feeling of doom washed over her, making it even more difficult to breathe. She'd heard someone interrupt her call with Edwin. Had it been suicide?

This might change everything, she realized. What if she couldn't meet Tommy at ten at the fire tower? She held her cell phone to her chest remembering their lovemaking at the old pine tree. As badly as she needed to hear his voice, she realized she couldn't chance calling him. She could hear more footfalls in the hallway. Ronan could be standing out there listening.

No, she'd just find a way to meet Tommy at the fire tower and give him the thumb drive. In the meantime, it sounded as if the guards had managed to awaken Fitz. She needed to change clothes and go downstairs. The best thing she could do, she told herself, was to act as normally as possible. It wouldn't be hard to appear shocked about Edwin's death. It would be much harder to accept that he'd committed suicide—and hide her true fear that Fitz was behind it.

She closed her eyes, thinking of the man who'd tried to help her and her father. But mostly thinking of Edwin's call and the sound of someone interrupting them—someone he'd feared. His own son?

Dropping her cell phone into her purse, she hurried to her laptop and inserted the thumb drive. She might not have much time, but she needed to know that this wasn't another of Fitz's tricks and that there really was something on this drive.

She could hear the sound of footfalls in the house, the commotion mostly in the guest hallway. Had he realized by now that he'd been knocked out?

There was only one file on the thumb drive. She clicked on it just an instant before there was loud knocking at her door again. Data. Lots of data, everything she needed, she hoped. Edwin had told her the truth. Hurriedly, she ejected the thumb drive and pocketed it in her jeans.

"I'm getting dressed," she called through the door—not about to open it again. She didn't trust Ronan. That was the problem with mad dogs. Sometimes they even turned on their owners.

But this time the voice on the other side came from

one of the other guards. "Mr. Mattson would like you to join him downstairs."

She glanced at the time. It would be daylight soon. What could Fitz want with her? "I'm getting dressed. Please tell him that I'll be down shortly."

She waited until she heard the man move away from the door before she hurried to change. Exhaustion pulled at her. It had been a nerve-racking night. She considered what to do with the thumb drive and decided keeping it on her was best. Her burner phone was in the car. She'd call Tommy on the way to the fire tower.

Dressed in a clean pair of jeans and a blouse, she pocketed the thumb drive, pulled on a jacket and went downstairs, taking her purse with her. As soon as she could, she'd go to Tommy.

Fitz was so adamant about them looking like a loving engaged couple, he would probably want her to go with him to talk to the police and make arrangements for his father's body to be taken to the funeral home.

But with Fitz she never knew what to expect. He could still be somewhat out of it because of the sedatives. She figured one look at him would tell her whether or not he knew what she'd been up to.

Chapter Twenty-One

Fitz tried to think. His head felt filled with cotton. "Coffee," he demanded once Roberto had been awakened and sent to the kitchen. "Keep it coming." The police had called with the news. They would want to see him. But they couldn't see him in this condition.

He caught a glimpse of himself in a mirror in the dining room and recoiled. He couldn't meet with anyone looking like... He narrowed his gaze at his reflection. He hadn't consumed that much alcohol at dinner. No, the way he was feeling wasn't from the wine.

At the sound of footfalls, he turned to see his lovely future bride coming down the stairs. Every time he saw her, he was stunned at how perfect she was. She'd always been like this, even as a girl. So self-assured, so adorable, so capable of just about anything.

The reminder sent a stab of worry through him. He touched the chain at his neck. When he'd awakened fully clothed as if from the sleep of the dead, the chain and thumb drive had been outside his shirt. He'd hurriedly stuffed it back in as he'd gone to the door to find the guards standing in the hallway looking worried. Apparently they had been banging at his door for some time.

"Sir, your phone is ringing and the police are on the

landline downstairs," one of his men had said, eyeing him strangely.

Fitz had had to fight to make sense of what the guard was saying. He'd turned back to his bed, shocked to see that he hadn't been under the covers. He hadn't even removed his clothing from last night. That was when he'd realized that his phone was ringing. He'd stumbled to the end table and grabbed up his phone. His father was dead. Suspected suicide?

He'd felt as if he'd missed more than a phone call. He'd lost hours of time and didn't have any idea how it had happened.

"I'm sorry to hear about your father," Bella said as she joined him.

He looked into her green eyes. It was like looking into a bottomless sea that beckoned him before the lids dropped, shutting him out. "Thank you," he said, his tongue feeling too large for his mouth. He turned and yelled into the kitchen. "Where is my damned coffee?"

"Let me go see," Bella said and started past him.

He grabbed her arm and shook his head. "Stay here with me." His voice broke, surprising him. He sounded like a man who'd just lost his father. He was taking this much worse than he'd expected. He and Edwin senior had been at odds for so long now…

She didn't argue. "Would you like me to go with you to talk to the police?"

The offer touched him and made him suspicious at the same time. She looked guilty of something. He would eventually find out, he told himself. Right now just keeping his eyes open was hard enough. Thinking hurt. "Thank you," he said, knowing he had no intention of taking her up on her offer. He'd go alone. Bella had spoken to his father recently. He couldn't trust that she wouldn't say something that might cast suspicion on him.

Roberto hurried out of the kitchen with the coffee. Also on the tray along with the cups and spoons were what appeared to be small cakes and a bowl of strawberries.

"I thought you might like something while I make your breakfast," Roberto said.

Fitz was touched by the man's thoughtfulness, until he realized that the gesture wasn't for him. The cook was beaming at Bella. He waved Roberto away and pulled out Bella's chair. "It seems you have a not-so-secret admirer," he said as he shoved her chair hard into the table.

She let out an *ooft* that made him feel better as he moved to his chair and sat down. Bella had recovered quickly. She busied herself pouring him a cup of coffee. Yes, she definitely felt guilty about something, he thought. He couldn't wait to find out what. Something more than Tommy Colt?

Just the thought of her with that cowboy made him grit his teeth. His head ached with a dull constant throb. He couldn't make sense of why he felt so…sluggish.

Ronan came into the room and motioned that he needed to speak with him. Fitz shot a look at Bella. Did she suddenly look pale? He believed she did. What now? he thought as he rose and excused himself to go speak privately with the man.

BELLA SIPPED HER coffee and tried not to act interested in whatever Ronan was telling his boss. She couldn't hear what was being said, but she saw, out of the corner of her eye, Fitz turning around to look at her.

When he came back to the table, he apologized for the

interruption and sat down. He seemed even more unco-ordinated than usual, as if his balance was off from the sedatives. She saw him frowning as if trying to under-stand what was going on.

Whatever Ronan had told him had him upset. She could feel waves of anger coming off Fitz like electrical currents. She braced herself, knowing that whatever the guard had told him, it wasn't good. She thought about her lovemaking with Tommy yesterday evening. She'd been so sure that she hadn't been followed.

Helping herself to some strawberries and one of the small cakes, she offered to dish up a plate for Fitz. He growled under his breath and shook his head, hardly tak-ing his eyes off her. The waiting was starting to get to her. Fitz sat rigid, staring a hole into her.

"I'm sure you're upset now that the wedding will have to be postponed," Bella said as she lifted her coffee cup to her lips.

Fitz roared, slamming his hand down on the table. Dishes and silverware rattled. His coffee slopped over onto the tablecloth, making him let out yet another oath.

He threw his napkin down on the stain as he appeared to fight for control. Was this about what Ronan had told him? Maybe his father's death had hit him harder than it had first appeared. Maybe he hadn't killed Edwin. Maybe it had been suicide after all and now it was interfering with Fitz's plans. Whatever the reason, his mood was worse than anything she'd seen before.

"Roberto," he called. "Please bring me another nap-kin." The cook responded at once and then quickly went back to making their breakfast plates. She watched Fitz carefully wipe coffee from the side and bottom of his cup before just as carefully folding the napkin and putting it aside.

One of his guards came into the room, stopping at the end of the table. Her heart dropped as she saw what he held in his hands—her laptop computer. The man set it down and left.

She shot a look at Fitz. He had been watching for her reaction and was now smiling. Picking up his cup, he took a sip of coffee and then another. She knew that the sedatives were probably partially to blame for the man's mood—but not all of it. His face was now composed but she could see fury just beneath the surface. It wasn't just his father's death that had him so upset.

Bella tried to remain calm but as she took another sip of her coffee she had to hold the cup with both hands to hide her trembling. Had he plugged in the thumb drive around his neck and found it empty? If so, he would know that she'd switched them. In which case, he would also know that she'd drugged him last night, which would explain why he wasn't thinking clearly.

She knew he was waiting for her to ask about her laptop so she didn't. Roberto brought out their breakfasts and she dug in, even though she had to choke it down. She could feel Fitz's gaze on her as she ate and pretended that everything was fine. She could feel her pulse just below her skin thumping. How much did he know? And what would he do now?

What she'd found on the thumb drive was more than bank and business records. There had been bank account numbers and passcodes for three foreign banks. She hadn't had time to find out how much money might be in each, but she suspected the money might be more of an issue with him than her destroying his hold over her.

"We are not postponing the wedding," he said calmly. He held out his hand. She looked from it to his face, uncertain what he might want from her. "Give me your keys."

Bella instantly bristled. "I will not."

"I'm afraid you now have no choice. Your…behavior with Tommy Colt will no longer be permitted. You are *my* fiancée. As such you will no longer sneak off to have sex with another man." She started to speak but he talked over her. "You will not be allowed to leave this house until the wedding this Saturday. If that cowboy comes around, he will be shot."

"You can't hold me here," she said with more conviction than she felt and saw in his expression that he could and would keep her here. She was now his prisoner. She thought about the burner phone hidden in her car and the thumb drive in her pocket. Tommy would be waiting for her at the fire tower at ten.

"Give me your cell phone and your keys. I already have your laptop and I've had the landline disabled. I don't want to have one of my men frisk you any more than I want to have them tear your room apart, but I will."

She reached into her purse, took out her keys and her phone and set them on the table, her mind racing. She had to get the thumb drive to Tommy. She had to at least call him. It would be just like him to come to the ranch if he didn't hear from her.

"What about your father?" she asked as Fitz reached across the table and scooped up her phone and keys. She'd actually thought that he'd been close to Edwin. But then again, Fitz had been blackmailing him—just as he had her father and her. Wasn't that why Edwin killed himself? If Fitz hadn't murdered him, she reminded herself.

Edwin had turned on his son. If Fitz had been the person she'd heard in the background on the phone…

"His last wish was to be cremated," Fitz said. "Given that he killed himself, I think a quiet family-only memorial after we get back from our honeymoon would be best."

She met his gaze. "But we aren't coming back from our honeymoon."

He had the good grace to redden at being caught in one of his lies. "Why would you say that?"

"Because you've already made arrangements to sell the ranch while we're gone," she said.

"We won't need it any longer," he said, defensively.

"As your wife, I'd be glad if I had a say in what happens to my family ranch," she said, refusing to cow down to this man. She would never be his wife.

Fitz laughed. "You have no say in anything. Haven't you realized that by now? I have both you and your father exactly where I want the two of you. We will be married Saturday and if you do anything to embarrass me, both of you will regret it to your dying day. Am I making myself clear?"

She swallowed. Fitz had her laptop, her phone and her keys. Unless she could get the thumb drive to Tommy, then Fitz would win. She couldn't clear her father—and the wedding was only two days away.

Chapter Twenty-Two

Tommy had been waiting for word from Bella. He'd gone to the fire tower and waited an hour before returning to the office where he now paced. "She should have called by now." He hated to think what Fitz might have done if he'd caught her attempting to take the thumb drive last night. The not knowing was killing him.

"She probably couldn't get away because of Edwin's suicide," James told him. Tommy knew that could be the case. Or it could be something much worse. If Bella had the thumb drive, she would do whatever it took to get it to him.

When his cell phone rang, he jumped and quickly pulled it out, praying it was Bella. It wasn't. It was FBI agent Ian calling from back East.

"Our face recognition program identified Caroline Lansing," Ian said. "Her real name is Caroline Brooks. She's a con woman and wanted in numerous states for fleecing rich older men. But with the information you gave us, we might be able to pick her up before she does it again."

"What about retrieving his money?"

"Sorry, he'd have to wait in line. I'm sure the money is long gone. But I doubt she was working alone. We have a lead on her. I'll let you know once we have her in custody."

"I suspect she didn't find this mark by accident," Tommy said. "If so, it would help the case I'm working on. The man's name is Edwin Fitzgerald the Third, better known as Fitz."

"You're thinking she might want to make a deal. I'll let you know."

He disconnected, feeling even more anxious. If there were a connection between Caroline and Fitz, she might implicate Fitz for a lighter sentence. Tommy held on to that hope.

Right now, he was more worried about Bella. He didn't dare call her cell. He'd already tried the burner without any luck. He didn't dare keep calling it. His only hope was that with Edwin senior dead, Fitz would delay the wedding.

FITZ WAS AS good as his word when it came to locking her up inside the ranch house. She wasn't allowed to leave. A guard had been posted at each door—including her bedroom.

"Ronan and Miles give me the creeps," she'd told Fitz. "I don't want to see either of them outside my room. You do realize that neither of them can be trusted, don't you?"

He'd laughed at that. "Talk about the pot calling the kettle black."

She'd held her ground and had been relieved when she hadn't seen either of them around. But she'd known they were still on the ranch and that if she tried to escape, they would be the most dangerous to come across.

There was no escaping though and Fitz knew it.

"What am I supposed to do over the next two days?" she'd demanded. "Stay in my room?"

"That's a very good idea," he'd agreed. "That way I'll know you're safe."

She scoffed at that. "I won't be safe until you're out of my life and my father's."

Fitz looked hurt. "I'd hoped we were past that by now. I've asked you to marry me."

"You've blackmailed me, moved into my ranch, threatened me with armed guards and now you're holding me prisoner," she said. "Let's not pretend that you're the victim here."

"Neither are you," he snapped. "You want out?" He picked up his phone. "I'll call the auditor who will call the FBI. They've been looking for enough evidence to put your father away. When they arrest Nolan, they'll find the drugs." Fitz shrugged. "You've always had a choice, Bella. Your father was a fool. If you hate me so much, then let your father get the justice he deserves and you can walk away."

He knew she couldn't throw her father to the wolves, no matter what foolish mistakes he'd made. Fitz knew that she'd never had a choice. She had the thumb drive but unless she could get it to the authorities…

No, she'd realized that there was only one way out. "I want to check on my flowers," she said the morning before the wedding.

"Is that really necessary?"

She stared at him. "Do I really not get any say in the wedding?"

He studied her for a moment, then relented. She could tell that he was hopeful she was accepting their upcoming nuptials. He started to pass her his phone, but then thought better of it. Getting up from the table, he went into the den and, after a few minutes, came back with her phone.

Bella knew he wouldn't let her leave the room to call the florist and was grateful when he got a call that at least took him away from the table. He didn't go far.

She hurriedly made the call. Susie Harper was a friend of hers and Bella was relieved when she answered. "It's Bella. I wanted to check on the bouquet."

Susie was silent for a moment. "The one that was ordered for you?" Before Bella could clarify, her friend said, "Tommy told me what you needed. With his help, it is ready to his specifications. Unless you want to change—"

"No," she said quickly. He must be planning to have a note inside the bouquet for her. She could tell that her friend desperately wanted to ask what was going on. "Thank you so much for doing that for me. I'll come by soon and we'll go to lunch and have a long talk."

"I hope so," Susie said, worry in her voice.

"You're a lifesaver," Bella said and hung up as Fitz cut his call short and returned to the table.

"Did you get what you wanted?" he asked.

She handed back the phone before he snatched it from her. "At least I'll have the bouquet I want."

"But not the groom," he said and cursed under his breath before saying he would be going out. "Do I have to warn you not to try to leave?"

She said nothing, just glared at him, wondering what she would find in the bouquet tomorrow.

FITZ COULDN'T WAIT for the wedding. Soon he would have everything he wanted. As it turned out, his father had done him a favor by taking his life. The man must have realized that if Bella agreed to be married to his son, someone still had to take the fall for the legal and financial problems with the partnership. If Fitz kept his promise and didn't give the Feds the books that made Nolan guilty, then he had to make it appear that Edwin senior was behind everything. His father must have come to that same conclusion.

With Edwin senior dead, it would be easier to let Nolan off the hook—unless Bella did anything to stop the wedding, Fitz thought.

But you aren't married yet, he reminded himself as he looked across the table at his fiancée later that evening. The past couple of days had been hell. If looks could kill, he'd be a molten pile of ash on the floor. She hated him.

Still he held out hope that if he kept his promise, she might come to love him. It wasn't like she had a choice. Once they were married, if she didn't come around, then he would punish her in ways she couldn't yet imagine.

That wasn't really what he wanted, though. He was in love with her—in his own way. The thought made him angry since he knew she was in love with Tommy Colt. He'd ached for this woman for years. Now, he told himself, he would have her any way he had to take her. Just the thought of their wedding night made him shift in his chair to hide his desire for her.

In another twenty-four hours, she would be his.

"There is something I've wanted to tell you," he said. He'd hoped to tell her this when they got married, but thought maybe if she knew it might soften her feelings toward him enough that tomorrow would go smoothly.

Bella looked up at him. It was the first time he'd let her come downstairs to dine with him. Instead, he'd been sending up her meals to her room. He'd hoped being locked in her bedroom would bring her to heel. He should have known better.

But this evening, she'd looked surprised when he'd tapped on her door and invited her down to the dining room. At first, he'd seen that she'd been about to decline out of stubbornness. Clearly she'd been going a little crazy in her room for all this time.

"I wanted to talk to you about something," he'd told her, giving her a way to accept gracefully. Grudgingly she'd agreed to have their last dinner together before the wedding tomorrow at ten in the morning. He'd opted for a morning wedding because he couldn't bear waiting all day. This way they would have a brunch reception and slip away to start the honeymoon.

Roberto, of course, had made her something special for this last supper before the wedding. Bella had been polite with Roberto, thanking him and even sharing just enough small talk to have Fitz gritting his teeth. She could be so sweet to other people. To Fitz himself, she snarled like an angry dog. But he assured himself that if he had to, he'd beat that out of her.

Now she stopped eating to stare at him as if waiting patiently for whatever he had to tell her.

He took a breath, let it out slowly and smiled as he cleared his throat and said, "I fell in love with you the first time I saw you." No reaction. "Seriously, Bella, I love you." She started to speak, but he stopped her, afraid of what she might say to ruin this moment before he could finish. "I hate the way I've gone about this." He saw disbelief in her expression. "I would have loved to have simply asked you out, but I knew…" He let out a self-deprecating laugh. "With our history from childhood that you wouldn't have gone out with me."

BELLA WAS GLAD she hadn't spoken in the middle of his touching speech. She saw Fitz's vulnerability unmasked in his face, in the nervous way he kneaded at his cloth napkin, in the way his eyes shone. She warned herself to step very carefully.

"I'm sorry too that this happened the way it did," she said. She couldn't very well say that she was glad he'd finally shared his feelings. She wanted to tell him all the reasons she couldn't stand the sight of him. But that too wouldn't help right now.

"I had no idea that you felt like this," Bella said, thinking of his awful threats as to what he planned to do to her once they were married. Fitz had always struck out in anger from the time he was a boy.

She knew whatever she said next could bring out that anger in him and make things worse. But she wasn't sure how to make things better without lying to him and agreeing to marry him.

"I have to wonder…" She met his gaze. She felt her heart begin to pound. Careful. "Is this how you envisioned it going?"

"I'd hoped that if we spent time together maybe…"

"It's hard to force something like this," she said.

"But in time…" He still looked as if he really believed that she would come to love him once they were married.

"What if our feelings don't change?" she asked quietly.

He tossed his blond hair back and she saw the change in his expression. "You mean what if *your* feelings don't change."

"It would only cause us both pain."

When Fitz smiled, she saw the bully he'd been as a boy and was now as a man. "I can promise it will be more painful for you."

Bella sighed and picked up her fork. Roberto had made her a special meal and she was bound and determined to do it justice. Also it was the first time she'd been out of her room.

She could feel Fitz's angry gaze on her and wondered how long it would be before he threw one of his tantrums. Fortunately, his phone rang. He let it ring three times before he shoved back his chair and stormed into the den to take the call. All she heard was him say, "I told you not to call me, Margo," before he slammed the door.

Bella looked toward the exits. Armed guards blocked both. She concentrated on her food. Tomorrow was the wedding. She'd found no way to get Tommy the thumb drive. She just hoped that whatever Tommy had put in her rose bouquet would save her.

Roberto came back to the table to see if she needed anything.

"Everything is wonderful, thank you," she said and dropped her voice. "Have you heard of anyone trying to get onto the ranch?" She saw the answer at once in his eyes. Her heart dropped and tears flooded her eyes. "Is he all right?"

The cook nodded. "I believe there was an altercation. Several of the guards needed to be patched up." He smiled then. "But when the sheriff came, the…intruder was escorted from the property."

Fitz came out of the den.

"Roberto was wondering if you needed anything else," Bella said, seeing that he suspected the two of them had been talking. The intruder would have been Tommy. She was so thankful that he was all right.

"I'm no longer hungry," Fitz snapped. "If you're finished, you should go back to your room. You need your rest. You're getting married tomorrow. I can have Ronan escort you." The threat had the exact effect he knew it would.

"I can see myself to my room." She rose and put down her napkin. "Roberto, thank you again for a lovely dinner," she called to the kitchen. With that she headed for the stairs.

Fitz followed her as far as the landing. He stood waiting as she entered her bedroom. A few moments later, she heard footfalls and then a key turned in the lock. She wanted to scream. Or at the very least cry.

But she did neither. She walked to the window and stared out at the ranch she loved, vowing she would do whatever it took tomorrow but she would never marry Fitz.

TOMMY'S ONE ATTEMPT to get onto the ranch and see Bella had been thwarted quickly. He'd known there would be guards. What he hadn't expected was to be accosted by two obvious thugs. He'd held his own in the fight even against two of them, but he was smart enough not to go back to the ranch alone.

As the wedding day had quickly approached, he'd become more concerned for Bella's safety.

"Fitz won't hurt her," James kept telling him. "He's planned this elaborate wedding and invited most of the county. If you're right and he's in love with her…he won't hurt her."

Tommy mostly agreed with James. "But we're talking Bella. She won't go through with it."

"How can she stop it?"

"That's what bothers me. I have no idea what she has planned," he said. "Fitz knows her, too. He'll be expecting her to do something. We have to stop the wedding before she does."

James sighed and nodded slowly. "You do realize that Fitz will also be expecting you to do something." He held up his hand before Tommy could argue. "I've already called Davey and Willie. They're coming in tonight. What we need is a plan."

Tommy nodded. "Whatever we do will be dangerous."

"I warned our brothers," James said. "This might surprise you, but they didn't hesitate even when I told them what we were up against."

The Colt brothers, Tommy thought as a lump formed in his throat. He'd always been able to depend on his brothers. But he'd never needed them as much as he did right now.

His cell phone rang. It was his friend with the FBI. "Tell me you have good news," Tommy said into the phone. Right now, he'd take all he could get.

"We have Caroline. She is willing to give evidence against Edwin Fitzgerald Mattson the Third, or Fitz as you both call him," Ian said. "Apparently the two had crossed paths when she'd tried to latch on to his father. Fitz told her about Nolan and gave her inside information that helped her take all of his money."

"So you're going to arrest Fitz?" Tommy couldn't contain his excitement. "Right away?"

"Probably not until Monday."

"That will be too late," he told Ian. "Is there any way

you can get some agents here tomorrow? Fitz is black-mailing Nolan's daughter into marrying him in the morning."

"I can try, but I wouldn't count on it. Have you talked to the local sheriff?"

"If Fitz had found out, he'd plant drugs on Nolan as part of the frame and blackmail. Bella was trying to get the evidence. But I've been unable to get near her the past couple of days. I'm really worried about her."

Ian sighed. "Let me see what I can do."

Chapter Twenty-Three

The wedding day broke clear and sunny. Fitz had one of the guards bring her the wedding dress and shoes.

"Your attendants will be arriving soon," the guard said. "Mr. Mattson suggested that one of them help you get ready."

She thought about his controlling behavior and was surprised he hadn't tried to see her before the wedding. Instead he wanted to send someone up to make sure she got ready?

"No, I can manage," she told him. Fitz had chosen her attendants, women she knew but wasn't close to. Again optics. The women were ones who would look good in the wedding photos. "Tell Mr. Mattson that I'm fine."

She'd awakened with a start this morning, heart hammering. Getting up, she'd checked to make sure she still had the thumb drive. Her fear was that Fitz would check his and realize that they'd been switched. It wouldn't take much for him to find it in her room, no matter how well she hid it. That was why she kept it on her except when she was sleeping.

Fitz had kept her from seeing Tommy before the wedding. But she wanted to make sure the thumb drive got into the right hands depending on how things went in the next hour.

She'd showered, put on her makeup and fixed her hair, gathering it up into a do on top of her head. She had to look the part. Fitz still had time to call the cops on her father. Timing was everything, she told herself, wondering how she was going to be able to stop him. Was he planning on giving her the thumb drive around his neck before the ceremony?

Or would he break his promise and still turn in her father?

At the knock on the door, Bella stepped to it. "Yes?"

"Your bouquet has arrived," a male voice informed her.

She opened the door a crack and the guard handed her the tiny white rose bouquet. She took it and closed the door. Her heart pounded. Tommy knew her, knew she would be desperate. He had put something in the bouquet, she told herself. She'd heard something in her friend's voice who owned the floral shop.

Carefully parting the roses, Bella saw something glint silver at the center hidden deep in the roses. But it was the note, the paper rolled up into a thin tube tucked in among the petals, that she pulled out and quickly read.

"This is only a last resort," the note read. "I love you, Tommy."

Heart in her throat, tears in her eyes, she reached into the bouquet and pulled out the deadly-looking slim blade. She swallowed, nodding to herself. Tommy knew her, he loved her. He knew how desperate she was or she would have been in contact with him. He'd given her a sense of power, last resort or not. She carefully slipped the blade back in between the tiny white roses.

A knock at the door. She took one last look at herself in the full-length mirror. The perfect bride about to head down the aisle to the wrong man. She dabbed at her tears, willing herself that there would be no more. She couldn't think of Tommy, not now, because just as he knew her, she knew him. He would do everything in his power to stop this wedding. She had to be strong. She had to survive this—one way or another.

Another knock. This time it was Ronan's voice she heard just outside. He would be getting impatient to walk her over to the barn where all the wedding guests were waiting. She looked down at the bouquet in her hand knowing that when the time came, she couldn't hesitate.

She checked to make sure the thumb drive was still tucked securely under her garter. Over the past few days she would have done anything to get the drive to Tommy, but Fitz had made sure that she had no way to get away—or get a message to the man she loved.

Bella still didn't know if Fitz was aware that she'd switched the thumb drives. She told herself he'd been so busy with the wedding arrangements that he probably hadn't given it a thought.

Had he known he would have torn up her room looking for it. Or maybe he would have realized she could have hidden it anywhere in the house and that he might never be able to find it.

It didn't matter now. It was too late for either of them to do anything about it. She took a breath, knowing she couldn't put this off any longer. Fitz would be worried that she might pull something before the ceremony. She'd seen all the extra guards he'd hired outside the barn. They were for Tommy Colt. Fitz was so sure he'd thought of everything and that nothing could stop this wedding.

Bella opened the door. Ronan looked upset that she was taking so long. She stepped out, moving past him, ignoring him. But she could feel him behind her. His eyes burned into her back where the fabric of her wedding dress left her bare. The man frightened her under normal circumstances and these circumstances were far from normal.

They went downstairs and walked the short distance to the barn where the wedding was being held. Vehicles were parked everywhere. She let her gaze sweep over them, taking in all the guards. Fitz had outdone himself and she suspected there would be even more on the way into the ranch—all to make sure that Tommy Colt couldn't get onto the property.

Her chest hurt at the thought of Tommy making another attempt to rescue her because if he did, she feared it would get him killed. She knew that Ronan and his friend Miles would have been ordered by Fitz to shoot to kill.

"Can't have any…trespassers on our wedding day," Fitz had said more than once over the past few days. "I'd hate to have any bloodshed. Ronan and Miles have promised to keep it at a minimum—unless necessary." The threat had been clear.

Bella thought of the blade in her bouquet. How ironic. *There would be bloodshed.*

As she and Ronan neared the barn, she heard the music and voices and spotted her attendants. They were all beautiful, slim and dressed in matching peach-colored gowns. Fitz had chosen well. Had there been photos of this wedding, they would have been quite gorgeous.

She gave the women a mere nod of her head as she stepped into the entry. The women had to be wondering why they'd been invited let alone why they weren't allowed to help the bride get ready for her big day.

Ronan moved past her to where her father was pacing nervously. He turned, looking both surprised and relieved to see her. He was dressed in a tux and looked quite handsome, she thought. He looked better than he had since she'd returned home, but he didn't meet her gaze as he came to stand next to her.

Bella stared straight ahead as she took his arm and waited as her attendants began the procession down the carpeted aisle between the seats that filled the barn to overflowing. A huge tent had been erected at the back of the house where Fitz had said the reception would be held.

He'd seemed disappointed that she hadn't wanted to see everything he'd arranged. She'd known she would never be going into the tent for the reception even before she'd seen the blade hidden in her bouquet.

"I'd rather be surprised," she'd told him. They hadn't spoken since dinner last night when Fitz had poured out his heart. She wondered if he really believed that he loved her or if it was just his excuse for what he was doing. Knowing that he was desperate for money, she figured that was more likely his true motivation.

But soon he thought he would have the ranch. With his father's death, he would have another third of the partnership. Or one hundred percent if he reneged on the deal and sent her father to prison.

He would however never have her, Bella told herself, knowing what she would do. Tommy had to have known how desperate she felt. That was why he'd seen to it that she had a way out.

Now as the attendants took their places, the aisle opening up, she saw Fitz standing next to his best man and a group of handsome tuxedoed attendants. She met his gaze. The look in those blue eyes was one of appreciation as he took her in.

But there was also relief on his face. He'd been worried that Ronan would have to drag her to the altar. That would have definitely messed up his optics.

But that was the problem, wasn't it? He knew her. He had to know that she didn't trust him to destroy any evidence that would send her father to prison. Just as he had to know that she wasn't going through with this wedding no matter what he did.

Did he really think this barn full of people would stop her? The man was a fool. He'd lied, cheated and bullied his way to this point. It wasn't going to get him what he wanted. He didn't know the first thing about love.

But Bella did. Just the thought of Tommy made her stumble a little. Her father placed his free hand on hers. She could feel him looking at her. She didn't have to see his face to know there was fear there. He didn't want to go to prison. They both knew it would be a death sentence.

But had she looked at him, she knew there would also be regret in his eyes. This wasn't what he'd wanted for his daughter. It wasn't what he'd wanted for himself. He'd lost so much, his business, his money, his only daughter. No matter how this ended, he would be a broken man.

There was nothing she could do about that, she told herself. She had to think about her own survival—and keeping her father out of prison. The thumb drive under her garter would do that—once she was arrested.

Bella tried not to think about taking Fitz's life. She despised him but not enough to kill him under any other circumstances. He'd asked for this, but that still wouldn't make it easy.

He was still staring at her. She met his gaze and suddenly he looked nervous. She almost wished he had his usual smirk on his face. It would make things much easier.

As she reached him, her maid of honor started to reach for her bouquet. She shook her head and sniffed the roses as she joined Fitz. The music stopped. There was the racket of everyone sitting down. The preacher cleared his voice. She could feel Fitz's gaze on her face as she held the bouquet close, as if she couldn't part with it.

Would he insist she hand it to her maid of honor? Would he take it from her? She couldn't allow that. Glancing up, she saw his expression and knew that the time had come.

She pretended to touch the soft petals of the baby roses. Her fingers brushed over the cool steel of the knife. She looked up at Fitz and sunk her fingers into the roses.

FITZ COULDN'T HELP being nervous as he watched his soon-to-be bride fooling with her beautiful bouquet as if she were as nervous as he was. That gave him hope that she'd accepted the marriage. Accepted him.

It had taken her so long to appear that he'd worried that she'd somehow tricked Ronan and escaped. She wouldn't have gotten far—not with all the guards he had on the property—but it would have spoiled their wedding day. That was the last thing he wanted.

While he was waiting, he'd looked over the crowd. Anyone who was anybody was here today. He felt a sense of pride that they'd all come. But that little nagging voice in his head reminded him that they had come for Bella, not for him. Everyone loved Bella, he thought and tried not to grind his teeth.

He'd been worried about Nolan showing up, but the man looked like the quintessential father of the bride in his tux. He must realize that his life was now in his soon-to-be son-in-law's hands. Fitz hadn't decided if he would let Nolan off the hook or not. That was up to Bella.

He'd met her gaze as she'd headed down the aisle toward him. He'd tried to sense what she was thinking. Her face looked serene, too serene, and that bothered him. Did she look like a woman who knew she'd been bested and wasn't going to make trouble? He could only hope, but he knew that until the pastor declared them husband and wife, he was going to be holding his breath.

When her maid of honor reached for her bouquet, Bella ignored her. Instead, she sniffed the tiny white roses before looking up at him. He'd seen something in her gaze that had threatened to loosen his bowels.

A shudder had moved through him as they'd locked eyes. His breath had caught in his throat and for an instant he'd felt…afraid. He swallowed now as he watched her fiddle with her bouquet. He tried to tell himself that she was merely nervous, something he'd never seen in her before.

He swallowed and was about to take the bouquet from her so they could get this over with when he heard a thunderous roar.

The guests heard it, too, he saw as he glanced toward the door. What in the world? He'd barely gathered his bearings when he recognized the sound. Horses. Dozens of them.

BELLA WOULD NEVER forget the look of panic and surprise on Fitz's face as the door to the barn burst open and

Tommy came riding in on a horse. The horse thundered down the aisle through the barn between the seats, coming to a rearing stop before the altar. The moment Tommy reached for her, she swung up onto the back of the horse.

The barn broke out in pandemonium as the two of them rode toward the exit door—which was now blocked by Ronan. She saw the gun in his hand and the look on his face. She could hear Fitz screaming for Ronan to shoot to kill.

She pulled the knife from the bouquet and leaned off to one side of the horse, drawing Ronan's attention. He hadn't seen the knife until she slammed it into him. Ronan's expression registered surprise as he dropped the gun and fell back. He got off one shot, but the bullet missed its mark, the report of the gunshot lost in the roar of horses and panicked screaming guests.

As she and Tommy Colt rode out of the barn, she tossed her bouquet over her shoulder. She didn't look back. The ranch yard was full of horses and riders. She recognized townspeople, neighbors, friends—who hadn't been invited to the wedding—all on horseback.

Some carried baseball bats. Others lengths of pipe. Most of the guards had backed down from what she could see. But Davy and Willie Colt were off their horses and involved in a fistfight with two of the guards.

The sound of sirens filled the air. Bella saw the sheriff and several more patrol cars roaring up the road. But Tommy didn't slow his horse as he headed into the woods at a gallop. She held on, wrapping her arms around his waist.

She looked back only once. Fitz stood in the barn doorway watching her ride away. The front of his tux was dark with what appeared to be blood. Had Fitz been hit by Ronan's stray bullet? Before she turned away, she saw him fall backward and disappear from view.

They hadn't ridden far when Tommy reined in and helped her off the horse. He swung down beside her and took her in his arms. She leaned into him and for the first time in forever let herself breathe freely.

"You're all right now," Tommy said as he loosened her hair and let it drop to her shoulders. His fingers wound into her locks as he drew her to him. She finally felt tears of relief flood her eyes as she looked into his handsome face. Of course, he'd come to her rescue. Hadn't she known in her heart that he would do whatever he had to. As she had done what she had to. Together, they were one hell of a team.

"I got the thumb drive," she whispered as she turned her face up to him.

"I never doubted it," Tommy said, grinning at her as he dropped his mouth to hers for a kiss that quickly deepened.

At the sound of someone approaching, they drew apart and turned.

"You remember Ian?" Tommy asked. "He's with the FBI."

She nodded, then lifted the skirt of her dress and slipped the thumb drive from under her garter. "I think everything you need is on it," she said, holding it out to the agent. "I hope this will help put him away." If he wasn't dead already. "At least, I hope it will clear my father."

Ian nodded as he pocketed the thumb drive. "They'll want a statement from you, probably at the Billings office."

"I'd be happy to give one," she said, surprised to hear

her voice break. She'd come so close to taking Fitz's life. As it was, she'd stabbed a man. Ronan could be dead for all she knew.

Tommy put his arm around her and pulled her close. "Fitz?"

Ian nodded. "I heard he was shot. He's being taken to the hospital."

"One of his own guards I think shot him," Bella said, her legs feeling suddenly weak. She leaned into Tommy's strong body, loving the feel of his arm around her.

Everything had happened so fast. It now felt like a dream. She feared she would wake up only to find herself standing at the altar with Fitz, her fingers searching for the knife in her bouquet.

"Are you going to be all right?" the FBI agent asked.

She nodded as she looked up at Tommy's handsome, familiar face. For so long she'd feared that she might never see him again. Or that Fitz and his guards would kill him. She smiled at the loving look in his eyes and felt her heart float up. "I'm going to be fine."

Chapter Twenty-Four

The next few days were a blur of cops, FBI and visits to the hospital where her father was recovering from a heart attack.

"I'm sure the stress played a major role," the doctor told her. "But he's recovering nicely. In fact, he's determined to get out of here as soon as possible."

Bella had been surprised by how quickly he'd recovered. When she entered his room later that week, she found him sitting up in bed. The change in him was nothing short of astounding. It was as if he was his old self again.

He smiled when he saw her. "Did the doctor say when I can get out of here?"

"He's keeping you a little longer." She studied her father and shook her head. He'd been so beat down before the wedding. Now though he looked ready to pick up the pieces of his life and move on as if nothing had happened. She wished she could put the past behind her that quickly.

"You and that Colt boy were brilliant," Nolan said. "I really thought you were going to marry Fitz." He shook his head. "I should have known better." He should have, she thought as he reached for her hand and squeezed it. "You saved your old man. Strange the way things turn out. Edwin…" He let go of her hand and looked away for a moment. "The police think he really did commit suicide."

Bella had been told the same thing. Edwin was facing prison for his part in framing her father. But also he had to know that Fitz might let him take the fall for all of it. She wondered what it must have been like for him to realize that he couldn't trust his own son, and worse, that he held some responsibility for creating this monster.

"The company is mine now," her father said after a moment before he turned to look at her again. "With Edwin and Fitz gone…"

So he was no longer broke. "What will you do?"

"Rebuild it," he said without hesitation. "I did it once, I can do it again." He sounded excited about the prospect.

She wondered how much the bad publicity would hurt the business, but she figured her father wasn't worried. He liked a challenge. She told herself that he was smarter now, at least she hoped so.

"You know they caught Caroline."

He nodded and avoided her gaze. "I loved her." He shrugged. "I hadn't realized how lonely I was for female companionship. Maybe I'll find myself a nice woman. Or not," he said with a laugh. "But you don't have to worry about me anymore."

She hoped not. If Nolan did find a woman, Bella would have Tommy do a background check, she told herself.

Her father grew quiet and for a moment he looked his age. "I'm so sorry I put you in that horrible position I did."

"It's over," she told him, putting her hand on his shoulder. He covered her hand with his own for a moment. "But you're going to have to stop calling Tommy 'that

Colt boy,'" she said, smiling. "After all, he's going to be your son-in-law."

Her father smiled, no surprise in his expression. "He's perfect for you."

She laughed. "Yes, he is."

Chapter Twenty-Five

Fitz opened his eyes. For a moment, he couldn't remember where he was or what had happened. A hospital. A nurse came running, followed by a doctor.

It all came back to him as he started to move, only to realize there was a handcuff attached to his left wrist and the bed frame. He closed his eyes. He could hear voices around him, but he preferred the darkness of oblivion.

He'd come so close to getting what he wanted. Bella. Just the sound of her name in his head made him wince in pain. His breathing was already shallow. His chest ached with each attempt to draw in oxygen.

He suddenly felt for the chain and thumb drive around his neck. Gone! All of his gold jewelry. He realized the doctor would have removed it once he reached the hospital. Did that mean the cops already had it?

He closed his eyes, wishing that he'd died.

At a sound, he opened his eyes to find a man standing over him. His first guess? FBI.

"I'm FBI agent Ian Brooks," the man said. "I have a few questions."

Fitz shook his head. "I have nothing to say."

"We have your thumb drive and a statement from Bella Worthington," the agent said.

"You have no right to take my thumb drive," Fitz said. "That's my private property and should be locked up downstairs with my other personal items."

"The thumb drive on the gold chain, is that what you're referring to? No, that one's blank. I'm talking about the one Bella Worthington removed from the chain you kept around your neck."

Fitz felt his insides go liquid. "That's not possible." He thought of Bella. She would have had to— Like a flash of lightning, it hit him. "I have nothing to say to you," he said to the FBI agent. "I want my lawyer. Get out of my room. Now!"

"We'll talk soon," the agent said and left.

With a curse, Fitz knew how Bella had done it. She'd drugged him. That explained why he couldn't seem to wake up with the guards pounding at his door and the phone ringing to tell him that his father was dead.

He slammed his fists into the bed he lay in. The bitch. She'd taken the thumb drive. When had she gotten it to the FBI? He couldn't believe this. He'd kill her once he got out of here.

If he got out of here.

He closed his eyes, fighting panic. He would get out of here. Bella thought she was so much smarter than him. He'd show her.

At a noise right next to his bed, his eyes flew open. He'd expected to find the FBI agent back. But instead it was a pretty young nurse.

With a shock, he saw that she had green eyes. Her hair was blond, but he could imagine her as a brunette. She looked more like Bella than Margo. She was the right age though and her body wasn't bad. He smiled at her.

"I see you're feeling better," she said.

He was feeling better. Seeing this woman, he told himself it was a sign. This wasn't over. He would beat the rap against him. He would have what he deserved. "What's your name?" he asked.

"Roberta, but everyone calls me Bobbi."

"Bobbi." He whispered her name. "I like that." He rattled the handcuff on his wrist. "This isn't comfortable. It shouldn't be on there anyway. I didn't do anything wrong." He chuckled. "They got the wrong man. But once I'm out of here, I'll clear it all up." He'd hire a good lawyer. Or the best he could afford. So much of what the cops had against him was hearsay, his word against Bella's and her crooked father's. Even what was on the thumb drive he could explain away as Nolan trying to frame him.

"In the meantime," he said to the Bella-like nurse, "if you could take off the handcuff—just so I can get some feeling back in my wrist…"

"I'm sorry, but it has to stay on except when you go for your MRI," she said, looking sympathetic. "I heard you were shot at your wedding?"

He nodded. "A terrible mistake. I can't wait to get out of this bed so I can clear it up. I was framed by a woman I thought I loved."

"I'm sorry," she said. "Now that you're better, I'm sure you can straighten it out."

"Oh, I will." He looked from her to the handcuff and then to the door. "What's the MRI for?" he asked.

"I'll let the doctor explain it to you," she said. "But don't worry."

He wasn't worried. Bella was the one who should be worried. Once he got out of here… He smiled at Bobbi and noticed she wasn't wearing a wedding ring. Not that it would have mattered. He would have her one way or another.

There was a noise out in the hallway. "I think they're ready for you," the pretty nurse said. "I'll have the officer come in now."

"Have you ever wanted to be brunette?" he asked.

She gave him a funny look but laughed. "Haven't you heard that blondes have more fun?"

Fitz chuckled. "Wait until you're a brunette and with me." Not that even this woman could satisfy his need for Bella. He would have them both. Only this time, he wasn't going to be so nice to Bella. He'd make her pay for this.

BELLA LOOKED UP at the sound of a vehicle. She'd spent a few days at Tommy's cabin by the river, not wanting to go back to the ranch yet. She told herself that the bad memories of Fitz would eventually fade. Tommy and his brothers had cleared all signs of Fitz from the ranch house, he'd told her, but she was happy being with Tommy out at the cabin. It was nice on the river. It was nice feeling safe and happy. She never wanted it to end.

But she had a business to run, and she'd decided to move the operation to the ranch. She had plenty of room there. And she couldn't hide out forever. Fortunately, when she'd walked in the front door, all the good memories of the place she loved came back in a rush.

Fitz was gone and forgotten. At least for a while. She'd heard that he was recovering from his gunshot but that when he'd collapsed from the wound at the barn that day, he'd hit his head. The doctor thought there might be some internal bleeding. She felt only glad that he was out of her life and tried not to worry what would happen if he were ever released from prison.

There was enough on the thumb drive to convict him of numerous felonies. Add to that kidnapping and blackmail and all that it entailed, and he shouldn't see freedom for a long time. He would hire the best lawyer he could. He would lie. She tried not to let that make her nervous.

Now she glanced out to see Tommy drive up in his pickup. She felt a smile immediately pull at her lips. Just the sight of him made her happy. She opened the door, then froze as she saw his expression. "What is it?"

He led her over to one of the porch chairs and they sat. "It's Fitz. He was being taken to get an MRI when he apparently tried to get away from the officer guarding him. He fell and hit his head."

"Is he…"

"He died. Hemorrhaged. Nothing they could do."

She stared at Tommy for a moment before he pulled her into his arms and held her. Fitz was gone. She hated the relief she felt and reminded herself that she'd been pushed to the point that she'd wanted to kill him and might have if Tommy hadn't shown up when he did.

Fitz had been misguided and power hungry, but it seemed wrong to be so thankful that a childhood acquaintance was gone. She told herself that maybe now he was finally at peace. Because otherwise, she'd known that he wasn't finished with her. He would have come after her again. Only the next time, she might not have been able to get away.

She shuddered and Tommy held her closer.

"You're all right now," he said. "We're all right." She nodded against his chest. "It's all rainbows and sunshine from here on out."

Bella laughed and looked up at him. "Rainbows and sunshine," she said and kissed him. As long as they were together, it definitely would be.

TOMMY WAS SURPRISED to find all three of his brothers waiting for him at the new office a few days later. "What's going on?" he asked, sensing trouble.

"It's official," James announced and held up Tommy's framed PI license. "I thought I'd let you put it on the wall." Some of the posters and photos of the cowboys in their family were now on the walls of the ground-floor office.

Tommy took the framed license and spotted the hook next to his brother's PI license. "You left a lot of room on that wall," he commented.

"For Davey's and Willie's PI licenses," James said, and his brothers laughed.

"Who said we were quitting the rodeo?" Willie said.

Davey was quiet. When Tommy had told him that Carla Richmond down at the bank had asked about him, he'd seen how his brother had brightened. "That all she said?" Tommy had suggested that maybe Davy should stop by the bank and see her sometime. Davy had said that maybe he would. He was smiling when he said it.

"Even if I gave up the circuit, I'm not becoming a private eye," Willie said, shaking his head. "It's too dangerous. I got shot at and thrown in jail for the night before James bailed me out and all I was doing was helping you steal a bride." They all laughed.

"I guess time will tell," James said and motioned to the front of the building. "Tommy, you should check out our new sign."

He stepped out the front door and looked up. Colt

Brothers Investigations. He couldn't help the sudden bump of his heart or the lump that rose to his throat. He was doing this.

Smiling, he stepped back inside. James had pulled out the blackberry brandy and the paper cups. They lifted their cups and the room suddenly grew very quiet. Tommy knew what they all were thinking about even before James made the toast.

"To Dad." His voice broke. "We haven't forgotten." They all nodded.

"We will find out the truth," Tommy said, and they all drained their cups.

Chapter Twenty-Six

Bella wanted to pinch herself. She couldn't believe she was standing in front of a full-length mirror again wearing a wedding dress. This one was of her own choosing though and so were the shoes on her feet and that smile on her face was real, she thought as she winked at her reflection.

She glanced over at the woman next to her. Lorelei was also wearing a wedding dress. They grinned at each other. It had been James's idea that they have a double wedding on the Fourth of July.

"I would love that," Lori had said. "This could be fun, unless you haven't completely gotten over your last wedding."

Bella had laughed. In the time that had gone by, she'd put Fitz and what had happened behind her. The FBI had cleared her father and he was rebuilding the business and doing better than even she had hoped.

"We could get married at the ranch," Bella had offered. "Maybe an outside wedding by the river." She hadn't been anxious to have another one in the barn and she'd realized that the Colt men didn't care where they got married—as long as they did.

She smiled to herself now, remembering the day

Tommy had saved her. "Marry me," he'd said as he'd dropped to one knee after Ian had left them in woods. "I love you and I should have done this a long time ago. Come on, Bella, it isn't like you aren't already dressed for it."

They'd both laughed. She'd taken his hands and pulled him to his feet. "Remember when we were really little and we would pretend to get married?"

"I didn't think you'd remember that," he'd said.

"I remember everything the two of us did growing up," she'd said, smiling. "You promised me an outdoor wedding by the river."

He'd laughed. "A promise is a promise."

"I will marry you this summer if you still want to get married. Who knows, you might decide being a PI isn't for you and go back to the rodeo. It was your first love," she'd teased.

"You're my true first love and always have been," he'd said. "I will marry you this summer by the river. In the meantime, can I put a ring on it?"

Bella had looked down at the huge diamond on her hand. She'd slipped it off without a second thought and hurled it into the pines. Tommy had shaken his head in surprise. "Some kids will be searching for treasure like we did at that age, and they'll find it in the dried pine needles," she'd said laughing. "Can you imagine it?" She'd seen that he could. "I just hope it brings them happiness."

He'd pulled her into his arms for another kiss. Then he'd opened the small velvet box he'd taken from his pocket. She hadn't needed him to get on one knee again. He'd taken the small diamond ring from the box, and she'd held out her hand. It had fit perfectly. She'd smiled down at it on her hand and then up at Tommy. "It's exactly what I wanted."

"Ready?" Whitney asked from the doorway, bringing her out of her reverie. It would be a small wedding, just family and a few friends. There would be a campfire afterward. There would be beer and hot dogs over the fire, Colt family style even though Roberto had offered to cater their weddings.

She and Tommy would be moving into the ranch after they were married and she hoped Roberto would stay on as she rehired staff both for her business and the ranch.

"I've never been more ready," Bella said now.

Whitney got tears in her eyes. "I'm going to cry. After everything you've been through to finally find the man of your dreams?" She wiped her eyes and handed Bella her bouquet. This time it was daisies, reminding her of spring and new beginnings.

Tommy and James were waiting for them at the river along with the pastor who would be performing the ceremonies. Both men were dressed in Western attire, including their best boots and Stetsons.

"Colt men," Lori whispered. "Aren't they handsome."

"Especially Willie," Whitney said, making them both laugh.

But Bella had to admit, seeing the four brothers together like this, it took her breath away.

She looked at Tommy. He had a huge smile on his face that made her laugh. She knew that they'd been heading toward this moment since they first met all those years ago. She was marrying her best friend, her lover, her future. She couldn't wait to become his wife and join his family.

"We are going to make some adorable children," she

said as she and Lori walked toward the altar they'd built by the river and Tommy waiting for her.

Lori giggled. "We've already started," she whispered.

Bella grinned over at her. "Congratulations. I suspect we won't be far behind," she said as she turned to meet Tommy's gaze. She was finally coming home to the one place she'd always belonged with the cowboy who'd stolen her heart at the age of four.

* * * * *

FOOTHILLS FIELD SEARCH

MAGGIE WELLS

For Sally, the Labrador we adore. Your search skills
may be limited to an unerring ability to find food, but
you certainly rescued us. Here's to all the pets and the
people whose hearts they own.

Chapter One

Brady Nichols's date for the Daniels Canine Academy tenth-anniversary celebration party whined when he took the sharp curve a shade over the speed limit. They were late. He'd been running a full thirty minutes behind schedule the whole day, and his date was not inclined to be understanding.

So, he was rushing, and Brady hated rushing.

"We'll be there in a minute."

She didn't look at him. No, she simply sat there, staring through the glass with such intensity he was surprised she didn't cut a hole clean through the windshield.

Idaho wasn't as overrun as Oregon and Washington had become in recent years, but still, he'd moved to Jasper to get away from Boise and all the complications the city held. He wanted a quiet life. He'd purposefully chosen a location where he didn't have to be constantly vigilant, and he'd never regretted his choice. But his quiet life wasn't actually very quiet, and he was getting tired of taking flak from the needy blonde beside him.

He let off the gas as they navigated the next curve, and the Daniels ranch came into view. "See?" he prompted, nodding to a car signaling a turn into Emma Daniels's drive. He glanced at the clock on the dash, pleased to find he'd managed to recover about ten minutes. "Here we are."

He swerved to park in the spot on the lawn the young

man wearing a yellow mesh safety vest indicated. He recognized the kid as one of the at-risk youths Emma routinely put to work at the DCA. Kevin? Kayson? No, Kyle. His name was Kyle.

Winnie let out a high-pitched whimper of excitement as he set the parking brake. Beside him, sixty-five pounds of pure happiness shivered with anticipation.

"There. We made it."

Winnie's sharp bark was one of pure joy, and he leaned over to pop the latch on the harness he used to keep her safely contained. His reward was a big, wet kiss. On the cheek, thankfully. Sometimes, in her exuberance, Winnie forgot they were partners first, friends second and the most significant being in one another's lives as a by-product of the first two.

He rubbed her silky ears, then looked her in the eyes as he stroked the dog's cheeks. It was a calming technique Emma had taught him when he first started working with the spirited yellow Lab. She'd been barely more than a pup with big paws, gangly legs and an eager-to-please attitude.

"Hold," he ordered, reaching for the door handle.

Winnie responded with another keening whimper of excitement, but stayed put. He climbed down from the truck and raised a hand to greet the young man in the vest. "Pulled parking duty, did ya?"

Kyle shrugged. "The safety vest is pretty lame, but it beats emptying trash all night like William. And poor Hugh, he's the designated scooper," the kid informed him with a wrinkle of his nose. "I figure most everyone who's coming will be here in the next half hour or so."

"Good turnout?" Brady asked as he opened the passenger door.

Kyle motioned for an incoming minivan to park in the spot beside Brady's. "Yep. Tons of food too. People have been bringing stuff, even though Miss Emma told them not to."

Brady smirked. "People around here hate to come to parties empty-handed."

He ran a comforting hand down the dog's flank. Anticipation had her muscles quivering, but she made no move to exit the vehicle. She wouldn't until he gave her the go-ahead. He waited until he was certain the van was parked, then snapped his fingers.

Winnie barely gave him a chance to step out of the way. Her nose was pressed to the grass the minute she landed. She was trained from a pup to specialize in search and rescue, so Winnie's first instinct was to sniff to get her bearings.

"Lots of your friends here today, girl," he said, clipping her lead onto the vest she wore. Crouching beside her, he snapped twice, and she plopped her butt to the grass, her full attention on him. He framed her face again, stroking her smooth cheeks with his thumbs. "I'm sure you're psyched," he said in a low, even tone Emma had trained him to use when not giving actual commands. At two years old, Winnie still had a few puppy tendencies. They were working on smoothing out the rough edges together. "Hang with me until we get situated, then you can run with the pack, okay?"

She blinked, but her amber-brown gaze never wavered.

"Good girl," he said approvingly.

"Is he your doggy?"

The question came at him on a gasp of barely contained awe and delight.

Winnie's gaze darted past him and her tail thumped the ground hard enough to stir the dust. Brady twisted, still in his crouch, and found a girl with long blond pigtails gazing at them in slack-jawed wonder. He pressed his hands to his knees as he rose.

"Yes, *she* is. Her name is Winnie, and she is a proud graduate of Daniels Canine Academy. She's here for her homecoming."

Winnie's tail shifted from thump to full swoosh, and the girl beamed her approval. "Wow! She must be real smart. Mama says Miss Emma trains only the smartest, bestest dogs."

"Your mama is right," Brady replied, unable to resist returning her gap-toothed smile. "I'm Brady, and I'm a policeman here in Jasper. Winnie is my partner."

The girl's eyes widened to the size of quarters. "She's a police dog?"

"She sure is. Say hello, Winnie," he prompted, giving the yellow Lab's head a single pat. At the signal, Winnie let out a bark of greeting, then panted with excited expectation.

"Jillian?"

A woman's worried cry had all three of their heads whipping around. Seconds later, another slightly taller, but equally coltish girl appeared around the front of his truck. "She's right here, Mama," the girl called loudly. Then she eyed him with wary curiosity. "She's talking to a man."

Brady tightened his hold on Winnie's lead when a long, lanky woman with a mane of corn silk hair skidded to a stop beside the girls, an enormous purse dangling from her arm, and a covered dish clutched in both hands.

"Jilly, I've told you over and over you can't run off—"

"But he has a police dog. He's a policeman," Jillian replied like this was all the defense she needed. "I was only saying hi."

Brady aimed a cordial smile at the mother. She looked vaguely familiar, but he couldn't quite place her. "I'm Brady Nichols, ma'am. I'm with the Jasper PD." He glanced down at Winnie, who'd shifted closer to his leg, exerting the barest pressure to her lead. "This is Winnie. She's here to see some of her old classmates."

The woman blew out an exasperated breath, then tipped her head in his direction. "Nice to meet you, Officer Nichols. You too, Winnie," she added.

Her expression warmed as she shifted her attention to the dog, and Brady drew in a sharp breath. The woman was beautiful, but her looks weren't her most potent weapon. No, it was the pure pleasure he'd seen in her eyes when she found herself on the receiving end of Winnie's winning doggy grin.

He'd forever be a sucker for women who loved animals.

Glancing toward the large white tent erected between the main house and the outbuildings, he said, "I'm glad I'm not the last to arrive."

"Oh no, we're chronically late," she said, her grimace wan.

Again, recognition niggled at him.

"I'm Jillian Marie Whitaker," the smaller girl volunteered. "Can I pet your doggy?"

"May I," her mother corrected.

Brady could tell by the well-rehearsed delivery this wasn't the first grammar lesson she'd given on the fly. "Sure," he said, bobbing a nod of assent. Jilly skittered forward, but he held out a hand to stop her. "Has anyone ever taught you how to approach a strange dog?"

She wagged her head so hard those long, silky pigtails whipped her face. "No," she replied. "I mean, no, sir," she adjusted, glancing over to her mother for approval.

Brady felt something in his gut loosen as he watched the silent exchange between mother and daughter. Turning his attention to the older girl, he motioned for her to join them. "Hi. I'm Brady. What's your name?"

"Brook," the girl answered shyly. Then, realizing her younger sister had set a more formal tone, she rolled her shoulders. "Brooklyn Ann Whitaker."

Matching her serious tone, he said, "Nice to meet you

both. All," he amended almost immediately. He saw their mother shifting from foot to foot and readjusting the weight of the bag hanging off her arm. "But maybe we can put the lesson on hold for a minute. It looks like your mom might need a hand." He stretched both arms out and signaled for her to pass over the covered dish. "I'd be happy to carry something for you, ma'am."

"Her name is Mom, not ma'am," Jilly interjected helpfully.

"Her name is not Mom," Brook retorted. "Sheesh, don't you know anything?"

"Girls," their mother said in a warning tone. Returning her focus to him, she gave him a half-hearted flash of teeth. "I've got it, thank you. And my name is Cassie. Cassie Whitaker. And no, I'm not telling you my middle name."

The well-rehearsed intransigence in her tone coaxed a bark of laughter from him. "No?"

"She won't even tell us," Jilly said in a confidential tone. "It's a big secret."

"It's ridiculous and I hate it," Cassie said, shaking her hair away from her face. "Come on, girls. We can meet the doggies later. I don't want Aunt Vera to come looking for us."

At the mention of the name, the puzzle pieces snapped into place. "Aunt Vera? Oh! Vera from the diner. You're Millard's niece," he said. "I thought I'd seen you somewhere. You've been helping out at the diner, right?"

"Technically, Vera's niece, but yes, I've been trying to help out here and there." The screech of a public address system coming to life yanked their attention to the tent, and worry puckered her brow. "I have to get this over there."

"You heard the lady, Winnie. Stop distracting these pretty girls."

He watched as Cassie Whitaker strode ahead, her gaze fixed on the crowd wandering in from all directions. Brook hurried after her mother, but Jilly appeared reluctant to leave Winnie's side. The stubborn set of her mouth spoke volumes about the rebellions she'd launch in the future, but for now, he wasn't willing to get tangled in one. He liked his life easy and uncomplicated, and a pretty woman with two precocious children were three complications too many.

"Go on now," he urged his new friend. "You get us in trouble with your mama, she'll never let Winnie run with the likes of you."

She must have enjoyed the notion of getting a grown man in trouble because she aimed her sunbeam grin at him again. "You think Winnie will let me run with her?"

"Definitely. You get on with your mama. Find us after dinner. I hear Miss Emma has a special obstacle course set up. That's where we'll be."

With a soft "Yay!" she gave Winnie a pat goodbye, then skipped ahead to catch her mother and sister.

Brady forced himself to tear his gaze from Cassie Whitaker's long, tanned legs, but it wasn't easy. The white denim shorts were more flattering than the T-shirt and jeans she covered with an apron when working at Millard's Diner.

Once they disappeared into the shadows of the tent, he steered Winnie toward the far end where he saw a few of his colleagues and Winnie's fellow DCA alums congregated. At his approach, his best friend, Dillon, raised his can of beer in salute.

"You came," Dillon said, gruff but sounding pleased.

Brady felt a blush prickle his cheeks but hoped his beard masked it. He wasn't a fan of the spotlight, no matter how small the circle. He rarely attended these town shindigs, mainly because he wasn't particularly adept at small talk, and so it was hard to imagine anyone would have missed his absence on this occasion.

"I did. The boss insisted," he added, nodding to the dog

at his side. Winnie and Dillon's dog, Bentley, a spirited Australian shepherd mix, exchanged sniffs in greeting.

"Do you good to get out. Mix and mingle a bit." Dillon gestured to Brady's face, then rubbed his own cheek. "Starting to look gristly in your off-hours."

"And since these are my off-hours, I don't need any commentary from you," Brady retorted.

"Saw you walking with Cassie from the diner," Dillon said. "Cute girls."

The switch in subjects was so abrupt, Brady gave his head a shake to settle the pieces into place. "Oh yeah. I didn't recognize her at first."

Dillon smirked. "Because you hardly look up from your plate whenever we're in there. You really need to learn how to cook for yourself."

"I can cook," Brady argued. "But I don't see the point in making a mess when it's only me. I have better things to do."

"Speaking of your to-do list, do you still need a hand tomorrow?" his best friend asked.

"Yeah, if you don't mind," Brady confirmed. He was starting to frame the interior walls on the house he was building, and though he'd devised an elaborate system of clamping and positioning lumber by himself, the task went much faster when there was a second pair of hands on the job.

"No problem, but I only accept cash, credit or pizza and beer. No personal checks."

"Pizza and beer it is," Brady confirmed.

The words had barely left his mouth when Barbara Macy, the woman who kept all the balls in the air for the Daniels Canine Academy, stepped to the mic. There was a sharp burst of static, then the piercing screech of feedback as she removed the microphone from its holder. The crowd let out a collective groan, and at his side, Winnie concurred with a soft keening sound.

Barbara spoke into the mic. "I keep telling Emma a live mic is better than a dog whistle, but I still can't get her to karaoke night at the Bart."

Brady chuckled with the rest of the crowd. Bartwell Brewing Company had purchased a karaoke setup complete with flashing lights and two microphones for duets, but few of the town's residents had been brave enough to jump onto the ministage.

"Thank you all for coming out," she said, beaming at the crowd. "Em said she didn't want a lot of fuss, but I think ten years of hard work, perseverance and excellence are worth celebrating, don't you?"

The crowd clapped heartily, and a few whistles, shout-outs and barks punctuated the applause.

She gestured to the tables overflowing with food and gave her head a rueful shake. "I could've sworn the invitation said food would be provided. I hope you all brought some plastic tubs to haul all this home. You know Emma is adamant about not feeding table scraps to the dogs."

"I'll take the leftovers," Jason Wright, the rookie on the Jasper PD squad and one of Emma's foster sons, called out. A few other men in the crowd were quick to volunteer their help as well, including chief of police, Doug Walters.

Ahead of them, Maisy Barton announced, "I brought zipper bags and plastic margarine tubs. A whole box of them!" Then she nudged her teenage granddaughter, who looked like she was hoping the ground would open and swallow her. "See? I told you people would want them."

Brady ducked his head and his mouth watered. He'd make sure he was in line for some of those leftovers. He was tired of microwave pizza pastries when he wasn't eating at the diner.

"I've asked the woman of the hour to say a few words, but in typical Emma fashion, she keeps trying to refuse."

Barbara gestured to Emma Daniels, who shook her head in stubborn refusal. Brady cringed inwardly as the assembled crowd called out encouragement, and Emma's face colored. He felt for the woman he'd come to consider a friend. Mortification was ten times worse when a person was shoved into the limelight.

Brady thought Emma might actually turn and walk straight out of the tent, but then Tashya Pratt leaned over and spoke directly into her foster mother's ear. Barbara continued to cajole Emma, although Brady could tell the trainer's focus had shifted entirely to the pretty young vet tech who'd returned home to work by her side.

He saw Emma mouth the word *Seriously?* as her brows reached for the sky.

Tashya beamed, then waved in their direction, gesturing for someone to join her. Brady saw Jason shouldering his way through the crowd toward the girl he'd loved since they were teenagers, his joyous expression a match for Tashya's, and now Emma's.

"Something's going on there," Dillon murmured.

Brady couldn't disagree. The crowd grew restless, murmuring to each other as Barbara's efforts to get Emma to say a few words appeared to be thwarted. But then Emma strode straight toward the PA system.

Barbara jumped when Emma practically yanked the mic from her hand.

"Thank you all for coming out," she said, her words booming through the speaker, her shout amplified enough to make several of the dogs in attendance plant their behinds firmly on the ground.

Brady chuckled when Winnie's rear landed on his foot. She clearly didn't care; her gaze, along with almost everyone else's, was pinned on the woman who'd been his dog's first love.

"Sorry," Emma said with a grimace. She gestured for Jason and Tashya to join her. "I do appreciate you all coming. I consider you all family, even if some of you only have two legs." The crowd chuckled, well aware she wasn't completely joking. "My whole life, you've all been so supportive. Of me, of my dogs, of the kids we've all tried to help over the years. This party is to celebrate life. Our lives, the lives of the dogs and of those we love." She glanced over at Tashya, silently asking for her consent, and the younger woman waved eager permission to proceed. "But I'm thrilled to tell you we have something more exciting than an anniversary to celebrate. Today, we get to share in a new beginning. So, lift your glasses and fill your plates. Jason finally put a ring on my girl Tashya's finger!"

The younger woman held her left hand high and waggled her fingers, showing off a ring so tiny Brady could barely see it from where he stood.

Beside him, Dillon groaned. "Engaged? Another one bites the dust."

Brady shot his buddy a worried glance, then returned his attention to the woman with the microphone. "To Jason and Tashya." Emma lifted her glass to toast the engaged couple, and others did the same. "I'm so happy I don't have to ground either of you for sneaking around anymore."

Chapter Two

Two hours later, Brady had his elbows braced on the top of a split-rail fence and a cold can of beer in his hand. He was feeling about as content as a man could get. His belly was full, he had his best pal by his side and his best girl was running around with a bunch of other dogs, showing her impressive skills.

Behind him, the tent glowed with strings of lights. He figured they were Barbara's doing. He couldn't imagine Emma even considering such a thing. She would have been too busy thinking about the training hours she was losing with the dogs.

Still, she seemed to be enjoying the party almost as much as everyone else was. Brady himself had eaten a heaping plate of barbecue, then gone for seconds, sampling a spoonful of most everything else, including all the desserts. There was nothing like a potluck to test a man's endurance. He was pretty sure he'd made a good showing.

Dillon leaned against the fence too. Brady had noted his friend was outpacing him two to one on the beers, but for the most part, Dillon seemed to be holding his own. Still, Brady worried. "You doin' okay, bud?"

Dillon hummed, his gaze fixed on the horizon where the mountains rose abruptly out of the patch of prairie the Daniels family had claimed long ago. "A-OK," he replied.

But his tone held a sarcastic edge. He wasn't fooling

anyone, much less his best friend. Dillon was all torn up over some woman named Rosie he'd met on a ski weekend.

"You've got to let it go, man," Brady said quietly. "Thinking about her is eating you up inside. You've got to let her go."

"Pffft," Dillon hissed. "Let her go? She's gone. I let her go."

"I mean, let the idea of her go," Brady persisted.

"The idea of her," Dillon echoed. "You been reading self-help books?"

The disdain in his friend's tone stung, but Brady kept his expression impassive as he stood beside the other man staring at the horizon. "Nah. I try not to read too much. My lips get too tired."

Dillon snorted a laugh, and both men fell quiet as they refocused on the action in the fenced arena. Their dogs and a couple dozen others ran through the obstacle course the DCA staff had laid out for them with joyous abandon. The enclosure was rife with lolling pink tongues, damp noses and wagging tails. As always, there'd been some growling and nipping as a new pack order was established, but no serious altercations.

The same could not be said for the impromptu game of softball the adults were playing in another part of the yard. At least the kids seemed to be content. A bunch of them were still lining up to play the yard games organized by the staff. Ring toss, bean bag throwing and a lawn bowling set complete with plastic pins and a foam ball.

A mix of adults and children stood along the fence separating humans from the dogs, watching the animals run the course and calling out encouragement to their favorites. Occasionally, he checked to make sure Winnie was playing well with the others. But his attention kept drifting to Dillon's somber quietness. He was trying to think of what to say next, what advice he could mine from the disintegration of his marriage to give his friend, but though he'd moved away from Boise and started a new life here in Jasper, he was no glowing example of moving on.

Sure, he had a new job and a new dog, and soon he'd have walls in his new house, but he was still another divorced police officer trying to scratch out a fresh start. He lived in a double-wide and ate pastry pizzas fresh from the microwave. He was certainly not the guy to give out handfuls of unsolicited advice.

A commotion over in the children's game area drew his attention. Cassie Whitaker seemed to be moving from one game to the next, questioning the children at each station. His focus had snagged on her more than a few times since they arrived. He couldn't help it; she looked so different than she did when she was working at the diner. Freer. Less frenzied and more…arresting. She had a fresh-faced, girl-next-door look, but moved with such assurance, no one would dare mistake her for anything but a grown woman who knew who she was.

Until now.

Now, she looked frantic.

Instinctively, he straightened to his full height when she spun away from the games area and set off toward the enclosure where he stood. But she wasn't looking at him. He watched, concern prickling his neck as she scanned the people lined along the fence. Then he realized her girls weren't with her.

"Something's happening," he said, nudging Dillon, then nodding toward the leggy blonde.

Dillon rolled his shoulders and lowered the can of beer to his side. Brady was glad to see his friend was steady on his feet, despite the beers he'd downed.

Cassie stopped at a cluster of people gathered at the opposite side of the ring, but whatever she'd asked, the answer had been nothing but head shakes and concerned frowns.

She moved in their direction, and Brady started toward her, drawn like steel to a magnet.

There was trouble.

She was troubled.

And he didn't like seeing her pretty face creased with worry.

He didn't examine those reactions too closely. Instead, he followed his instinct and let his feet carry him to her side. He paused beside the group of people she'd stopped to question and overheard her describing her two girls to them. In detail. Right down to the color of the elastic bands holding their hair in pigtails. Cassie twisted her fingers into knots when she was met with yet more negative responses and expressions of concern. His gut tightened.

"What's wrong? Did something happen to one of the girls?" he demanded, blocking her path to the next group of people at the fence.

"Oh. It's you." She looked at him like he was a genie who'd appeared from a magic bottle. Then she clutched his arm. "Wait. You said you're a police officer, right? What was your name? Brendan?"

"Brady, ma'am," he corrected, refusing to acknowledge the sting of being so forgettable to this woman. "Lieutenant Brady Nichols with the Jasper PD."

"I'm sorry. Brady. Brady," she repeated trying to get it to sink in even as she looked past his shoulder to scan the area around them. Her gaze returned to his. She was twitchy. Distressed. "I can't find my girls. I've looked everywhere," she said, panic making her voice slide into a higher register. "Everywhere." She shook her head hard in frustration, then brushed a strand of hair stuck to the corner of her mouth away impatiently. "I told them they could go play games, but not to go anywhere else. I've asked everyone working the games, but no one's seen them."

Brady took her arm. "I'll help you look for them." He

jerked a thumb at Dillon, who had followed close behind him. "This is Dillon. He's with the JPD as well." He looked at his friend. "We're looking for two girls, ages—"

"Nine and seven," Cassie provided.

Dillon immediately pulled out his phone and began typing a note. "Two girls, ages nine and seven," he repeated. "Names?"

"Brooklyn and Jillian," Cassie provided. "Brook is nine. She was supposed to keep an eye on Jilly."

"I'm sure she is," Brady assured her. Turning to Dillon, he said, "Both blonde. Both wearing their hair in two long, uh…" He gestured to the sides of his own head, then pulled his hands downward to indicate long hair.

"Pigtails," she supplied the word, though it came out watery.

Brady peered down at her, his heart flipping over at the sight of tears pooling in her eyes. He tamped down the urge to comfort her and kept his expression carefully blank as he focused on getting the pertinent information. "Can you repeat what they were wearing?" Brady asked, keeping his tone gentle. "Jillian had something pink on, right?" He wanted to kick himself for not paying closer attention to her kid.

"Yes," Cassie said eagerly. "Both girls are wearing white shorts and short-sleeve tops. Brooklyn's is blue with a unicorn on it, and Jilly's is pink with a glittery puppy dog." She turned big hazel eyes to Brady, her expression a plea for understanding. "She's been wanting a dog forever, and I… It's a lot having the two of them on my own. I can't imagine a dog. It's one of the reasons I told Aunt Vera we'd come today. I wanted to give her the chance to meet the dogs," she finished with a shrug.

Brady placed a gentle hand on her shoulder, hoping to give some comfort. "I'm sure Winnie enjoyed meeting her. And she couldn't have picked a better dog to meet first because she's Officer Winnie, a trained search and rescue dog. Whenever we have hikers get too far off the trails—" he pointed to the woods leading into the foothills of the mountains "—Winnie goes and finds them and brings them home safe."

She raised a horrified hand to her mouth, and Brady quickly pivoted away from the possibility of a search. "But I don't think we need a full search. I saw a bunch of kids hanging out around the dessert table, snitching cookies and poking their fingers into the whipped cream on the pies. Why don't you go check there while Dillon and I ask around a bit? They may have gone to the tent to find you," he suggested.

Cassie's head whipped toward the tent, and she pressed a hand flat against her chest. "Brook does have a sweet tooth," she said hoarsely. "She'd eat nothing but candy and cookies all day long if I let her."

Brady let his hand fall to his side. "But I'm sure you don't let her." Her gaze flew to his, and he shrugged. "You seem like a good mom. The kind who makes her kids eat vegetables and gets all the tangles out of their hair at bedtime. I can't imagine it's an easy job, so cut yourself some slack. And once we find them, we'll make sure to tell them they can visit Winnie or Dillon's dog, Bentley, whenever they're downtown. The dogs are always happy to meet with members of the public."

Dillon scoped the area. "I'm gonna start over at the softball game and see if anyone's seen them, then I'll circle around this way. Brady, you cover the dogs and the kids' games again while their mama checks the dessert table." He switched his attention to Brady. "They couldn't have gone far without someone noticing them wandering away. Not out here."

Brady watched as Cassie hurried to the tent, no doubt hoping to find her girls sneaking treats at one of the rapidly emptying tables. When Brady met Dillon's worried gaze, he found his friend's mouth set in a grim line. "You don't think they're eating dessert," he stated flatly.

"Who knows?" Dillon shrugged. "I hope so, but there are so many people here. It's hard to weed through them all."

Brady gave a nod. Not too long ago he'd been the new guy in town, eyed with suspicion and greeted with wariness for months after he'd made the move to Jasper. Emma Daniels trained dogs for police departments and federal agencies. She dealt with people who reached far beyond the insular circle of Jasper, Idaho. There had indeed been many people who were not locals attending the festivities.

"I get you. Let's move on this," Brady said brusquely. Placing two fingers between his lips, he whistled sharply. Winnie stopped frolicking with the German shepherd she'd chosen as her playmate. He whistled two more short bursts, and she ran to the rail where he stood. "Come," he said quietly, and she shimmied out beneath the bottom rail of the fence.

Despite his worry, he chuckled at the dog's single-minded determination. "You could have used the gate." Pulling the looped lead from the post beside him, he clipped it to her harness.

Dillon stepped to the fence and shouted, "Bentley, come!" The Australian shepherd immediately abandoned the Frisbee he'd been carrying in his mouth and dashed toward Dillon.

With their dogs by their sides, the two men took off in different directions. Brady paused long enough to glance at the tent and saw Cassie moving from table to table asking the occupants nearby if they'd seen her girls, and bending to peek beneath each one.

He covered the remainder of the spectators watching the dogs and went to the area where the children's games were arranged. At the bean bag station, Piper Lambert, one of the DCA staff who'd helped train Winnie, shook her head sadly. "No, I told Cassie I haven't seen them. I hope she finds them soon. It's so worrisome when they wander away," she said, a frown puckering her brow.

Then a boy who had been inching closer to Winnie shook his head. "They didn't wander away," he said. "Their daddy came and took 'em for a walk. They went thataway." He extended a hand to point to the mountains darkening in the rapidly falling dusk.

Chapter Three

Chapter Three

"No. No, no, no, no, no," Cassie Whitaker said adamantly.

"No, it wasn't your husband?" Brady asked, hoping to stop the trembling woman in front of him from shaking her head so hard. He was almost afraid she'd concuss herself.

Behind him, Dillon mumbled, "I'm going with no."

"He's not my husband anymore," Cassie asserted brusquely. "He doesn't even live around here. He lives in Billings, Montana. There's no way he came here. I'm not even sure he has a clue where we are."

Brady's brow creased. "He doesn't have any kind of visitation arrangement with the children?"

"No."

"She's batting a thousand with the noes," Dillon murmured.

Casting a quelling glance over his shoulder, Brady said, "What's your ex-husband's name? Can you give us an address or phone number? A description? Anything you can think of off the top of your head would help. Dillon can make himself useful by trying to run him to ground," he said, cocking an eyebrow at his friend.

Brady slapped the grip on Winnie's lead against his thigh as Cassie rattled off the information. When she was done, he cast another glance out at the rapidly darkening sky and said, "Do you have any clothes the girls might have worn today? You said something about sweatshirts. Do you have their sweatshirts here?"

The urgency in his tone must have registered for her because she strode quickly to one of the few remaining tables still set up in the tent. He watched as she pulled a tangled wad of clothing from the enormous tote bag he'd seen swinging from her arm earlier. Emma and some of the Daniels Academy folks followed in her wake.

"Jilly's is clean, but Brook tends to run cold. She had hers on in the car earlier. She doesn't like the air-conditioning blowing on her."

Brady waggled his finger between the two sweatshirts, then chose the slightly larger one. "This one?"

Cassie bit her lip. "Yes. Oh, Brookie," she said in a husky whisper. "She'll be cold."

Brady took the sweatshirt from her. Turning to Barbara and Emma, he said, "It's getting dark, but I think Winnie and I can take a quick walk across the field to see if we can find any scent."

Emma Daniels agreed with a brusque nod. "Is your phone charged? Do you need a flashlight?" she asked without further conversation.

Brady touched the phone case clipped to his belt. "Yes, ma'am, and no. Thank you," he added as an afterthought. "I'll be right back."

He led Winnie from the tent out into the open pasture between them and the wooded foothills of the mountains. Once they were away from the circle of lights, he stood and waited until their eyes adjusted. Then he leaned down and held the small soft sweatshirt out for Winnie to sniff.

"Here, girl. Remember your friends from earlier? We've gotta go find them."

He spoke in a hushed but commanding tone he knew the Lab responded to best. Obediently, Winnie went to work, snuffling around in the folds of the fabric until her muscles tightened and her fur rippled with anticipation.

"You got 'em?" he asked the dog.

Her floppy ears twitched forward and her brow wrinkled. She strained against the lead ever so slightly, but didn't move. Smiling, he gave her head a pat, unlatched the lock on the retractable lead and said, "Let's go find them."

The two of them took off across the field covered in stubbly grass at a jog. Two minutes in, the retractable leash had stretched as far as it could. She far outpaced him with her four-legs-to-two advantage.

If it weren't so close to dark, he might have let her off the leash, but while she was well trained, she was also still young and stubborn. Sometimes, Winnie had a mind of her own and hadn't quite learned how to obey an order she didn't agree with. He couldn't risk losing her to the dark as well.

The grass gave way to brush, then brush thickened to include sapling trees that stood as tall as he did. Their pace slowed markedly. Winnie paused to sniff various points in the undergrowth, and he took in some of the slack on the retractable leash. Under the cover of trees, the darkness started to close in around them more rapidly. Fearing they might not be able to pick up a trace, Brady shortened the distance between himself and Winnie until they stood side by side again.

Through the darkening gloom, he could see the dog's worried frown. He stroked her head reassuringly. "It's not you. You're doing great."

She needed only those few words of reassurance. Winnie pressed her nose to the ground again and started working the area around where he stood in a small circle. He gave her as much leeway as the clearing would allow, but soon he'd have to call it quits for the night. Hopefully, whoever the girls had left with had taken them into town, and one of the people combing the streets of Jasper would be sure to spot them.

He was about to signal for Winnie to call off the hunt when the dog went stock-still. Brady froze as well, barely daring to breathe. He waited patiently, certain she would not act until her olfactory senses told her she had something real. Within seconds, she lifted her head, her ears perked and she lunged forward, leading him off to his left.

Brady jogged through the scrub, branches hitting him in the face as he struggled to release the clasp on the lead. Once she was free, he followed her through the thickening trees as close as he could, hanging back enough to keep her in sight but not distracting her from her primary focus. They'd gone about a hundred yards when she let out a low woof to warn him she was about to take off in earnest.

Brady quickened his pace, his heart rate accelerating at the possibility of locating the girls. Panting, he jumped over a fallen log and thrashed at protruding limbs as he ran, heedless of the scratches forming on his forearms.

But then, Winnie gave another bark, this one shorter and sharper. A bark of frustration.

He was so fixated on following the direction of her call in the new all-encompassing dark, he hadn't registered the clearing he approached until he stumbled out of the woods onto a dirt road, tripping on an exposed root as he burst forth. Winnie barked again as he fell to the hard-packed dirt and gravel. He muttered a curse in response.

Mere yards away, his dog circled an area near the side of the road. Rolling to his knees, Brady tapped the flashlight icon on his phone and surveyed the area. It appeared to be one of the many gravel and dirt tracks cut by the forestry service over the years. This particular one seemed to have fallen down a few notches on the maintenance list. He pushed to his feet and dusted the dirt from his jeans as he walked toward the circling dog. At his approach, Winnie sighed and looked at him, her brow furrowed. A high, keening whine escaped her.

He reached down and gave her head a consoling pat. If Winnie was giving up, the trail had gone truly cold. He held his phone high to take in the area once more, then directed the flashlight at the road.

Tire tracks heading into the hills.

Whoever had taken Cassie Whitaker's girls had driven. On foot, they could be anywhere, but roads were rough and limited in the foothills. They wouldn't make it far. He saw no signs of a turnaround. No flattened scrub or crumpled saplings on either side of the narrow lane. It was possible whoever it was had taken the road higher into the mountains, but most of these roads only led as far as forestry service outposts. He'd have to get the records from town to find out where this particular lane would dead-end.

He'd have to wait until morning to look for better clues.

The dog whimpered again, and Brady dropped to her side. Stroking her cheeks, he looked directly into those amber eyes and spoke calmly. "Good girl. You are a good girl. Good work." He rubbed her head once more, then clipped the lead to her harness. "Come on. We'll head downtown and see what we can figure out tonight, but I promise, you'll be on the case tomorrow. You're gonna need a good night's rest."

The dog resisted enough to show she was as dissatisfied with the result as he was, but followed obediently. The walk to the Daniels ranch seemed to go much faster than the climb into the mountains, even though he had to use the more circuitous route along the road. Dread pooled low in his belly. He returned from searches empty-handed all too often, but he'd never grown immune to the looks of profound disappointment on loved ones' faces when they saw him and Winnie returning alone.

The lights under the tent had been shut off, but every

lamp in the old ranch house was ablaze. There were also at least a dozen cars parked close, including three Jasper PD units. As he circled around the pasture to the front of the house, Brady cast a glance at the far field where two vehicles sat abandoned—his truck and Cassie Whitaker's minivan.

He approached the building, his stomach twisting into a knot. He'd barely climbed the first step when she spoke from a dark corner of the porch.

"No luck?" Cassie Whitaker asked, the question tremulous.

Since he wasn't returning with two blondes on his arms, Brady saw no point in soft selling his failure. "No, ma'am, but I promise you, Winnie and I are gonna be out first thing in the morning." He took a step closer, squinting to make out her features in the dim light emanating from the house. "You shouldn't be out here alone."

"Too many people in there, and none of them the ones I want to see," she returned.

He made a grunt of understanding. "We did pick up their scent crossing the field and into the woods."

She let out a strangled "Oof," but managed to suck it in quickly. "You think whoever it was took them into the woods?"

"Maybe. It's only a guess," he hastened to add. "The trail went cold at one of the fire lanes. Most likely, whoever they're with had a vehicle parked there. We have to remember they could be holed up somewhere in town," he said, extending a dim ray of hope.

The corner of her mouth curved down, and she shook her head sadly. "They're not in town. Your boss is in there talking to Emma right now. They've looked everywhere and no one's seen them."

"Yet," he added. "Doesn't mean no one will," Brady reminded her. "I think the good news is whoever they're with is somebody they know. Hopefully somebody they trust. No one saw them struggle or heard them yelling or crying, so I think this may be the case. Hopefully, they are with someone who won't hurt them."

"You'd think," she muttered, a bitter note in her tone. "But we don't know many people here yet, aside from Aunt Vera and Uncle Millard."

"If you don't mind, I'd like to go into the station. Dillon's working on tracking down your ex, and we'll have better access to resources there." He glanced over at the brightly lit house. "I'd say we shouldn't impose on Emma any further, but she'll be doing everything she can to help find them. Everyone will be," he asserted. "Jasper is a small town, and they take care of their own."

"I'm not sure we're one of their own yet," Cassie replied huskily.

"You are. Your grandparents lived here, right? Your mother and aunt grew up here. Vera may not be a ray of sunshine, but people still love her." He gestured for her to rise. "I'll give them the heads-up we're leaving. You can either ride with me or follow me downtown."

After a flurry of goodbyes and reassurances from the people still hanging around the Daniels ranch, including the chief himself, they walked across the darkened field. The grass lay flat, the only proof it had been the parking area hours earlier. The moon was high and bright now, but not quite bright enough to search. The night breeze cut through his T-shirt. Those girls would be cold, and the worry sat like a lump of ice in his gut.

Winnie trotted at his side, off her leash since it was the three of them alone. As they approached the vehicles, Cassie spoke.

"Thank you for doing this," she said earnestly. "I wasn't… I wasn't particularly friendly earlier," she said, glancing over at his truck.

The light from the moon was enough to outline the worry and regret etched into her pretty face. "You were fine," he said firmly. "I wouldn't expect any parent to take too kindly to their kid talking to a strange man."

The corners of her mouth sloped down. "I've been talking to Jilly about stranger danger," she said with a short, bitter laugh. "I guess those lessons haven't stuck."

Unable to refrain any longer, Brady reached out and placed a hand on her shoulder. When she jolted, he gave it a gentle squeeze and withdrew, signaling he meant the gesture as nothing more than a comfort.

"I'd tell you not to worry, but that would be futile," he said with a self-deprecating chuckle. "If you weren't worried, I'd think there was something wrong with you."

She absorbed his assertion. "Would you take me to the spot where…?"

She didn't say "where you lost them," but he felt the unspoken words like a gut punch. Drawing in a sharp breath, he inclined his head, even though the thought tied his stomach into a knot.

He gestured to her minivan. "Sure. Why don't you ride with us, then we'll get your car and head into town?"

"Okay." She ducked her head and made her way to the passenger side of his truck. He reached for the handle and opened the door, but she didn't climb in. Instead, her gazed was fixed on the harness he used for Winnie. "Should I get in the back?"

"Oh. No, sorry." He unhooked the harness and tossed it in. Opening the half door to the rear seat, he said, "Winnie, up."

The dog obeyed without hesitation. Once she was settled, her muzzle resting on her paws, Brady gave her a pat and murmured, "There you go. Good girl." He closed the rear door, then gestured to the vacant seat. "Help yourself."

"What? You don't want to order me to jump?" she asked

as she grabbed the handle above the door and stepped into the truck.

Happy to hear a touch of sass in her tone, Brady stood in the open passenger door as she reached for the safety belt and then clipped it in place. She raised her eyebrows and he smirked. "There you are. Good girl." He gave the roof a pat, then closed the door on her husky chuckle.

Chapter Four

Cassie had spent a couple weeks with her grandparents in Jasper almost every summer of her childhood, but she never strayed too far from town. As an adult, she'd gone down many an unpaved road leading to hiking trails and points of river access, but she'd never had a chance to follow this particular road. The gravel lane was so rutted, they bounced around in the cab, trying to maintain equilibrium. She was glad she hadn't tried to drive her minivan. Poor old thing would never have made it.

They'd ridden in silence, but it wasn't the uncomfortable kind. It was sort of…full.

Full of worry. Full of wondering. Full of concern.

She could feel the frustration practically rolling off both the man beside her and the dog behind them. They clearly wanted to act. Cassie was so appreciative of their determination she was tempted to cry. But she wouldn't. Couldn't. She didn't have time for an emotional breakdown. As a mother, she was an absolute expert on shoving her own feelings aside in order to focus on what needed to be done.

Until she'd moved to Jasper, no one cared about her girls the way she did. Certainly not their father.

"It wasn't Mark," she said, her words low and throaty, as she watched the scrubby brush zoom past her window.

A bitter laugh escaped her, but there was no point in trying to sugarcoat anything. Brady and his friend Dillon would find out exactly how useless her ex-husband was in due course.

"He has a drinking problem. It pretty much consumes him. He hasn't tried to see the girls once since we left. I can't imagine him going to this extreme. Too much effort," she concluded, chancing a glance at the man beside her.

He gave a short nod. "I'm sorry," he said gruffly. "It must have been rough on you and the girls."

"Actually, leaving Mark was one of the easiest things I've ever done," she said simply. She didn't wait for any follow-up questions he might have.

"After the divorce we moved to Bozeman." She gazed out the window again, though the shapes beyond the glass grew more and more indistinct in the deepening dark. "I actually liked the life I built in Bozeman. I had a good job and a nice apartment," she said her, tone tremulous. She swallowed hard. "I'd even started dating again. Talk about a mistake."

"Mistake?" Brady asked as he let off the accelerator and the truck rolled to a halt on the steadily rising incline. She waited until he set the brake to speak.

"I'm concerned one of the men I dated in Bozeman might be behind this," she said, letting the words form as the idea took shape in her mind. "I'd hoped he'd lose interest if I didn't answer anymore, but…"

"But he didn't," he prompted when she trailed off.

"No," she replied, not offering anything more.

"What makes you think it might be this guy? What's his name?" he asked, the questions coming at her faster than she anticipated.

"Keith," she supplied. "Keith Norton. As for the why, it was a messy sort of breakup."

"Messy how?" Brady asked.

"I could see it wasn't going to be a long-term thing for us, so I ended it." She clamped her mouth shut, unsure how much more she wanted to share. After all, she had no real reason to suspect Keith other than his persistence.

Brady reached over and touched her forearm with two fingers. The movement was purposefully nonthreatening. Nothing more than a means of getting her attention. Still, she couldn't look directly at him. She stared straight ahead through the windshield at the narrow red dirt-and-gravel road illuminated by the truck's headlights.

"Is this it?" she asked, hating the break in her voice but unable to muster the strength to hold it together.

"Hard to say exactly in the dark," Brady said. "I figured we'd get out of here and let Winnie have a sniff around."

Cassie waited impatiently for him to get down to it. At last, he snatched something from the center console and reached for the handle on the door. She watched as Brady rummaged under the seat of the truck and pulled out a heavy-duty flashlight. He clicked it on and off, checking to be sure the batteries were still strong. Then he opened the door on his side of the truck, and Winnie jumped down to stand by his side.

"I'm going to leave her off lead, if you don't mind," he informed her.

Cassie shook her head hard. "Are you kidding? She could do whatever she wants as far as I'm concerned."

Warmed by her appreciation for Winnie's skill, he patted the dog's head. "But won't," he said, shifting his attention to his partner.

Cassie watched as he dropped to a crouched position and spoke directly to the dog. It reminded her of the way she spoke to Jilly. Focused. One-on-one.

He stroked Winnie's face as he talked, his cadence and demeanor gentle but firm. "Right, girl? I need you to stay on track, okay?" he murmured to the dog.

Cassie's heart leaped into her throat when she saw him offer Brook's sweatshirt to the dog to sniff. The Lab's ears thrust forward and her poor head wrinkled. She kept snuffling as Brady rose to his feet, and gave her a pat on the head. "Go on. Search," he prompted.

Standing by the front bumper of the truck, Cassie watched the dog press her nose to the dirt and start working the area. If it weren't her girls they were searching for, Cassie would have been more fascinated by the process and the dog's methodology, but her girls were missing, and it was hard for Cassie to do anything but stare into the darkened woods surrounding them.

"She's good." The compliment came out rusty, but she needed to say something. The chirp of crickets surrounding them was becoming unbearable.

Brady cast a sidelong glance at her. "She was almost a DCA washout," he informed her. "Emma was having a hard time finding someone who could connect with her in a way Winnie responded to positively. She was still a puppy and a bit all over the place."

"And the two of you connected?"

"Yep." He chuckled. "I never considered myself a dog person. Didn't have one growing up. Didn't work K-9 when I was on the force in Boise, but when I met Winnie…it was all over."

Cassie kept her eyes fixed on the Labrador caught in the headlight beams. The dog kept her nose to the ground, looking determined. She moved about five more feet along the lane, then stopped, lifted her head and let out a soft woof. Brady moved toward her. "There's the spot. She lost the scent there," he informed Cassie.

She hurried behind him. "Where does this road lead?"

"It's a fire lane. There is a whole maze of them, most overgrown, but interconnected. They usually lead to a ranger station or a fire lookout. We'll have to get the maps out when we get down to the station."

She watched as he pulled out his cell phone and opened

a mapping application, dropping a pin in the spot where they stood. When he swiveled the screen to her, she saw their location coordinates displayed in the message box. He'd literally marked the spot.

Cassie turned in a slow circle, narrowing her eyes as she peered into the ever-deepening darkness beyond the headlight's beams. Logically, she knew there was no point in them trying to go on tonight, but logic wasn't playing a big part in her way of thinking right now.

Reading her thoughts, Brady placed a gentle hand on her shoulder. "The best thing we can do is go down to the station, do some research and prepare for the morning. I promise you we will be out at first light."

The sincerity in his tone made her swallow hard. "I understand," she croaked. "I'm sure you're right, but…"

"You're anxious. Believe me, if it made any sense for us to get out there right now, we would. We'll go down to the station and see if there's any new information."

"If you don't mind taking me to my car, I'll follow you," she said. "I want to have my car."

He bobbed his head once. "You think you're all right to drive?"

"Yeah," she said briefly, then yanked open the passenger door.

Brady watched as she strapped herself into the seat. Winnie barked and Cassie was not surprised when he kicked it into gear. Once Brady had Winnie loaded into her harness, Cassie gave the dog a pat. "Thank you."

Winnie replied with a low hum of a growl.

Clearly, the dog was as frustrated as she and Brady.

He glanced over his shoulder after he executed a tight three-point turn on the narrow lane. "We're going to find them, right, girl?" Winnie turned her head to look at the woods where they'd lost the scent. "First thing tomorrow, I promise."

Cassie waved, but she had no doubt her expression was as somber as Winnie's.

Chapter Five

Brady's eyes kept flicking to the rearview mirror, and his mind raced as he led Cassie into Jasper. The woman was clearly in shock. But rather than crumpling under the weight of what was happening, she seemed to grow more…steely.

He figured it had to do with being a single parent. Every single mom or dad he knew had this miles-deep well of calm they could draw on in times of extreme stress. It fascinated him. He never thought he was much of a kid guy himself, but he had friends, and a few had become parents. He was glad he and Lisa never had kids. Their divorce had been messy enough all on its own. Dragging innocent children into the mix would have made it worse.

Lisa hadn't been the type to settle down once the wedding was over. Oh, she loved the whole white dress and rigamarole. All the attention. But settling into married life? She chafed against it from the beginning. Resented the days when his work hours ate into what she considered their time. Hated the danger inherent in his job even though he had been a cop when they'd met.

He understood how hard it was on the spouses, so he listened to her complaints with as much patience as he could muster, but after a while he realized her grievances with his career choices had nothing do with his safety and more to do with their lifestyle.

Lisa had been five years younger. She wasn't done with

her partying. Other than shopping for home decor, she wasn't much interested in anything domestic. He never expected her to turn into a television housewife, but it would have been nice to have a meal prepared occasionally, or the laundry done when he got off a long shift.

He let off the accelerator as they entered the town. A quick check of his mirrors showed him Cassie had done the same. The streets of Jasper were dark now. Only the occasional lamp glowed in windows as they passed. The businesses were all locked down for the night. Steering around the town square with its floodlit gazebo and trio of flagpoles, he tapped the brakes and hooked a right onto Main Street.

The parking lot adjacent to the Jasper Police Department held only a few cars. The cruisers driven by the officers on duty were gone, but they had a dispatcher working overnight. As usual, he spotted Dillon's truck parked in the space farthest from the door.

His friend was here even though they were both technically off duty, but in a town the size of Jasper, when a situation such as this arose, it was all-hands-on-deck. The other canine officer, Cal Hoover, was a family man, but Brady knew he'd join the search the second they called. He parked next to Dillon, then waited until Cassie pulled into a space as well.

He glanced over at his partner and found Winnie dozing in her harness. Periods of intense searching zapped the usually energetic dog. Reaching across the seat, he stroked her smooth head and gave one of her silky ears a gentle tug. "A few minutes longer, girl. Let's go in and see what Dillon's got, then we'll go home and get a couple hours of sleep." He peered into the dog's drowsy amber eyes. "Sound like a plan?"

Winnie huffed a sigh, then nestled her face into his palm,

demanding a few more strokes. He obliged her. After a final pat, he reached for the driver's door and climbed down from the truck. He attached the lead to Winnie's harness, then gave her room to jump down.

Cassie sat in her minivan, her hands wrapped tight around the steering wheel and her gaze locked on the brick wall of the police station. She was obviously deep in thought, and he hated to interrupt her, but every minute they spent gathering information brought them closer to finding her girls.

He wanted to hear what Dillon had unearthed on the ex-husband. And he wanted to get whatever information he could on this Keith Norton character Cassie seemed to think was more of a threat. In his experience, victims of harassment often had a heightened sixth sense when it came to their safety, and he'd worked enough domestic calls to take her concerns seriously.

Protocol said they had to cross one off before they could move on to the other, but regulations didn't mean he couldn't start gathering more intel.

Beside him, Winnie let out a soft whine. She was undoubtedly thirsty and ready for a rest. He could go ahead on into the station and get his dog situated, but something about Cassie Whitaker's rigid posture held him there.

She was barely holding it together. Who could blame her? He certainly didn't. But for his purposes, and for the sake of the investigation, he needed her to hang on a bit longer. Wincing to himself, he stepped over to the van and rapped on the window with the knuckle of his index finger.

Cassie jumped and he grimaced. When she looked over at him wide-eyed and wary, he gave her an apologetic wince and mouthed the word *Sorry*.

He noted her slumped shoulders and decided he needed to get her inside and get what information he could from her. When she opened her door, he automatically offered a hand to help her from the van, and to his surprise, she took it.

CASSIE HAD NEVER been inside the Jasper Police Department, but she'd been in others. When she left Billings, she vowed to herself she'd never visit another. Now, here she was. The low brick building sat squarely on Main Street just off the square. It had a solid kind of midcentury construction that somehow managed to look modern and old-fashioned all at once.

She forced herself to take three deep breaths after switching off the ignition.

Her girls were gone.

Her girls were her everything.

It felt like someone chopped both her arms off at once. What was she going to do if anything happened to them? How would she go on?

For the last few years, her entire world was a bubble built for three. In the months following her divorce from Mark, all she could do was focus on rebuilding. She wanted to give them the stable home they deserved, and maybe find a smidge of peace for herself.

Thankfully, Jilly didn't remember much about living with their dad, but Brook... Brook had seen too much. As a matter of fact, her older daughter had been the reason she finally said enough is enough and left.

It was one thing to live a life you didn't deserve; it was another to have your children witness it.

Mark, her ex-husband, had been an alcoholic, an ugly drunk who'd had no qualms about using his words to wound. Cassie had been about to leave him when she discovered she was pregnant with their second child. Feeling well and truly trapped, she stayed.

Until the night he went too far.

A tap on her window jolted her from her thoughts. She looked over to see Brady standing on the passenger side of her van, watching her with a cautious expression. She reached for the handle on her door.

She gathered her purse, opened her door, and hopped down from the vehicle. "Sorry, I was woolgathering."

Brady gave her a commiserating look when she came around the front of the car. "Understandable. It's been a lot to process." He swept an arm toward the building. "Let's go in and see what Diaz has found."

Diaz? It took a minute for Cassie to realize he was referring to the other officer at the scene. Dillon. He had introduced himself as Dillon Diaz. "You both have police dogs. Is Officer Diaz your partner or something?" she asked as they approached the front of the building.

One corner of Brady's mouth twitched. "Winnie is my partner. The department here isn't really big enough to pair us off. For the most part, we all work together. I'll be the lead on this case, since it's a search and rescue, but Dillon and all the other officers will pitch in where they can."

"Oh. Yeah. Makes sense," she said as she passed through the door he held open for her.

She glanced down when Winnie brushed against her leg. The yellow Lab trotted beside her. Apparently, she decided Cassie needed backup more than Brady. She studied the dog Jilly had been so excited to greet mere hours earlier, then cast a shy glance at Brady. "Can I pet her? Is it okay?"

He nodded. "She's not on an active search at the moment, so I'm sure she would love a good rub behind the ears," he said with a wry grin. "Truthfully, she's kind of a needy girl, so she'll take whatever you give her."

Cassie reached down and stroked the dog's head, her fingertips grazing Winnie's silky years. "I've always heard you weren't supposed to pet service dogs on duty."

Brady shrugged. "True. But when she's focused, she's focused. You saw her out on the trail. She knows what her job is and she's good at it." He looked down at the Lab leaning heavily against Cassie's leg and gave a rueful chuckle. "And she's also keenly aware of when she's off duty."

"I'm glad." Cassie cringed as the words clogged in her throat. "I'm also glad she's off duty right now, because I sure could use some comfort."

Brady pointed to a chair beside the desk. "This is mine. Have a seat."

She took in the computer monitor covered in sticky notes and overflowing inbox as she lowered herself onto the hard wooden chair.

He shifted his attention to the dog, waited until she met his gaze, then pointed to Cassie. "Stay with her."

The Lab plopped down next to the chair, and placed her chin on Cassie's thigh. A surprised laugh of delight escaped her despite the crushing worry. "Oh wow."

"Good girl," he said to the dog. He shifted his attention to Cassie. "She takes cuddling seriously as well. Can I get you anything? Coffee? Water? Soda?"

She wanted to say "My kids," but she knew it wouldn't be fair. This man was trying to help as best he could. She had no cause to make him feel bad even though she felt wretched. She kept her answer short, hoping to avoid word vomiting her every thought all over the poor guy. "I'm good."

He hooked a thumb over his shoulder to the next desk, where Dillon Diaz sat speaking into a telephone. "I'm gonna grab us all a bottle of water. Hopefully, Dillon will be off the line by then and give us an update on where we are with your ex."

He glanced down at her hand on the dog's head. "Pet her as much as you want. It will never be too much for Winnie." He started to turn, then stopped. "Oh, and she really enjoys a nice solid hug if you need one."

The offer startled another laugh from her. "Oh, I need one."

Brady snapped his fingers twice. The dog lifted her chin and fixed her gaze on him. "Hug it out," he commanded.

Winnie gave an enthusiastic thump of her tail, then rose on her hind legs. She placed her paws squarely on Cassie's lap, smiling as the two of them came face-to-face.

Cassie couldn't help but think of how delighted Jilly would have been to be on the receiving end of one of Winnie's hugs. Unable to contain it one second longer, she buried her face in the dog's soft neck, and the dam burst with a sob.

Chapter Six

Brady skirted his way over to Dillon's desk, hoping to put himself between the weeping woman and the other man. She'd had a hell of a night and deserved at least a few minutes of privacy.

"Any luck on the ex?" he asked. Dillon shook his head as he ended the call. "Phone's going straight to voice mail. I'm guessing it's either dead or he doesn't accept calls from unknown numbers. I left a message but with no real details."

Brady sat down in the chair alongside Dillon's desk. "The mother doesn't think it's the ex," he stated flatly. "Apparently, there was some guy she dated after the divorce who didn't take the breakup well. I don't have all the details, but I have a feeling he's been pursuing the relationship despite her moving to Jasper."

Dillon clicked his mouse and opened a fresh document. "You think we have a stalker situation going on?" he asked as he typed in the words, "Second possible suspect—Whitaker kidnapping" at the top of a page.

Seeing the word spelled out on the screen gave Brady a jolt. Kidnapping was a federal offense. Federal agents would probably be on the case midmorning. Something about the prospect of handing the case over made his stomach tighten. It wasn't simply a local department's desire to hang on to a case. He'd met these girls. He looked into those big, hopeful eyes. He watched them hug and shower love on Winnie. Turning his head, he saw Cassie Whitaker straightening in her chair, wiping her eyes with the heel of one hand while stroking Winnie's damp fur with the other. This case was personal. The last thing he wanted to do was hand it over to the Feds.

To Dillon, he said, "I'm going to get as much information on the ex-boyfriend as I can. Keith Norton is the name, and apparently they met after she moved from Billings to Bozeman, Montana."

Dillon typed the information into the notes document he'd started. "I'll run the usual searches and see if anything hits on the name. Keep me in the loop if you get anything more from the mom."

Brady rose and tapped two fingers on Dillon's desk. "Winnie and I will be heading out at first light—"

"Bentley and I will be there with you," Dillon said, glancing down at the dog sleeping beside his chair. "And three dogs are better than two. I'll call Hoover and make sure he brings Ruby too."

Brady clapped his friend on the shoulder. "Thanks, man." Crouching down to pat Dillon's dog, he said, "Rest, Bent. We're going to go at it hard first thing in the morning."

The dog's ears twitched and his tail thumped once, but it was all the acknowledgment he was given.

Snagging some bottles of water from the fridge, he walked to his own desk and extended one wordlessly in Cassie's direction.

She accepted it, her cheeks coloring as she ducked her head. "Sorry about the, uh, meltdown."

Brady dropped into his own chair and looked directly at her. "Absolutely no need to apologize. It's the people who are too calm that worry me."

Cassie's brows shot skyward and she looked at him quizzically. "What do you mean?"

"Nothing," he answered a shade too quickly. He cracked the seal on one of the bottles and tipped the contents into the dog bowl beside his desk.

He wanted to kick himself. He was trying to build trust with her, and the last thing he needed to do was make her think he doubted her in any way. Still, it was a legitimate line of thinking. Some parents did stage the abduction of their child. But he knew in his gut they weren't dealing with such a case here.

There were a thousand different motives for kidnapping, but the outcomes in these situations were limited to a handful. The best was when the child was found safe and returned to a loving family. Good, but not great, were the cases when the child was found unharmed, then shuffled over to Child Protective Services. Worse was when the child was found, but not safe. But the worst of all were the cases when the child was never found.

"Nothing," he repeated more forcefully. "I'm running various scenarios through my head."

"And one of those scenarios concerns me arranging to have my own children taken?"

"You would not be the first, but no, we're sure you didn't," he stated firmly, holding her gaze.

She didn't flinch. If anything, her stubborn chin rose a notch. "Good, because someone took my babies and I want them home with me now," she said, enunciating each word for emphasis.

"Dillon has not been able to reach your ex-husband. We're going to pursue contacting him through the night, but as the children's father, he will be considered the number one suspect until we can eliminate him from the list."

Brady didn't bother to boot up his computer. Instead, he pulled a notepad out of one of the desk drawers and plucked a pen from a cup. Clicking it a couple times, he found her staring at him intently.

"But I want to get some information on this Keith Norton guy. Everything you can think of about him. If we're able to clear your ex, I want to have a bead on this guy, if I can."

"I met him at work. But I didn't start dating him then." She stopped, then gave her head a shake. "I took a temp job as a receptionist for a dental practice, and he was one of the dentists. I only worked there for a week, then landed a permanent job. A few months later I had the brilliant idea to try some online dating."

Color came into her cheeks, but she didn't avert her gaze. "I was still pretty new in town and hadn't met many people outside of work or my apartment building."

He bobbed his head. "I get you."

"Keith and I were a match, and since we'd already met each other, I thought it might be the safer thing to do," she said, wrinkling her nose at the thought. "Anyway, we dated for about six weeks. Dinner or the occasional movie. There was a high school girl who lived in the apartment next to mine who was willing to babysit. I thought I had a really good setup." She let out a sigh, then went silent.

Brady continued scribbling notes on his pad until he caught up with her. "Sounds reasonable enough," he said gently. "Go on."

"Keith only met the girls a couple of times when he came to the apartment to pick me up. I didn't like the thought of exposing them to anyone I was seeing until I thought the relationship might work, but logistically it seemed to make more sense for him to drive a couple of times. Or so he said," she spoke with a hard edge to her tone. "In hindsight, I think maybe he wanted to see where I lived. He made a point of wanting to meet the girls, so I introduced them, but they didn't spend hours together or anything. When you're a parent, you're always worried about who you're letting into your kids' lives, you know?"

Brady continued to write. "Absolutely."

"The last couple weeks we were seeing each other, life got hectic and I didn't have much energy left over for dating. He started to get pushy, and I made it clear the girls would always be my priority—"

Brady's head lifted. "Can you tell me what you mean by pushy?"

"Nothing physical," she said quickly. "More phone calls and texts. He even emailed a couple of times, trying to nail down when we might get together. I felt bad, but Brook had a cold, then gave it to the rest of us. The last thing on my mind was going out. I tried to explain to him, tried to tell him I'm the one who takes care of all three of us when we're sick, but he used it as an excuse to come over. He wanted to bring chicken soup, and I didn't have the energy. I told him I was too tired, and he didn't take it well."

"What did he do?"

"He came over unannounced with a bag of take-out chicken soup in his hand. I didn't want to open the door because I was sick, and the girls were sick, and the place was a mess." She shook her head, her lips tightening. "I looked like death warmed over on a plate, so I asked him to leave it at the door, and he started shouting about how he wasn't some kind of delivery service, and how it wasn't out of line for a guy to want to take care of his girlfriend."

She looked at him squarely.

"It bothered me he considered me his girlfriend. I wasn't in the right headspace for a relationship, and I didn't want to be. My marriage was a hot mess, and while I enjoyed having some adult companionship, I wasn't looking for anything serious. I even put it in my dating profile," she said, jabbing a finger at the notepad, insisting he make note of it as well.

"But he wanted to get serious," Brady filled in.

"I didn't think I was leading him on, but apparently Keith disagreed. Over the next few weeks, I changed my phone number and stopped replying to his emails after sending a polite one saying I didn't think things were going to work out."

"Then what happened?" Brady asked, because he'd taken enough of these statements to get the notion something had to have pushed her to flee Bozeman for Jasper.

"One day I got off work and went to get the girls from after-school care." She drew a shaky breath. "When I got there, I found Keith at the front desk arguing with the woman in charge. He was claiming he should have been on the list of people approved to check them out. The only people I had on my list were me and Kayla Mikelson's mother. She's the girl who lived next door and would sometimes babysit for me."

Brady focused intently on her. "What did he say when he saw you?"

"He tried to play it off like we'd arranged for him to get the girls, but I'd forgotten to put him on the list. I didn't want to make a scene, so I said something about how I was able to make it after all, thanked him and told him he could go. He was smart enough to get out of there."

She took a deep, shuddering breath. "I waited a while, looking at all their projects and artwork and stuff, hoping he'd be long gone when we came out. Thankfully, he was." She glanced down at the hand buried in the scruff of Winnie's neck. "I called Aunt Vera on my way home. She's the only family I have. My parents were killed in a car crash not long after I married Mark. She told me to pack my stuff and get to Jasper. My grandparents' house was vacant, and she said Millard would let me work at the diner until I found something permanent."

Leaning down, she pressed a kiss to the top of Winnie's head. Then, she whispered her secret into his dog's floppy ear, saying, "We left Bozeman as soon as I could pack my car, but somehow, he always keeps tabs on me."

"How do you mean?"

"I changed phone numbers, but he managed to get the new one and started calling and texting again." She sighed and slumped down in the chair, like merely talking about the man sapped her energy. "I've changed my number twice now. I also closed all my social media accounts, thinking maybe he was tracking me through a mutual friend or something."

She paused until he met her gaze. With a meaningful glance over at Dillon, she pitched her voice low.

"Here's the thing. I get why you have to look at Mark first, but I can tell you he doesn't care what happens to me or the girls. He's a drunk. A mean drunk, and not a good guy to be married to, but his first thought is always about his next drink."

Brady flinched when she reached across and tapped the pad where he'd been scrawling notes. He looked down at everything he'd written. His handwriting was a barely legible mix of print and cursive. He'd be hard-pressed to make out some of the words in the morning. Then she spoke with a soft surety that startled him from any worries over his penmanship.

"Keith," she whispered. "If anyone from my past did this, he would be the one."

Chapter Seven

Given what she'd shared with him about the former boy-friend, Brady was inclined to agree with Cassie's assessment. Still, they couldn't search until morning, and his captain wasn't going to let him go off on too many tangents until Mark Whitaker was located.

But her story, combined with the steady determination in her hazel eyes, sold him on the notion of Keith Norton as the guy. The person who'd lured the girls from the party was someone they knew. According to the volunteers they'd spoken to, and the boy who'd seen them leave, they hadn't fussed about exiting the games area with him.

He drummed the pen against the pad. The temptation to try to lure this Norton guy out was strong. But if he did have the girls, if he was fixated on Cassie, would it put them in more danger if he knew she suspected him? If she'd changed phone numbers, would she still be able to reach the man?

"Do you still have his phone number?" Brady winced. He'd meant to be gentler with the request, but he was tired, and this might be something.

But Cassie didn't hesitate. She pulled her phone from her pocket and unlocked it. "I've kept it. I also have screenshots, archived emails and all of it," she said as she swiped at the screen.

He must have made a sound of surprise because she lifted an eyebrow.

"In less than a decade, I've managed to get involved with two of the most despicable men I've ever met. I've learned a few lessons, Officer Nichols."

As she said the last, she thrust the phone at him. The contact page labeled Dr. Keith Norton had a lock icon at the top. Nearly every field was completed. Name, address, email, various phone numbers. It appeared she had collected as much data on the man as she could find.

"It's Brady," he corrected. "And do you mind if I send this to my phone?"

"Please do."

He transferred the information to his own number, then saved his contact information to her phone. "I saved my contact info for you, in case you need me," he informed her.

"Thank you."

He eyed the information she'd gathered on her former paramour, weighing whether he should ask her to put herself out there. Bracing himself to be shut down, he went for it. "Are you willing to try to reach out to this guy?"

She squirmed when he handed her phone to her. "You want me to call him?"

He could see she was uncomfortable with the idea. "I'm thinking maybe. We could try to pinpoint his location."

"He's smart about technology. I doubt he's carrying his phone," she said, frowning at the number on her screen. "He tags every photo he takes. He knows his phone has GPS."

"Maybe not, but it could be worth a try to see if we can determine whether he's even in the area."

She gnawed on her bottom lip, then gave a decisive nod. "Okay. How do we do this? I don't want to call him from this phone. I don't want him to have this number."

Brady pushed away from the desk. "No problem. Give me a minute."

He walked over to Dillon's desk and waited until his friend looked up from his screen.

"Hey, do we still have any of those burner phones we used to trace calls when we were tracking those dealers?" he asked, referencing a methamphetamine bust they'd helped assist with a few months prior.

Dillon glanced at a metal cabinet in the corner of the room. "Yeah, there are a couple in there. We'll probably have to update the software to make sure we can run a trace on them. Then we can triangulate any signal we get."

Brady started in that direction. "I'm going to get one. Would you check the software? We want to try to ping this ex-boyfriend's phone and see if we can get coordinates in the vicinity."

Dillon shot to his feet. "Good idea. We'll have her try the ex-husband's phone too. It's better than nothing."

"I agree." Brady walked to the cabinet, then called over his shoulder. "Cassie? Do you have a phone number for your ex as well?"

He pulled a pay-as-you-go phone still in its package from the supply cabinet and tossed it to Dillon. His friend caught it and went to work plugging the phone's information into the software on his computer. When they made it to his desk, he saw Cassie had a contact labeled simply Mark showing on her phone.

"This is the latest number I have, but I have no idea if he's still using it. He tends to forget to pay his phone bill. After a while, the cellular companies cut him off and he has to move on to a different one."

"We're going to try something with some software we have. It may not amount to much, but it's something," he said with a shrug.

Cassie handed over her phone again. "I'll do anything. I don't have any idea how I'm going to make it till morning."

At her feet, Winnie let out a small snuffle as if she'd

heard and agreed wholeheartedly, even though the dog was clearly half asleep.

Brady felt the exact same way. "It's always better to feel like you're doing something rather than nothing. Let's try this, then we're all going to head home and get some rest. Dillon and Bentley will be heading out to search with us first thing in the morning."

Dillon approached holding the newly programmed phone, and she eyed it warily. "What do you need me to do?" she asked, wringing her hands again.

"You don't need to say anything," Brady assured her. "We're going to dial the number and on the off chance he answers, mute it. But it will be an unknown number, so even if he lets it go to voice mail, hang on. We're hoping the software will get a ping on the phone receiving the call. From there, we may be able to determine where it's located. You don't have to speak at all," he said. "As a matter of fact, it's better if you don't."

"Okay," she agreed. "I'm not so worried about Mark, but what if Keith has something on his phone capable of finding this one?" she asked, nodding to the burner phone.

Dillon shook his head. "The software we use scrambles everything. If he tries to pin it down, all it will show is a data farm in Silicon Valley."

The three of them leaned over the desk as Brady punched in the numbers for Mark Whitaker's mobile phone. It rang and rang until finally voice mail connected, and a gruff-sounding man said only, "Leave a message. Maybe I'll call you."

The three of them stood in silence, letting the recording spool out on the voice mail until the service tripped over to an automated recording asking them if they were satisfied with the recording. Brady glanced over at Dillon, and the other man gave a silent nod. He disconnected the call, then waited until the screen went dark again. He looked over at his friend.

"You got a location?"

"Yep," Dillon said. "Looks to be someplace in the middle of Billings, Montana. I'll get the coordinates and pinpoint a more exact address. In the meantime, let's try the numbers for the other guy," he suggested.

Brady chanced a glance at Cassie and found her twisting her fingers together in her lap. "Okay so far?" he asked.

"As okay as I'm going to be," she said grimly. "Let's do it."

"Ready?" he called to Dillon.

"Go for it," the other man replied.

Brady dialed the first number Cassie had listed on Norton's contact page. As expected, the call went to voice mail. They held their breath, allowing the recording to take in the silence for as long as it would allow, then Brady disconnected when Dillon knocked on his desktop.

"Bozeman, Montana," he announced a minute later.

Cassie let out an explosion of breath. "Oh God. I don't know if I was wanting him to answer and be here, or if I wanted it not to be him." Her head swiveled and she stared at him, her eyes wide with panic. "Which would be worse? Somebody we know or a stranger? But they wouldn't go off with a stranger. I've taught them better," she insisted.

"I'm sure you have," Brady said calmly. "But let's not assume anything until we try these other numbers you have here. If he's as smart as you say he is, he may have left this most recent phone at home. Or it's not his only phone."

Cassie lifted a trembling hand to her mouth, but nodded her assent. Brady glanced at Dillon and asked, "Ready to run another?"

"Ready when you are," his friend replied.

Brady punched in the second phone number and got a recording saying it was no longer in service. He let it play out in hopes something might register on the software, but Dillon only gave a short shake of his head.

"Okay, on to the next," he murmured under his breath.

Brady dialed the third and final phone number, and they all waited as it rang and rang. At last, the voice mail kicked in and they let the recording run on as long as they could.

Behind him, Dillon rapped sharply on the desk three times. Brady disconnected the call and whirled. "You get something?" he demanded.

Dillon scribbled a couple of things on a notepad, then began typing furiously on his computer keyboard. "White Feather, Idaho. Getting the GPS coordinates. I'll get the address and see if I can send the sheriff out to the location."

Cassie slowly lowered her hand. "Oh, my God. It *is* him," she said, her voice throaty with disbelief.

When she looked at Brady, her expression was a mixture of hope and fear so potent, he felt both viscerally.

"I don't think he'd hurt them," she said in a whisper. "He's not a violent man. At least I don't think he is. Mark could get out of control, so I was attuned to the signs, and I never saw anything violent in Keith," she said, almost to reassure him more than herself.

But Brady was fixated on what she said about her ex-husband. "What do you mean Mark could get out of control?"

Cassie closed her eyes, drew in a deep breath, then exhaled slowly. "He pushed me around... Never punched me or anything, but there were a couple of times he shoved me into things—furniture, doors, whatever. He drank too much. One night we were having a fight and Brook came out of her room. We'd woken her. He pushed her aside... hard..." She stopped on a tangled sob.

"Take your time," he said in his most soothing tone. He nudged the bottle of water closer to her, and Cassie reached out and grabbed it like a lifeline. Brady watched as she unscrewed the cap with trembling hands, took a small sip and then carefully replaced the cap.

"He shoved her into a wall and I lost my mind. I went at him, kicking and screaming and throwing punches until he finally fell. Then I pulled my daddy's old hunting rifle from the closet and told him I'd load it and unload into him if he ever touched one of my children again."

"Take a sip," he urged, his tone low and soothing.

She did as he suggested, then blew out a breath. "I packed the girls, the gun, and left. I can still hear him standing in the driveway yelling about how I'd be crawling to him by the next morning. I'd never be able to make it without him…blah, blah, blah." She wet her lips, then met Brady's gaze steadily. "I did. We never went home again. No one hurts my girls."

"I have no doubt."

Chapter Eight

He said it with such quiet certainty, Cassie found she had no room for disbelief. Which was good. She spent far too long doubting herself and her ability to be a good mother to her girls. And though some could argue her current predicament might indicate she wasn't exactly mother of the year, Cassie refused to accept the blame for somebody else's actions. Being married to an abusive alcoholic had taught her a thing or two about personal responsibility. She was not going to blame herself for this situation.

"What do we do now?" she asked, sounding considerably steadier than she felt on the inside.

"Dillon's going to call the sheriff's department and have them do a drive-by to see if they can get anyone who has seen Keith in the area. I'm gonna need you to give me as good a physical description as you possibly can."

Cassie barked a laugh. "I can do better."

Snatching her phone again, she scrolled through her photos until she came across the one Keith had insisted they take together. They'd had dinner at a popular local restaurant, and then had gone for a walk after sharing a dessert. She'd been startled when he stopped another couple on the sidewalk and asked the woman to snap their picture, but she hadn't objected. The gesture had seemed impulsive and romantic. Until the woman had handed his phone to him and Keith had expertly enhanced and cropped the photo with a few taps of the screen. He'd texted it to her and urged her to save it to her camera roll. She did, then promptly forgotten about it until now.

Brook and Jilly had had a dance recital the following weekend, and the photo of her and Keith was soon swallowed by dozens of shots of her daughters dressed in cowgirl costumes and sparkling with glitter.

Brady eyeballed the photo. "This is helpful." He tapped the phone screen and quickly sent the photo to his own phone. Then he clicked his pen once more. "I'm guessing from the photo about five-eleven or six feet?" he asked, all business once again.

"I'm five-seven, so I'm going to say somewhere closer to five-ten or five-eleven. I don't think he was over six feet tall."

Brady scribbled it down. "Build?"

Cassie winced. She and Keith had been intimate exactly twice, but given the current context, it was hard to imagine she was describing the same man. He'd seemed so...normal. Forcing herself to focus on recounting facts as she knew them, she drew a deep breath and said, "Lean, somewhat muscular, but not bulky. He was a runner. Kept talking about training for a triathlon, but I don't think he's ever gotten far. It was all talk. A lot of things with Keith were all talk."

"A shade under six foot, lean build but not skinny," Brady repeated. "Any distinguishing marks, tattoos, scars, anything notable?"

She shook her head. "No. He was a pretty average-looking guy. Handsome enough. Looked like a guy out of sitcom central casting for nice-guy-slash-dentist-or-doctor. Brown hair, brownish eyes, not too fair, not too tan. Everything about him was sort of medium," she concluded.

"What about how he dressed? Anything unusual there?

Did he wear a hat? Was he a ball cap guy or one of those who fancied himself a cowboy?"

She shook her head. "No hats. Didn't like to have his hair messed."

"Got it." Brady clicked his pen, then tapped the tablet. Turning to look her directly in the eye, he said "You've done well here. You've given us far more information than most people can. We have a lot to go on."

She knew his words were meant to comfort her. It was a compliment. A pat on the head meant to reassure her, but his kindness only made her previous choices seem worse. What kind of woman needed to keep a dossier on a man she dated for barely two months?

The kind who'd been through the wringer with another man.

"I got an address and sent it on to the sheriff's department," Dillon called out from behind him. He rose from his desk, and Bentley rose as well. "We're going to head home, but as soon as I get any word from the sheriff, I'll relay it to Brady and he can pass it along to you." He and Bentley walked over to Brady's desk, where the two dogs exchanged a sniff.

Brady extended a hand to his friend. "Appreciate your help, man."

Dillon raised a hand. "Anytime." He checked his watch. "See you at about five thirty?" he asked.

"I'll be by about five fifteen," Brady informed him. "It should be getting light by five forty-five. I want to be at the road when it does."

Dillon extended his hand to Cassie. Shocked, she took it and gave it a firm shake, but to her surprise, Dillon covered hers with his other hand, enveloping her in a warm grip.

"I'm not going to tell you not to worry because I don't believe in asking for the impossible. I *am* going to tell you we will not stop—" he tipped his head toward Brady and then looked down at the dogs at their feet "—until we find your girls. And we will."

Cassie drew her hand away slowly, and curled it into a fist over her heart. "Thank you."

Dillon stepped away. "Call you as soon as I hear anything on the ex," he said in parting.

The door closed behind him, and Cassie became hyperaware she was alone with Brady Nichols. She fidgeted in her seat, and Winnie scrambled onto her front paws, her expression concerned as she leaned into Cassie once more. "Wow, she *is* intuitive, isn't she?" she said with a laugh.

"When Emma was training her, it was a tough call to decide whether she'd be better off doing search and rescue or counseling and emotional support."

"She seems to be a pro at both."

Brady chuckled. "Winnie is a dog of many talents. Not only is she a search and rescue expert, and a part-time empath, but she also excels in devouring enormous dog bones and has occasionally gnawed on large pieces of furniture."

"Large pieces of furniture?" she asked, brows raised.

He shrugged. "I never liked the couch anyway."

Cassie laughed out loud, and the sound startled her so much she had to cover her mouth with her hand. Winnie lifted a paw in silent plea for some attention. Shaking her head, Cassie leaned forward and used both hands to stroke the fur over the dog's head and down her neck. "Am I comforting her or is she comforting me?" she asked him in a low, amused tone.

"Whatever works," Brady told her.

"She's wonderful," she murmured as she hugged the dog again.

"You'd be questioning your assessment if she ate your couch," he said dryly. "We should all get home. We have a busy morning coming."

"Aren't we gonna wait until we hear from the sheriff?"

"My number is in your phone. I will text you as soon as I get any news, but we all have to get what rest we can. Tomorrow's going to be a busy day."

Cassie stood, but she didn't reach for her bag. "I don't want to go home without them." It was the truth, though she was embarrassed to have blurted it out. She could not imagine walking into her house without Brook and Jilly by her side.

"Is there anywhere else you can stay tonight?"

"Aunt Vera said I could stay there," she said, gathering her bag, relieved to have decided at last.

She pulled her keys from the depths of her purse. When she met his gaze again, she felt something settle deep inside her. She wanted to say more, but she wasn't sure what. Jingling her keys in her palm, she glanced at him, needing one last dose of reassurance. "You'll call?"

He inclined his head. "The second I hear anything."

"Thank you. Good night."

She stepped outside and a brisk breeze cut through her thin summer clothes. She ducked her head and climbed into her van, her limbs feeling like they were filled with wet cement. Cool moisture streaked from her eyes. Dashing the tears away, she tossed her bag onto the passenger seat and tried to ignore the sickly sweet scent of juice spilled onto the carpet. She started the engine, but her phone chimed.

She thrust her hand into the outer pocket of the bag and fumbled until she could get the text to open.

Sheriff's dept rpts no one home at addr, no vehicle. ?ing neighbors with the help of your pic. Try to sleep.

Try to sleep. The last part made her want to snort, but it caught on a sob. Brady Nichols could walk out of the building any second now, so she typed only a brief reply in thanks, then threw the van into Reverse and swung out of the spot. He'd seen her cry enough for one night. As she pulled out of the parking lot, she vowed she'd hold herself together better tomorrow. Poor Winnie had a job to do, and she wouldn't be able to help find her girls if she had a distraught mother crying into her soft fur.

After hooking a right and pointing the van toward her aunt and uncle's house, Cassie decided to rethink her stance on getting a dog for the girls.

Chapter Nine

Cassie parked in front of her aunt and uncle's house and entered through the kitchen door, which, as usual, they'd left unlocked. Frowning, she twisted the dead bolt. It was stiff from disuse and didn't align correctly, but she threw a hip against the door and the bolt slid home.

The house was cloaked in darkness, save for the light above the stove. She'd closed the door as quietly as she could, hoping she wouldn't disturb her aunt and uncle's sleep. They rose at four thirty each morning to start preparing the diner for the breakfast rush, and the last thing she wanted to do was cut into their rest.

Leaving the light on, she tiptoed through the kitchen to the hall, but a voice from the darkened living room stopped her in her tracks.

"I take it there's no news?"

Cassie jumped and whirled, pressing her hand flat to her chest to hold her thumping heart inside her rib cage. She squinted into the darkness and saw Aunt Vera seated on the worn sofa, her hands wrapped around a mug. "Oh, my goodness, you scared me," she said in a rush.

"Sorry, baby girl."

The endearment, the same one the usually no-nonsense Vera used for her great-nieces, made a lump the size of her fist lodge at the base of Cassie's throat.

She swallowed hard. "I'm sorry. I thought you'd be in bed, and I was trying to be quiet."

"Who can sleep?" Vera replied gruffly.

Cassie stepped into the darkened room. "Hopefully Millard?" Cassie said tiredly. Her uncle was a good man, a kind man, but he guarded his sleep jealously and was notoriously cranky if he didn't get at least seven hours in the sack.

The corners of Vera's mouth twitched as she patted the cushion beside her in invitation. "He's in there sawing logs."

"Good." Cassie lowered herself to the sofa beside her aunt, and to her surprise, Vera stretched an arm around her, gently urging Cassie to lean into her. Too tired to resist getting what comfort was offered, she toppled over until her head rested on Vera's lap.

"No, there's no news," she whispered, nearly choking on the words. "They're trying to locate Mark but not having any luck."

Vera snorted. "Mark. He'd never stir himself enough to help himself to his children," she said disdainfully. She reached over and placed the mug on the end table. "I'll tell you who I'm worried about—it's that Keith fella," her aunt insisted. "I told the chief he was the one they need to be looking for when we were at Emma's place, but I don't think he was paying me any mind."

Cassie sniffled but had to stifle a laugh at the thought of her opinionated and outspoken aunt being ignored. Vera didn't mince words, but most of the residents of Jasper were used to her bluntness.

"I agree. I told Officer Nichols all about Keith, and I'm pretty sure they're going to focus in on him too, but they have to make sure Mark is in the clear first since he's their father."

Vera shook her head, her expression mournful. "It's a sad, sorry day when folks can't let their kids run around here in Jasper. You expect to hear about things like this happening in the big city. Heck, I thought even Boise was fairly safe, but now…"

"It happens everywhere," Cassie said, hoarse with fatigue and emotion.

The two women fell silent. Vera ran a hand over Cassie's hair. The gesture was another surprise in an evening chock-full of them. Vera was awkward and self-conscious with her affections, which, to Cassie's mind, made them even more endearing.

"You want a cup of tea? Something to help you sleep?" her aunt offered.

Cassie drew in a steadying breath. "No, thank you. Tea will only make me jittery." She forced herself to sit on her own, freeing her aunt of her weight. "You should try to get some sleep. I think I'm going to lie down and wait for the dawn."

Vera hoisted herself from her seat with a groan. "There are clean sheets on the spare bed. At least try to close your eyes. You'll want them well rested so you can help look for your girls," she said with a nod. "Folks will be out early. Millard and I will keep everybody fueled from the diner. Aside from the official search, a few of the guides from the outfitters are going to lead small groups on the hiking trails."

Cassie swallowed past the tightness in her chest. "I appreciate everyone's help."

"It's what folks around here do. We look out for each other," Vera said briskly. "You're one of ours, whether you've been living here your whole life or not. We're going to find your girls, and we're going to bring them home."

Vera placed a hard peck of a kiss to the top of Cassie's head, then shuffled toward the hall. "Now, get to bed," she ordered.

Cassie's heart thudded as she listened to her aunt's shuffling steps. She sat on the sofa for a few minutes more, simply staring into the middle distance and allowing the quiet of the house to close in around her. Thank goodness she didn't have to go home. Her grandparents' house, the house she shared with her girls, would be an entirely different sort of quiet, and it wasn't one Cassie thought she could handle.

Heeding her aunt's advice, she forced herself to rise and head down the hall as well. True to form, the guest room was neat as a pin. The wedding-ring-patterned quilt had been folded down, and faded floral sheets awaited her. Cassie stripped off the clothes she'd been wearing all day and slid between them in nothing more than her underwear. The pillowcase smelled like fabric softener and sunshine. Clutching the spare pillow to her chest, she rolled onto her side and allowed silent, shuddering tears to flow.

She must have cried herself to sleep because the next thing she knew, gray light filled the room and someone was knocking on the front door.

Startled, she sprang from the bed. She didn't bother to dress. Her heart hammering, she yanked the quilt free and wrapped it around her. Holding the bundle of covers closed at her throat, she hurried toward the door. Out of habit, she checked through the sidelight first. Brady Nichols stood on the top step wearing dark tactical gear, sturdy black boots and a vest identifying him as a member of the Jasper PD. No jeans or T-shirt in sight. She fumbled to open the single lock charged with holding the big, bad world at bay.

She yanked open the door. "Have you heard anything?" she demanded in a rush of breath.

Brady's eyes widened when he took in her state of undress. But to his credit, he fixed his gaze directly on her forehead as he shook his head.

"Nothing about the girls. I was coming to tell you your ex-husband has been located. He spent the night as a guest of the Billings Police Department. We got the confirmation this morning. They've been holding him for drunk and disorderly conduct."

"No shock there," Cassie muttered.

"Norton has been bumped to number one on our list, but we need you to try to think if there's anyone else we should be looking at."

She shook her head. "No, there's no one else. And he's here in Idaho. What more do you need to convince you?"

"It's not a matter of convincing anyone. I want to be sure we're covering all the bases. I spoke to Dillon and they've found a vehicle they believe may be Norton's truck. They're running the plates now."

"His truck? Keith drives a car. A sedan," she said, her brow furrowing in confusion.

"There's a truck with a Montana temporary tag parked near the old ranger station. We're heading out there now."

Cassie blinked. "What do you mean heading out now? Without me?" She stared at him in bafflement. It never occurred to her the search would go on without her being there.

"It's better if you stay here. We can move faster without civilians on-site," he said, meeting her eyes.

"I'm not a civilian. I'm their mother."

"I'm aware, but—"

"No. No, you're not going out there without me." Leaving the front door wide-open, she backed into the house and took off at a run. In her haste, she let the quilt drop as she headed down the hallway, uncaring whether she'd flashed Officer Nichols or not. In the spare room, she yanked on her clothing. "Don't you dare leave without me," she shouted, then grimaced.

A glance at the clock by the bed told her Millard and Vera were likely already gone. She said a quick prayer of thanks for small favors and pulled her shirt over her head. Shoes dangling from her fingers, she finger-combed the snarls from her hair with her free hand as she headed for the front door. "I am their mama. I'm the one who they're gonna want to see the minute you find them."

Brady had stepped inside and allowed the screen door to close behind him. "No doubt. But I thought I would call you once we found any sign—"

Cassie charged straight at him. She'd go through him if she had to. She was getting in his car. "No, sir. I'm going."

He deftly sidestepped her in the nick of time. "Listen, I understand—"

"Pull the door closed behind you," she called over her shoulder. "Millard and Vera will have already left for the diner, and I can't leave their house standing wide-open."

"Ms. Whitaker, I can't—"

"I think we're on a first-name basis now, don't you?" She headed for the passenger side of the officially marked K-9 unit he was driving and reached for the door handle. "Is Winnie in back?" she called out to him.

Brady pulled the front door closed and hurried down the concrete steps, the screen door slamming hard as he came after her. "Yes, but you can't climb in and ride along. This is an official investigation."

"And I'm officially their mama, and I'm not letting this go on without me being there. Period. Now, we can stand here and argue until the sun rises and sets again, but the clock is ticking." She opened the door, tossed her shoes inside, then jumped in after them, slamming the door on Brady's protests.

Chapter Ten

This had disaster written all over it. Brady drove toward
the fire lane where they'd lost the trail the previous night
with his jaw set. Dillon had called to say he was already on
his way with Bentley. Cal Hoover and his dog, Ruby, were
coming too. The chief had texted a heads-up that the FBI
field office in Boise had been notified of the abduction.
The ticking clock in his head grew louder. If he and Winnie wanted to be in on the search and rescue, he didn't have
daylight to waste arguing with the mother of the victims.

But boy, was he gonna hear it from the guys.

"You didn't want to bring me, but I can't sit there and
wait," she said, breaking the taut silence.

"It's not a matter of what I want," Brady explained.
"There are procedures I have to follow." He drummed his
fingers on the steering wheel, already anticipating the ribbing coming his way. But then, maybe he could mitigate
some of it by keeping her out of sight. "When we get there,
you have to stay in the vehicle. Our dogs are trained, but we
want to give them as few mixed signals as we possibly can.
Having you out there will add another scent to the mix."

"I'm not going to do anything to jeopardize your search
for my daughters," she said stiffly. "But if you think I'm
going to sit home waiting for you to call, you've lost your
mind."

"Yes, you've made your stance abundantly clear," Brady

answered in the same tone. "My primary concern is to keep the search area pristine. We have a new possible point of entry. If you go running willy-nilly into our search, it's only going to complicate matters."

"I've never run willy-nilly in my entire life," she replied tartly.

"Okay." He glanced at her again. "As long as you understand there are reasons I can't let you go traipsing off into the hills. There's a methodology to doing what we do. I want to be clear."

"Crystal clear," she said.

Brady pulled off the main highway onto the dirt lane leading into the foothills. He turned onto the fire lane, but ascended about a mile farther into the woods. The road widened slightly when the old ranger station came into view. He lifted his foot from the accelerator and allowed the tires to roll to a grumbling halt behind a pickup truck parked in the center of the lane.

"Montana temporary tag," she whispered.

Anxious to keep her focused until their backup arrived, he parked the SUV at an angle, effectively blocking the pickup in. "Have you ever seen this truck?"

She shook her head hard. "No. Never."

"Keith Norton does not own a truck?"

"Not that I'm aware of, but this one is obviously used," she said, gesturing to the vehicle. "Keith is a dentist. He makes a good living. He could easily afford to buy a used truck."

"Probably in cash," Brady murmured. "Tell me more about him. You said he's a runner. Does he hunt? Camp?"

She wagged her head hard. "No. God no. The opposite." The corner of her mouth lifted in a disdainful smirk. "He's a city guy. Not at all outdoorsy. I wanted to go for a hike when we were first seeing each other. I picked a supereasy trail, thinking it would be nice to walk and talk. All he did was complain."

"Complain about what?"

"The heat, the bugs, the dirt—" she waved a dismissive hand "—all of it." She paused when she caught sight of the rugged terrain beyond the small cabin. "He isn't the kind of guy who likes to get mussed."

"So sleeping out of doors—"

"I can't imagine he would."

"He never returned to the house in White Feather. The county sheriff had an eye on it all night."

"Maybe they slept in the truck?" she hazarded. "I should go look, see if there's any trace of the girls—" Cassie reached for her door handle, and he placed a staying hand on her arm. "No, ma'am. You stay in the vehicle, remember? Those are my conditions," he said, holding her belligerent gaze.

"Brady—"

"No. We wait for backup before we approach the vehicle, then you wait in here. If you can't agree to my terms, I will turn around, drive you to town and dump you there."

They glared at one another.

"Cassie, I need you to work with me here. Stay in the car. I promise you as soon as there's anything to tell, you will be told."

Their intense stare-down lasted a few more seconds. The sound of vehicles approaching snared her attention. She watched wide-eyed as three other vehicles—marked and unmarked—maneuvered around them to block the truck in from every possible angle. Finally, she acquiesced with a nod.

"You better have my contact information open on your phone and saved to your favorites," she warned. "We're talking speed dial ready. You get me?"

He reached for his own door handle, not allowing himself to dwell too long on the way she said his name. "Trust us. I promise you Winnie and I want to find them every bit as much as you do."

He closed the driver's door and moved to the lift gate of the SUV. He saw her turn in her seat, her eyes glued to him as he unhooked Winnie's restraint.

"Tell her we're gonna find her girls," he ordered the dog.

Winnie let out a low woof, and Brady was pretty sure he heard a soft sob escape Cassie when he slammed the lift gate closed.

THEY WERE TWO HOURS in and at least a mile from the cabin when the hairs on Brady's neck prickled. He stilled, and Winnie paused too. She lifted her nose from the mulchy ground and sniffed the air, her ears flicking forward as she caught something of interest on the wind.

"I feel it too," he said, speaking softly to his partner. "I think they were near here, don't you, girl?"

Winnie sniffed some more, her snout raised high and her forehead wrinkled in concentration. Brady didn't interfere. He didn't rush her or do anything more than stand by her side. He had all the faith in the world in this dog. Suddenly, Winnie jerked to the right and took off into the underbrush, straining at her lead. With a practiced flick of his thumb, Brady untethered the dog, allowing her to follow her nose at her own pace.

Fighting his way through the ever-thickening underbrush, he kept his attention fixed directly ahead of him. Barely three minutes passed when a sharp bark cut through the sound of his own labored breathing.

The radio affixed to his collar crackled, and Chief Walters asked, "Was that Winnie?"

Brady keyed the microphone. "Ten-four. She's onto something."

A burst of static came across, then Dillon's call came

through. "Ping your current location so we can tighten the scope."

Brady did as his friend suggested, relaying his approximate position to the satellites orbiting the earth while he moved steadily in the direction of his dog's increasingly agitated barks.

"You get me?" he asked into the mic.

A second later, his fellow lieutenant, Cal Hoover, replied, "I have you."

"Ten-four," Dillon chimed in.

Brady checked his compass. "Winnie is heading almost due west. There's a bluff ahead, so I'm not sure what she—" He paused when he burst through a clump of undergrowth and saw his dog barking at the jagged rocks. About seven feet above the clearing, there looked to be a small crevice in the rock formation. Winnie's gaze was fixed on it with level-five Labrador intensity.

"There's a cave," he spoke the words quietly into his mic.

"Await backup," the chief ordered.

If asked, Brady would say he couldn't hear the man over the ruckus his dog was making. But if they found the Whitaker girls, the chief wouldn't ask too many questions. He was good about looking the other way when it was expedient.

Lowering his hand, he snapped his fingers once. Winnie toned her barking down to a stream of steady woofs. If there was anyone there, her barking would have already sent them deeper into the crevice or flushed them out, but he didn't want her to stop entirely. His team would use her barks as a beacon.

Climbing over the smaller boulders at the base of the rock face, he groped for a handhold. Five minutes and a few curses later, he leveraged himself high enough to peek over the ledge into the cave. There, he saw a small white sock, a pink elastic hair band and nothing more than a few footprints in the dust covering the rock.

"Crap."

He braced an elbow on the ledge and made a grab for the bits one of the girls had left behind. Jilly, he guessed, judging by the size of the sock and a heart-squeezing flash of memory. She'd had her long blond hair in two of these ponytail holders. And, presumably, she'd had two socks on as well, but he couldn't swear under oath.

Something wasn't adding up for him. For the life of him, Brady could not figure out exactly what the end game was. If he were going to kidnap a couple of kids, he would have hightailed it to the highway, not driven deeper into the wilderness. His gut told him Brook and Jilly were not who Norton—if it was indeed Cassie's former boyfriend— was after. Did he still have them, or had the jerk dumped the girls out here? What if he was camped out at Cassie's house while they were here searching?

A surge of hot panic shot through him as he climbed down onto the jagged rocks. Breathless, he pressed the button on his mic. "Does someone have eyes on Cassie Whitaker?"

A second later, Chief Walters's laconic drawl came through loud and clear. "You mean the civilian you have riding shotgun in your official vehicle, Lieutenant Nichols? Yes, I do."

Brady didn't have the inclination to be embarrassed by the subtle dressing-down. "Yes, sir. Keep tabs on her, will you? I don't think the kids are the end game here."

"What have you found, Nichols?" the chief asked, as Cal Hoover burst out of the woods, his dog, Ruby, at his side.

Brady held the sock and the hair tie, glanced at the cave one last time, then gave his head a shake to indicate the place was empty. Pulling the microphone from his shoulder, he spoke directly into it. "Sir, I have evidence they were in a cave on the northeast side of the outcropping, but nothing more at this time."

"I have an ETA of thirteen hundred from the federal agents," the chief informed him gruffly.

"Ten-four. We'll keep going until relieved," Brady replied. Or until they found the girls.

"I have an eye on things here," Chief Walters assured him.

"From the footprints I could see, it appears they are on the move," he reported.

"Then you get moving too. I'd like to put the lady's mind at ease. Once the Feds get here, she'll have to start this whole process over again."

"Ten-four. Me too, sir."

He crouched in front of Winnie and stared into the Lab's amber eyes until he was sure he held her full attention. Then he offered the sock for her to sniff. "Here, girl. Find," he commanded.

Winnie put her head down and paced the area in a slow, methodical circle. Brady watched her carefully, then offered a sniff of his findings to Cal's dog, Ruby. The German shepherd hadn't had time to take a good snort, when Winnie whipped her head to the right, barked twice and bounded into the woods again.

But this time, she was heading away from the mountain.

Chapter Eleven

Cassie appreciated the steadying presence of Chief Walters, but… She shot him a sidelong glance. "There's something they aren't telling me, isn't there?"

"There are likely a lot of things we aren't telling you, ma'am," the chief replied. He smoothed the rough edges of the comment away with a kindly pat on the arm. "Those are my best people. If they can't find them, the Feds are coming right behind with *their* best people. We're doing everything we can possibly do to get those girls home safe."

"I don't doubt it, Chief," Cassie said in a rush. "I feel so… I'm a mom," she said, holding her hands out in help-less futility. "I'm the one who does things. I'm not the one who waits."

He gave a brief nod. "They're on the right track. Believe me."

Chief Walters was right: she had to trust Brady would come through for her. Brady was the man who'd listened to her chronicle her pathetic excuse of a love life without batting a judgmental eyelash. Brady offered her reassurances and had spoken so gently and patiently with her girls. Until they moved to Jasper, Jilly and Brook hadn't had many good interactions with men outside of a school setting. They were just warming to her uncle, and Millard was one of the mildest men she'd ever met. Biting her lip, she paced the length of the SUV. Brady had been the first man she'd ever seen them approach without trepidation. But, of course, Winnie had been the real draw there.

She'd once been close to her father and enjoyed her uncle's company, but after what she'd been through with Mark, it was difficult not to be guarded. Perhaps she hadn't given Keith the chance he thought he deserved, but she had to go with her gut instinct when it came to who she allowed near her children. And her gut had told her Keith wasn't the kind of man they could trust.

But Brady Nichols might be. Brady was calm and steady… What would it be like to be with someone whose mood she didn't have to gauge constantly? Her relationship with Mark had been explosive from the start. She'd been young and mistook their pent-up energy for passion. She didn't realize he was simply an angry, disappointed man until it was too late. And Keith, a man who had every reason to be content with his life, seemed to always be grasping. He wanted more than she could give him, and when she refused, he decided to take it.

A burst of radio static interrupted her thoughts, and she whirled to face the older man. He had been careful to keep his communications with his team away from her, but she'd heard Dillon's excited report: "Winnie's got something. Brady and Cal are tracking her. Bentley has an injured paw. We're heading to base."

"I'll radio Jenny and ask her to call Dr. Beaumont or Tashya to meet us here and take a look at Bentley. Easy does it heading in."

"What? What does Winnie have?" Cassie demanded when he finished transmitting the call.

"I have no idea," Chief Walters replied calmly.

He glanced down at his phone, and she saw two blue dots moving across the screen from left to right. "Is it them?" she demanded. "Where is she headed? Are they coming this way or are they moving away from us?" she asked, peering over his arm.

"The dots are Cal and Brady," he corrected. "Winnie and Ruby are out in front of them."

"What did he mean Winnie had something?"

"They are heading slightly closer, but mostly east, which is good. The terrain is much easier."

"East of the mountain? Toward the river?"

"Not far," he said gruffly. "But in the general direction. Excuse me, I need to make a call," he said, then stepped away, giving her his back to make it clear he wouldn't be answering any more questions.

Cassie twisted her fingers into a cat's cradle of worry, but stuck close to the chief as he radioed dispatch to put in the call for veterinary services.

"Nichols, what's your status?"

A tense minute passed, but at last Brady's breathless reply came with a crackle of static. "In pursuit, sir. Wish I had four legs and about half my height. Winnie's plowing through like a brush cutter."

"Keep us updated."

Cassie moved closer to the chief, heedless of allowing the man any personal space as they watched the dots moving across the screen, then head toward the bottom.

"Coming this way," he murmured. "Bet they're following Spring Creek."

"Spring Creek?" Cassie repeated, trying to conjure the area maps she'd been studying in preparation for her job as a guide for Blaze's River Tours and Rafting. "It feeds into the Salmon River, right?"

He nodded. "Most creeks in this area do. Spring is mostly fed by snowmelt. It's summer now, so it shouldn't be much more than a few inches deep, but since it's on the northeast side of the hills, it stays wet most of the year."

A crackle of static erupted from his radio, but then nothing followed.

"Should they be done this soon? What does it mean if they're heading in? Do the dogs need to rest or something?" She paced as she fired question after question at the man. "I mean, they'd radio if they'd found them, so this is probably not good news, right?"

"They aren't necessarily headed for base," the chief told her, but he kept his gaze locked on the screen.

Minutes passed, tense and silent. Then they saw the blue dots pause in one spot and hover. "What does it mean when they aren't moving?" she demanded.

"Could be they found something. Could be a waterbreak," he answered tiredly. Then he stabbed at the screen with one blunt fingertip. "Diaz is almost here. We'll see what he has to say." They both swiveled in the direction Dillon's dot indicated, but he didn't appear. When she leaned in closer to peer at the phone, he stepped away and shot her a warning glance. "Get any closer, and people will start to talk."

"Sorry," she whispered. Cassie forced herself to close her eyes and draw a deep breath. "I'm sorry," she repeated, feeling marginally calmer. "It's been hours."

He gave her shoulder a none-too-gentle pat. "There's a lot of ground to cover. Believe me, you want them to be as thorough as possible."

"I'm sorry. I'm…" she trailed off, completely at a loss to explain her emotional state.

"Keyed up," he provided. "Like I told you, they are the best," he said reassuringly.

"I appreciate everything you all are doing. I hope you know I do," she hastened to add.

"It's our job, ma'am, but even if it weren't we'd be out there. We're going to find your girls." He frowned at the blue dot representing Dillon Diaz. "Diaz should have been here by now. Sometimes, the GPS can lag out here," he explained. "Hard to get an exact bead on them."

Static came through the speaker again, but once more only silence followed. The crunch of gravel and dirt announced the arrival of another vehicle. Parked behind the others, Tashya Pratt climbed out of a Jeep, a jam-packed duffel bag with a veterinary caduceus emblazoned on the side.

"I hear Bentley is hurt," she called to them as she approached, her long legs eating ground. "Doc Beaumont had an emergency at the clinic, but I can help."

Seconds later, Dillon crashed through the brush behind them, his dog, Bentley, cradled in his arms. "Here," Dillon gasped. "And remind me to buy him the diet dog food," he said, sagging as he came toward them with the fluffy Australian shepherd.

Tashya returned Bentley's good-natured doggy grin. "He's not a bit overweight, are you, B.?" she cooed as Dillon deposited the dog on the open tailgate of the nearest JPD vehicle. "No, you are perfect, aren't you, boy?" she said, her hands moving over the fluffy dog.

Cassie watched as the young woman confidently checked the dog from head to tail.

"It's his right front paw," Dillon said. "Cut on a sharp rock, but possibly sprained or a broken bone."

"I will get to his paws," Tashya said in a singsong tone. She stroked her hands down Bentley's hip and cooed encouragingly to the panting dog. "Give a man a dog, and he thinks he's a vet tech," she teased.

"I know my dog," Dillon grumbled, but gave Tashya the room she needed to go through her routine.

When she did get to the Aussie's right front paw, Bentley gave a sharp yelp to indicate his partner hadn't been wrong. Cassie found herself wanting to add her own soothing coos to Tashya's, but a barrage of insistent barking filled the air.

Dillon's head swiveled. "That's Ruby," he said, spinning in the direction of the barking.

Chief Walters looked down at his phone and then gave it a frustrated shake. "GPS must have been frozen."

"It's not a magic eight ball, Chief," Dillon said, smirking at his boss's insistent shaking.

Before either of the men could stop her, Cassie stumbled out from behind the vehicle and took off in the direction of Ruby's barks.

"Ma'am—" the chief called after her.

"Cassie," Dillon shouted.

Shaking her head in refusal to heed their warnings, she stumbled over rocks and roots, then paused when she heard movement to her left, but all she saw was a flash of light blue that was quickly swallowed by the greenery surrounding her.

She plowed headlong into the brush, heedless of the branches and twigs tearing at her clothing. They found them. Cassie knew it in her gut. She knew it in her heart. She knew her daughters were with Cal and Brady and their dogs, and she wasn't going to wait one second longer to see their faces.

Another short burst of barking made her course correct a little to her right, and she shouted with all her might. "Brooklyn! Jillian!" She knew her babies probably couldn't hear her, but she needed to say their names aloud.

Another round of barking ensued, these ones deeper, more growly and not as sharp as the others. It had to be Winnie.

Something surged through the dense growth behind her, and she jumped and whirled. Dillon Diaz glared at her in disbelief. "You can't go running off into a search scene," he chastised.

"They've got them. I can feel it. I need to get to my

girls," she insisted as she took a step away from the glowering officer.

"They've got them, but whoever took them could get you," Dillon argued.

Winnie barked again, and when Cassie swung her head in that direction, she saw two dark-clad figures moving through the woods.

"The GPS and the radio relay were sketchy where they were at," Dillon explained. "Brady's report came through the second after you took off."

Cassie barely heard a word of Dillon's explanation. Frankly, she didn't care. All she wanted to hear was her children's voices. "Brooklyn! Jillian!" she cried again.

"Mommy! Mama!" the girls chorused in reply.

When their voices touched her ears, she crumpled to the soft leaf-mulched ground. "Oh, my God," she whispered. "Oh, thank God."

Behind her, Dillon let out a sharp whistle, and seconds later the two men appeared, each holding a dirt-smudged blonde. Jilly clung to Brady's neck like a koala, but more surprisingly, Brook had abandoned her usual reserve in favor of snuggling Cal. She lifted her head from his shoulder as they came into a small clearing.

"Mommy," she croaked.

Cassie stumbled to her feet and ran toward them. "Are you hurt? Are they hurt?" she demanded, looking from the girls to the men. "Oh, my poor babies," she said in a rush. She pressed a kiss first to Jilly's forehead, then to Brook's. Her elder daughter didn't shy away from the affection as she had so often lately, which troubled Cassie almost as much as it thrilled her. Both girls lunged for her, nearly toppling Cassie, Brady and Cal to the ground in their exuberance.

Jilly slipped into her arms and Cal adjusted his hold on Brook enough to allow her to lean in close. Cassie couldn't stop squeezing them both, needing to confirm they were real and not some wishful thinking she'd conjured.

"Mommy, Winnie and Ruby finded us," Jilly reported, nearly shouting in her excitement. Her daughter glanced over at the dogs standing beside their partners, hero worship written all over her face. "We were by the river and they found us," she continued. Then she wrinkled her freckled nose. "Winnie and Ruby had to sniff my sock. So gross!"

"Your socks are gross," Brook inserted weakly.

"Your socks are perfect. Beautiful." Cassie swiveled her head from one girl to the other, pressing fervent kisses to their grubby cheeks.

From behind her, Brady said, "They both appear to be unharmed, but they were out all night, so we should get them to the hospital for a thorough checkup. They stayed in the cave where I found Jilly's stuff. Brook says Norton took off this morning and never came back."

"I dinnent like him," Jilly announced.

"Me either," Brook chimed in,

"He said I talked too much. Brady's my boyfriend," Jilly said, gazing over at the surprised man adoringly. "He doesn't think I talk too much. I'm gonna marry him and live with Winnie. Brookie can marry Cal."

"I'm already married." Cal chuckled as he shifted Brook's weight. "Besides, I suspect you ladies might only want us for our dogs," he said dejectedly.

Serious as ever, Brook shook her head. "We can be friends," she said solemnly.

Cal beamed at the girl in his arms. "I'd like to be your friend, Miss Brooklyn. Now, let's get you down to one of the cars so your mama can have a good look at you." Cassie babbled her thanks as she followed them, but Cal brushed her gratitude off.

"It's our job, ma'am." Cal answered with a good-natured

smile. They all pushed their way through the trees to get to the lane.

Brady jiggled Jilly to get her attention again as he passed the abandoned pickup, his gazed fixed on the chief's car, which was parked in the rear and off to the side. "If you ask real nice, I bet Chief Walters will put the swirling lights on when he drives you into town."

Confident her eldest was in good hands, Cassie quick-stepped to keep up with them. She gasped when Brady halted suddenly and she found herself standing too close. She looked into his warm brown eyes, but failed to find words good enough to express her thanks.

"Brady, I—"

Wordlessly, he shook his head, then took Jilly from her. "Let's get them to the ER so the docs can have a look. I'll follow you down, and fill you in on what we found." Brady caught Chief Walters's eye. "Sir? Can we get someone here to watch this truck? We couldn't find any signs of Norton, but the girls confirmed he was the one who took them from the party."

The older man reached for his radio. "I'll call down and get the rookie—uh, I mean Jason—to come this way to surveil the truck. Dillon's going to follow Tashya to the veterinary clinic."

"Looks like it's a cut on his paw," she called out to the group. "But I want to get an X-ray to be certain there's no break."

"Thanks, Chief. Cal's going to start the report. I'll be in to add to it once I get statements from Cassie and the girls."

"Sounds like we have a plan." Chief Walters raised a hand and waved it in a circle. "Saddle up. We need to get everyone seen to, and I need to let those federal agents know the girls have been found."

Chapter Twelve

The doctors wanted to keep the girls overnight for observation, to be sure there were no adverse effects of their exposure to the elements. Cassie thanked God this had happened in June, and not January. She hadn't left their side until both girls had dozed off and Aunt Vera came in to sit with them.

"Brady Nichols is sittin' in a chair out in the hall," Vera informed her in as hushed a tone as she could manage. "Looks like he's been dragged behind a horse for a few miles."

She knew he'd been waiting to fill her in and to get her take on things away from impressionable ears, but she hadn't been able to tear herself from her girls. Drawing a deep breath, Cassie rose. She needed to talk to Brady, but she didn't want either of the girls to wake and find anyone but her at their bedside.

"Will you stay with the girls while I go talk to him?" she whispered.

Vera set her purse down. "I drove your van over. Millard will be around in a half hour to get me." With an expression of distaste, she eyeballed the plastic container of salad one of the nurses had brought to her. "I should have thought to bring food. Funny how it's always the last thing on my mind."

"Probably because you look at it all day." Cassie waved her aunt's concern away. "I'm too tired to taste anything anyway. Let me go out to talk to Brady, then I'm going to hit the hay."

Cassie slipped into the corridor, careful to close the door silently behind her. Her heart melted when she took in the sight of Brady sitting in a hard molded-plastic chair. Like the girls, he and Cal had straggled out of the woods dirty and decidedly worse for wear. But Brook and Jilly had been bathed, and patched and outfitted with fresh hospital gowns and socks with nonskid treads.

Vera hadn't been wrong in her assessment. Brady still wore the uniform he'd set out in early that morning. His beard looked thicker after only a day's growth, and his short hair was rumpled. He sat with his eyes closed, his hands laced loosely in his lap and his head tipped against the wall. But something about his posture and breathing told her he wasn't sleeping.

He stirred when she slipped into the seat beside his. Without thinking, she reached over and pulled one of his hands from his lap and squeezed it tightly between hers. It was hard to believe she'd met this man less than forty-eight hours earlier. She already trusted him more than most anyone she knew.

"Brady," she whispered, choked with emotion.

He didn't withdraw his hand, but he did sit straighter in his seat. "How are they?"

"Sleeping," she reported. "You should be too."

"I wanted to talk to you," he said hoarsely.

"You're exhausted," she said, chafing his hand between hers. "We can talk later," she promised.

He shook his head. "I need to fill you in on what we found."

She felt the corners of her lips twitch but kept her expression serious as she asked, "You don't think the girls have filled me in enough? They spent the night in a cave. He left them there alone."

He ducked his head and checked his notes. "I know. But I also want to make sure you have some other facts right."

"The facts can wait until you get a few hours of sleep. Besides, don't you have a report to complete?"

"I dictated most of what I had to say into a voice memo and sent it to Cal. The chief said I could fill in any other blanks and proof the report tomorrow."

"The chief is a smart man." She realized she was still holding his hand and let go of him with a self-conscious laugh. "Sorry."

Brady flexed his fingers. "Nothing to be sorry about."

"Any word on Keith?" she asked, both anxious and hopeful.

The downward turn of Brady's mouth told her there was word, and it wasn't good.

OF COURSE, SHE'D ASKED the question he'd been dreading straight out of the box. His stomach sank, and any pleasure he might have found in her touch was extinguished like a match dropped into a bucket of water.

"I'm sorry to tell you this, but sometime between when we left the scene and when our officer got there, the truck was gone." He sighed. "We can only assume it was Norton. We were already spread thin with three of us on the search. He must have been watching us from someplace in the woods, waiting for a window of opportunity," he said. "We put out an APB to all the surrounding counties and fed the information on the truck to the Jasper grapevine. If he's still in the area, no one has seen him."

Cassie gazed at him in open-mouthed shock, then snapped her jaw shut. "I can't believe he got away."

Brady grimaced and gave a helpless shrug. "I'm sorry. We're not a big department, and we have limited resources." He scrubbed a tired hand over his face, but the minute he let it fall, Cassie reclaimed it, sandwiching it between both of hers once more.

"Don't you dare apologize to me. Don't you dare," she ordered.

"Everybody around here is going to do everything possible to catch this guy and get him put away. Vera and Millard have printed off the picture you gave me, and they're distributing it from the diner. They've made copies, and every business in town is handing them out like candy."

Cassie sucked in a sharp breath. "Oh, my God. I can't believe people are doing all this."

"It's a small town. Everyone wants to help. We got sloppy thinking he wouldn't come for the truck at the first opportunity. We should have made sure there was no gap in the surveillance. I promise you it's not going to happen again."

Cassie let out a startled laugh of disbelief. "You did what you could do."

"Still, it's not safe for you and the girls until we find him."

"It's not like you can post an officer on me 24/7," she said, weariness heavy in her tone.

"Maybe, maybe not. Either way, this part of the hospital stays too busy for him to approach you here. Even if he did, one of the federal agents is sticking close by," he said, nodding to a brawny man dressed in navy blue trousers and a white shirt. He leaned against the counter of the nurses' station, but his eyes were alert.

"He's going to want to talk to the girls. Since this was an abduction, it technically falls under federal jurisdiction. He's going to need to ask a few questions to be able to update things on his end. In the meantime, they've cleared him to hang around the hospital until morning. We'll take the watch from there."

"Okay," Cassie said hesitantly. "But I'm not going to

wake the girls so he can talk to them tonight. If they wake up, I'll get him, but until then he's going to have to wait."

"I think we're all good with letting them sleep," Brady said. He waved to the other man, and the agent came over. "Agent Westley Sims, this is Cassie Whitaker. She's Brooklyn and Jillian's mother."

The agent pulled his identification from his pocket and held it out for Cassie to inspect. "I'm terribly sorry for your trouble, ma'am. I understand the girls are resting now. I'm going to stay here overnight, and if anytime in those hours you see fit to let me have a few words with them, I sure would appreciate it. I need to touch base with Boise first thing tomorrow and coordinate with the local authorities in the search for Mr. Norton."

Cassie gave him cordial nod. "It's nice to meet you, and thank you for not asking me to wake them. I figure they're probably going to be out until after suppertime, but I doubt they make it through the night." She shrugged. "They may not have slept at all last night."

The agent inclined his head. "I won't ask you to wake them until tomorrow morning if they don't come around on their own. Sound reasonable?"

"Yes, thank you. More than reasonable." She looked at Brady, seemingly oblivious to the fact she still held his hand between both of hers. "You and I can talk later. I really want you to go home and get some rest. They're going to put a cot for me in the room with the girls, and I don't plan on budging again." She gave a choked laugh. "Heck, I may not let them out of my sight until their eighteenth birthdays. Maybe not ever."

"No one could blame you," Brady reassured her. Reluctantly, he extracted his hand from hers and rose from the chair with a groan. "Okay. I'm heading home to take a hot shower and try to catch a few hours of sleep myself. You have my number in your phone. Call for any reason at all."

Cassie pressed her lips together to stifle a protest, but said only, "I will. I promise."

Brady gestured to the chair, then at Agent Sims. "If I were you, I'd try to sweet-talk one of the nurses into a spare desk chair. These things could be used as instruments of torture."

The federal agent smirked. "I've got more experience at sweet-talking nurses and kidnapping cases than you have scruffy whiskers. Don't you worry about me."

Cassie stood too, then gazed at the floor, her forehead puckering. "Where's Winnie?"

"Dillon has her at his house."

Her hand flew to her mouth. "I forgot to ask how Bentley is," she said, clearly horrified.

Brady shuffled. "You may have had a thing or two on your mind. Bentley's fine. Got a cut on his paw and lost a toenail. Nothing broken."

"Oh, poor baby," she said in a rush.

Warmed by her unabashed affection for the animals, Brady inclined his head. "He's going to be okay. We're all going to be okay."

With a nod, Agent Sims returned to the nurses' station to give them some space. Grateful for the man's circumspection, Brady reached for Cassie's hand and held it between both of his. "Promise me you'll call if anything spooks you," he insisted. "Anything at all."

"Promise me you'll sleep," she countered. "You can text me in the morning."

He released her hand. He drew a deep breath as he pulled away, summoning the power to set his body in motion again. "Okay. I am going to sleep, but only because you want me to."

Cassie laughed out loud, the sound of it bouncing off the sterile walls of the hospital corridor. "I also want a cheeseburger. Can you make one appear?"

Brady made a show of searching his pockets and patting down the utility vest he still wore. "Darn, I'm fresh out of cheeseburgers."

"Looks like I'm gonna have to eat the salad they brought from the cafeteria for me," Cassie said mournfully. "Good night, Lieutenant Nichols. Sleep well."

Brady turned on his heel, unoffended by her dismissal. He was dead on his feet. Pulling his phone from his pocket, he tapped the screen until Dillon's number appeared. When his friend answered, he asked, "Can you handle one more houseguest tonight? I don't think I can drive all the way out to my place."

Dillon murmured something to one of the dogs, then replied. "Sure, no problem, man. You hungry?"

"Starving."

"I threw a couple burgers on the grill. I think we deserve a double after the day we've had. I can throw a couple more on," Dillon offered.

Brady stopped outside the sliding doors and looked at the hospital facade. "Can you make about three more, and are you willing to deliver?"

Chapter Thirteen

A knock startled her awake, and Cassie rubbed the sleep from her eyes and saw Agent Sims poke his head through the door. She started to rise to greet him, but found both girls had crawled onto the rollaway cot with her at some point during the night.

"I'm sorry to wake you," he whispered, "but I really do need to take a statement, and they're starting to bring breakfast trays around."

She waved in acknowledgment, then glanced at the girls snuggled into her. "Give us fifteen minutes."

In those precious few minutes, she managed to rouse the groggy girls and herd them into the adjoining bathroom. Faces washed, teeth brushed and hair combed, they were ready to entertain guests. A woman with a volunteer tag clipped to her scrubs bustled in carrying two covered trays stacked one on top of the other.

Brook and Jilly returned to their beds, but the novelty of being served a meal on a rolling table had been exhausted the night before. Their excited chatter had died away too. She watched as Brook prodded the pale scrambled eggs with her fork, and Jilly waved a limp piece of bacon, trying to make it fly like a bird flapping its wings. It was painfully obvious Jilly didn't have it in her to really sell her stunt.

Sighing, Cassie pushed aside the cot she'd folded in half

and secured with a strap to the side and dragged a chair between the beds. "Girls, there's a man here—"

Brook dropped her fork with a clatter, and Jilly stopped flapping the strip of bacon. "What man?" her youngest asked with uncharacteristic wariness.

Cassie's heart squeezed. Would they ever be able to recapture what innocence they had before Keith Norton upended their world? Would any of them ever feel safe again? She hated him for stealing her daughters from her, but would resent him for the rest of her life for snatching their innocence away too.

"A nice man," Cassie said, calm and cool, though she seethed inside. "His name is Agent Sims, and he wants to talk to us all about what happened."

"I don't want to talk about it anymore," Brook said, her expression turning mulish.

"His name is Agent?" Jilly asked, her expression perplexed. "I've never met anybody named Agent."

Cassie shut her eyes and inhaled deeply, counting to three as she exhaled. "No, agent is not his name. It's his job. Like Officer Nichols, or Dr. Beaumont. He's a special agent with a, uh, place called the Federal Bureau of Investigation. When someone takes a kid without asking their mommy if it's okay first, they help look for them," she explained.

"But Brady already finded us," Jilly pointed out.

"And we talked to Brady's boss guy," Brook chimed in, her jaw still set.

"Yes, well, they work for a different place and had to get their own story. Now, Agent Sims wants to hear your story."

Brook narrowed her eyes mutinously. "What if we don't want to tell it again?"

Cassie reached over and snatched a piece of cold toast from her daughter's tray. "Sometimes we have to do things we don't want to do," she said, relying on a familiar refrain.

Jilly caught on right away "Like clean our room," she said, dropping the hapless bacon onto her plate.

"Exactly." Cassie devoured the triangle of toast in two more bites as she walked to the door. Holding on to the handle while she chewed, she fixed the girls with her I-mean-business stare. "We're going to be helpful and polite to Agent Sims, then I will text Officer Brady and tell him we're ready to go home."

The interview with Special Agent Westley Sims didn't take long. He covered much of the same ground Chief Walters, Cal and Brady had, but in a much more direct way. The girls chafed against answering more questions at first, but soon warmed to sharing the dramatic tale of their rescue again. Cassie looked forward to telling Brady and Cal they had achieved superhero status as far as her daughters were concerned.

Sims pressed the button to stop the recording he'd made of their interview, and Cassie stood. She only intended to see the FBI agent to the door, but at a jerk of his head, he indicated he wanted her to follow him into the corridor.

"We're searching for Keith Norton. The temporary tag on the truck seems to be registered to a woman named Marcia Thomas. Does the name ring a bell?"

Stunned, Cassie's jaw dropped. "Uh, yes." She swallowed hard, then cleared her throat. "Yes, um, Marcia is the office manager at Bozeman Dental, the practice where Keith works."

Agent Sims put his phone away and pulled out a notebook. "There's the connection we need." He closed the notebook, then shoved it into the same pocket as his phone. He ran a hand over his face, and it occurred to her he had stayed awake all night watching over them. "Do you mind passing the information along to the locals?" he asked, gesturing toward the double doors at the end of the hall. "I'd like to get on the road."

She looked to find Brady Nichols striding toward her. He wore a uniform, but not tactical gear. "No, I... Yes, fine. Please," she stammered as an unexpected wave of relief pulsed through her. "Is it safe for you to drive?"

The other man waved her concern away. "I've got a few more hours in me." He rose when Brady approached. "I'll be hitting the road, but I'll be in touch." He offered his hand to her first, then moved to Brady and did the same.

"Thanks for your help on this," Brady replied.

Cassie waited until he left, then shifted her attention back to Brady, her mind racing with the information about the truck, unable to parse out the exact nature of Marcia and Keith's relationship. "The temporary tags on the truck are registered to a woman who works in Keith's office," she blurted.

He inclined his head. "Marcia Thomas," he confirmed. "We've already got someone from Bozeman PD heading out to talk to her."

She shook her head, boggled. "Marcia is..."

Brady watched her carefully. "Involved with Norton?" he prompted when she stalled out.

"Old enough to be his mother," she said, wide-eyed. "She's married. A grandmother. Leads a Sunday school class." She frowned as she tried to work it all out in her mind. "Do you think he stole the truck from her? I don't remember Marcia driving a pickup, but I didn't work there long." She wrinkled her nose, trying as hard as she might to make the pieces fit. "She's not really the truck type." He looked at her quizzically, and she shrugged. "Older woman, wears lots of floral dresses, drinks hot tea year-round."

"And do you think she has a thing for Norton?" Brady asked.

"A thing?" Cassie grimaced. "Not like a crush. More of a sort of hero worship. She thinks anyone with Doctor in front of their name walks on water."

"But he's not exactly the kind of doctor who saves people's lives," Brady said dryly.

"I don't think she makes the distinction." Cassie shrugged. "For some people it's all about the title and prestige." She waved a hand toward the door of the hospital room. "Speaking of prestige, your fan club is waiting for you."

"Fan club? Are you telling me I made a good impression?"

"Only slightly less than godlike. They wanted me to give them my phone this morning so they could order capes for you and Cal," Cassie said, fixing him with a droll stare.

"Capes?"

"Because you're superheroes," she explained. "Anybody who saves anybody is worthy of the title as far as the under-ten crowd is concerned."

He flashed a self-deprecating smirk. "If only it worked so well with the over-ten crowd."

She rolled her eyes and reached for the door handle. "I doubt you have any trouble, Lieutenant."

Both girls cried out with pleasure upon seeing Brady follow her into their room. Cassie stood nearby and watched as he answered their rapid-fire questions concerning his whereabouts, and what Winnie, Ruby and every single one of the other people they'd met from the search team were doing. He held his own under the interrogation.

It wasn't until Brook fell silent, allowing her younger sister to continue the barrage, that Cassie's maternal radar pinged. When there was a pause for breath, her older daughter asked the question uppermost on everyone's minds.

"Did you catch the bad guy?"

There was a beat of charged silence, then Brady gave his head a slow shake. "Not yet, but we will."

Brook's stare was a mixture of apprehension and speculation. His answer even put a damper on Jilly's enthusiasm, but Cassie wasn't as worried for her. Her baby always bounced back quickly. Brady looked around, clearly at a loss. Feeling bad for him, Cassie diverted the conversation.

"So, we're waiting for the doctor to tell us we can go home. We all had a good night's rest, and we hope you did too, don't we, girls?" she prodded.

They each dutifully answered with a mumbled "yes, ma'am," but the previous jubilation filling the room had lessened considerably.

As Cassie searched for a neutral topic, Brady swung around to face her. "Did you get my delivery last night? I was too shot to do anything but snarf one down for myself and fall face-first onto Dillon's foldout couch."

Cassie recalled how good it felt to fall asleep with a full belly, a warm blanket and the soft sighs of her daughters surrounding her. The rollaway cot was nothing to write home about, but compared to a night of worrying and wondering, it was as plush as a cloud.

"Yes, thank you. It was exactly what I needed." She touched his arm. "And please thank Dillon for me too. I was half asleep when he came in, and I have no clue if I even said thank-you. I pounced on the burger like I was feral, though."

He grinned. "We're glad to be of service," he replied.

"I'll tell Vera you two get breakfast on me when you visit the diner."

"Not necessary." He shifted nervously from foot to foot. Cassie got the distinct impression he wanted to be anywhere but standing in their hospital room. Figuring she needed to let him off the hook, she gave his arm one last squeeze. "Thank you for coming by to check on us. My aunt dropped the van off, so as soon as the doctor clears us, we'll be by the station to finish anything you need, then head home."

He tipped his head to the side, debating whether he should speak his mind. Feeling they were well beyond any pretense, Cassie mimicked his tilted head and asked, "Was there something you wanted?"

"Listen, I don't want to overstep any bounds or anything, and this might sound kind of, um, sexist? But I don't mean it to come across that way."

"Well, now I'm intrigued," she said, crossing her arms over her chest. "What's on your mind?"

"I was thinking I would feel better, and hopefully you would feel better, if maybe I…" He trailed off and rubbed the nape of his neck in a fidgety, vulnerable way. The uneasy movements made her soften inside. Then he inclined his head toward the door, indicating they should step away from the girls to speak more privately.

She followed him. "What is it?"

"I guess I was thinking I could go by your house and check to make sure everything is secure, I mean with your permission." He shoved his hands into the pockets of his uniform pants. "People have been keeping an eye out for Norton's truck, but I'm not sure anyone's going to check the property itself to see if he's been around there," he said in a low voice.

Cassie blinked. She'd been so relieved to see the girls, she hadn't thought much about the continued threat to their safety. "Yes. Please. If you don't mind," she hastened to add.

"I wouldn't have offered if I didn't mean it," Brady reassured her. "I'll go by there now and meet you at the station." Turning to the girls, he called out, "I gotta go. Winnie is pretty jealous if I talk to other girls for too long."

Both Brook and Jilly laughed, but Cassie could hear the hollowness in their giggles. It made her chest ache and filled her with a righteous fury she wished she could rain down on Keith Norton. He'd not only stolen her girls, but he'd also taken away the precious safety and security they'd sought here in Jasper. She hadn't done anything to deserve this. Her girls certainly hadn't done anything to warrant having their lives risked and the possible trauma from this experience. And what did he think would happen between them? Did the man actually believe this was the way to get in good with her? Was she supposed to pack up her kids, move back to Montana, and date the man who stole her babies? Oh no. Never in a million years. If he thought she'd have anything to do with him after what he'd put them through, he was sadly mistaken. No, the police would find Keith Norton, and he'd better hope the law got to him before she did.

Chapter Fourteen

The door had barely closed behind Brady when Adele, the nurse on the morning shift, came bustling in wearing scrubs printed with cats holding umbrellas and dogs tumbling from the sky. The girls' displeasure in Brady leaving was quickly forgotten when faced with such fabulous fashion sense. Cassie dropped into the chair and heaved a sigh, wishing this whole nightmare could end so she could simply take her daughters and go home.

Adele ran through her tasks with brisk efficiency, then cheerfully informed them Dr. Stenz was on duty this morning and making his rounds now. Not long after, a grandfatherly man with a shock of white hair and half-moon-shaped reading glasses came in to give the girls one last going-over as he signed their release papers.

But they weren't done yet. A social worker stopped by to speak to the girls about their experience, then provided Cassie with a printed list of resources available to kids who had suffered a traumatic event. They were wrapping the interview when Cassie received a call from Agent Sims wanting to clarify she had definitely never seen the pickup truck Norton left parked in the fire lane leading into the woods.

Then Chief Walters made his entrance.

But rather than bringing news or hammering them with questions, he simply grinned at the fresh-faced girls. "I thought I might escort the ladies of the hour to their car."

Brook and Jilly preened as they were loaded into wheel-chairs, peppering the chief on whether he had a dog, and if so, why didn't his dog go to work with him? He told them he did, but Bruno was an old hound who'd flunked out of the Daniels Canine Academy after wandering off one too many times, so he now spent his days keeping a watchful eye on the chief's refrigerator.

The two nurses pushing the chairs parked them near the sliding glass doors with a flourish. They waited under the watchful gaze of Chief Walters until Cassie brought her van around. Once the girls were buckled in, she thanked the chief again for all he and his team had done to recover her daughters. But the grim expression on the older man's face as he gazed at the screen of his phone stopped her.

"What is it?" she demanded without preamble.

His head jerked. "What makes you think it has anything to do with you, Ms. Whitaker?" He gave her a wry smile to soften the rebuke. "I am responsible for the whole town, not just you, ma'am."

A hot, prickly rush of embarrassment crept up her throat and made the tips of her ears burn. "I'm sorry," she responded quickly. "I guess I'm in my own bubble," she said, gesturing to the van and their immediate vicinity. "Trust me, I understand not everything is about me."

He stepped away. "You've been through a lot these last few days. I think I can forgive you a smidge of self-absorption," he said, his eyes narrowing and his lips curving into a teasing grin.

"I do appreciate everything you've done." Cassie lifted her hand in a wave.

"Don't forget to go by the station on your way home," he reminded her. "I know you're all tired of being questioned and prodded, but I'm sure at least one or two of the dogs will be there."

"That's all they'll need to hear," she assured him as she

climbed into the driver's seat. "Thank you again. I can't thank you enough."

The chief touched the brim of his hat like a cowboy in an old Western. "Just doing my job, ma'am."

On a laugh, Cassie slammed the car door and started the engine. They hadn't even made it out of the hospital parking lot when the girls began bickering. What would have annoyed her two or three days ago now sounded like sweet music to her ears. In the cup holder her phone buzzed, and she saw a text notification, but she refused to check while driving. Her old van wasn't equipped with all the latest technology, so whatever it was would have to wait.

The girls were at it full tilt when she swung into the parking lot adjacent to the Jasper Police Department. She parked in the same spot, but it felt like months had passed rather than days. She switched off the engine, and their complaints with one another morphed into groans of tired frustration.

"Why can't we go home?" Jilly whined.

"How many people do we have to tell?" Brook asked derisively. "Can't one person write it down and pass it on to everybody else?"

"No, I'm afraid not," Cassie commiserated. Then she whipped out another tried-and-true mom line. "Sorry, chickees. I don't make the rules—I only follow them."

She climbed out of the van, grateful the lame momism seemed to work. Brook unhooked her seat belt the second Cassie slid the door open, but Jilly, annoyed she was still required to use a booster on her seat due to being slightly underweight for her age, remained stubbornly strapped in.

She claimed that if she was so small she had to sit in a baby seat, then she was too much of a baby to unbuckle her own seat belt. Most days they argued about it, but today, Cassie was almost pathetically happy to unclip it for her.

Loath to let either of the girls stray too far from her, she planted a hand on their heads and playfully propelled them toward the front of the station. Once they stumbled through the glass doors, the three of them were laughing again.

A woman at the front desk beamed at them. "Well, there they are! You girls are practically celebrities around here," she said, clapping her hands together and coming out from behind her desk. Turning to Cassie, she spoke in a hushed tone. "I'm Teresa Norwood. I've worked here since dinosaurs walked the earth, and I've never... Well, that doesn't matter. I can't tell you how happy we all are to see your girls safe. Thank goodness." Turning to the girls, she leaned down. "Would anyone like a cup of cocoa?"

Almost in unison, the girls answered with a murmured "yes." Brook added a polite "please," and Jilly belatedly tacked on a whispered "ma'am" at the end.

Teresa gestured for the girls to follow her. "Oh, you don't have to 'ma'am' me, sweetheart. You can call me Miss T. Everybody else does. Now, who here likes cinnamon rolls?" When the girls' faces brightened, she shot Cassie a questioning glance. Not looking abashed for failing to ask permission, but more to ask if she was interested. Cassie's stomach growled, the triangle of toast long forgotten.

"I made some fresh this morning," Teresa said coaxingly. "Do you want one too?"

Cassie nodded enthusiastically. "Oh yes, ma'am, Miss T. I most certainly do."

Teresa tilted her head toward the room where the officers' desks were aligned. "You know which desk is Brady's?" she asked.

Cassie pointed to it, and Teresa beamed again. "Good. You settle yourself in. He radioed our dispatcher, Jenny, a few minutes ago to tell her he was heading in and asked if you could wait for him. You go ahead and have a seat there while the girls and I make sure these rolls are nice and warm."

Cassie was still processing when the older woman stooped to talk to her daughters. "Winnie is going to be beside herself with excitement when she sees you two. You are all she has talked about all morning."

The girls giggled as they followed the older woman into what appeared to be a small break room off the main office.

Cassie made her way to Brady's desk and dropped heavily into the chair beside it. The only other officer in the room was Cal Hoover. He'd given her a wave, then indicated the cell phone wedged against his ear, implying he couldn't talk. Glad to have a minute alone, Cassie closed her eyes and let her chin fall to her chest. More than anything, she wanted to sleep in her own bed. If she could sleep at all.

She practiced the deep breathing exercises the counselor she'd seen in Bozeman had taught her, hoping to center herself. She'd almost made it through her fifth slow inhalation and exhalation when Cal interrupted her brief meditation.

"Marcia Thomas says she has never owned a pickup truck," he announced from across the room.

"I didn't think she was the type," Cassie said, sitting straighter. "Did she say why there are temporary tags in her name on one parked near the spot where my missing daughters were found?"

One side of his mouth curled and he rose from his chair, stretching his long, lanky frame. "As a matter of fact, she did. Turns out, one of the doctors who works at the practice she manages bought it from her brother. He asked if she could handle the registration for him, but she didn't have some of the information she needed, so she put it in her name with the understanding he'd transfer it over when he had a chance."

"And the doctor's name happens to be…" she prompted.

"Keith Norton."

"Shocker." She said the last in a deadpan tone, but inside she was ready to kick the mealymouthed jerk all the way to the Idaho-Montana state line. Or better yet, feed him to the Feds. "I don't suppose she had any idea where we could find Dr. Norton," she said dryly.

Cal gave his head a mournful shake, then stooped to glance at his notes. "No. According to Ms. Thomas, the good doctor is supposed to be visiting his brother in Tacoma this week."

"Keith Norton is an only child," she informed him stonily.

Brady walked through the door, his expression grim. Cassie rose from her seat to go meet him halfway. "What? What's wrong?"

He shook his head and gestured for her to reclaim the chair she'd abandoned. He dropped into his own seat adjacent to hers and laced his hands behind his head, tipping his face to the ceiling.

"This town, man," he muttered. "It's like they're living in some kind of dreamworld where nothing bad ever happens."

Cal smirked. It seemed this was an old refrain.

"What do you mean?" Cassie asked, feeling defensive.

The other officer explained. "Brady likes to rant once a week about how nobody around here locks their doors."

"I do," Cassie said without hesitation. "I lock my doors and my windows."

Brady stared at her with such intensity she wanted to squirm, but she held it together. "You're sure you do? Front and back doors?"

Cassie raised her eyebrows. "Absolutely. A person doesn't go through some of the stuff I've gone through without learning how important basic safety precautions can be," she told him dryly. "I always double-check the doors and windows when I leave, and then lock the front door with my key from the outside."

Brady's interest sharpened. "And you're certain you did on the day of the party?"

"Yes," Cassie spoke emphatically. "As a matter of fact, I had to go in again to find Jilly's shoe. It was on the patio." She glanced at Cal, communicating the sort of understanding you could only find in a fellow parent. "I remember dropping the shoe as I reset the lock on the door." Then the implications of Brady's questioning finally broke through her brain fog. "Why? Was the door unlocked?"

Brady hesitated only briefly, then nodded. "It doesn't look to have been forced, so I assumed you hadn't locked it."

"You assumed wrong."

"What kind of a lock is it?" Cal asked.

Cassie shook her head. "Standard lock on the doorknob. I meant to install something stronger, but I haven't gotten around to it yet."

Brady scribbled something in his ever-present notebook, then said to Cal, "Might be a fairly easy kind of lock to pick," he commented.

When the other officer made note of the observation, Cassie leaned in and added, "Particularly if you're a dentist and used to working with small, precise instruments."

Brady looked around. "Where are the girls?"

"Teresa has them in the break room, pumping them full of cocoa and about twenty pounds of sugar," Cassie reported.

"Would you be open to leaving them here? We can ask Teresa if she'd mind keeping an eye on them while we head over to the house to see if anything's been disturbed. I didn't go farther than the kitchen because I honestly didn't think we were looking at a possible breaking and entering."

Cassie raised a shoulder. "Sure, if you don't think Teresa would mind."

Brady launched himself from his seat. "It shouldn't take

long. I'll go ask her now. And I'll ask the girls to give Winnie a good brushing and rubdown. Tell them she needs some pampering after yesterday's excursions."

"Perfect," she agreed.

Cal backed away. "You'll fill him in on what we discovered about the registration?" he asked Cassie.

"I will." She wrinkled her nose. "I still need to figure out whether I buy her explanation or not. Marcia is a super–straight arrow. I can't imagine her falsifying an official government document."

"Do you think she's covering for him?" Cal asked.

Cassie tossed his question off with a shrug. "Anyone's guess. It's a strange situation. I don't believe she'd say no to anything he asked her to do, because as far as she's concerned, all the doctors walk on water. On the other hand, I can't imagine she did it without qualms." She chewed her lip as she considered the possibility. "She's a by-the-book sort of person. How did she sound on the phone?"

"Nervous," Cal said, his eyes narrowing. "I get what you're saying about not being the type to falsify information. Perhaps she really did think she was doing both her brother and Norton a solid," he answered grimly. "Either way, she did you and your girls no favor."

Cassie stood as Brady emerged from the break room and gave her a thumbs-up.

"I appreciate your due diligence on this," she said to Cal. "It probably is as she said, but maybe she'll think twice about who she trusts. A call from a police officer saying her name was on the registration for a truck used to perpetrate a crime could not have gone over well with her."

Cal chuckled as he resumed his position at his desk. "No. I have to say she was pretty agitated about it."

Brady looked between them quizzically, then hooked a thumb toward the door. "You can fill me in on the way. I want to get this over with and I don't want the girls to get too antsy."

Cassie felt her shoulders drop. It was nice to be around somebody who cared about her girls as much as he did her. "Let's get to it, then."

Chapter Fifteen

Brady parked his SUV a block from Cassie's house. When she looked at him quizzically, he killed the ignition and shrugged. "It's a marked car. I don't want him getting squirrelly if he sees it."

"Squirrelly," she repeated with a laugh. "He hasn't seemed overly worried about the law catching him to this point, but sure, probably a good idea," she conceded.

They walked down the sidewalk in silence, but when they reached her neighbor's house, he indicated they should take a shortcut through Mrs. Garbowski's yard.

Cassie put a hand on his arm to stop him before he could place a foot on the neatly trimmed turf of the woman's lawn. "Mrs. Garbowski doesn't like people walking on her grass," she explained. "She's particular about weird things. If I let mine get above optimal two-inch height, she's after me to mow it."

Brady chuckled. "I discovered most of this earlier, but when I showed her my credentials and explained why it was important for me to cut across her property, she gave her permission."

Cassie snorted, but followed him across the lawn around the side of the older woman's home and through her backyard. "I can't imagine how much charm and sweet talk you had to pour on to make this happen," she said, eyeballing the other woman's house as they crossed the boundary from her yard onto the slightly more unkempt lawn surrounding Cassie's grandparents' former home.

Brady held out an arm to indicate the invisible property line. "I can't believe there isn't a fence."

"My grandpa wanted to put one in, but Mrs. Garbowski wouldn't agree to fencing her side of the property. He always said there was no point in building one two-thirds of the way around the yard."

Brady laughed. "Nope. Absolutely no point."

Cassie led the way to the shallow back steps, through the screen door and into a small mudroom. They stopped at the door. She hesitated, then reached for the knob and twisted. When it swung open easily, her jaw dropped in disbelief, but she didn't balk.

"We can take a minute if you aren't ready to go in."

She glanced over at him. "What if he's in there?"

Brady rested his hand on the utility belt near his sidearm. "With your permission, I'll do a sweep of the whole house. You can come in once I know it's clear."

Cassie shuddered, then gestured for him to proceed. "By all means, permission granted."

Brady opened the clasp on his belt to withdraw his service weapon. Holding it aloft, he moved through the kitchen, his head swiveling as he took in everything he could. There was a door beside the refrigerator he could only assume led to a pantry. Placing his back against the wood panels, he lowered his gun into position and reached for the knob. He opened it slowly, allowing his firearm to take the lead. It was indeed a pantry, but there were no runaway kidnappers stored in there.

He swept through the living room, his heart rate kicking into overdrive as he took in the barely contained chaos of a home well lived in. A family home. How dare this jerk violate what should have been their safe space?

He moved his way down the hall, poking his head

around open doorways, his service revolver blazing the trail. Brady worked methodically, feeling slightly abashed when he whipped around one doorway and found himself pointing his gun at the biggest stuffed unicorn he'd ever seen outside of a county fair.

Brook's room, he guessed, scanning the neat stacks of books and the toys stored in a large plastic bin. He moved on. Sure enough, the next room was a messy mishmash of ballerinas, stuffed dogs, unicorns, of course, and some truly frightening dolls with cartoonlike facial features. Definitely more Jilly's style.

He checked the hall bath next, making sure to pull the shower curtain all the way so he could be certain no one lurked in the tub. Then he moved down to the end of the hall into what appeared to be the master bedroom.

The bed was neatly made. There were few mementos or personal effects scattered around. He imagined Cassie had left whatever bric-a-brac she'd collected in her adult life in Montana, and hadn't had the inclination to fill the room with any more than what she absolutely needed.

A shallow tray on the top of the dresser contained bits and pieces of jewelry and a few hair accessories. The furniture itself was heavy and old-fashioned. He assumed it was left behind by her grandparents, because he certainly couldn't imagine Cassie Whitaker walking into a furniture store and selecting this particular suite.

Lowering his gun a few inches, he made his way over to the en suite bath. A shower framed in trendy 1980s brass and glass made it easy to see the room was clear of unwanted guests. But a ripple ran the length of his spine when he moved to leave and noticed someone had scrawled a warning on the mirror.

It read simply, "I'll be back for you."

Brady eyed the basket of cosmetics on the vanity and

retreated, mindful of the need to preserve the scene. "Over my dead body," he muttered.

Spinning on his heel, he stalked through the house to the kitchen, where he found Cassie nervously fiddling with the coffee maker.

She gave him a wobbly smile. "I could use a cup. How about you?"

"No, I think we'd better not," he told her.

"You didn't find anyone hiding under the beds, did you?"

She graced him with a tremulous but hopeful smile. He hated to be the one to wipe it off her face.

"There's nobody currently here, but I can tell you he has been here."

Cassie's hand trembled as she set the plastic scoop she'd been using to fill the coffee filter down on the counter with a thud. Grounds scattered on the laminate countertop. "Are you kidding me?"

"I wish, but I rarely joke about breaking and entering." Brady tried to mask his impatience, but it must have shown on his face, because she shook her head quickly and began sweeping the spilled grounds from the countertop with the side of her hand.

"Right. Of course not," she said. "I can't believe he's been here."

"I'm going to call in a crime scene unit to try to see if he left any fingerprints, but I don't think it's safe for you and the girls to stay here."

"No. Right. Oh, my God," she said, each word reaching for a higher octave.

"Do you think you could stay with Vera and Millard?"

She shrugged. "I'm sure we could. We'll have no choice, really," she said grimly. "I hate to do it to them, though. They keep such early hours, and the girls are so noisy. It's not a good mix. Certainly not any kind of long-term solution, and it's hard to know how long it will take to catch him."

"Hopefully, we won't need long-term, but I understand what you're saying," Brady said with confidence borne of pure determination. "We'll figure out something else. Let me radio this in."

Freeing the mic from his lapel, he pressed the key to open the channel. "Jenny, can you have Cal grab Ruby and head to Cassie Whitaker's place?"

"Cal?" the dispatcher asked, clearly puzzled by the request. "Do you need him to bring Winnie too?"

Brady met Cassie's eyes, then gave his head a slight shake. "Leave Winnie there with Teresa and the Whitaker girls for now. It looks like our suspect may have been on the premises. We'll need a crime scene unit for the interior, and I'd like Cal and Ruby to search the perimeter."

"Ten-four," came the reply from the dispatcher. A crackle of static followed, and then Jenny said, "I'll call the county guys for the forensics. They have a bigger team and can probably get the processing done faster."

"Good thinking. Over."

Brady reattached the microphone to his lapel, then looked down at Cassie. "I think you should gather whatever clothes and other essentials you and the girls need, but I'm going to ask you to touch as little as possible inside the house. I'm aware your prints are all over the place already. We just don't want to risk any overlapping."

Cassie raised a hand to indicate he didn't need to say more. "Gotcha."

She stood in front of him, wringing her hands, her bottom lip caught between her teeth. The urge to wrap her in his arms was nearly overwhelming, but Brady wasn't about to overstep his bounds. Particularly not with a woman who'd been through what she'd been through.

"Maybe I can rent one of the cabins from Blaze's River

Tours instead of going to Vera and Millard's." She winced. "Of course, they'd have us if I asked, but we're so disruptive to them. And the girls would be like elephants learning to tiptoe."

"I understand." He jerked his head toward the hallway and said, "Go gather what you need, and we'll think of something. But please don't go in the master bath. If there's anything you need from in there, we'll have to buy it new."

Cassie stared at him, her jaw dropping open. "The bathroom? What did he do?"

"Nothing gruesome," he assured her. "But he left you a message. It's also the one room where we have the best chance of lifting fingerprints since we're fairly sure he was in there touching things," he concluded. "It's only going to be upsetting to you to see it."

Cassie stood straighter. "Shouldn't I be the judge of what I can handle? If the message was left for me, I should see it."

"Trust me on this. He only wants to get into your head." He leveled her with a steady gaze. "Do not let him in."

She eyed him mutinously, then her shoulders sagged. Her quiet "Okay" was more than an acquiescence. With a single word, she told Brady she trusted him. And he was not at all oblivious to what a big issue trust was for her.

"Thank you," he said, inclining his head.

She frowned. "For what?"

"For believing me. If there were something I thought you could decipher or some deeper meaning, I'd take you in there myself, but he's only trying to scare you. Thank you for not giving him the satisfaction."

Cassie gave a short bark of laughter. "Oh, I'm plenty scared," she said as she started down the hall. "Right now, I'm more mad than scared."

Brady followed her as she strode from room to room, packing a small backpack full of clothes for each girl, grabbing their spinning toothbrushes and sparkly toothpaste from the bathroom off the hallway, then finally moving to her own room. Mad was good. He could work with mad. He was glad she wasn't crying again. Watching her cry into his dog's fur tore him to shreds.

He stayed close to her. Not because he didn't trust her not to open the bathroom door he'd so carefully pulled closed, but because he didn't want to let her out of his sight. The realization struck him like a blow. Without thinking, he was about to make an offer with the potential to earn him an honest-to-goodness slap across the face.

"Listen, this might sound…odd, but I have a suggestion."

Cassie paused in the process of pulling a stack of T-shirts from a drawer. "A suggestion?"

"Rather than spending money on a cabin, why don't you and the girls stay out at my place?"

Chapter Sixteen

"Your place?"

Brady grimaced, but he couldn't blame her for the skepticism in her tone. He lifted a hand to stay any immediate protest, then stepped into the room. "I live a few miles outside of town. Not far from the Daniels ranch. I bought a large piece of property out there, and I'm building a house." He rubbed his neck, wondering if it sounded like he was trying to impress her—which he may have been, but that honestly wasn't his motivation. "Right now, I'm living in a double-wide mobile home I bought used. It's kind of dated, but it has three bedrooms. If the girls don't mind sharing, it would be plenty of room."

He paused, trying to gauge her blank expression for any indication of how this might be landing. When she didn't say anything, he went on in a rush.

"Think about it. You would be out of town. We wouldn't tell anybody but your aunt and uncle and the Jasper PD where you were staying. You'd be with a policeman and a trained police dog," he said with a shrug. "What could be safer?"

"What happens when you go on duty?"

Brady pondered the possibilities. He had no doubt in his mind he could convince the chief this plan was a good one. And even if he couldn't, he had plenty of unused leave coming his way. If the department didn't want to go along, he'd take the days off. He needed to put in a few hours working on his house.

"I can figure things out. As a matter of fact, it might be better if you talked to Vera about not taking any shifts for the next few days. I believe Norton is sticking close, and in my opinion, you need to consider keeping a low profile."

"Hiding," she said flatly.

"Better to frame it as keeping yourself and your girls safe," he said gently.

She sighed and her shoulders slumped. Brady knew he'd won the argument, but it didn't feel good. Rather than gloating, he focused on logistics.

"What's your schedule looking like with Blaze's?"

She shrugged. "I pretty much go in whenever I am free. I'm a trainee, and an hourly employee. Since I can't take any tours out alone, I wouldn't be messing with anyone's schedule but my own."

Brady searched her expression for a hint of wariness about him. "See? It's a good plan. You and the girls need to disappear for a few days. We can even put it about town he got scared and moved on." When she tipped her chin stubbornly, he pressed gently. "I'm not saying you should, but gossip spreads like brush fire around here. A whisper or two in case Norton is listening in somewhere."

"For the record, I didn't leave Bozeman because I was scared of Keith Norton. And I didn't leave Billings because I was scared of my ex-husband. I moved on because I want to live my life and raise my girls in a place we feel safe and secure. But I don't run away because I'm scared. I'm tired of men trying to tell me what I can and can't do."

"I hear you," he assured her. "I'm not trying to tell you what to do. I'm only making suggestions."

Cassie stood there, the pile of shirts clutched to her chest. "I understand," she said at last. "I don't mean to sound ungrateful. It's a generous offer, but I don't think you have any idea what it's like to live with two young girls underfoot."

"You are absolutely right," he admitted with a grin. "But my gut is telling me to stay with you. Close to you. And I'm willing to deal with a few days of chaos if it means we all sleep better at night." He paused. "Trust me, Winnie isn't going to let anybody near my place without everybody knowing it."

"Winnie the superdog," she said fondly.

"I told her about the cape, and she's looking forward to it." Brady shoved his hands into his pockets and rolled onto his heels. "She's as brave a beast as there ever was. At least until a thunderstorm comes rolling through."

"The girls don't like them either," Cassie told him. "Maybe they could all huddle together and I'd get to sleep solo for once."

Brady didn't allow himself to dwell too long on the image of Cassie Whitaker sprawled across the double bed in his spare room. He gave a businesslike nod, pulled his hands from his pockets and stepped out of her bedroom. "I'm going to make a call and let you finish packing. In the meantime, I'll try to figure out how we're going to fit two girls and one bed hog of a Labrador on the foldout futon in the third bedroom."

"Trust me, they'll find a way," Cassie called after him.

He gathered the backpacks she'd left in the hall, but lingered near the master bedroom as he called the station to report the break-in. He needed to be sure she didn't try to sneak a peek at the lipstick-scrawled threat on the bathroom mirror. Minutes later, he found Cassie shoving handfuls of what he could only assume were her undergarments into a duffel with a Blaze's River Tours and Rafting logo emblazoned on it.

She saw him watching and her cheeks stained a faint

pink. "I'll need a new toothbrush and deodorant and stuff," she informed him.

"We can handle a run to the Stop & Shop," he assured her. "We'll also need to get some food you and the girls like to eat. I'm not much of a cook, so my meals at home mainly consist of breakfast cereal, microwave dinners and the occasional steak I can throw on the grill."

Cassie's face brightened. "I can cook. I love to cook." She zipped the duffel bag, shouldered it and then gave a decisive nod. "The girls and I will cook for you while we're there."

Brady grinned. "Sounds like a deal." He scratched his neck. "I guess I should apologize ahead of time. I can't really remember what condition I left my place in." When she gave him an amused glance, he shrugged and avoided her gaze. "Mainly I've been working on framing out the new house, but then…" He trailed off, not wanting to make her feel guilty for being the reason he hadn't been home in days.

"But then Keith Norton stole my daughters and you did everything humanly possible to get them home to me safe and sound," she said tartly. Blowing her hair away with a huff, she straightened and looked him dead in the eyes. "Brady Nichols, you never have to apologize to me for anything. Ever."

He grinned at her. "Be careful about making blanket statements to a guy. We remember those."

She snorted. "Probably the only things you ever remember a woman saying."

"Hey, now—"

"I'm only teasing." She pulled the bag from the end of the bed, cast a glance at the door to the adjoining bath, then straightened her shoulders. "You didn't have to worry about me sneaking a peek. If there's anything the last ten years has taught me, it's to not take the things men say when they're in the midst of a tantrum to heart."

"I understand." He ducked his head, slightly abashed by being so transparent. "Sorry."

"Again, no apologies needed. And you certainly don't have to worry about questionable housekeeping. The girls and I will pitch in. We'll also be helping to make a mess of it, so you'll see, everything will even out in the end."

The hopeful look on her face unlocked something inside of him. "I'm looking forward to it. Winnie is great, but not much for conversation."

"Okay, well, gird your ears. You're going to have plenty of chatter coming at you." She abandoned the bag and walked over to the dresser and picked up a small blown-glass figurine of a ballerina. "I bought this for my nana at the mall in Boise one year when I was about Brook's age."

"Did she like ballet?"

Cassie shook her head. "Not particularly. And I didn't dance. It was one of those kid gifts you buy your grandma because you have no clue what old people like. My parents gave me money to buy Christmas gifts, and I picked out the thing I thought was prettiest."

"She kept it."

"Of course. She was my nana." She glanced over at the closed bathroom door and rolled her shoulders, "And now I've brought this ugliness into her house."

He jerked with surprise when she pivoted and hurled the delicate figurine at the closed bathroom door. It shattered into thousands of tiny pieces which embedded themselves into the carpet. Cassie watched the shards settle there. "I guess it's too much to hope he'll come around barefoot."

"Probably a long shot," Brady agreed gruffly. "Feel any better?"

"It didn't hurt." Striding to the bed, she looped the strap on the duffel over her shoulder. "Okay," she said briskly. "I have everything I need from here, and you've got yourself a passel of houseguests invading your space." She cast one last glance at the closed bathroom door, then gave a visible shudder. "Let's get out of here."

"I called in and told Jenny to tell the technicians to be subtle about approaching the house," he said, following her down the hall. "They can enter through the rear door. We'll leave it open. It's possible he'll show up again. We'll make sure someone is keeping an eye on the place. Any neighbors we should inform?"

Cassie shook her head. "Only Mrs. Garbowski next door. I don't want to worry her. She's ninety-two and watches too much true crime on television."

"Gotcha."

She huffed a breath. "I doubt he returns. Keith may be a jerk, but he's a smart jerk."

"Okay then."

She paused in the living room and took one last look around, her expression mournful. "I used to visit every summer. I would stay with my grandparents for weeks and basically run wild." She slid him a sidelong glance. "They were—are—some of my best memories. But this house has felt strange without my grandparents in it, and now…" She swallowed hard, and Brady clutched the straps of the two backpacks he held tighter, hating to see her distress. "I guess I'll worry about where to go next later," she concluded.

Moved by her emotion, Brady took a step closer. "He can't steal your memories. This is still your grandparents' house, and soon it will feel like a safe place again," he assured her. "Your girls will grow up here. Maybe not running wild," he added with a pointed look. "But kids are resilient. Eventually, they will accumulate as many happy memories as you have of the place, and it will balance out the bad."

"I hope so," she said, a wistful note in her tone.

He gestured to the door. "This is a good town, Cassie.

It's full of good memories for you and has plenty of adventures in store for the girls. I promise you we're gonna do everything we can to help make it feel safe again."

She put her hand on his arm. He felt the now-familiar jolt of attraction zing through him but quickly squelched it. He'd invited this formidable, yet still vulnerable, woman to bring her children to his house and stay. He wasn't about to do anything to make her feel uncomfortable there.

"Thank you," she said in a whisper. "You always seem to say exactly what I need to hear."

He ducked his head, pleased but embarrassed by the compliment. "I hope so."

She gave his arm a gentle squeeze, and it was all he could do to keep from jumping straight out of his skin. "We haven't known each other long, and certainly not under the best of circumstances, but I consider you a friend, Brady. I trust you. I trust you with my life, and more importantly, with my girls."

He blinked, wondering as he stared down into those wide hazel eyes if he'd been firmly and permanently placed into the friend zone. He hoped not, but he knew she couldn't be thinking about becoming anything more than friends. For now, he was grateful for her candor.

"Thank you. And I feel the same way about you." Recognizing he couldn't feel exactly the same because he wasn't entrusting her with his life or children, he gave a self-conscious scoff of a laugh, then gently tugged his arm from her grasp, unable to withstand the electricity pulsing through his veins one second longer. "I mean, I consider you a friend. I'm glad we're friends."

Cassie gazed at him watchfully for a beat longer, then gave him what had to be her first genuine smile since they'd arrived. "Okay then, friend. Let's go tell the girls they're going to have a slumber party with Winnie."

She glanced over her shoulder as they headed for the

kitchen door. "Do you happen to keep any noise-canceling headphones handy? If not, we'd better buy some earplugs when we stop at the store, because when we tell them, you will be subjected to squealing guaranteed to hit decibel levels you'll wish only Winnie could hear."

Chapter Seventeen

Brady Nichols's place wasn't anything like what Cassie had envisioned. Not that she'd spent hours picturing his home, but based on what she knew of him—a divorced guy in his late thirties, living alone with his dog—she hadn't expected his place to be so…clean. The layout was pretty standard. A living room with a single shotgun hallway leading to three bedrooms and a full bath. A good-sized eat-in kitchen had a window above the sink and a door that led to a deck. Through the window, she could see the skeleton of the home he was building for his future.

His warnings about the state of the place were unnecessary. It seemed comfortable, if a bit dated. She couldn't imagine a guy Brady's age picking out some of the furniture. And other than a few dishes soaking in a sink of long-cooled water and a fine layer of dust in the living room, the place was spotless.

Of course, with her girls there, it wouldn't stay neat for long. She bit her lip, feeling torn about invading this man's world. He had no clue what he was in for.

Brady and Winnie led her daughters into a bedroom with a large futon sofa and a home office setup complete with a laptop sitting open on top of the wood-and-glass desk.

"Whoa, we get to stay here?" Jilly asked, plopping down on the sofa and giving a couple of experimental bounces.

"You do. It folds down into a bed," Brady explained, spotting Brook's dubious glance.

Cassie oh-so-casually moved to the desk, closed the laptop and stooped to disconnect the power cord. Brady shot her a quizzical look, and she shrugged as she straightened, the laptop clutched to her chest like a shield. "Trust me, you'll thank me later."

"Is that a computer?" Brook asked, right on cue. "I wanna use it!"

Cassie shook her head, cutting off any response Brady might have. These were her daughters and she would set the rules for them. "This is not our computer. Therefore, no, you cannot use it without asking for Brady's permission." She handed it over to the man in question. "My recommendation is that you do not grant permission unless you like having crumbs in your keyboard and a smudged-up screen."

Brady nodded solemnly, then his face broke into a wide grin. "I actually don't mind either of those things. But I do think maybe it would be better if you used it only when your mom or I can be around to oversee things. Sound like a deal?"

Brook's response was subdued, but she bobbed her head empathically. "Yes, sir," she replied.

"You can call me Brady," he told her.

Her grin flashed to full wattage, and Cassie had to blink away tears. Brook was always so serious. Her smiles felt like a gift on the best of days, and now mere hours after suffering one of the worst days in her young life, she was gracing Brady with one of the brightest smiles Cassie had ever witnessed from her eldest daughter.

"I can?" Brook asked, looking pleased by being invited onto such grown-up footing. She glanced hopefully at Cassie, waiting for parental consent.

After all they'd been through together, and the close proximity they would be in for at least a day or two, asking them to call him Officer Nichols seemed excessive. "If he says it's okay, it's okay with me."

"Computers are stupid," Jilly announced. She promptly flopped down onto the floor and sat cross legged, extending her arms open wide. "Dogs are so much better. Can I play with Winnie?"

"Again, Winnie is not ours," Cassie was quick to interject. "She's also a working—"

But the yellow Lab interrupted her lecture by pushing her way through their legs and sitting down directly in front of her younger daughter. The two eyed each other hopefully, then Jilly wrapped her skinny arms around the dog's neck in an exuberant hug.

"Not too tight now," Cassie warned automatically.

"Thank you," Jilly whispered into Winnie's fur. "Thank you for finding us."

Cassie's heart clenched. They'd been hanging out with the dogs at the station for hours, but now Jilly's narrow shoulders shook with tears as she hugged Winnie. Cassie's knees gave out and she knelt beside her, rubbing her narrow back.

"She's the bestest dog in the world," Jilly pronounced.

Cassie couldn't argue the sentiment. "Winnie is definitely our heroine," she said in an emotion-choked whisper. She glanced at Brady and found his expression wistful. Maybe even affectionate.

He cleared his throat. "Maybe while you girls stay with us, you'll help me make sure Winnie gets her dinner on time and her water bowl is clean?"

Jilly stared at him, hero worship written all over her face. "Oh yes," she exclaimed, nodding almost as enthusiastically as her sister had. "We'll help any way we can, won't we, Brookie?" she asked, turning to her big sister for confirmation.

Brook reached out to pat Winnie's head and stroke the dog's soft ears. "Yeah, sure. We love Winnie."

"When Momma says we can get a dog, I want to get one like Winnie," Jilly announced.

Brady chuckled. "Live with her a few days and you might want to look around a bit more. Labradors are great, but they take a lot of training," Brady said in a warning tone. "They're good pets, but they can get kind of lazy if you don't work with them a lot."

"Oh, we'll work with her," Brook said eagerly. "We'll need someone to show us what to do."

"Lucky for you, Winnie is a bit of a show-off," he said, his tone warm with affection.

"Okay, we need to get settled in and give Brady some space," Cassie insisted. "We went by the store on our way to get you guys. We're having tacos tonight."

The announcement was met with a chorus of "Yay!" which Winnie joined in on with a bark.

Brady grinned. "Tacos are a yay from me too."

Satisfied she made the right call, Cassie stood and moved closer to Brady's side. "I suggest you remove anything else from this room you might not want destroyed," she spoke in hushed tones. "They're curious girls and they tend to have fairly few boundaries."

Brady's grin grew wider. "I don't mind. Winnie and I are gonna enjoy having some company, I think." He glanced to where his dog had collapsed in front of the girls, allowing them to rub her belly and scratch behind her ears. The Labrador's pink tongue lolled out the side of her mouth, but her gaze still traveled to Brady as though she were checking to see if accepting their adoration was all right.

He laughed and said firmly, "Winnie, stay."

Cassie saw the tension literally melt away from the dog's prone posture. She pressed her head against Brook's knee and rolled over, her paws stretched in ecstasy as the girls continued their exuberant rubdown.

Ducking her head, she walked down the short hall toward the kitchen. Being in such close proximity to Brady Nichols was both wonderful and disconcerting. Wonderful because the man was a comfort. Disconcerting because he was a man, and hadn't she learned enough lessons where men were concerned?

"I'll get the groceries unpacked," she said, hoping to put enough distance between them to get her thoughts in order again.

But to her consternation, Brady followed. "I'll show you where everything is."

As she plunged her hand into one of the many bags they had carried in from her van, she glanced over her shoulder, taking in the decent-sized kitchen and eating area. "I really didn't expect this place to be so spacious. It's nice. I was worried we'd be on top of you." The second the words were out of her mouth, her cheeks heated. The last thing she needed to do was start tossing innuendo around. She hoped Brady didn't take her comments out of context.

Thankfully, he seemed oblivious. She watched as he stowed packages of ground beef, chicken, and bags of frozen chicken nuggets into what appeared to be a freezer desperately in need of defrosting.

"Are you kidding me? My mouth is already watering at the thought of tacos." He waited until she looked over at him, then gestured to the boxes of frozen entrées in the iced-over freezer. "I'm not much of a cook."

"We'll be happy to earn our keep," she replied. "I'm no gourmet, but I've managed to keep those two alive for a few years. Maybe I can show you a thing or two, get you out of the frozen-entrée rut."

He chuckled and let the freezer door swing shut. "You can try, but I spend most of my off-hours working on the house. It's easier to nuke something than spend time in the kitchen preparing a meal for one." He waved a hand toward the window above the sink, and Cassie moved closer to take a better look at the large wood-framed structure they glimpsed as they pulled to the double-wide.

"I can't believe you're building a house. Amazing," she said as she let her gaze travel over the size of the foundation he'd laid out for a structure. It was much larger than the mobile home he lived in currently. "It looks like it's going to be pretty big."

He pointed to some of the exterior walls he and his friends erected. "Almost twice the square footage of what I have here. More than I need, but I didn't want to build something I'd have to add on to in order to make it marketable if I ever wanted to sell."

"Sell?" she asked, surprised by the notion. The house wasn't even built yet and he was already thinking ahead about putting it on the market?

Brady shook his head. "I have no plans to move anytime soon, but I figured if I was going to build a house, I was going to build one that would appeal to someone other than me."

"Wow." The thought of him casting his mind so far into the future was boggling to her. She'd been living day to day, week to week and month to month for so long, she couldn't imagine thinking beyond those markers. Brady was planning for a future ten, twenty or even thirty years out.

Cassie moved away from the window and focused on the array of shopping bags. "Smart thinking," she said as she pulled a box of crunchy taco shells from one of the bags. She shook her head. "I have no earthly idea where I'll be a month from now, much less years into the future."

"You don't plan to stay in Jasper?" he asked as he unpacked the next bag.

"I had hoped to," she confessed. It came out huskier than

she'd intended. She cleared her throat, shook her head, then shot him a shaky smile. "I'd hoped this town would be the refuge for the girls it had been for me when I was young, but now… I don't know. Will the girls ever be able to move past this? Will I?"

Brady stopped and faced her head-on. "You will."

Chapter Eighteen

She was saved from needing to reply by the ringing of his cell. Brady's brows knit as he accepted the call and pressed the phone to his ear. He walked out the kitchen door for more privacy, and Cassie tried to ignore the twist in her gut. She couldn't simply assume every call he received was connected to her circumstances, nor did he owe her any insight into his personal life.

But she would be lying to herself if she didn't admit she was curious. As she finished putting the groceries away, she thought over the conversations they'd had, parsing them for any details she could winnow out. No, she wasn't mistaken. He hadn't mentioned anyone special in his life. Nor had he alluded to any desire to have someone. Sure, he might be building a big house out here on this pretty piece of property, but it didn't mean he envisioned a family to fill it. In fact, he'd spoken pretty plainly about his thoughts concerning resale value.

The certainty in his tone when he said she'd be able to move past their current predicament was heartening. She didn't know him well, but her gut said Brady was a straight shooter. He wouldn't blow hot air at her. If he thought she and her girls could get past Keith Norton's invasion in their lives, then he truly believed it.

She pulled out the brownie mix and went on the hunt for a mixing bowl. In a lower cabinet she found a large ceramic bowl with flowers printed around the outside and a chip in the lip. She placed it on the floor at her feet, and scanned the assortment of battered old pots and pans. When she heard his heavy footsteps she asked, "I don't suppose you have a cake pan, do you?"

Brady shook his head, but then indicated the disposable aluminum roasting pan he'd tossed into the cart at the store. "No, but I saw the brownie mix and grabbed one of these," he said, a hopeful gleam in his eyes.

One corner of her mouth curved as she eyed the deep roasting pan. "Ah, I see. Unfortunately, I would've had to purchase two boxes of mix to make a pan that big work."

"Really?" Brady asked in a tone so crestfallen, she was tempted to drive to the market to buy a second box of mix.

"Never mind. I can buy a smaller pan and we can bake them tomorrow."

Frowning, he jerked his head to the side, signaling for her to step out of the way. She did, and he dropped to his knees in the spot she'd vacated. "I have to have something that'll work."

Determination furrowed his brow. Apparently, Brady wanted those brownies. The clatter and scrape of pots and pans being moved and rearranged in an increasing crescendo of desperation made her want to laugh out loud. She bit her lip instead. Something told her Brady Nichols would go running to the store again rather than ditch the idea of brownies.

"Hey, will this work?" he asked, his voice sounding oddly hollow from the inside of the cabinet. A second later, he pulled out a battered pie plate.

Unwilling to disappoint him, she took the pan he held aloft like a trophy. "Yes. I think I can make it work."

"Excellent," he hissed, sitting on his heels. "Tacos and brownies. My heart might not be able to handle any more excitement tonight."

His words were light, but there was something in his grim eyes that set alarm bells ringing in her head. "What? What is it?"

"Huh?" He froze for a split second, then placed the bowl she'd unearthed onto the counter with the pie pan inside it.

"Something's bothering you," she insisted.

He pressed his palms to his thighs, then lurched to his feet with a grunt of exertion. "It's, uh—" He rubbed his neck, clearly conflicted.

Cassie was coming to recognize the nervous gesture and respected it. She took a step closer to him. "If it's personal, you can tell me to butt out, but if it's something to do with the case, I need to be in the loop."

He raised dark eyebrows, pinning her with an assessing stare. "At this point, I'm not sure if it's anything."

"If it has anything to do with my daughters, then it's something."

"It's not directly about the girls," he said, but his gaze slid away from hers.

Evasion was not his strong suit. It was one of the things she liked most about Brady Nichols. He couldn't lie well, even if he wanted to. "Okay. If you want to play semantics, I can too. If whatever it is concerns anything to do with Keith Norton, then I have to be informed," she amended. "I'm the one who knows him."

Brady heaved a sigh. "I don't want to say anything because it could be absolutely nothing," he hedged.

"Brady…" she said in the same tone she used with the girls when they were trying to get around her.

"There's an old, abandoned lumberyard. We patrol it fairly regularly because there was some trouble out there not too long ago. That was Jason Wright calling. He's the young guy who got engaged the night of the, uh, party at the DCA."

"The night Keith Norton abducted my children," she corrected, each word hard as a rock.

"Yes." Brady ran his hand over his hair, then gave his neck a squeeze. "Jason says he's spotted some evidence someone may have been in the lumberyard recently."

She opened her mouth, but before she could get a word out, he waved his hands to stop her. "We have absolutely no proof or reason to believe it might have been Keith Norton in particular. Lots of people pass through these parts. People moving from one spot to another. People trying to get away from civilization."

"But it could have been Keith," she said in a rush, determined to wedge in the words.

Brady inclined his head in acknowledgment. "Jason and one of our other officers, Ava Callan, are checking the place more carefully. So far, it's some litter left behind, but if they find anything hinting it may be Norton, they'll be sure to give me a heads-up right away."

Cassie fixed him with her sternest mom glare. "And you'll give me one," she stated flatly.

Brady stared at her, his jaw tensing until the tiny muscle in the corner jumped beneath his beard. "If there's anything you need to be aware of, I'll be sure to tell you," he promised.

Cassie heaved a sigh and turned to the counter, where she pried open the box of brownie mix. Pulling the chipped mixing bowl closer to her, she said, "I guess that'll have to be good enough. For now." The two of them held each other's gaze, both wordlessly trying to convey their immovable will.

In the end, Cassie couldn't have said which one of them would have won if Jilly hadn't interrupted. "Mama, can Winnie and I help you make the brownies?"

Chapter Nineteen

Brady rose early the next morning, put on his uniform and had Winnie in her harness before he realized he would be leaving Cassie and the girls in his house unattended. He stood in the front entry listening to their morning chatter bubble out of the kitchen, completely torn about what to do.

A part of him really wanted to be on the job. A bigger part of him needed to be involved in the search for Keith Norton. Jason and Ava hadn't been able to find anything more than scattered evidence of someone being in the abandoned lumberyard, but nothing tying the detritus left behind directly to Norton.

Brady wasn't surprised. The man was smart. He'd cover his tracks. Leaving the truck at the end of the fire lane had been a lucky stroke for them, and they'd bungled it. They should have impounded the vehicle immediately. But the truck itself wasn't his main concern. The man had managed to thread the needle on their surveillance once. His adversary seemed to be one step ahead of them. It made Brady uneasy.

His gut told him Norton was still in the area. The girls hadn't been physically harmed. The message on the mirror made it clear Cassie was the one Norton was after. Having spent a scant couple of days in the woman's company, Brady could understand how a man could get so sucked into her orbit. It would be hard for any guy to watch a woman so strikingly self-possessed walk away. Something about her unapologetic confidence made a man want to strive to be better. To be needed. But unlike Norton's kind, Brady ached to be wanted as much as he was needed.

He wouldn't mind one bit if a woman like Cassie decided he was the one for her. She was beautiful, but easy and natural. He liked the way they interacted. Liked how they could talk openly and honestly, but could also sit comfortably in silence. Even when her tension and worry for her daughters had to have been crushing her.

The fact that she was a mother didn't lessen her attractiveness but rather enhanced it. Seeing the way she faced life head-on, but still remained soft enough to give her girls everything they needed, was extremely appealing.

Brady knew he was far too susceptible to the lure of her, so his first thought upon waking had been to get out of there. He needed to give himself some space to breathe and to get his thoughts in order. If she didn't plan to stay in Jasper, there was no point in trying to start anything.

He wanted to put down roots. The structure behind the trailer was proof of permanence. He wanted the family he'd been denied in his marriage. He'd always wanted a family. Was building a house large enough to accommodate one. He wanted the quieter small-town upbringing for his kids. Basically, he'd wanted everything his ex hadn't. He'd picked this place, this life, on purpose. Jasper was where Cassie came when she needed refuge. He hoped it wasn't a convenient pit stop on the way to something different. He planned to be one of the old goats hanging around the town square watching the passersby and yammering a constant stream of commentary.

His were simple life goals, but they made him happy thinking about them. Usually. But thinking about them both with and without Cassie Whitaker in the picture stirred some emotional turmoil.

Stroking Winnie's head, he looked down and gave the dog a pat. "I think we could use some distance today, don't you, girl?"

She must have tuned in to his plan using her I'm-a-mom supersensory hearing, because Cassie appeared in the kitchen doorway. "Heading to work?"

Though she phrased it as a question, the observation came out sounding more like a statement. "Yeah, I have a shift this morning and I want to review what's going on with the investigation. Will you be all right here by yourselves?"

Cassie's chin lifted an inch. "Of course, we will." Then she seemed to catch the defensiveness in her tone, and her expression softened. "You haven't had breakfast," she pointed out. "Hang on a minute."

He didn't usually eat breakfast, but she disappeared into the kitchen without giving him a chance to say so. A minute later, she reappeared cradling a napkin-wrapped pancake in her hand.

He glanced down to see she had layered scrambled egg with two strips of bacon, then drizzled maple syrup onto it and curled the edges upward. She presented it to him with a flourish. Breakfast eater or not, Brady's mouth watered.

"I figured since you were such a fan of last night's tacos, you wouldn't mind a sort of twist on them," she said, looking eager to please.

He took the offering from her. "No, ma'am. This looks fantastic."

Cassie beamed down at Winnie. "I have something for you too," she assured the dog as she conjured one of the small crunchy bones Brady kept in a jar on the counter as part of Winnie's training reward system.

He didn't have the heart to tell Cassie he didn't give his dog treats on a just-because basis. Winnie accepted the offering gingerly, then glanced at him for permission. Unable to deny her, he nodded and Winnie chomped down on the bone with such glee, they both chuckled at the dog.

"Good girl," he said automatically.

Cassie moved a step away, then put her hands in the pockets of her shorts. "I'm sorry, I probably should have asked first, but she is a good girl, and she deserves all the treats in the world as far as I'm concerned."

"I get you, but yeah. I try to save those for training and working situations."

Her eyes flared with rebellion. "Well, she did keep watch over the girls all night."

"She did," Brady concurred, letting her off the hook. He patted his pockets, checked the utility belt to be sure he'd clipped his phone in with the rest of his equipment, then jangled his car keys. "You have my number. You'll text if anything at all bothers you." He stated the last as fact, not a request, his gaze fixed on her in an unwavering stare he hoped commanded acquiescence.

To his relief, Cassie didn't make a fuss. "Absolutely."

"Good. And it goes both ways," he assured her. "I'll text you if I find out any new information."

"I would appreciate being kept in the loop."

Brady lifted the makeshift breakfast taco in salute, then turned toward the front door. "You girls have a good day. Make yourselves at home, and don't worry about making a mess of the place." He pointed to the skeletal structure behind the double-wide. "This is temporary."

Cassie grinned at him. "Maybe this evening you'll give us a tour of the site? I'd love to see what you have planned for the house."

Her genuine interest sent a wave of warmth through him. No, his instincts were right. He needed to put distance between himself and this entrancingly earnest woman. Through sheer force of will, he tamped down the pride aching to burst out of him.

"I'd be glad to," he replied casually.

"Have a good day," she called after him.

The words were so simple. Her wish for him such an everyday sort of sentiment it made his chest tighten. He wanted to hear them each time he left for work. Stepping out onto the small porch with Winnie hot on his heels, he answered gruffly, "You too." With his gaze fixed on his vehicle, he called over his shoulder, "And lock the doors behind me."

"Oh, don't you worry, I will," Cassie assured him.

At the foot of the steps, he paused to listen until he heard the click of the locks on the front door. Then, and only then, did he allow himself to raise the pancake-wrapped breakfast taco to his mouth and take a large bite. The explosion of sweet and salty under his tongue nearly sent his brain into overload.

How would he ever be able to stomach microwave meals again?

A bit of a scrambled egg fell to the ground, and Winnie stared down at it, prepared to lunge if only he'd give the go-ahead. Brady sighed contentedly as he chewed. "Okay, fine. Eat," he commanded.

The dog wolfed down the bit of egg and gazed at him with hopeful amber eyes.

Brady shook his head, then pointed toward the truck. "Not gonna happen. And don't get used to extra cookies either," he warned her. "You're the hero of the hour so you're getting a few bonus treats, but we'll be on austerity measures from here on out," he said, trying for a stern tone.

Winnie's pink tongue lolled out the side of her mouth as she trotted alongside him, glancing at the food hopefully. He walked slowly, taking huge, greedy bites. Somehow he managed to fold the pancake just right and the syrup seemed to be holding things together as he snarfed the last couple of bites.

Winnie looked crestfallen. He chuckled as he opened the door and gestured for her to hop in. But she was a crafty dog. She gave his syrup-sticky fingers a few surreptitious licks while he secured her harness.

"We're both going to gain ten pounds in the next week. And what kind of search team would that make us?" he asked his partner. "We'll be crashing through those woods like a bowling ball."

Winnie simply panted in response. She had absolutely no problem with this possibility.

Chuckling to himself, he closed the passenger door, wiped his hands on the now sticky napkin Cassie had wrapped around the taco, then slid into the driver's seat.

Thankfully he had some antibacterial gel in the console to remove the rest of the syrupy residue. Once they were all set, he started the truck and cranked the wheel. The clearing he'd made in front of the trailer was wide, even if the lane he'd cut for access to the property wasn't. Sometimes his friends would help on weekends. Gradually, they'd carved out ample parking. But he never expected to be maneuvering around a minivan so soon.

Chapter Twenty

On the drive into town, he forced himself to think of all the next steps he had upcoming with the house rather than the attractive woman and two vulnerable children he'd left alone in his double-wide, miles from the nearest neighbor.

As he drove past the sign marking the Jasper city limits, Brady kept his eyes peeled for anyone who didn't look like they belonged. Familiarity was one of the perks of a small town. Even with the tourists who flocked to the Salmon River, it was easy to tell they were there with a purpose.

Though he hadn't lived in Jasper long, he knew many of the town's residents well enough to exchange a wave. Plus, gossip was a major form of currency around these parts, so if Norton had shown his face at any of the local establishments, there was a good chance he'd hear about it. There was no doubt in his mind nearly everyone was aware of the kidnapping and that the perpetrator hadn't been caught. Jasper would be on high alert.

At the station, he parked his truck next to Dillon's, collected his partner and headed for the front door. He tried to pretend he was reporting for duty like he would on any other day. But this was not a normal day. He felt tense and jittery. Winnie was attentive. And when they stepped into the station, he could feel the kinetic energy coursing through the place.

"The chief would like to see you," Teresa said in a low tone.

Brady suppressed a groan. "Sure. Of course."

It stood to reason the big boss would want a full report on everything Brady knew at this point, but he had to assume Captain Rutledge would be sitting in on the meeting. As the chief's heir apparent, Arthur Rutledge was wheedling his way into more and more top-level conversations within the department. And having Rutledge in his business was almost as annoying as the questions Brady was sure the man would ask.

He raised his hand in greeting to his fellow officers as he and Winnie wended their way through the warren of desks. He caught Dillon's eye and angled his head in the direction of the chief's office. His friend grimaced for him. Stopping by his desk, he deposited his keys and wallet in the center drawer, then removed Winnie's lead. The dog curled on the bed beside his desk, her eyes fixed on him as she settled in.

"Good girl. Stay."

Winnie rested her chin on her front paws and let her eyelids droop. After all, Labradors loved an early-morning nap. Heck, they loved anytime naps, Brady thought, chuckling to himself as he made his way to the chief's office. It was a marvel his partner got anything accomplished at all, given her affinity for a good snooze. Dogs were amazing creatures.

He paused outside the office door, then rapped twice with his knuckles.

At the bellowed "Come in!" he reached for the handle.

Brady opened the door and found Rutledge lounging in one of the chairs across from Chief Walters's desk. He tamped down a flare of annoyance and gave each man a cordial nod. "Good morning."

Rutledge did nothing but nod, but the chief gave him an encouraging smile. "Morning, Nichols. I trust you had an uneventful night?"

Brady thought about the pleasant evening he'd spent with Cassie, Brook and Jilly. The girls had been quiet at first, but with Winnie nearby, Jilly was quick to bounce back. However, both girls stayed close to their mother, Brady had noted. Even Brook. Though, as the elder, she held herself aloof. She was nine and not a baby anymore, she'd reminded him, offended by his offer to pour her a glass of juice.

But yeah, it had been a good night. An uneventful night, thank goodness. The tacos had been delicious, and the brownies hit the spot even if they were thick and unevenly baked from being prepared in a pie plate. He didn't mind. The fudgier the better as far as he was concerned. All in all, the evening passed in a haze of exhausted camaraderie. Somehow the four of them had formed a unit. Five of them, really, because Winnie was more a part of the group than he was, he suspected.

"Everything went well. The girls seem to be settling in, and I think it helped to have Winnie nearby. They like the dog, and she can be pretty comforting when she wants to be."

"She's a service dog," Rutledge interjected briskly. "You shouldn't let them treat her like a family pet."

Brady's jaw tightened. There was no point in arguing the finer points of canine training with Arthur Rutledge. The man didn't see the value in the K-9 partnership they'd formed with the Daniels Canine Academy, and more than a few of the officers were concerned Rutledge would do away with the program altogether once he was in charge.

He inclined his head in acknowledgment, then turned his attention to the chief. "I've spoken to Ms. Whitaker about requesting some sessions with therapists who came to see the girls in the hospital. It would be great if they could speak to them again today, if possible. I think the more they talk about what happened, the better off they'll be."

Rutledge snorted softly but didn't say anything because

the chief was already nodding emphatically. "Yes. It's important kids talk about things. Otherwise they bottle their emotions up."

Chief Walters steepled his fingers. "I put in a call to county services already, so you may want to make sure Ms. Whitaker is aware someone will be reaching out to her."

"Will do." He turned his attention to Rutledge. "Any new leads, Captain?"

Rutledge darted an encompassing gaze to Chief Walters, then returned his attention to Brady, who did his best not to bristle. The man supposedly had direct responsibility for this investigation, but he didn't seem to be ready to share whatever they'd been discussing with him.

When there was no answer forthcoming, he pushed with the information he had. "They didn't find anything conclusive at the old lumberyard, but there are some other spots around town Winnie and I could check out. Maybe the mill? I could ask around some at the local businesses to see if they've seen Norton. I think we should also alert the folks out at Blaze's. Some of their fishing cabins are pretty remote, and if they're not checking them daily, he could have used one of them as a squat."

Rutledge waved a hand. "Already on it with Blaze's and the other businesses. If you want to take the dog out to the lumberyard and the mill to have a sniff around, it couldn't hurt," he said, shifting his gaze to the chief, who nodded approvingly.

Rutledge might not have been a fan of the canine additions to their department, but he was no fool. He knew Chief Walters was the one who instigated the program, and he wasn't going to stomp on it in front of the man.

Brady opted to take him at his word. "Will do. Should I bring anyone with me, or—"

Rutledge shook his head. "No. We can't assign any additional resources to this until we have something concrete to investigate," he said, his tone a shade too brusque for Brady's liking. "The Feds are already involved. They have more to work with than we do."

Thankfully, the big guy stepped in. "As far as JPD is concerned, this is your case, Brady," he interjected. "If you find something where you think you need additional resources, we'll provide them. Until we have something that indicates the need for more manpower, we'd like you to take the lead on it."

Brady appreciated how Chief Walters's years of experience had shaved the edges off. His order was essentially the same as the one Rutledge had given, but was completely different in tone. "Yes, sir."

He turned to leave the office, but froze when Rutledge called after him. "Oh, and Nichols?"

Brady glanced over his shoulder. "Captain?" he responded, refusing the call the man *sir*. He hadn't earned his respect as of yet.

"We're willing to let this go on for a couple more days, but if there are no signs of Norton in the area, we will need to turn our attention to the usual matters again."

Brady's hand tightened on the doorknob. The urge to look at the chief to see if the older man approved this plan was strong, but Brady was also savvy. The future of his career would lie in Rutledge's hands one day. Openly defying or second-guessing the man's decisions would not play well. The captain was the kind of man who kept score.

"Understood," he replied tersely. "I'll go check out those locations and keep you briefed on my findings."

"And we appreciate what you're doing to keep Ms. Whitaker and her daughters feeling more secure. I hope having them as houseguests isn't putting you out too much," the chief added, eyes twinkling.

"No, sir. No trouble at all."

Brady pulled the door closed behind him, shut his eyes

and let out a huge exhale. It bothered him that Rutledge riled him so much. Arthur was a good officer. He wasn't corrupt or self-serving. But the man's ambivalence toward the K-9 program, a program that had turned out to be life-changing for Brady, made him chafe. Rutledge's innate obnoxiousness made him an easy target for animosity among the officers who worked for him, though. Brady hated how easily the guy could push his buttons.

Keeping his gaze straight ahead, he walked through the maze of desks until he reached Dillon's. "So, I hear you've all been pulled off the Whitaker case."

His friend's gaze never wavered from Brady's. "Yeah. You know how it is." He shot a glance at Rutledge's empty office. "But, you know, keep us posted." Got it. Dillon wouldn't be working the case in any official capacity, but if Brady needed him, his buddy would be there.

Brady glanced over to where Cal Hoover watched them with a scowl on his face. "Yep, moving on to other things," Cal said gruffly. "Maybe we'll hand out some speeding tickets today."

Brady chuckled as he shook his head. "You guys have anything I can add to the file?" he asked, not liking the troubled look in Hoover's eyes.

Cal shook his head and shifted in his seat. "No. Nothing concrete. I've got a creepy feeling. He's been too quiet. No one has seen anything, and that's not normal around here."

Brady had the same itch between his shoulder blades. There was more happening than they knew about. Norton was going to make a move, and the suspicion sent shiver after shiver down Brady's spine. "Nobody is aware they're staying out at my place, are they?"

He shifted his gaze between the two men, but Dillon broke first with a shrug. "Nobody *knows*," he said, emphasizing the word, "but, of course, some people know."

Brady wished the riddle didn't make sense to him, but

he'd lived in Jasper long enough to both admire and disparage how well the grapevine worked. He also knew not everybody on the grapevine was good people. "Well, if you talk to one of those people, would you make sure they keep the information quiet. Norton could still be around. That was the whole point of them staying out at my place."

"We will be sure to remind them, but the people who may be clued in are people we can trust," Dylan assured him.

"Let's hope so," Brady said grimly. "In the meantime, any suggestions for where I might go kicking over some dead logs?" he asked both men.

Cal gave a shrug. "We've asked about everybody who's got a business here in the downtown area, and nada. The lumberyard was our first indication of anything possibly Norton related, but the search was inconclusive."

"Some people steer clear of the places cops go," Dillon said. "I think you should check out the places we *don't* frequent to ask a few questions."

Brady nodded his agreement. There were a few businesses outside the immediate vicinity of downtown Jasper. They weren't the places he and the other cops went to grab a beer after work or stopped in for lunch. Some were more attuned to the tourist trade Blaze's River Tours brought in, but there were also a couple of establishments where elements of society who didn't necessarily appreciate a police presence gathered. "Good call."

He raised a hand in farewell, then returned to his desk to collect Winnie. "I'll keep you updated," he called over his shoulder to no one in particular.

But it was Teresa who spoke as he snapped Winnie's lead onto the harness.

"Please do," she ordered, holding a key fob to one of the department's SUVs.

Winnie followed him toward the receptionist's desk at a

trot. Teresa was always good for a scratch behind the ears. The older woman obliged the dog, then said, "Here," as she held out a plastic container filled with his favorite chocolate chip cookies. "Take these too. For energy."

Brady accepted the gift with a grin. "You're the best," he told her, pressing a hand over his heart.

"And don't you forget it," she said as he and Winnie pushed through the double doors.

"Never," Brady promised, then headed out to hunt for Keith Norton.

Chapter Twenty-One

He drove through the empty lots of the former JPG Lumber, his eyes peeled for any sign of activity, but failed to spot anything. He and Winnie stopped to search the area where Jason said he'd found the litter and other evidence of someone in residence, but the dog could not pick up any scent outside of the immediate area. Whoever had been there had driven in and driven out.

Determined to widen his circle, he drove out to the old mill. A few years ago, somebody had bought the property and tried to convert it into an ice cream parlor meant to attract tourists heading to and from the Salmon River. Apparently, business had not been as brisk as the owners had hoped because the ice cream parlor closed in the same season, and as far as he knew, no one had maintained the property. The second they jumped down from the SUV, Winnie had her nose pressed to the ground, but her ears remained flat against her head. Brady stood and surveyed the historic old place. There were plenty of places for someone to hide. They checked all the doors and windows, but nothing looked to be disturbed.

He gave Winnie plenty of lead to take him in any direction that caught her fancy. But while the dog found many scents of interest, none of them piqued her curiosity enough to warrant more than a cursory search of the perimeter.

At the car, he made sure to fill Winnie's portable water

bowl to the brim, then chugged a bottle himself. The day was warm and the sun was high. Sweat dampened his uniform shirt, and he could feel droplets trickle down his temples. He ran the cool plastic bottle over his forehead. He exhaled loud and long, wiping away the mixture of sweat and condensation with his forearm. There were no signs of Norton here, and the longer he was away from home, the more uneasy he grew.

The property he purchased outside of town seemed idyllic with its wide-open pasture and the untamed woods he'd chosen as the backdrop for his newly built home. Now, all he could think was Cassie and the girls were too isolated out there. It was miles to even the Daniels place, his nearest neighbor. Setting his bottle on the roof of the SUV, he and Winnie moved into the shade provided by the vehicle, and he pulled his phone from the clip on his belt and began to text.

Everything okay?

Brady hadn't realized he was holding his breath until the flashing ellipses appeared, signaling typing on the other end.

Depends. How do you feel about beef stroganoff?

His thumbs flew over the screen.

I feel strong approval for beef stroganoff. Is there anything I can get for you while I'm in town?

The three dots appeared, then disappeared, then they appeared again.

I guess I'll use this roasting pan. We can have ice cream for dessert.

Involuntarily, Brady turned to look at the abandoned ice cream parlor. It hadn't been a bad idea. He would have enjoyed taking Cassie and her girls out for an ice cream cone after dinner.

He had to stop thinking about those sorts of things. They weren't dating. She wasn't staying at his house because she liked him and wanted to be with him. They were together only because some guy had decided he had the right to invade her life.

Turning his attention back to his phone, he began typing again.

Ice cream sounds great. I'll text later to see if you need anything else from the store.

Her reply appeared almost instantly.

I have a car.

His jaw clenched as he stared at her reply. Of course, she did. He wasn't holding her captive at his place. But surely she understood the need to keep a low profile around town. He looked down at the screen, and the dancing dots reappeared and a second message from Cassie came through.

Sorry. Knee-jerk reaction. It's better if we stay here and lay low for a couple of days.

Thumbs poised, Brady composed multiple answers in his head, but decided simpler was better.

Call if you need anything.

Then he reattached the phone to his utility belt, opened the door for Winnie to hop in and secured the dog in her harness. "Winnie, you can't let me go thinking we have something more to go home to, okay? I need you to keep me in check." The dog panted contentedly, and he stroked her head. "It's you and me, right, girl?"

Bending to collect her water bowl from the disintegrating gravel parking area, he murmured to himself, "I need to remember. It's just you and me."

Brady had decided early on to make the Shaker Peak Bar and Grill the last stop on his general search for Keith Norton. He'd been avoiding it. He'd gone out with the woman who tended the bar a couple of times not long after moving to Jasper, but nothing ever developed between them. Much to Alyssa's chagrin.

Situated midway between town and the access to the Salmon River, Shaker Peak attracted a good number of out-of-towners to go along with the day drinkers who parked themselves on the stools and whiled away their days in a bar.

He left the vehicle running to keep Winnie cool as he went inside. Hopefully, he'd be able to get in and out with no more than a few cursory questions and answers.

Alyssa rocked onto her heels and crossed her arms over her chest as she gave him a pretty effective stink eye. "Well, well, well. Look what the doggy dragged in," she said in a mocking tone. "How's your girlfriend? What was her name again? Wendy? Ginny?"

Brady approached the bar with no hitch in his stride. "Hello, Alyssa. You're looking well. Business good?"

Alyssa, who never wanted to take the high road, rolled her eyes. "Booming," she said, casting a glance at the three grizzled men parked at the other end of the bar. Brady took a look around and saw only a single table of young college-aged guys obviously fresh from a day on the river. Besides them, there were no other occupants.

"What can I do for you?"

Brady wasn't offended by her brusque manner. He appreciated her getting right down to brass tacks. Unclipping his phone, he found the picture of Keith Norton and held it out for her. "Have you seen this man?"

He watched her face carefully. He could see recognition kicked in. He also had a creeping feeling again as she averted her gaze and snatched a damp towel off the bar.

"Can't say as I remember," she replied.

"Alyssa," he said, gentling his tone. "Have you? It's important."

She clutched the damp towel as she crossed her arms over her chest again, but she still wouldn't meet his eyes. Instead, she focused on the door behind him. Maybe she was expecting someone to save her from his interrogation.

No one did, and there was no way Brady was leaving without getting what she didn't want to tell him out of her.

"This have something to do with those girls everyone's goin' on about? The ones who were taken?" she demanded.

"This is the man who took them," he answered without equivocating. "Have you seen him?"

"I didn't hear anything about it until Mavis Clausen came in here at lunchtime whining about how her nerves were shot," she informed him. "I told her she didn't need to make excuses to me, but then she started spilling her guts about how some horrible man had snatched two kids right out from under the noses of nearly everyone in town." She scoffed. "Including most of our police department."

Brady refused to take the bait. "You *have* seen him," he said, his tone flat but insistent.

She glanced over at the trio of barflies. He wondered if she was looking for backup or escape. They were too engrossed in dissecting the baseball game airing on a muted television mounted above the bar. "Maybe I have. Not sure."

"You are too." Brady thrust the phone out until it was an inch from her nose. "When? What did he want?"

She batted his arm away. "Stop."

Brady lowered the phone, but leaned in. "What did you tell him?"

She shrugged, but then her shoulders crept toward her ears as she crossed her arms again, her fingertips biting into her bare biceps. "He came in last night looking for the blonde who works down at the diner every once in a while. Vera's niece. Said they were old…friends."

Brady ignored the emphasis she put on the last word, needing to keep his cool. "What did you tell him?"

"Nothing. I told him she sometimes worked at the diner. He asked where she stayed, and I told him I thought she was living in her granny's old place, but I doubted she was home."

Then at last she met his eyes. "I heard you two are staying together, so I told him he might be able to find her with her policeman boyfriend," she said, drawling the last two words.

Brady closed his eyes on a cringe. "Did you give him any names?"

She shook her head. "Why would I? If he's stupid enough to still hang around after I told him his lady friend is shacking up with a cop, then he doesn't have the sense God gave a goose."

Brady didn't see the point in pursuing the line of questioning anymore. Whatever damage had been done, he couldn't undo it, so he gave Alyssa his most stern cop stare and spoke in a flat tone. "Cassie Whitaker is not my girlfriend. She is a nice lady whose daughters were taken from her by a man who appears to be stalking her," he said, speaking slowly and succinctly. "I'm sure as a fellow woman you can understand how afraid she must be. But this man was bold enough to walk off with her girls in the middle of a party most of the town, and as you pointed out, most of the police force, was attending." He let those stark facts sink in for a beat, then added, "If he does show himself again, I would appreciate you giving somebody at the station—doesn't have to be me—a call."

With nothing left to say, Brady turned on his heel and strode toward the door. He needed to talk to the chief about sticking close to home for a couple days.

Chapter Twenty-Two

Cassie had to wait until the girls left the room to add the sour cream to the stroganoff. For some reason they were convinced it was gross, and if they saw her add it, they wouldn't eat it. All things considered, they'd had a pretty good day at Brady's place. She'd straightened here and there, and enlisted the girls' help in deciding what they could cook to fill their hero's freezer.

Jilly had voted for chicken noodle soup, her personal favorite, but Brook's sophisticated taste ran more to the lasagna end of the spectrum. After they'd inspected what she'd already procured from the store, Cassie texted a short list to Brady. He had replied to it with a terse Will do.

The brief response set her teeth on edge. A part of her thought the sight of lasagna noodles on the list might have stirred more excitement in the man, but maybe she overestimated the lure of her culinary skills. Now she was worried he wouldn't like her invading his space in such a way. The notion hadn't occurred to her until she discovered the mother lode of plastic leftover containers stored in the bottom cabinets. It appeared Brady Nichols was not above relying on the kindness of others when it came to scoring a home-cooked meal. And she didn't have to stretch her imagination to figure some of those meals were likely prepared by single women auditioning for the role of personal chef. The thought of other women feeding Brady made her irrationally irritated.

She'd placed the stroganoff in the oven to keep warm when the front door opened and Winnie barreled into the house. The big yellow dog made a beeline for her water bowl, sloppily lapping the liquid in great, greedy gulps, then gazed at Cassie. The dog seemed unperturbed. Maybe she came home to a strange woman in the kitchen every day. Cassie had no idea what Brady's lifestyle might be. For all she knew, he was a serial dater.

Thankfully, a chorus of squealed greetings rent the air, jarring her from her thoughts.

Winnie bounded off to the left to meet the girls halfway down the hall, and Cassie found Brady carrying bags of groceries into the house.

Instantly contrite, she rushed to relieve him of some of the burden. "I would have helped carry those in."

"No problem." He sniffed the air, then gave a gratifying groan of approval. "Man, this is probably something Winnie and I shouldn't get too used to. We've never come home to the house smelling so good."

"Oh." The compliment sent a warm flush to her cheeks and made her ears burn. "I'm glad it smells good. I thought you might like something nicer than tacos from a kit."

Brady placed the remaining bags on the counter and turned to her. "Are you kidding me? Those tacos were gourmet compared to the frozen burritos I usually nuke."

She laughed. "I'll add the stroganoff leftovers to your collection of frozen entrées. The girls and I were thinking we could help stock you with some better options." She cocked her head to the side. "What do you think?"

"I think, yes, please," he responded with gratifying swiftness.

"Jilly voted for chicken noodle soup, and Brook thought you might like lasagna, but we're open to making whatever you want," Cassie said as she slid her hands into the battered oven mitts she'd found in a drawer. "I didn't want to overstep, but we want to show our appreciation to you for letting us stay here."

"There's no need."

"I've seen the sad state of your freezer. There's great need."

Brady's expression settled into a grim line of concern she was growing far too familiar with. He shifted his weight, scratching the corner of his jaw. It was a good thing the man hadn't set his sights on being a professional poker player. His earnest expression practically telegraphed his every thought.

"What is it?" she demanded.

He shot her an exasperated look. "Either you're a mind reader, or I need to work on my acting skills."

"It's hard to raise kids without being able to read people's expressions. My girls are like tiny tornadoes. When it comes to reading a room, I've gotten pretty good at dialing in to the barometric pressure."

He chuckled. "I bet you have."

"What's bothering you, Brady?"

His head jerked and she realized she'd never called him by his first name. At least, not like that. Somehow, it sounded intimate, and possibly overfamiliar. The heat in her cheeks intensified, but she hid it by ducking to extract the pan from the oven. "You might as well tell me. I won't let you rest until you do."

"Is that how you get them to clean their rooms?"

She caught his wry tone as she straightened. Placing the stroganoff atop the stove, she turned to look him square in the eye. "It's how I get them to do anything. It's my mom superpower." And in saying so, she widened her stance and planted her fists on her hips, staring him down as she did with the girls. "I think this arrangement of ours is going to work better for all of us if we speak our minds."

She wanted to retract the words almost immediately. They had no "arrangement," and she couldn't actually speak her mind. Couldn't tell him she found him to be the most attractive man she'd met in…forever. Not only because he was a winner in the looks department, but also in terms of personality and integrity. She'd stupidly dumped all of her dirty laundry about the ugliness of her previous relationships on him. Why would a man like Brady want to take on a woman with as much baggage as she was hauling around?

"You're right." He drew a deep breath and bent his head to the side to stretch his neck in a way she was coming to recognize as a prelude to bad news. "Keith Norton is still around town. I don't have any evidence other than a sighting as of yesterday, but I'm pretty sure he hasn't given up."

"He wouldn't," she stated flatly. "Why would he? He's already put too much on the line. He won't stop until he gets what he wants."

"He wants you," Brady stated flatly.

Cassie snorted. "No, he thinks he wants me because I didn't want him. He doesn't really want me. He wants to win," she said grimly.

"Either way, he's got you marked as his prize."

Cocking her own head to mirror the tilt of his, she studied the man beside her. "I'm damn tired of men acting like they get to lay claim to me."

"No man has the right," he said without missing a beat.

"Exactly. You get it, but you're not like other men," she said with a scornful sneer.

But what she said was true. Brady was not like other men. He was calm and steady. He was her port in a storm, but he was also as easy to be around as the yellow dog he called his partner.

He gave her a skeptical glance, and she shrugged. "You aren't," she insisted. "It's what makes you a good cop. Makes you a good man. You have integrity and self-confidence most other men, at least those of my acquaintance, act like they have but rarely do."

He swallowed hard. "Thank you," he said gruffly.

"It's the truth. And the truth is always easy to share." She held his gaze for a beat too long, then forced herself to turn away, busying her hands at the sink. "Go on and change. Vera dropped off some green beans left over from lunch at the diner. I called her because I couldn't remember the last time the girls ate something green, and I wasn't thinking too clearly when we went to the grocery store. Anyway, after dinner, the girls and I would like a tour of your house, if you don't mind."

He pushed away from the counter, looking pleased. "You're really interested in my house?"

She bobbed her head enthusiastically. "We stood on the deck trying to guess what rooms would be where when it's finished, but it's hard with no actual walls." Reaching for the skillet she'd used to make the stroganoff sauce, she glanced over at him, eager to reassure him they had been careful not to overstep any boundaries. "Don't worry, I wouldn't let them go out there. I told them it's a construction site and there could be dangerous things around."

He blew out a breath and ran his hand through his hair as he turned to look out the kitchen window. "There is. Let me go out and pick up some tools and such. I'll give you the grand tour after we eat."

"Sounds like a plan," she said as she poured the sauce over the beef and noodles.

Dinner was boisterous. The four of them sat crammed together at the tiny round table in Brady's eat-in kitchen. Of course, the girls complained mightily when they saw the green beans she'd spooned onto their plates, but when

Brady helped himself to a second spoonful there was a marked shift in attitude. He'd bought a loaf of crusty bread from the grocery store's bakery aisle, and they all ate thick hunks of it slathered with butter.

She sat back and for the first time in hours, let her shoulders slump. She liked how easy Brady was with her daughters. He didn't talk down to them like so many adults did with children. Which probably explained why her girls responded to him with such ease.

She'd been worried. No doubt they'd deal with some tough moments thanks to the trauma Keith Norton had put them through, but right here and right now, everything was good.

The bread was warm, soft and fragrant, the stream of chatter from her girls, a reassuring soundtrack for the meal. Brady laughed at one of Brook's comments, and she felt her lips twitch into a smile. She glanced over at Brady and found him watching her with an expression of mild concern.

With a quick shake of her head, she indicated there was nothing wrong. Picking up her fork, she granted herself permission to enjoy the comfort of both the food and the company.

Her girls were safe. Brady was here, and so was Winnie. All was well.

Chapter Twenty-Three

Conversation was slow to start, but once Brady began telling stories about his early days working with Winnie, the girls became more animated. Even Brook, who was a much tougher audience than her younger sister. By the end of the meal, the noodles had been consumed, most of the green beans had somehow disappeared, though she suspected a good portion were slipped under the table to Winnie, who lay waiting patiently at Brady's feet, and the mood was relaxed. Cassie felt truly at ease for the first time since they walked into the party at the Daniels Canine Academy.

Brady had coaxed the girls into helping him clear the dishes when she heard her phone chime. Glancing around, she spotted it on the countertop faceup in the midst of the upheaval she'd created in putting this meal together. Brady's head turned too, and she knew he'd scanned the notification because his entire body stiffened. He set the plates down on the counter with a clatter, and she rose from her chair.

"What? What is it?" she demanded, stretching her arm out in a gesture for him to hand over the phone.

It chimed three more times in rapid succession. Brady waved her into her seat and checked the notifications again. Then he looked at Cassie with troubled eyes as he pressed the button to lock the screen again. But he didn't hand it over. She sank down into her chair, and he pivoted to the girls, who were jostling for position at the sink.

"Hey, since your mom worked so hard at cooking this great dinner, and I'm sure you girls helped," he added, fixing them with a pointed stare.

They hadn't helped at all. Cassie had to stifle a grin as she watched them wrestle with telling the truth or letting him go on believing they'd been angels.

Thankfully, he plowed ahead, oblivious to their consternation. "How about I put you to work too? Go put on long pants and your sturdiest tennis shoes, okay?"

Brook frowned and glanced at the window dubiously. "Long pants? It's summer."

Brady grimaced an acknowledgment to the season. "I know, but we always wear long pants and sturdy shoes when we're near a construction site," he informed them gravely. "It's important for the safety of the crew. If you want to be on my crew, then you've got to wear the uniform." He looked at Cassie, then pointed at the window with the view of the home under construction. "I wanna show you what my house will look like."

The girls took off for the room they were sharing, jabbering all the way about who was gonna be the boss of who on Brady's crew.

They both winced when the bedroom door slammed shut. Brady grabbed the phone and handed it to Cassie. She wanted to compliment him on how good he was with her daughters, but her curiosity couldn't be contained. Unlocking the phone, she opened her messaging app to see the stream of texts that had obviously upset Brady.

Don't you think you should come home?

I'm tired of chasing you around.

This town isn't that big.

Do you think I can't find you?

Cassie tried to suppress the shudder of terror that raced down her spine. At a loss for what to say, she asked the question she'd had looping through her head for days. "What is it about me?" She spoke barely above a whisper, her gaze fixed on the phone. "How do I always get mixed up with these guys? I think I'm a good person. I work hard, I'm doing my best to raise my girls the best way I can…to make them good people—"

She choked on the last word. Tears filled her vision, but she pressed the heels of her hands to her eyes to stop them. She didn't want to cry. She was angry, not sad or scared. She was stronger than tears. She wanted to find Keith Norton and drag him off into the woods. Leave him there scared and unprotected. Terrify him the way he'd terrified her children.

A blur of black moved into her field of vision. She lowered her hands, frustration bubbling inside her when she felt two hot drops spill over her lashes and course their way down her cheeks. Keith had made her see red, but now all she saw was Brady kneeling in front of her, strong and steady, his expression sincere.

"It isn't you, Cassie. It's them. None of this is your fault. There are as many good people out there as there are bad people." He stopped, tensing his jaw against his own emotions.

What were they exactly? she wondered. Did he feel the same anger and frustration roiling inside her? He must have.

He drew a deep breath and exhaled slowly before pressing on. "Unfortunately, you've run into a couple of pretty bad ones. But it isn't you. You haven't done anything wrong."

A sob rose up and strangled her. She placed her hand

over her mouth to catch the damn thing. She wasn't going to cry. Forcing herself to take deep breaths in through her nose and out through her mouth, she held Brady's gaze until she felt she could speak.

When she did, her voice cracked, but she held the tears in check. "How can you be sure? What if I'm some kind of a magnet for trouble?" she asked, allowing this calm, steady man to hear her deepest fear.

She trusted Brady when she had no reason to trust any man. And she'd upended his entire life with her drama.

Brady dropped back and landed on his rump. Winnie commando-crawled out from under the table. She gave his cheek a sniff, then turned to face Cassie. The dog sat patiently staring at her, clearly intending to take over where her partner wasn't getting the job done.

She put out a tentative paw, and Cassie broke.

Laughing and crying all at once, she hugged the dog the way she wished she could hug Brady. "Oh, sweet girl. I don't want to get your fur all wet again."

Brady looked at her from his spot on the floor. "Labradors are water dogs. They don't mind getting wet."

Bracing the dog's soft cheeks between her palms, Cassie stared into Winnie soulful eyes. "Thank you. You're such a good girl. I won't even tell the boss man there about the green beans you've been eating all night."

Brady chuckled. "There are worse things they could have been giving her," he said with a shrug. "But we're gonna have to talk about table scraps."

The dog turned and shot him a baleful look. Sometimes he thought she understood every word he'd said. Brady gave her midsection a brisk rub. "Labs tend to put on weight, so I have to watch her diet pretty carefully. She needs to be agile when moving through tight spaces."

Cassie wiped the remnants of her tears from her eyes. Straightening her shoulders, she gave him a brisk nod. "I'll explain to the girls. Hopefully, we'll be out of your hair soon and you won't have to worry about having such bad influences around." She forced herself to stand. "You're a good girl," she said, giving Winnie's head one last pat.

Brady's expression sobered as he scrambled to his feet. "You're staying here until Norton has been caught," he stated in a no-nonsense tone.

Cassie didn't see the point in fighting him when she had absolutely no intention of leaving until his stated outcome had been achieved. "Of course, we are. I can't think of any place the girls and I would feel safer than right here with you and Winnie."

Her cheeks heated with the admission, but she refused to look away. It was the truth, and the trials and tribulations of her past had taught her that pride was a cheap commodity.

And truth was worth its weight in gold.

Brady held out a hand for her to shake, prepared to seal their pact. Cassie took it, loving the way the warmth of his fingers enveloped hers. She was not a tiny or incapable woman, but there was something about Brady's presence. He made her feel protected but not diminished.

Shaking her head to dislodge those thoughts, she glanced at her phone. "Should I block the number?"

Brady gave his uniform pants a cursory brush, then shook his head. "No. I think it's best to let him see the text came through and was read. The last thing we want is for him to disappear for a while. We want him to stay right here until we can catch him. Otherwise, you'll be waiting and watching, wondering if he plans to return." Brady reached out and gave her shoulder a squeeze. "This is scary, but you came here to build a new life. I want you to be able to get on with your life without needing to look over your shoulder constantly."

Cassie pushed the phone to the corner of the counter. "Okay. I'll leave it open, but I'm not going to respond."

"He will see the read receipt. It'll be good enough. He's getting anxious to find you. I spoke to the chief this afternoon, and I'm going to be taking a couple of days off to stick close to home."

Cassie shook her head, her ponytail flying. "Oh, Brady, you don't have to take vacation days. We can take care of ourselves."

"You absolutely can, but until this is over, Chief Walters and I think it would be best if either Winnie or I are on-site." He looked her straight in the eye. "He's going to make a move soon. I feel it in my bones."

"You don't think he'll find us out here, do you?"

He pinned her with a stare. "I think he's going to go anywhere you are. I am too." He paused, wondering if she was playing his words over in her mind. "But I don't mean in a creepy way," he added quickly.

She grinned when she saw him tug at one pink ear. "Right. No, I get you. And thank you. Your noncreepy presence makes us all feel a lot better."

Chapter Twenty-Four

Cassie dressed in a pair of dark skinny jeans and hiking boots for the excursion to the backyard. The girls had also complied with Brady's uniform regulations, though she doubted any of his regular helpers rocked rhinestone unicorns on the legs of their jeans or silky flowers appliquéd to their rear pockets.

When they stepped out onto the deck, they found him waiting at the foot of the stairs wearing a faded gray T-shirt and jeans he'd obviously worn to paint at some point. Cassie did her best not to ogle the man as he plunked two bright yellow hard hats onto the girls' heads.

They were too big, of course, which sent them into gales of giggles. Brady grinned as he took the hats and adjusted them to their smallest fit. Once he was satisfied, he scooped two more hard hats up off the ground. He placed a white one covered in scuff marks on his own head, then handed her a dull blue hat that appeared to have seen many years of service.

"Sorry, I had to scrounge through what I had around."

Cassie tried the hat on for size. It fit decently enough, though she was sure she didn't look anywhere near as cute as the girls did in theirs. "Nothing we can't cure with glitter glue and some stickers, right, girls?" she asked, shooting him a mischievous glance.

The girls cheered their approval for the plan, but Brady

shook his head. "I'm afraid I can't allow glitter glue and stickers. You're wearing Dillon's hat, and he is definitely more into airbrush painting." He gestured for them to join him in the yard with a wave of his arm.

"Come on down." As they started down the steps, he spoke reassuringly. "I put away most of the tools and any miscellaneous hardware I could find laying around the place, but it's really important you girls never play out here without either me or your mom with you. There are dangerous tools out here. I would be upset if you were hurt, and Winnie would probably never forgive me." He jerked his head toward the dog, who had settled herself in a sunny patch of grass a few feet away. "Do we have a deal?"

Both girls nodded, their bright yellow hard hats slipping down over their eyes and making them giggle again. Jilly's tumbled to the ground, but she scooped it from the dirt and slapped it onto her skull with such force Cassie winced.

Brady laughed. "Easy, now. I don't need you hurting yourself with the safety equipment either."

With another wave of his arm, he herded them in the direction of the house under construction. "As I said, I planned a pretty big layout. Mainly because I didn't want to have to add on to it later if I want more room." He glanced down at Brook and flashed her a conspiratorial grin as he tapped the top of her hard hat. "Go big or go home, right?"

"Right," Jilly cried enthusiastically.

As they moved to stand in front of the partially framed structure, he gestured to an opening at the center. "This will be the front door. I plan on building a wraparound porch. At least three sides, if not the whole house. I'm still debating about what to do in the rear of the house. I'd hate to have to clear too many more trees. They're one of the reasons I bought the place." He pointed to his left. "There's a trail down to Cade's Creek."

"Nice," Cassie murmured.

"I might go with more of a side yard," he continued, gesturing to the open area to their right. "I'm thinking of putting in a pond or a pool."

"Oh!" Jilly gasped.

Brook bounced with excitement beside her. "A pool! A pool!" she exclaimed, clapping her hands together.

Brady stroked his chin, then smoothed his neatly clipped beard down his throat. "You think?" he asked, cocking his head to the side, surveying the area and weighing the possibilities. "I was thinking a small pond would be cool. I could stock it with some fish, maybe build a dock to sit on in case I want to toss a line in."

The hopeful note in his tone made Cassie's heart pound. She could envision him sitting on his imaginary dock. "Sounds nice. And you can also swim in a pond," she added for the girls' benefit.

Brook stilled, staring at Brady solemnly. "A pool would be prettier."

Brady pursed his lips, like he was seriously taking her point under consideration. "Yes, a pool would be prettier. But Winnie loves a pond. She likes to swim."

Jilly's whole demeanor changed at the mention of the dog's name. "Oh yeah. Winnie would like a pond better," she agreed like she was an authority on his dog's swimming preferences.

Brady steered the conversation to the house again. "Okay, follow me." They fell into a line like ducklings, with Cassie bringing up the rear. She wanted to be sure the girls didn't stray too far off whatever path Brady determined was suitable.

He led them through the maze of walls, pointing out which rooms would be where, but she was hard-pressed to visualize the final layout. His enthusiasm was distracting. *He* was distracting. When the brief tour was over, she asked, "Do you have actual plans drawn out?"

"Yeah. I took my ideas into an architectural firm in Boise, and they gave me a set of blueprints."

"But you designed it yourself," she said, impressed.

"For the most part." He shrugged. "One of the architects made a couple of suggestions, which made sense. I was open to input."

"Amazing."

Cassie didn't mean it was amazing he designed the house himself, but his willingness to be open to input from others. Another way that Brady Nichols stood apart from other men. When they returned to the double-wide, Brady collected their hard hats in a stack and set them on the deck. In the waning evening light, Cassie could see the weariness around his eyes, and she decided Brady might appreciate some space to relax. Clapping her hands to get the girls' attention, she made a shooing motion toward the door. "Okay, dessert then bath time," she announced.

The girls groaned when she mentioned the bath, but Cassie ignored it as usual. "You know the drill." She leaned down to whisper to Jilly, whose bottom lip stood out in a pronounced pout, "You don't want Winnie to think you stink, do you?"

She scooped out bowls of ice cream for all of them. She smiled when Brady seated himself at the table, clearly as excited about dessert as the girls were. She took her own bowl and dropped back into the chair she was starting to think of as hers. A dangerous presumption, she knew. But here, seated at this small table with these three people, she felt safe.

The scraping of spoons against empty bowls brought her out of her haze. Giving the table a firm pat, she announced, "Okay. To the bath, ladies."

Jilly was off like a shot, calling out her demands for bubblegum-scented bubble bath. She'd spotted the bottle Cassie had purchased on their grocery store visit, and seemed to be determined to use it all as fast as possible.

She turned to look at Brook and caught the older girl rolling her eyes in exasperation. "Can I take a shower instead?" she asked in a hushed tone. "I'm getting kind of big for baths."

Cassie's heart clenched. Another rite of passage. Another reminder her eldest was a big girl now, and running headlong into those preteen days where they would start to clash.

"Sure," she said, running her hand over Brook's long ponytail. "Let me get Jilly out of the way, then it's all yours."

Brook followed her sister into the trailer. She swallowed down the lump of emotion, focusing on the spot where the sun set beyond the trees.

"Too fast," she murmured to herself.

But Brady heard her and stepped closer. Truthfully, she'd forgotten about Brady until he placed a comforting hand on her shoulder. "Nah, she's only trying to be different."

Cassie shifted to look at him. She appreciated his attempts to make her feel better, but she had far more experience at turning from a girl into a young woman than the man beside her.

"I'd better go supervise, or Jilly will dump the entire bottle into your tub."

He gave her room to move past him. "Yeah, good idea. I bought this place as is, and I'm not sure how well the plumbing will handle being bubble-gummed," he said, pulling a face.

Loath to miss the sunset lighting the woods, she turned to him. "We'll be out of your hair soon, I promise," she said.

"I grabbed a bottle of wine at the store, if you'd like a glass once the girls are in bed," he said, speaking over her promises.

Their eyes met and held. Brady broke the tension.

"You're not in my hair. I like having you here. I didn't realize how quiet the place was," he said sincerely.

A squeal reverberated through the trailer, and Cassie grimaced. "Certainly not quiet anymore. Thanks for the tour, and a glass of wine would be great."

Chapter Twenty-Five

By the time Cassie got the girls settled, full dark had come to the foothills and Brady Nichols had moved to the porch. Padding silently through the house on bare feet, she double-checked the locks on the kitchen window and the back door to be sure. Then she tugged the hem of her T-shirt down and made a futile attempt to press the wrinkles from her shorts with the steam from her sweaty palms.

Running back to her room to primp would be too obvious, so she unleashed a long sigh and smoothed her hair before stepping out onto the porch. A single citronella candle burned in a bucket at the far end away from the steps. Brady sat on the top step, his long legs stretched out in front of him. He had a bottle of beer on the step between his knees and an old-fashioned jelly jar filled with pink wine beside him. She smiled when she saw he'd taken the trouble to cover the top of the glass with a paper napkin.

He looked up when she set foot on the porch. "I didn't want to turn on any lights. We'd attract every bug from here to Boise."

"Good thinking." She pointed to the jar of wine. "Fancy stemware," she said, unable to suppress a grin. "If I didn't know any better, I'd think you were trying to impress me."

"Maybe I am." Brady reached over and picked up the wine he'd poured for her. Whipping the napkin off with a flourish, he raised both eyebrows and announced, "Only the best for you, *mah-dahm*."

Cassie snickered and accepted the jar. "Thank you, kind sir," she said, settling down beside him. "The girls have been making you play Princess and the Dragon too much."

"I'm hoping it'll be my turn to be the dragon soon," he said, his expression impressively neutral.

Chuckling, Cassie tipped the jelly jar to her lips. The wine was cool and fruity. The perfect antidote to the sticky warmth of the hectic summer day. A wry smile twisted her lips. "It's funny, I never think to buy myself wine."

"I have beer, if you'd rather have one of those," Brady said, tensing to rise. "And, you know, water and stuff."

She shook her head hard, and he paused as if in suspended animation. "The wine is perfect. Thank you."

They sat together in companionable silence for a few minutes. Cassie gazed out into the velvet darkness, mesmerized by how thick and warm the night felt as it closed in around them. Part of her knew she should be wary. She was out in the middle of nowhere, alone with a man who was practically a stranger. But she wasn't scared.

She stole a glance at Brady out of the corner of her eye. He was staring into the deep, dark distance as well.

"I'd forgotten how close the night feels when you're away from the lights of town." She hesitated for a moment, then plunged ahead, finishing the thought. "Like it's a tiger crouched *right there*, ready to pounce."

He jerked as if she'd poked him, then shifted away from her ever so slightly. "We can go back in if you'd feel safer."

But she didn't feel unsafe. For the first time in a long time, she felt absolutely secure. And at that moment, all she wanted to do was sit on those narrow porch steps with this handsome man and bask in the comfort of his presence.

"No, it's beautiful."

"I wouldn't blame you for feeling a little twitchy. I'd

never lived anywhere but in a city until I moved out here," he told her, his lips curving into a bashful smile. "The first few nights I lived here, I must have jumped out of my skin at least a half dozen times."

Heartened by his confession, she beamed up at the carpet of brilliant stars gracing the summer sky. "Is that why you decided to get Winnie? So you'd have a companion?"

"Maybe partly," he conceded. "The department has close ties to the Daniels Canine Academy, and I was always impressed with what these dogs can do. When they asked if I wanted to train to be a handler, it might have crossed my mind that I wouldn't be out here alone anymore."

"I can't believe a big, strong man like you would be afraid," she teased, affecting a husky parody of a drawl.

But whatever Brady was going to say in response was interrupted by the buzzing of her phone. She looked down at the device, wariness crawling up her spine as she watched it vibrate across the wooden stair, inching its way closer to Brady's beer bottle.

Brady looked down too. "Unknown caller?"

She shrugged. "I get as many of those as anybody does, I guess. Except now, I always wonder if maybe it's Keith rather than someone trying to sucker me into loan consolidation or sell me a car warranty."

Brady nodded solemnly. "Do you ever answer them?"

She shook her head. "No. I figure if it's somebody who really needs to speak to me, they'll leave a message."

Brady nodded. "I get one every once in a while, but they're not too bad for me." He toasted her. "Maybe they sense I'm a cop."

He lifted his beer bottle to his lips and took a long pull. Cassie caught herself staring at his Adam's apple as he swallowed and forced herself to look away before he caught her gawping.

Grasping for a change of subject, she latched on to the

one that was always uppermost in her mind. "The girls really love staying here. Winnie's curled up at the foot of their bed, and they're arguing over which one of them she's protecting."

"Both of them," he said without hesitation.

Cassie nodded. "I told them that, but they're not in the mood to share right now, so I'm afraid that Winnie is going to have to pick sides."

Brady chuckled. "I wonder—"

His speculation was cut off by the vibration of her phone again. They watched as the notification flashed on the screen. Cassie stiffened when she noticed the area code: 406.

The call was coming from Montana.

Brady must have felt her tension because he immediately went on high alert. "What? What is it? Do you recognize that number?"

"No," she reassured him quickly. "It's just, that's the area code for Montana."

"Where? What area of Montana?" he demanded, setting the beer bottle down with a thud.

She shrugged. "The whole state."

"The whole state?" he repeated, incredulous. "A state that big only has one area code?" he asked.

Cassie smirked. "Big state, small population."

"But you don't know the phone number," he pressed.

She shook her head. "Like I said, I get some of those autodialers. I bought this phone in Montana, and lots of them have software that clones phone numbers with similar exchanges so you'll think it's someone you know calling."

His shoulders slumped, but at last he nodded a concession. "Maybe we should go in," he suggested, his voice gruff.

They probably should. It seemed foolish and dangerous for them to be sitting out in the open like this. Especially with Keith still out there. Anger surged through her, and impulsively she reached over and placed a hand on his forearm to restrain him. "No. I want to enjoy this glass of wine and this nice night. I want to sit here in the quiet and just...be."

His brow furrowed, but he nodded slowly. "Do you... Should *I* go inside?"

The soft sincerity of his question gave her the courage to look directly at him. "No. I want to sit here and enjoy this nice, quiet summer night with you."

They subsided into silence once again. Cassie sipped her wine, smiling as the crisp liquid tickled her taste buds. It was nice of him to have thought to buy a bottle. Then again, *he* was nice, so it made sense for him to be thoughtful as well. And sitting there with him, all warm and solid beside her, was somewhere beyond the definition of nice.

"Brady, I—"

Whatever she was going to say was disrupted by a chime indicating that her last caller had indeed left a voice mail.

Growling with frustration, she set her jelly jar down and snatched the phone from the step. "Seriously, if this is someone trying to sell me vinyl siding, I'm probably going to lose my ever-lovin'—"

"How dare you sic the cops on me," a deep voice erupted from the speaker. "Who do you think you are? You told them I stole my own kids? I can't steal my own kids—they're my kids," Mark Whitaker said, slurring heavily. "I can see my kids whenever the hell I feel like seeing my kids. If I wanted them, I could just come take them, and you couldn't say anything about it, Miss High and Mighty. You can't sic the cops on me. I'm their father. I have rights. You think twice before you go pointing the police in my direction. My own damn kids," he mumbled before the recording came to a stop.

Cassie stared at the phone, her cheeks aflame and the blood pulsing loud in her ears. She closed her eyes and wished as hard as she could for the porch to cave in and swallow her up.

"Oh, my God," she whispered.

"I take it that was your ex," Brady said as he thrust to his feet.

Cassie's head jerked up and she watched as he stepped down onto the gravel drive and began to pace back and forth in front of the stairs.

"Uh, well, yeah. That was the prize known as Mark Whitaker. Can I pick 'em or can I pick 'em?"

"First of all, he cannot come and take his children anytime he feels like it," Brady insisted, holding up one finger as if there would be multiple points to his argument.

"He's not going to come and get his children," she assured him. "He hasn't attempted to see them since the day I left. He's just mad because I gave somebody an excuse to question him."

"Second, if he thinks he wants to get anywhere near you or those kids, he's going to have to get through me," Brady said as if she hadn't spoken.

Now, maybe on any another night, Cassie would have appreciated the sentiment, but on this night she was fresh out of patience for male posturing.

"No, he would have to get through *me*," she corrected. He opened his mouth, and she held out her palm to stop him. "I am their mother. I will take care of my children. And while we appreciate everything you have done, and continue to do for us, we're not in the market for a white knight."

Her last assertion seemed to draw him up short. Brady stopped pacing and pivoted to face her squarely. "I'm not trying to be some kind of white knight," he argued. "I'm only saying—"

"I know what you're saying, and it's very kind of you, but I will remind you that *I* am the last line of defense between anybody and my children," she stated unequivocally.

Brady blinked, then took a step back. "Right. Of course. I didn't mean to imply anything else."

Clutching her phone, Cassie rose on unsteady legs. "Listen, it's been a long day." She gave a short laugh. "It's been a long week. Month. Year." Bending over, she picked up the jelly jar and held it aloft in salute. "Thank you for the wine, Brady. You're a good man." She raised the jar to her mouth and drained the thing dry in three gulps. Smacking her lips as she lowered it, she flashed him a satisfied smile. "Sometimes you're too good to be real."

"I'm not that good," he retorted.

She knew he wanted to say more, but at that moment, the phone buzzed in her hand. Again, the 406 area code preceded another string of unfamiliar numbers. Turning the screen to face him, she said, "You're far too good to have to deal with me and all the nasty baggage I tote around with me."

Pressing the button on the top of the phone, she held it down until the option to power it off appeared. With a swipe of her thumb, she ended their night. "Good night, Brady. Sleep well. Tomorrow is sure to be another doozy of a day."

With that, she turned on her heel and slipped back into the house. Shoving her blessedly silent phone into her pocket, she headed straight for the hall leading to the bedrooms. When she peeked in the first doorway on the left, she found the girls curled up together like kittens, and their guard dog blinking blearily. Cassie exhaled long and soft when Winnie gave her a reassuring thump of her tail, then settled her chin on her paws again.

"Such good girls," she whispered to the three of them. "Sweet dreams."

Minutes later, she was scrubbed clean and stretched out on the guest bed, wide-awake and listening for things that bumped in the night. The last thing she heard before drifting off to sleep was the creak of Brady's footsteps as he paused outside each of their bedrooms, then quietly closed the door to his.

Chapter Twenty-Six

Brady enjoyed having the Whitaker girls at his place. Or maybe it had been him and Winnie alone out there for too long. Whatever the reason, having them stay under his roof charged him up. They were like firecrackers, adding spark to the day and keeping everyone on their toes.

The day after Mark Whitaker's call, things had been a bit tense with Cassie, so he focused more on the girls. He put Brook and Jilly to work. First, it was stacking small pieces of scrap wood off to the side of the deck. Then, when they grew restless, he took them around to the front of the trailer where a small flower bed planted with evergreens was slowly being overtaken by weeds. For once, he was grateful for the never-ending list of tasks he never got around to tackling. What he considered a trial, they saw as a treat.

Jilly was gleeful at the thought of being allowed to destroy something without getting in trouble. She was born to be a weeder. True to her nature, Brook moved at a slower, more methodical pace. Brady wasn't surprised when he came to check on them and found Brook had refused to pull some of the weeds because they were flowering.

"They're too pretty," she insisted, gazing at him with sincerity lighting her face.

He couldn't disagree with her assessment, so he left the landscaping to her more appreciative eye. When he came around again, he found Cassie settled down in the dirt beside them. He couldn't help remembering how his ex-wife had tossed a houseplant someone had given them as a gift into the trash because she thought it would be "too much trouble."

He commented on Cassie's willingness to get her hands dirty, and she laughed at him outright, her eyes dancing with amusement.

"I'm training to be a river guide and a hiking trail expert. You think I'm afraid of your landscaping?"

Brady could only shake his head as he walked away, grateful the tension from the previous evening had dissipated. She wanted to be a river guide. The notion of her heading off into the wild with a bunch of strangers both terrified and intrigued him. Sure, he'd made a study of her lithe, athletic grace, but it was still hard for him to believe such a beautiful woman derived so much pleasure from the outdoors. His ex-wife, Lisa, had been anything but the outdoorsy type.

Cassie and her girls were a refreshing contrast.

He kept himself busy through the morning by doing parts of the framing he could handle on his own. When the sun had reached its apex, he knew they should find cooler modes of entertainment.

He walked into the kitchen to find Cassie preparing an assembly line of sandwiches. Two of them were peanut butter and jelly, but the other two were piled high with sliced deli meat and cheese. She glanced over her shoulder and waved a butter knife in greeting when she saw him. "I was about to yell out there to ask if you like mayo or mustard on your sandwich," she said.

"Actually, neither," he admitted. Walking over to the fridge, he opened the door and pulled out a bottle of ranch dressing. "I usually squirt some ranch on there. Gives it extra zing."

Cassie looked at the bottle of salad dressing, then down at the jar of mayonnaise on the counter. "Ranch," she said slowly, almost tasting the world. Then she thrust her hand toward him. "Such a guy thing, but not necessarily a bad idea."

Brady handed the bottle over to her, then shoved his hands into the pockets of his jeans. "I'm full of them."

"Listen, Brady, I'm sorry I got a little prickly last night. Living with Mark… Well, let's just say it wasn't the best thing for my self-esteem—"

"No need to apologize," he interrupted.

"No, there is." She turned to look him in the eye. "I have a bit of a chip on my shoulder when it comes to the girls. Or more like, when it comes to me being a good mom."

"You're a great mom," he said quickly.

"I try," she answered with a wan smile. "But I know I get a little sticky about it sometimes." She made a cringing face. "Vera called me out on it, and as much as I hate to admit it, she's right. I tend to take the independence thing a step too far."

She placed her hand on his arm. His gaze flew to hers. "You have been nothing but good and generous with us, and I want you to know I appreciate you."

He gave a solemn nod. "It's my pleasure. I like having you here."

His statement hung in the air a moment too long. Cassie drew her hand away, curling her fingers into a ball as she turned her attention back to the sandwiches.

Kicking himself for making her uncomfortable, he switched gears entirely.

"Anyway, no worries. We're good, right?"

"Yeah, right. Definitely okay."

"Great." He clapped his hands once, then rubbed his palms together. "So, I was coming in to see if maybe you and your squad would like to go with me to do some fishing down at Cade's Creek. There's lots of shade there, and the trail is an easy walk through the woods."

Cassie's face lit up. "Sounds great."

"There's a nice spot on the bank. If you want, we could make it a picnic."

"Oh, the girls will be so excited," she said, looking up from her work with a grin. "I'll get the food together. You go tell them what the plan is."

Minutes later, Brady realized she tricked him into delivering news that was sure to have taken years off his hearing ability. The girls both squealed and jumped around him like their legs were spring-loaded. He disentangled himself with the excuse of needing to go change into some shorts as they were talking a mile a minute about all the fish they would catch and how they'd ask their mom to cook them for supper.

Pleased with himself, Brady quickly changed and hurried out to find them assembled near the door. "I guess you're ready."

"We're ready," Brook and Jilly chorused.

Jilly kept a steady run of chatter as he carried the cooler Cassie had packed and led their merry band around the partially constructed house and down the trail leading to the creek.

Once again, Cassie found herself in the rear of their contingent, a couple of fishing rods and a tackle box in hand. Winnie darted ahead of them, scoping the path with her supersnozzle and clearing the way for their safe procession. But Brook grew quieter and more withdrawn as they neared the water.

He claimed to need a minute to rest, and they stepped into a small clearing. Cassie was busy restraining Jilly, who insisted she should run ahead to keep Winnie company, but Brady was focused on Brook. She was almost completely silent, her expression wary and her body language closed. Brady shot a glance at Cassie.

Cassie hushed Jilly with a stern, "No, and that's final."

He stepped away as she abandoned the fishing poles and other equipment in favor of wrapping her arms around Brook's shoulders.

"Are you okay, sweetie?" she asked, keeping her tone light even though her eyes were searching, intense with worry. "Too hot to walk?"

She looked at her mother, her eyes wide and frightened. "I don't like it here."

Cassie hugged her, though her expression said she wasn't entirely clear as to what triggered Brook's apprehension. She appeared to be ready to give those tender emotions a gentle prod when Winnie let out three sharp barks.

Brady straightened. Those weren't happy barks. Those barks meant business.

"Here in the woods? Or at Brady's house?" Cassie probed, her focus locked on her daughter.

Brook shook her head so hard, her entire body twisted with it. "No, I love Brady's house." She looked down at her dusty sandals, then admitted, "I hate the woods."

"All woods or just these woods?" Cassie pressed, but gently.

"All woods," Brook answered in a lisping whisper.

"Okay, then, we don't have to go through them," Cassie asserted, glancing up at Brady.

"You know what?" he said, straining to keep his tone light. "I think I got too hot working on the house and walking down here. I'm getting a headache," he added, holding himself still as Winnie sounded the alert again.

"Aww," Jilly groaned, sensing the outing was about to get nixed.

Cassie tipped her head to look at him, concern written all over her face. "Are you okay? Do you need water?"

Winnie barked again. Three barks. Short, stubborn and insistent, and Brady took a step in the direction of the sound.

Cassie rose to her feet, keeping a hand on Brook's shoulder and reaching out to corral Jilly. "Oh."

"Do you mind if we eat lunch at the house and save the picnic for another day?" Anticipating Jilly's protest, he grabbed the abandoned tackle box and practically shoved it into her skinny arms. "I promise we'll go another day."

Winnie barked again, and both girls turned toward the sound.

Not wanting to freak Brook out any more than she already was, he forced a neutral expression. "She gets excited about the water too." He scooped the poles from the ground and thrust them at Brook, figuring she'd do better with a task. "You girls head to the house. I'll go get her and grab the cooler on the way home."

Cassie placed a hand on each girl and propelled them toward the house, impervious to Jilly's complaints. Brady leaned in at the last second and handed her his house key. "Lock the doors after you."

She gave a barely perceptible nod and nudged the girls ahead. He waited until they were around a bend, then quicktimed it down the rough trail to the stream.

He burst from the tree line as Winnie let loose another barrage of barks.

"I'm here. I'm here," he wheezed, skidding to a halt. He scanned the area but couldn't spot anything amiss. "What is it? What do you have?"

Winnie circled a spot not far from him, then walked toward the trail.

"You got something? Has someone been here?"

He forced himself to take calming breaths and focus on the scene around him. There was no trash or sign of any disturbance of the earth. No one had pitched a tent or built a fire. Winnie pawed the ground, then looked at him expectantly. Unfortunately, his sense of smell was not nearly as keen as hers. But she was trained to discern one human scent from another, and the last person she'd searched for had been Keith Norton, when they checked the lumberyard.

He swore under his breath as he took another look around. "I've got nothing to go on here, girl," he said, holding his hands out in a helpless shrug. "Go. Show me where he went."

Not needing to be asked twice, Winnie turned and bounded toward the trail leading to his property. To the place where he'd sent Cassie and the girls.

A gushing stream of self-recrimination ran through his head as he and Winnie sprinted through the underbrush. They had almost made it to the clearing when Winnie veered to the right. But he couldn't follow her lead. Not until he knew they were safe inside. Brady sprinted directly to the door. Cassie must have been watching from the kitchen window because he heard the locks click. The door opened as he hit the top step.

"What did she find? Was it Keith?"

Brady panted, but shook his head. "I'm not sure. Nothing there, but maybe." He glanced over his shoulder and saw Winnie snuffling around in the woods between the trail and the country road. He whistled, and she lifted her head. Two sharp bursts had her sprinting to the house.

Cassie turned away and without another word she opened the freezer, extracted a handful of ice cubes, and dropped them into Winnie's water.

"Where are the girls?" he asked, twisting the bolt into place.

"Brook is lying down. I asked Jilly to keep an eye on her." Her lips twisted. "She's pretty pleased to be her sister's keeper for once."

"I forgot to grab the cooler," he said, still trying to catch his breath.

"Forget it." Pivoting to the fridge, Cassie extracted the meat, cheese and ranch dressing. "Sit. We'll have our picnic right here."

Chapter Twenty-Seven

Sensing trouble, Winnie stuck close to the girls for the rest in the day. When they sat down to eat their reconstructed sandwiches, the Lab sat right beside Brook. Again, Cassie marveled at the empathy the dog seemed to have. She wondered if this was something Emma Daniels had worked with Winnie on, or if it was a God-given gift.

Either way, she was thankful Winnie had such a sharp sense for reading the emotions of those around her. Brady said not all dogs did. But his Winnie was as much about the rescue as she was the search, and Cassie was grateful as she watched Brook wind her thin arms around the dog and bury her face in Winnie's neck.

"I think it should be my turn to hug Winnie now. I haven't hugged her since this morning and she's probably missing me too," Jilly interrupted, oblivious to her older sister's distress.

"I'm sure she is," Cassie said, gently placing a hand on Jilly's head to still the girl.

Brady gathered the plates she'd used for their sandwiches. "I think this picnic was a better idea. I don't really like sitting on the ground anyway," he said a shade too cheerfully. "Ants. Every picnic's uninvited guests."

Cassie almost snickered at the idea of a man like Brady being bothered by a few pesky ants, but she caught herself.

"I don't like ants in my pants either," she said gravely. "Makes me have to do a dance."

"You can't dance." Jilly's laughter bubbled out of her, and soon Brook and Cassie were chuckling along with her.

Cassie might have been insulted by the accusation in her daughter's tone if she weren't so relieved to hear them laugh. "Of course, I can dance," she insisted, highly offended. "Everyone can dance. I bet even Brady can."

"I'm a great dancer."

To prove his skill, he boot-scooted to the sink, then proceeded to do a sort of shuffling cha-cha-slide as he squirted dish soap into the running water. Then and there, Cassie knew she was feeling something more than gratitude to the man who'd literally saved her family.

But she wouldn't dwell on that now. Despite Brook's minimeltdown and Brady's worries about Keith finding out where they were staying, it turned out to be a good day. Or as good as any day was going to be given their circumstances.

Brady had kept the conversation verging on downright silly through the relocated picnic, and Cassie couldn't have been more grateful for the distraction he provided. After lunch, she'd called the therapist recommended by the hospital, spoke to her about Brook's fear of going into the woods, and scheduled an appointment to visit with her the following week.

In the meantime, the woman gave Cassie a few different strategies for getting Brook to talk about what happened when she and Jilly got out of the cave where Keith had left them. She also had some advice on how to help her daughter cope with her emotions when they became too overwhelming. Cassie took copious notes on the last one, planning to put some of those tips to use for herself.

She'd thrown together a homemade pizza for their supper. She'd added a bag salad, and a batch of slice-and-bake cookies to use as the carrot to get her kids to eat the salad. It wasn't the most balanced meal she'd ever prepared, but she felt like they could all use something simple and tasty.

Cassie watched the girls follow Brady and Winnie around the yard like ducklings. He was so good with them. So patient. But she couldn't let her daydreams get too far ahead of her reality. They were temporary guests here. Their abandoned picnic served as a stark reminder of the threat looming over them. Over her.

With a weary sigh, she turned away from the window. She was about to call the girls in for their bath when a text came through on her phone.

It's rude not to answer phone calls, but that's okay. I'll see you soon.

"Keith." She drew in a sharp breath then let it out slowly. Her ex-husband might be annoyed with her, but certainly wasn't going to rouse himself enough to come looking for them. The message had to be from Keith. "Not if I see you first, creep," she muttered.

The door opened, and Brady herded his helpers inside. Oblivious to their chatter, she pointed to the phone on the counter and pointed the protesting girls down the hall. "My code is six-two-three-one," she called over her shoulder. He shot her a puzzled glance, but she simply pointed to the phone again and said, "Six-two-three-one."

She ushered the girls into the hall bath, only half listening to complaints over having to bathe again so soon. Running on autopilot, she used the dirt embedded under their fingernails as proof enough for the need. In truth, she just wanted them close to her.

She was stripping a yammering Jilly from her clothes when Brady's voice reverberated through the door.

"Don't worry yourself over it. It's a mind game."

"I hate games," she shouted over the roar of the water filling the tub.

"I love games," Jilly chirped. "Can we play Uno? I'm so good at Uno," she bragged as she settled into the tub. "Get in with me, Brookie."

All too aware Brook considered herself too big to share a bath with her baby sister these days, Cassie was glad her elder daughter stripped down without a fuss. They were getting too big too fast, and needing her less and less every day. She wanted to be the one they turned to for everything, always. She knew all too soon, they'd edge her out as a member of their magical threesome. Truth be told, she didn't mind the girls' clinginess these past few days.

Cassie handed her elder daughter the bottle of body wash once she was settled in the tub, then she addressed Jilly's question. "I'm not sure if Brady has Uno," she answered, careful to keep it noncommittal.

She sat with her back against the vanity, half listening as the girls debated the merits of various games while steam filled the small bathroom. She shook herself from her stupor and leaned over to turn off the taps. The last thing she wanted was for Brady to discover he had no hot water if he wanted a shower.

"Okay, go ahead. Just a quick dip," she said briskly. "We'll wash hair tomorrow."

The girls cheered at being spared the threat of shampoo in their eyes. As usual, Brook was all business. She finished rinsing the soap from her arms and she stood, letting the water cascade off her and leaving her sister to linger.

She handed her daughter a surprisingly fluffy towel. She caught a whiff and instantly recognized the scent of fabric softener.

"Brady says he's gonna let us hammer," Brook announced as she wound the towel around her body and sat down on the bath mat next to her mother.

"Did he?" Cassie said distractedly. Leaning in, she pecked a quick kiss to her big girl's head and inhaled sharply.

"Yep," Jilly confirmed. "With real hammers and nails."

She was about to quiz them on how this promise had been extracted when she heard a commotion coming from the other end of the house. Winnie began to bark incessantly, and Brady shouted a stream of expletives decidedly unsuitable for impressionable young ears. Both girls turned to look at her, their expressions wide-eyed with wonder and shock.

"Uh-oh," Jilly said under her breath.

"Cassie! Cassie!" Brady called from outside the bathroom door.

Scrambling to her feet, she pressed her cheek to the door. "Yeah? What is it? What's wrong?" she called through the thin barrier of the hollow-core door.

"The house is on fire!" he shouted to her.

"What?" She waved frantically for Jilly to get out of the bath. Brook jumped to her feet and wrapped her own damp towel around her sister, practically hauling the younger girl over the edge of the tub.

"Don't go outside," Brady ordered.

Cassie scowled at the door, her hand flying to her mouth. "What? But we're on fire," she shouted. Swiveling her head to fix the girls with a stern stare meant to hold them in place, she opened the door a crack and called over Winnie's frantic barking, "Brady? Shouldn't we evacuate?"

"Not this house. The new house," he clarified, breathless. "Here," he said, shoving her phone into her hand. "Lock yourselves in."

Winnie continued to bark, racing back and forth in the narrow hall. The white walls glowed a terrifying shade of orange.

Her breath caught in her throat as she pressed the three

digits, then held the phone to her ear. She slipped out into the hall and craned her neck to sneak a peek out the kitchen window. A towering flame danced from one of the high support beams and licked at one of the outstretched limbs of a nearby tree.

The dog continued to bark, the sound growing rough and hoarse with each volley. Above it all, the keening wails of her daughters reached out to her. Pressing the phone to her ear harder, she plugged the other ear with her index finger.

At last, Jenny, the county dispatcher, came on the line. "Jasper emergency services. Police, fire or medical emergency?" she said briskly.

"Fire," Cassie blurted. "Fire! Brady Nichols's new house is on fire."

"Brady's house?" Jenny said, the shock in her tone evident.

"Not his current house. The house he's building is on fire," Cassie clarified.

Unable to wrap her mind around what she was saying, she rushed to the kitchen window to look again. She needed to be sure she hadn't imagined the sight of his dream home in flames while she cowered in his double-wide.

She hadn't.

She saw Brady struggling to pull a garden hose free from its coil. The fire looked too far gone for a hose to do much good, and her heart broke for him. "Brady's trying to spray the flames with a hose, but we need help."

"Help is on the way." Jenny paused. "Can you stay on the line with me until they've arrived?"

Cassie backed away from the window. "Yes, but I have to go into the other room. I was giving my daughters a bath," she explained.

"Keep the call connected in case I need to ask any questions," Jenny said, her voice comfortingly calm.

Cassie sneaked one last glance at the window and saw

the most pathetic stream of water ever to shoot from a hose dribble out then shrink to a drip on the dry ground at Brady's feet. She realized in an instant the hose must have a hole in it.

"It looks like there's a hole in his hose or something," Cassie reported briskly. "Tell the fire department to hurry—"

She turned to leave the kitchen, but the words died in her throat when she stepped into the hall and saw Keith Norton standing square in the front doorway. As subtly as she could, Cassie lowered the phone from her ear. "Keith, what are you doing here?"

It was a stupid question, she knew, but she needed to stall. She needed to get to safety. More than anything, she needed to get between this man and her girls.

Chapter Twenty-Eight

Brady swore another blue streak as he looked down at the shredded garden hose in his hand. It had been a warm summer, but not hot enough to put so many cracks in a brand-new hose. Winnie's barking became more frantic. He turned away from the dancing flames consuming his hard work to look at the secondhand trailer meant to be a refuge for Cassie and her family.

The family he'd left unattended.

His stomach dropped and his fingers opened. The shredded hose fell to the ground, tangling around his feet.

He'd left them alone, and his hose hadn't cracked from baking in the sun. As he circled the house, the sweeping beam of his flashlight caught on something metal in the woods. Whirling, he swung the beam around until it shone on a red pickup truck parked on the other side of the clearing.

"Son of a—" He took off for the front door in a sprint.

"Cassie!" he called as he bolted into the double-wide. Winnie's ferocious barks nearly drowned out the sound of terrified wails. Almost, but not quite. Reaching into the coat closet, he yanked his utility belt off the high shelf where he'd stored it since two small children invaded his life and his home. He freed both his Taser and his service revolver from their nylon compartments.

Easing into the living room area, he crept forward cautiously. "Cassie! It's a trap," he called to her, though he was sure Norton was already in the house. Winnie stood at the opening of the hallway, her eyes fixed on someone in the narrow passage, and her barking incessant and aggressive. Brady couldn't see him, but it was clear she had Norton cornered.

"I'll shoot the dog," a man shouted from the end of the hall.

Brady closed his eyes, praying Cassie and the girls had managed to barricade themselves in one of the rooms. He didn't believe Norton would shoot Winnie. If the man could kill an animal, he would have done so already. Still, Brady didn't see the point in showing his cards quite yet.

"Don't harm the dog," he called out. "Winnie, down."

On command, the Labrador pressed herself to the floor, but remained poised to pounce. If Norton did have a gun, he wanted Winnie to be as small a target as possible.

Winnie did not stop barking.

Norton spoke again, shouting over the snarls and barks. "I mean it. Make it stop or I'll shoot the damn thing."

Brady moved closer to his partner and spoke in the low, commanding tone she responded to best. "Winnie, quiet."

The Labrador barking came to an abrupt halt, but Winnie wasn't above letting out a high-pitched, keening whine he assumed meant she was not happy with the command. Norton would think he got what he wanted. It was the best Brady could do until he could determine whether the man was truly armed or not.

"I'm a police officer," he called out. "Lieutenant Brady Nichols of the Jasper Police Department, and this is my home." He paused long enough to let the information penetrate. "You are a trespasser in my home. I am armed. If you are armed as well, I suggest you drop your weapon and step out into the open immediately."

"I'm not going anywhere until Cassie is where she belongs," Norton said, an edge of belligerence in his tone.

Brady inched closer to the corner of the hallway. "I'm serious, Norton. We have all your information—where you're from, where you've been. If you are carrying a weapon of any sort, I strongly suggest you drop it now."

"Mama?" one of the girls called in a voice trembling with fear. He wanted to throttle Norton for traumatizing those two sweet, innocent girls in his quest to make a point with a woman who clearly didn't want him.

"Hush, baby," Cassie said from somewhere down the hall. "Hush now, it'll be okay, Brady's here. And Winnie."

Her vote of confidence was all he needed to galvanize him into action. He snapped his fingers once and Winnie sprang into action, barking as loud as he'd ever heard as she ran straight at her target. Brady swung around the corner, his weapon leading the way.

Thankfully, both he and Cassie had closed the bedroom doors. Norton cowered at the end against the wall, too frightened of Winnie to have the guts to try either of the doors. Instead, the man stood pressed against the full-length mirror the previous owner had hung there, his hands raised high above his head.

"Call off your dog. Call off your dog," he said, his demands sharp with panic.

"Winnie, heel." Brady trained his weapon on the man, and smirked when he saw his dog stop with her muzzle within a breath of the man's crotch. She stood with her fur raised along her spine, her eyes fastened on Norton's zipper. He followed Winnie into the narrow passageway. "Cassie? Are you and the girls all right?" he called, not taking his eyes off of Norton.

"We're fine," Cassie yelled. Her words were muffled, and he prayed she was behind a closed and locked door. "But Brady, he has a knife."

No sooner did her words penetrate than Brady saw Norton swing his hand down. He caught the glint of a blade as Norton slashed at his dog, but Winnie was faster than her assailant and her senses more attuned to danger than any human could imagine. The dog shifted onto her haunches, managing to avoid the arc of the knife, but Norton's reflexes weren't nearly as good. The momentum of his swing meant the kitchen knife he held tight in his fist sliced into his own thigh.

Norton crumpled, crying out in pain and dropping the knife as he doubled over to clutch his leg with both hands.

Brady rushed closer, kicking the knife out of Norton's reach with the heel of his work boot. He didn't lower his weapon. "Oh, now you've really made a big mistake," he said, his tone deadly calm and chillingly soft.

Norton looked at him, his expression a mixture of anger and anguish. "I'm injured," he said, biting off each word.

"Self-inflicted wound," Brady corrected. "You injured yourself in an attempt to assault an officer of the law," he clarified, enunciating each word to be sure they sunk in through the man's thick skull.

"It's a damn dog," Norton ground out between clenched teeth.

"She is Officer Winnie, a duly sworn member of the Jasper Police Department. An assault on her will bring additional charges, though I don't think you'll get off too lightly with the Feds when it comes to the kidnapping attempt."

"I didn't kidnap the girls. They walked away with me. Their mother and I are going to get married," Norton snarled. "They know me. They came with me because we're going to be a family."

Brady shook his head. He wasn't going to argue with a man who was clearly delusional. "You have the right to remain silent," he said as he heard sirens approach in the distance. He finished running through Norton's rights, as footsteps pounded on the porch steps. He was happy to put the safety on his weapon as Jason Wright rushed past him, gripping a set of handcuffs.

"All clear here?" Cal Hoover asked when he and Ruby entered the scene.

Brady's shoulders slumped. "We're all fine," he said brusquely. "Norton injured himself with a knife." He turned to his friend and offered his firearm handle first, his hand trembling as the aftereffects of the adrenaline rush pulsed through him. "Here, can you hold this for me?"

Cal took the gun from Brady. "We're going to step out of here," Cal informed him. "This hallway is tight, and Winnie looks fairly wound up."

Brady glanced at Winnie and saw his dog still hadn't shifted into a position of ease. "Winnie, down, girl. Sit."

At last, the Labrador's rump hit the floor. But she wouldn't take her eyes off Norton while Jason Wright secured the cuffs in front of the injured man.

"JFD is working on your house," Jason informed him. "They pulled in right in front of us." He moved to Norton's injured side and pushed himself under the man's arm. "EMTs are outside. I'll have them take a look at this paper cut, then we'll take him down to the station."

"Cassie," Norton called out as Jason pushed him past the closed bathroom door. "Cassie, let me explain. Give me a chance to ex—"

His words were cut off when the bathroom door flew open and Cassie Whitaker shot out like a bullet fired from Brady's gun.

"Explain? You want to explain kidnapping my daughters and holding them out in the woods overnight in the cold and dark? Are you going to try to tell me you didn't think they would be scared? Or maybe you wanna tell me about how they ran away from you and got lost in the woods, but were still smart enough to find the creek and follow it toward town," she said, raspy with unspent emotion. "There's nothing to explain, Keith. There is nothing between us. We were never serious. I was never going to marry you. Never." She stared him right in the face, a portrait of defiance. "You've stalked me, stolen my children, terrorized us. There's nothing in this world that can make me come within ten feet of you. We will never speak again, Keith. Ever."

Having spoken her piece, she stepped into the bathroom and slammed the door so hard the entire place shook.

Cal let out a low whistle as Jason propelled a sputtering Norton past him. "Man, if a dressing-down like that doesn't make things clear for you, nothing will," he said to the cuffed man.

When he was sure Jason and Norton were out the door, Cal turned to Brady with a nod and said, "How about I take Winnie out for a run in the woods and let her work some of the adrenaline off? We'll head for the road, since the crew is working on putting out the bonfire you've got going on out there." He gave his head a sad shake. "I sure am sorry about the house, Brady."

Brady looked up, numbness setting in as his synapses slowed. "Winnie, go. Go with Cal and Ruby."

The dog followed his order, but not without casting one last, worried glance at Brady. "You're a good girl. The best. Now, go with Cal."

Chapter Twenty-Nine

Once they had gone, Brady stepped forward and knocked on the bathroom door with the knuckle of his index finger. "It's me. Let me in?"

There was a pause, then Cassie asked, "Is everyone else gone?"

Her question was muffled. When he cracked open the door, he found them huddled together. The girls were clad in cotton nightgowns stuck to them where the damp ends of their hair dripped. They were wrapped around their mother like koalas clinging to a tree. "It's me," he assured them.

As always, Jilly was the first to shift gears. Peeling herself away from Cassie, she hurtled into his legs. "Winnie saved us."

Without thinking, Brady reached down to smooth her silky hair, tempted to point out he'd played a small part in holding Keith Norton until backup arrived. But as far as Jilly was concerned, he was merely the guy who scooped kibble for Wonder Winnie, and that was okay with him.

"Winnie is the best."

"So are you," Cassie said, voice hoarse with tears and residual anger.

He glanced over at her. "Thank you." He drew a steadying breath, then said, "We'll book Norton into custody here, but the Bureau will likely take over the case. I'm assuming he'll be moved to Boise for holding."

"Can they send him farther?" Cassie asked with a watery half smile.

"Like to the moon?" Brook grumbled, nuzzling deeper into Cassie.

Jilly immediately latched on to the idea, tipping her small face to his. "Yeah! Like on a rocket."

Brady stared down at her, marveling at the girl's resilience. "Yeah, I think Boise is about as far as we can say for sure, but I'll suggest an interstellar incarceration."

"Sounds too cool for Keith," Cassie grumbled. "He needs to be sent to a place decidedly warmer and fierier—"

She stopped, her eyes widening as she scrambled to her feet, Brook clinging to her. "Oh, my God, Brady, your house!" Standing on her toes, she craned her neck to look out the small window above the tub. But all she could see was the orange glow of fire. "Your beautiful house," she said, fresh worry creasing her brow.

Brady shook his head to indicate there was nothing to be done. Crouching, he swept Jilly into his arms. "I'm not worried about the house."

"But—"

"It's wood and nails, Cassie," he said, the gruff finality in his tone cutting through her arguments. Cradling Jilly's head in the palm of his hand, he found solace in her trusting embrace. "It doesn't matter. All that matters is we're all safe."

Tears filled her big hazel eyes. "Thanks to you."

"Winnie did it," Jilly corrected, her face nuzzled into his neck.

Brady was more than happy to let his partner take the credit. The warmth in Cassie's gaze was more than enough for him. "That's right. Winnie will want you girls to help her make a statement."

He did his best not to turn his head to look at the fire as he led them out of the bathroom and into the smoke-filled twilight. He didn't have to look to know exactly how bad the scene behind the trailer would be. The flames had been subdued, but all around them, firefighters continued to shout instructions to one another. A second truck had arrived minutes after the first, but his gut told him their efforts would be too late. Even as Cassie fell into step beside him with Brook clasping her mother's hand tightly, Brady was beginning to accept the reality of his home being beyond saving.

"It's going to be a mess here tonight," he informed Cassie. "Will you be able to stay with Vera and Millard?"

She turned, her gaze following a pair of firefighters in full turnout gear as they sprinted around the corner of the trailer. "I guess we could, but with Keith in custody, I think I'd rather go home. Do you think we can?"

His heart clenched at the hopefulness in her tone. Home. To the house where her grandparents had lived. Home, to the place where she and her daughters would make new memories. If they stayed here.

Lowering Jilly to the ground beside Cal's SUV, he said, "Yeah. Of course. I don't see why not."

"I think the sooner I have the girls in their own beds, the better."

"You're probably right," he agreed, though the words came out gravelly with disappointment. He hated to see them go. All of them. It was bad enough contemplating one night, but now… She was right. There was no reason for them to stay with him. Except he wanted them there.

Mentally kicking himself for letting his own selfish feelings get in the way of what might be best for her poor, traumatized girls, he kept his mouth shut tight as they made their way to the vehicles.

"Do we have to go to the police station again?" Brook asked, trepidation making her voice quaver.

Brady knew they would have to take a statement from Cassie and the girls, but he hadn't thought far enough ahead to request their interview be done as far from where Norton was being held as possible.

Cal stepped out from the other side of the van with Winnie and Ruby straining at their leads and saved him from floundering. "No, miss," he replied, all Western civility. "Unlike some people, you are not under arrest. You are our star witnesses." He met Brady's troubled gaze, and Brady gave a grateful nod. "As such, I think it means you get to choose." Turning to Cassie, he said, "We can conduct our business at your house, if that's okay with you, ma'am."

"Our house would be great. Thank you."

"Can Winnie spend the night with us?" Jilly asked, her face lighting with hope as she turned to Brady.

A sad smile twisted his lips. "I'm sorry. She'd like it a lot, but she needs to stay with me. We're partners, remember?"

Both girls looked crestfallen. He felt like an ogre, but Winnie was first and foremost a working dog, and as such, constant reinforcement of her routine was essential. "But you are welcome to visit us whenever you like," he said, his gaze drifting to Cassie's and holding. "Anytime. We'll miss having you around."

Cassie returned his stare long enough to make his heart start to hammer. But then she shifted her attention to strapping her daughters into her van. "We will definitely visit, sometime. Maybe even bring Brady some brownies baked in a regular baking pan," she said, injecting a note of forced cheer into her tone.

"I take brownies any way I can get them," he said, matching her false brightness.

When the girls were buckled in, and Cal went to secure Ruby in his vehicle, Brady followed Cassie to the driver's door. "Are you okay to drive?" he asked, glad he didn't need to mask his worry for the sake of the girls.

She gave a laugh, but it sounded more like a sob. "I can't

believe you're asking if *I'll* be okay." Shaking her head, she gestured to the chaos surrounding them. "Brady, your house—"

"I told you, the house can be rebuilt." He stepped closer and stared straight into her wide, troubled eyes. "You and the girls are safe. That's all that matters to me."

She wet her lips, and the temptation to kiss her was so strong, he had to make himself move away.

"Thank you," she whispered.

Unable to conjure too many coherent words, he simply jerked his chin in acknowledgment, then reached past her to open the door for her. The sounds of the girls bickering in loud whispers was music to his ears. He'd spent the better part of the last week of his life wrapped in the cocoon of their world, and now he was sad to leave it.

"You go on now. I'll see to this and gather up your stuff and we'll get it over to you." She hesitated, and he gave her a tired smile. "It's okay. I'll see you soon," he promised, though he barely recognized his own voice.

Cassie's lips curved. "See you soon," she promised as she slid behind the wheel.

Brady closed the door, then gave it a final pat. The girls waved as Cassie drove carefully through the vehicles littering his front yard. The lights from the fire engines bounced off the windows of the minivan.

Winnie nuzzled his hand with her damp nose and gave a soft whine, letting him know she was nearby. He stroked her head absently. Cassie's brake lights flashed before she turned onto the road.

He spotted a small hand pressed against the side window in a gesture of farewell. He realized from the positioning of the seats, it had to be Brook and something inside him broke.

Behind him, the home of his dreams was going up in smoke, but somehow, it wasn't as hard as watching the family who'd captured his heart drive away into the night.

Chapter Thirty

It took a couple of days for Cassie to gather everything she wanted to give Brady as a thank-you gift. Secretly, she was hoping he was missing her every bit as much as she and the girls missed him.

Cassie was glad Cal Hoover had been the one to take their statement. The girls had been through enough, and being interviewed by the man who'd helped carry them to safety after the night they were lost in the woods made it easier for them to get comfortable with him. Almost as comfortable as they'd been with Brady. But not quite.

And it felt weird to be in her grandparents' house without them. The place didn't feel right. It wasn't her place. And even with two lively girls, something was missing.

Someone was missing.

Cassie walked out of Saunders's Hardware with big bags of donated building materials with a small, smug smile on her face. "It's nice they're going to help, Mama," Brook said approvingly.

"We're all going to help," Jilly chimed in. "I can hammer. Brady said he was gonna show me how to hammer when we were helping him pick stuff up the other day. I bet he'll let me."

Cassie chuckled at her daughter's confidence and enthusiasm. "I bet he will," she agreed.

They turned the corner and found Dillon Diaz lounging against the side of a pickup truck loaded down with an unusual assortment of tools and equipment. Cassie looked at him questioningly.

Dillon shrugged as he pushed away from the vehicle. "I've been collecting everything anyone was willing to give us to use. The truck with the lumber should be arriving shortly. We should probably get a move on," he said briskly.

Cassie shepherded her girls to the van parked across the street. They followed Dillon's pickup truck north out of town. When they got to the crossroads that led to the Daniels ranch, Cassie hooked a right instead of a left. Her breath hitched when she caught sight of the line of cars turning into Brady's driveway.

Once she and the girls had pulled in, there were easily twelve vehicles parked at odd angles. She was attempting to calm the girls when the man himself stepped out onto the small front porch. Brady shook his head in bewilderment as his friends and neighbors climbed from their vehicles.

Cassie was glad for the cover the crowd created. She wasn't exactly sure how Brady would feel about seeing her or the girls. After all, it was their fault the house he'd been building with his own hands had been turned into a pile of ash.

Captain Walters had been the one to tell her Keith Norton had indeed been transferred into federal custody and taken to Boise for holding. Hearing he wasn't even going to spend one more night in Jasper was a relief. Brook and Jilly had been perturbed when Special Agent Sims came to the house for yet another official interview, but they were becoming old pros at the question-and-answer game.

A part of her worried her children were becoming all too inured to the extraordinary circumstances surrounding them, but the minute the federal agent was gone, they turned into her little girls again—bickering, playing and seeking her out for comfort and counsel as needed.

The commotion of car doors slamming and shouted greetings jarred her from her thoughts. She switched off the engine. Brook and Jilly were too fast for her to contain them, but she didn't mind so much. Anxious to see Brady again, Cassie threw off her seat belt and bailed from the van. The dog at Brady's side sighted them before he did. Winnie gave three happy barks, then launched herself off the porch.

Brady looked perplexed by his dog's sudden defection. He snapped his fingers, called and whistled, but it was to no avail. Winnie had her targets in sight. Cassie witnessed the moment he spotted her daughters. He froze for a second, then he beamed so unreservedly it nearly cracked her heart wide-open.

He waved to them, but she could see his head moving from side to side, scanning the crowd as he came down the steps himself. She hoped he was looking for her.

Some would say it was ridiculous for her to feel so attached to a man after only a few days, but those days had been intense. She knew a woman with her history should be wary. But when their gazes met and held, all her doubts disappeared.

He was happy they came.

So was she.

The previous night she'd told Vera she was comfortable with Brady, but it was more than the ease between them. She trusted him with a surety she felt in her bones. And after a couple days of space, she could admit she wanted him. More, she wanted him to want her. And her girls.

All she needed was the guts to tell him what was in her head and her heart.

But, as was his way, Brady made things easier for her straight off the bat.

"Hey, I missed you," he said, his grin unwavering as he

approached. Her lips parted, but no sound came out. The next thing she knew, he was holding her tight against him.

"We missed you too," she whispered, aware her choice of pronoun was a bit of a cop-out, but unable to resist shielding herself if even in the smallest way. She chuckled self-consciously as he loosened his hold enough to look at her. "Though I bet it was a lot quieter."

"Too quiet," he said gruffly. "I liked having you here." He gave her arms a squeeze. "All of you."

"Well, here we are, invading your space again," she said with a watery laugh.

"Cal tells me we've handed everything over to the FBI in terms of the kidnapping. Norton will also have charges of malicious vandalism, breaking and entering and terroristic threatening to contend with, but the investigation is closed and he's the lawyers' problem now."

Cassie shot a look at the double-wide Keith had managed to infiltrate and shuddered. "Brady, I'm so sorry I brought all this to your door. Literally." She gave a short laugh and half-heartedly tried to pull away, but he held firm.

"Don't. Don't apologize for something you didn't do. I'm sorry I wasn't thinking more clearly. He should never have gotten through my door."

"Your house—" she started.

But he cut her off with a quick, hard kiss. Whistles and catcalls erupted around them, and they parted on her soft gasp. Brady pressed his lips together and scowled, but it wasn't enough to make them stop.

But he didn't let her go. His arms wound around her and he pulled her into his warm embrace. "I should apologize, but I don't want to," he whispered into her ear.

"I don't want you to," she said on a rush of breath.

He retreated enough to look her in the eye. "It's too much, too fast, and we were thrown together by circumstance," he said huskily. "I get all this logically, but right now, the logical part of my brain is on hiatus. I've been wanting to kiss you for so long."

"I, uh, me too. You," she stammered.

At a sharp bark, she whipped her head around and saw her daughters staring at them. Jilly, for once in her young life, appeared speechless. Brook, looking horrified by their behavior, cried, "Ew!"

But, despite her protestations, her elder daughter's eyes looked bright and, for the first time in too long, hopeful.

"Oh, Winnie!" Jilly cried, then threw her arms around the panting dog's neck in an exuberant hug. "They love each other!"

Brady's dog showed her approval with a wide doggy grin. She thumped her tail so hard puffs of dust rose.

Cassie's face heated, but she forced herself to look at Brady. "The critics seem divided," she managed to joke.

He shook his head. "Nah, one of them is trying to play it cool, and the other two couldn't act nonchalant if they tried." He left one arm slung over her shoulder as he surveyed the chaos she'd once again rained down on him. "What's all this?"

"Oh!" Pressing her hand to her flaming cheek, she turned to look at the sea of beaming faces watching them with avid interest. "I, um, everyone wanted to help."

"Help?"

"Dillon told me he and some of the other guys were out here clearing debris and checking the foundation. He said things looked solid, so like I said, people wanted to help. Vera and I talked to some of the folks who came into the diner, and Millard has a friend who works with a construction company out of White Feather. They had some lumber left over from a project they had finished. They're dropping it off here—" she paused as the roar of an engine and the hiss of air brakes filled the air "—now, I guess," she concluded with a laugh.

Brady blinked in apparent disbelief as all around them people started strapping on tool belts and wrestling ladders, table saws and other equipment from truck beds. Cassie turned to check on the girls. She bit her lip as she took in the mayhem, then met his warm brown gaze. "I have to tell you something," she said in a whisper meant only for his ears.

Brady's arm tightened, holding her close to his side. "Yeah?"

The hopeful lilt in the single word buoyed her. Stretching onto her toes, she whispered in his ear, "My middle name is Pandora."

His brows shot high, and an incredulous tilt to his lips. "You're kidding."

She shook her head. "Now you're in on my deepest secret," she told him gravely. "I can be a whole passel of trouble, Brady Nichols."

"Cassandra Pan—"

"Would you look at the teeth on that table saw," she cried out, cutting him off.

Brady chuckled, then kissed her temple. "It's safe with me," he assured her.

"I trust you."

Brady gave her another squeeze. "I can't believe you did all this," he said, his eyes wide with wonder.

Behind them, someone let loose with an indelicate snort. "She isn't Wonder Woman," Vera groused as she trundled past holding what appeared to be a tray of sandwiches. "Plenty of folks helped."

Millard followed in his wife's footsteps, a giant stainless-steel urn in his hands. "Hey, Brady," he said in his usual easy manner. "This here's coffee, but I have a couple cases of bottled water too. The folks at the Stop & Shop are sending over some of those sports drinks as well."

Cassie beamed at Brady's bewildered expression. "Vera's right. Everyone wanted to help."

"But you organized it. I see your fingerprints all over this operation."

He gathered her into his arms and bent his head toward hers, but she braced her hands on his chest to hold him off for one more minute. "It wasn't all me. Dillon did a lot of it."

Brady glanced over to where his best friend was directing groups of volunteers like a seasoned construction foreman. "I appreciate the effort, but I'm not kissing him."

"Emma Daniels helped a lot too."

As if conjured, Emma appeared with the teenage boys who worked for her over the summer. "I just wanted a break from cleaning out kennels," she announced, giving Brady a playful nudge as they walked past. "And don't you dare try to kiss me. I'll sic Winnie on you." The trainer turned and walked backward a few steps, her eyes alight with amusement. "You know she still thinks I'm her alpha."

Brady laughed, but tightened his hold on Cassie.

"But you want to kiss me," Cassie murmured when their gazes met again. She needed to confirm the first kiss hadn't been an impulse on his part.

"Absolutely, I do."

"Ew," Brook said loudly. "He's gonna kiss her again."

"I want him to kiss her," Jilly announced loudly. "I want him to kiss her so we can live here in his new house so Winnie can sleep with me every night."

Cassie squeezed her eyes shut, mortified, but the touch of Brady's lips against hers had them popping open wide again.

He flashed a wide, rakish grin. "I think that sounds like a great plan, Jilly," he answered, still holding Cassie's gaze.

"You can't mean—" she began to protest.

"I can, and I do." Without giving her a minute to recover, he released her and turned to scoop a giggling Jilly into his arms. With the smaller girl settled on his hip, he ran a hand over Brook's hair. Despite her protestations about public displays of affection, she moved into his side without hesitation. He met Cassie's gaze steadily. "It'll take a while to get the house built, but we can use the time for us all to get better acquainted. I think it's a great plan."

When Brook stretched her arm out toward her, Cassie stepped into the four-way embrace. "So, this is how it's going to be, huh?" she asked, tears blurring the edges of her words. "You three ganging up on me?"

"Four," Jilly corrected. "Don't forget Winnie."

Cassie felt something brush her calf and glanced down to see the Labrador sit right between her leg and Brady's, her pink tongue lolling as she gazed adoringly at the tangled knot of them.

"Of course not," Cassie whispered, reaching down to pet the dog's head. "We could never forget Winnie. After all, she's the one who introduced us."

* * * * *

COMING SOON!

MILLS & BOON

THE HEART OF ROMANCE

A ROMANCE FOR EVERY READER

MODERN
Prepare to be swept off your feet by sophisticated, sexy and seductive heroes, in some of the world's most glamourous and romantic locations, where power and passion collide.

HISTORICAL
Escape with historical heroes from time gone by. Whether your passion is for wicked Regency Rakes, muscled Vikings or rugged Highlanders, awaken the romance of the past.

MEDICAL
Set your pulse racing with dedicated, delectable doctors in the high-pressure world of medicine, where emotions run high and passion, comfort and love are the best medicine.

True Love
Celebrate true love with tender stories of heartfelt romance, from the rush of falling in love to the joy a new baby can bring, and a focus on the emotional heart of a relationship.

Desire
Indulge in secrets and scandal, intense drama and plenty of sizzling hot action with powerful and passionate heroes who have it all: wealth, status, good looks…everything but the right woman.

HEROES
Experience all the excitement of a gripping thriller, with an intense romance at its heart. Resourceful, true-to-life women and strong, fearless men face danger and desire - a killer combination!

To see which titles are coming soon, please visit

millsandboon.co.uk/nextmonth

LET'S TALK

Romance

For exclusive extracts, competitions
and special offers, find us online:

f facebook.com/millsandboon

🐦 @MillsandBoon

📷 @MillsandBoonUK

Get in touch on 01413 063232

For all the latest titles coming soon, visit
millsandboon.co.uk/nextmonth

JOIN US ON SOCIAL MEDIA!

Stay up to date with our latest releases, author news and gossip, special offers and discounts, and all the behind-the-scenes action from Mills & Boon...

 millsandboon

 millsandboonuk

 millsandboon

It might just be true love...

MILLS & BOON

Desire

Indulge in secrets and scandal, intense drama and plenty of sizzling hot action with powerful and passionate heroes who have it all: wealth, status, good looks…everything but the right woman.

MILLS & BOON

MODERN

Power and Passion

Prepare to be swept off your feet by sophisticated, sexy and seductive heroes, in some of the world's most glamourous and romantic locations, where power and passion collide.

MILLS & BOON
MEDICAL
Pulse-Racing Passion

Set your pulse racing with dedicated, delectable doctors in the high-pressure world of medicine, where emotions run high and passion, comfort and love are the best medicine.

Eight Medical stories published every month, find them all a